Sam Carrington lives in Devon with her husband and three children. She worked for the NHS for 15 years, during which time she qualified as a nurse. Following the completion of a psychology degree she went to work for the prison service as an Offending Behaviour Programme Facilitator. Her experiences within this field inspired her writing. She left the service to spend time with her family and to follow her dream of being a novelist. *One Little Lie* is her third psychological thriller.

Readers can find out more at http://www.samcarrington.blogspot. co.uk and can follow Sam on Twitter @sam_carrington1

BY THE SAME AUTHOR

Saving Sophie
Bad Sister

ONE LITTLE LIE

SAM CARRINGTON

avon.

Published by AVON
A division of HarperCollins*Publishers* Ltd
1 London Bridge Street
London SE1 9GF

www.harpercollins.co.uk

This paperback edition 2019

First published in Great Britain by HarperCollins*Publishers* 2018

A catalogue copy of this book is
available from the British Library.

ISBN: 978-0-00-832848-1

Set in Minion by Palimpsest Book Production Limited,
Falkirk, Stirlingshire

Printed and bound in the United States of America by
LSC Communications

For my sons, Louis and Nathaniel.
You make me proud every day.

PROLOGUE

19th March 2014 – Exeter Crown Court

'It took approximately eight hours for Sean Taylor to die.'

She listened as the man spoke, her heart beating a little faster, her eyes blinking a little more than necessary. She shifted in her seat. Her bottom was numb, her legs heavy. She didn't *want* to hear the details. She *needed* to. Her gaze fixed on the coroner; she couldn't move her limbs and escape the courtroom, couldn't close her ears to the words.

She had to know.

'The stab wound to the back of his neck entered between cervical C5 and C6, causing complete severance of the spinal cord. Not immediately fatal, but it would've paralysed him.'

A tight band constricted her chest wall, threatening to squash her heart. Still, she listened.

'He lay, unable to move, in his own blood for hours. It wasn't until the tide came in fully that his life was finally taken.'

'So, cause of death was drowning?'

The man's left eye twitched. It was visible even from her seat in the gallery. 'Well, officially, yes – suffocation from water was the decisive factor. But, clearly, the stab which caused—'

'That will be all, Doctor Varsey. No further questions.'

The young man in the dock was standing very still – like a shop dummy, frozen in position by the person who put it there. Unmoved by proceedings. His mop of blond hair fell in loose curls, covering his eyes. Blocking his guilt from view. How could this unremarkable eighteen-year-old have caused so much devastation?

She swallowed.

He deserved what was coming to him. Didn't he? A lifetime in prison.

A life for a life.

But he wasn't the only one who needed to be punished.

PART ONE

PART ONE

CHAPTER ONE

Alice

Wednesday 31st January 2018

The chairs form an almost perfect circle. I manoeuvre the last two so they have equal distance between them. It's important I try to maintain the personal space of those who'll be seated here. Satisfied, I step back to check. Only one chair is different – double the room either side of it – separated from the rest of them. It's also the only soft-furnished chair, the others being brown plastic.

This is my chair.

I'm their leader. I need to be seen easily by all the members – all eyes will need to be able to find mine. Eye contact is so important. That's how they can see my empathy. My pain. Share it all with me.

Ten minutes left to wait.

It's taken a few months of organisation: a lot of online chats, convincing others there was need for in-person interaction rather than virtual, finding an appropriate venue. Hopefully there'll be a good turnout; at least six. I've optimistically put out ten chairs. Not a big group, but that doesn't matter. Not to begin with. It will grow, once people realise how much they're gaining. How much help and support it will offer them. And then they'll travel from further afield to be a part of my group, a part of each other's lives.

Five minutes.

A fizz of excitement bubbles inside my stomach. Most people wouldn't understand that. Not with the type of group I'm running.

But this means a lot to me.

This is going to help redeem me.

'Hello.' A quiet, hesitant voice drifts in from the outer door of the church hall.

I straighten, my muscles hardening for a few seconds before I recover. I deftly smooth my black pencil-skirt with both hands, and pat my hair – the new curly style is taking some getting used to. I take small, quick steps towards the voice.

'Welcome, I'm Alice Mann, come on in.' I'm relieved to hear the words effortlessly flowing from my mouth as I thrust my hand into the palm of my first group member. The robust, ruddy-faced woman gives a shaky smile in return.

'Wendy,' she manages, her eyes flitting around the church hall.

I can tell she's nervous. I must put Wendy at ease quickly, to make sure she stays; doesn't turn tail at the first opportunity, or only attend this first session and never return.

'A church,' Wendy says. 'Is it appropriate?'

'Well, the church *hall*, to be exact,' I say, as confidently as I can. 'It's the only venue I could secure locally.' I pop my arm around Wendy's shoulders and guide her to a chair.

I did wonder if this would be the best place, but I'd been limited. And this only cost £25 for two hours. It's not like we're in the actual church. But anyway, isn't God meant to forgive people their sins? And the people coming to my group aren't the ones who've sinned. I keep this thought to myself.

The sound of footsteps catches my attention. A sigh of relief forms but dies in my throat. At least it's not going to be just the two of us. That would be a disaster. I smile as I greet four more people: three women and one man. I hope he won't be the only male. It's important to have a good selection.

After a few minutes of mumblings, squeaking of metal legs on the wooden floor, shuffling of bodies into a comfortable position – the room falls silent.

I can hear my own breath as it escapes my lips.

Six people, including me. All here for the same thing.

'Welcome to the group.' My enthusiastic voice fills the high-ceilinged room, and I almost jump – it sounds loud, unfamiliar. 'I'm really pleased you've made it here today.' I take a moment to look directly at each of the group members in turn. 'I thought we'd start by going around the circle, each giving a brief introduction, start getting to know each other.'

A few people drop their gaze from mine. They don't want to be the first to speak, the first to verbalise the reason they're here. It's easy, online, you see. To talk in a chat room, remain anonymous, unseen. This is different, and it'll take a while before they build up trust in each other. In me. It will take time before they can be themselves. I can relate to that. I'm not even at that stage myself, yet.

I'll start. I am the leader, after all.

'Okay. I'll begin.' I take a large lungful of air, and slowly expel it before speaking again.

'My name is Alice. And my son is a murderer.'

CHAPTER TWO

Connie

Connie Summers all but sprinted up the hill towards the building that housed her psychological therapy practice, puffs of breath clouding the cold space in front of her. Eight months ago, she'd struggled to walk it – extra weight gained through long periods of stress-related binge-eating had taken its toll and prevented her from even ascending stairs without gasping for air. But when her new housemate had moved in, so too did a new regime: healthy eating, gym sessions, hikes over the moors. Detective Inspector Lindsay Wade had brought the best out in Connie.

Not everything in Connie's life was rosy, though. The weight of worry still hunched her shoulders and tugged at her thoughts – still meant she couldn't fully relax. Even now, as she strode past the familiar Totnes shops, flashbacks permeated her mind in short, sharp bursts. The images – bright, vivid and unwelcome – came to her when she didn't even realise she was thinking about the events that had shaken her so profoundly last year.

Connie hadn't fully recovered from the aftermath of her involvement in the Hargreaves' murder, and she doubted she ever would. It was bad enough that she'd been one of the professionals responsible for the decision to release Ricky Hargreaves from prison, when days later he reoffended by raping a woman, but to then be dragged into Ricky's murder case a year later when she'd begun to put her prison career behind her – it was like the red-blood icing on a poisoned cake. She'd lost clients, quite literally, due to a cruel twist of fate: the lethal mix of her previous work with offenders and her own father's criminal links. The innocent faces of the young woman and her little boy – both now dead – were still at the forefront of Connie's mind. She'd also struggled financially – her failure to drag herself to work every day, coupled with an inability to motivate herself to build her business back up, took its toll. This wasn't only a direct effect of Hargreaves, but also her family's own dubious past, its secrets unexpectedly revealing themselves, causing her thoughts to spiral uncontrollably for a while. Lindsay moving in had helped, enabling her to afford the mortgage repayments and the rent on her business premises. But it wasn't the main reason Connie had suggested the arrangement. A friend was what she really needed.

Despite the memories haunting her walk to work, Connie was looking forwards to starting the week by welcoming a new client. Having completed the journey from the train station through the narrow side streets onto High Street and up the hill towards East Gate Arch, all in a dazed fog, Connie came back to the moment as she reached her building. She shook her head to clear it, took a breath and unlocked the blue front door. After taking a few steps across the reception area, she dashed up the stairs, giving a cursory glance at the newly installed security camera as she went. She unravelled her scarf and slung it, together with her coat, on the stand in the corner of her upstairs consulting room. The gentle clanking of the radiator filled the room – she'd timed it to come on at 8.45 a.m., so it was comfortable by 9 a.m. Connie went back downstairs to make a coffee, to let warmth replace the chill of the room before beginning her day.

Mug cradled in both hands, the heat penetrating her cold fingers, Connie leant back in her chair and listened to her answerphone. The third message made her sit forwards abruptly, spilling her coffee over the desk. *What the hell?*

'Long time no speak, Con,' the overly cheerful female voice said.

Connie reached forwards to delete the message before it played out, her finger hovering over the button. Curiosity prevented her from pressing it.

'I know this might be a long shot,' Jen paused, and Connie heard a sigh before she carried on. 'But we're in the shit here, really. You know how it is: lack of staff, too many prisoners to assess, parole board breathing down our necks. We're swamped.'

A worm of dread began its journey through her stomach. She knew where this was heading.

'So, anyway. The psych department has had permission to draft in some help, by way of independent psychologists popping in to carry out some of the backlog of reports. Obviously, I thought of you. You're local, know the job, the prison. It makes sense. There are only a few men to assess, but the money will be good.' There was another pause. 'I thought perhaps you might appreciate a bit of extra income at the moment?'

Yes. She would. But, there was no way she'd be returning to HMP Baymead, no matter how much they paid her.

'Think about it, eh, Con? Would be great to see you. Give me a call!'

10

CHAPTER THREE

Connie

'It might not be such a bad idea,' Lindsay said, sitting on the sofa with one leg tucked under her, both hands nursing her second mug of coffee.

'Really? After everything that happened there? After leaving because of the fallout?' Connie took a long, drawn-out breath. Even thinking about it was increasing her anxiety levels. Although if she was being honest, those levels had been elevated ever since listening to Jen's message yesterday. The decision to leave her lead psychologist position at HMP Baymead had been the best move for her – she'd been off sick for months before she resigned, the fear of making another error of judgement too much in the end. She'd needed to feel as though she was contributing to something good, so made the focus of her new practice counselling those who'd been affected by crime. Victims, not offenders.

'Think about it logically. And, you know – financially . . .' Lindsay raised her eyebrows so they disappeared beneath her red fringe.

'Yeah, I need the money. But I'm really not sure it's worth putting my well-being at risk by going back in there. When I left, it was for good.'

'Okay.' Lindsay shrugged. 'Say no, then.'

Connie narrowed her eyes. 'Are you trying reverse psychology on me, Wade? That's not your area.'

'No. Although, I am quite good at it. Picked it up from the best.' She wrinkled her nose and smiled.

'Well, stop it.' Connie got up from the sofa and walked to the window. A crisp, white layer of frost covered the ground. She shivered. She wasn't ready for this. Not ready, nor willing to go backwards.

'How many reports is Jen asking you to complete?'

'A few.' Connie made quotation marks with her fingers.

'So what's that, in terms of time within the prison walls?'

'Three, maybe four days. I'd only need to see each prisoner for two sessions, I reckon. Then the rest could be done at home.'

'So not even a week. Easy money, then.' Lindsay's voice softened. 'I'm here, you know, to support you. It wouldn't be like before.' She got up and strode towards Connie, embracing her in a quick, tight hug. 'I must get going – don't want to be late for the morning briefing. Mack will take the lead without me, and I can't have him feeling too important.'

Connie listened as Lindsay's footsteps hurried through the house, grabbing her coat and bag. She heard the jangling of keys, then the slam of the front door. She didn't relish the silence of the house when Lindsay wasn't in it. She watched from the window as Lindsay got in her car and drove off, waving, as she always did.

Lindsay didn't understand the battle Connie was having inside her head. Not fully. It wasn't only the thought of going back into the prison causing her anxiety, it was the responsibility of compiling the written reports. What if she got it wrong again? And by worrying about being too positive about the prisoner, she'd probably err on the side of caution and perhaps not give a balanced, objective report. Just in case. Whatever way she played it, she would be wrong. And she wasn't prepared to chance having another person's life – or death – on her conscience.

Connie flung herself back on the sofa and lay with both arms crossed above her head. The money *would* come in useful. Lindsay was right about that. Having her as a support, knowing she'd have someone other than her mother to lean on, was reassuring. Lindsay hadn't let her down – she'd been through the Hargreaves situation with her. She'd been the detective inspector on the case, and, after the initial frostiness between them, they'd come together for the common cause.

And then Lindsay had saved her. Literally saved her life.

She trusted Lindsay implicitly.

Connie pushed herself up. She'd give herself another day or two to consider it before calling Jen. For now, she had her own work to focus on. Her new client yesterday had been a woman whose son had been convicted of murder four years ago, and she'd presented with huge guilt issues. Her life had been upturned, she'd been hounded from the town she'd lived her life in, and although she was making progress in Totnes, she couldn't get over the knowledge her own flesh and blood – a boy she'd brought up – could've ever committed such a heinous crime.

After the initial consultation, it had become clear to Connie that she had an ethical dilemma on her hands. Her new client, Alice Mann, had spoken of her son's crime and an alarm of recognition rang in her head.

Her son was Kyle Mann.

And Connie knew him.

CHAPTER FOUR

Alice

My knees are wobbling. I'm glad I chose a long skirt – only I know they're shaking as I reach to press the doorbell. I know it's working because I can hear the tacky tune it plays within the house. I wait for movement, looking through the patterned glass of the door. I lick my lips; the roughness catches my tongue. I can't swallow either, all moisture has left my mouth and throat.

Maybe no one is in.

I'm not going to be able to ring again. My heart is already dancing along at a rate that can't be good for me. This is my second attempt. At least I managed the bell this time. Last week I only got as far as the gateway. This is progress.

I turn, and, disappointed in my weakness, walk away from the house.

I see a flutter of a curtain as I pass by the house next door. A nosy neighbour, no doubt. I wonder if they saw me last week, too.

Oh well. Doesn't matter if they did. I'm not doing anything wrong. In fact, what I'm trying to do is make things right. It's all I want. I'm doing well so far, I reckon. I've set up the support group, I've even begun therapy myself. I've made huge leaps.

None of it was my fault. I didn't make him do it.

I repeat this mantra a lot. I cannot be held responsible for his actions.

But I am accountable for my own. And while I didn't *make* him do it, I didn't stop him either. That's what they said in the newspapers. What people gossiped about at the post office, in the local shops. I saw it, heard it.

It's always the mother who gets blamed. Something she did, or didn't do, when the child was growing up; some sort of neglect during that delicate stage of development. Lack of attention, lack of love, lack of stimulation. The list is endless. Who even decides this stuff? Who has the right to question the parenting skills of others? Probably some stuck-up university toff. What do they know about parenting?

I did my best.

Or is that another lie I tell myself every day?

'Hatred stirs up conflict, but love covers over all wrongs,' I say quietly, making a sign of the cross on my chest as I slowly head back to the bus stop.

I get off the bus at a different stop than usual. I don't want to go home. I can't face that right now.

I slip and slide up the road towards the café at the top end of Fore Street. I wish I'd worn trainers instead of these ankle boots. The sole has little traction, and although there are only a few frosty patches on the pavements, I feel vulnerable. What if I fall and break an ankle?

I'm being silly. It's not like I'm old, with brittle bones. I shouldn't be worrying about stuff like this. I'm only fifty-five. If it hadn't been for these past four years, I'd feel a lot younger, I'm sure. This has prematurely aged me.

The familiar sensation of prickling begins at the top of my nose, my eyes water. The cold makes them sting.

Don't cry. Feeling sorry for yourself isn't helping anyone. Neither is feeling guilty.

My preferred table in the corner of the café, practically hidden from view, is taken. *Now what?* I hesitate. It might be better to leave. But no one really knows me here. My face won't be recognised. I am anonymous. With a confidence I'm unsure of the source of, I position myself at the table by the window.

It's only when I have ordered my latte that I allow myself to look outside. I can see the psychologist's building from here – down the hill a bit, on the left, before East Gate Arch. I have another session with Connie Summers on Monday. Our first meeting involved a lot of background information, a setting up of expectations. Talk of objectives and goals.

I told her about Kyle.

I don't mind talking about him. It makes me feel better to talk about what he did. I told Connie that, and wondered if she thought me odd. I bet she thinks I'm off my rocker. Maybe I am. It's not normal to feel better when talking about how someone murdered another mother's son, is it?

But I am beginning to feel better. Talking about it is all I can do at this present time. And now I have two outlets. Two opportunities to make right.

The third way will come. Any day now, I'll be brave enough. It's building, this inner strength I've found.

Soon, I'll be strong enough to face her.

CHAPTER FIVE

Connie

Alice Mann was quite still. She didn't fidget, didn't flit her eyes about; she wasn't nervous in her demeanour. She appeared calm, confident – keeping her eyes squarely on Connie's as she told what seemed to be a well-rehearsed retelling of her story. Her experience of finding out her son had committed a murder. Connie's decision to accept Alice as a client despite her earlier misgivings was made after carefully deliberating the pros and cons. Now, as she sat opposite Alice, listening to how her son's actions had such far-reaching implications, Connie felt confident she'd made the correct choice. She could help this woman. She could make a difference to her life.

'I tried, you know? I tried so hard to encourage him out of his bedroom, to go out with his friends, not just chat to them over the internet. I literally took his door off its hinges once – I wanted to know what he was up to, all those hours with his eyes fixed on that screen, earphones plugged into his ears – it wasn't healthy. He could get nasty, would shout at me to leave him alone. So, you know, I let him put the door back on eventually. Not like I had much choice, as I couldn't stand up to him physically. You understand?' Alice took a breath.

Connie took advantage and jumped in before she set off again.

'It sounds as though you had a difficult time with Kyle. Had his behaviour been challenging before, or was it new?'

'Oh,' Alice sighed, 'it had been since his dad left, about two years before . . . you know. Anyway, I noticed that he was beginning to take on a different character, really. Like he was now the boss of the house. He took over where his dad left off. Looked after me, in his own way.'

For the first time during the session, Alice lowered her head, staring at her lap. She traced the flower pattern on her skirt with her index finger. Connie noted a small bald patch at the crown of her head, or maybe it was where her dyed ash-blonde hair had become white-grey at the roots. What did she mean by 'looked after me, in his own way'? She made a mental note to come back to that in a later session.

'That must've been hard, to manage on your own. Did you seek any help?'

Alice gave a guttural laugh. 'Help? What kind of help? He wasn't a child, he was sixteen. No one was interested in helping.'

'You said before that he was always in his room, that you tried to get him to interact with others, but failed. How then did he come to commit the murder?' Connie spoke softly, in an attempt to take the hard edge off her question.

'Well, they said the victim was someone he met online.' Alice straightened. 'On some stupid gaming site. He spent hours on it. I could hear his low voice, even through the soundproofing he'd put on the walls. Always chatting – you know, on the headphone mic, into early morning.'

'What was he talking about?'

'Not sure. On the few occasions I was allowed to be in his room when he was talking, it was mostly about the game. Tactics, medi-packs – or something like that . . . Killing. The game was about killing.' Alice closed her eyes. 'It was only a game, though. How could I have known he was going to go one further – take it into real life?'

'Do you think you *should* have known?' Connie said.

18

'I'm his mother. Yes, I should've known. I should've seen something bad coming. Done something about it.'

'What do you think you could've done to prevent it?'

'Talked to him. Given him more of my time; attention.' She sighed again, gently shaking her head. 'I don't know. Something. I could've done *something*. Instead, I went for the easy life, the easy option. When he was in his room, I could relax, I didn't have to worry about any conflict. If I gave him what he wanted, we could get on with each other.'

'What he wanted?'

'Yes. Privacy, to be left alone. Not to be challenged about anything. Not to go on about him getting a job. No *nagging*.'

Connie thought back to her own tempestuous teenage years. Her behaviour had got out of hand after her brother Luke was stabbed. She became unruly, disobedient. Promiscuous. Her parents' numerous warnings and well-meaning interventions – their constant *nagging* – went ignored. The consequences of that had been far-reaching and had followed Connie into her adult life. A shudder shot along the length of her spine as the memory of That Night flashed in her mind. All she'd wanted after that was to be left alone – shutting herself away in her bedroom with only her shame and rock music for company. She'd not spoken to her mum or dad for days on end.

Hadn't Alice's son behaved like a lot of teenagers? How could she have known, really, that he would go on to commit a terrible crime? Unless there were other indicators. Perhaps Alice wasn't telling the whole story, yet. Connie had the feeling there was a lot more behind Kyle's behaviour. It was one thing to kill in a game, quite another for that to escalate into killing in real life. Despite what the anti-gamers wanted people to believe, it was not common for violent games to make a violent person. There was usually something already *in* them, or something predisposing them to violence.

Like growing up with an abusive parent.

19

CHAPTER SIX

Alice

I think that went well. Connie is going to be helpful, I feel sure of that. I must be guarded, though. Be careful not to tell too much; think about how I'm saying things. She's smart – she's going to chip away, use her psychological knowledge to get under my skin. Attempt to get to the root of my issues. I want that as well, to a degree. But I need to protect my son, still. I know what he did is bad, and to some, unforgivable. But he's my flesh and blood. A product of me. And *him*.

We created him, and I nurtured him. Despite what I try to tell myself, it's my fault he's turned into this monster.

The walk back to the house is slow. The sun is shining, and it's quite pleasant – a mild day for February – but I feel heavy. Cumbersome. I stop a few times, looking into random shop windows. I know I'm not really seeing anything. My eyes don't focus on the displays. It's like I'm looking past them into the distance. Into my past. My future. Both are equally messed up.

I need to jolt myself out of this mood.

Should I attempt another visit to her house? I think getting to the next stage will pull me out from under this dark cloud. It's been over a week since I was last there. Standing at her door full of dread, but with an inkling of hope.

20

Hope is what I need right now.

I turn and head back to the lower end of town. I'll get the bus, go there while I'm feeling bold. No guarantee she'll be there, of course. I should try to figure out her schedule so I don't waste these bursts of courage by getting there and her being out.

I need to be more organised if I'm to achieve what I want.

CHAPTER SEVEN

Connie

Connie stared at the phone, one hand twiddling a piece of her sleek black hair around and around her fingers. She'd just looked at her accounting records – it didn't make for good reading. Her client base was growing, but slowly. She needed an injection of cash for advertising.

A piece of A4 paper was placed next to the phone with two columns: one showing the 'pros', one showing the 'cons' of going back to Baymead to do the reports. Connie picked it up. The only thing in the pros column was 'extra money'. Not really the best reason for stepping back into the lion's den, she mused. Maybe another pro could be that by going back, facing her demons, she'd be able to move on more successfully. Had she really put everything that happened behind her or was she avoiding anything that brought the memories back?

Connie had often thought about her actions, examined them, considered what else she could've done – should've done – and, each time, she concluded that she wouldn't have handled Hargreaves any differently than she had back then. She wasn't the last gatekeeper either – as the psychologist, she'd merely handed her report to the parole board for them to make the final decision of whether to release him or not.

Still, Connie never shook the feeling that her favourable report gave considerable weight to proceedings, and ultimately led to the rape of a woman. The ripple effect of her involvement had caused so much hurt and pain. If she went back, would something similar happen again? But then, could she go through the rest of her life worrying about whether a single action of hers could cause something bad to happen?

It had in the past, she reminded herself.

She sighed and tried to refocus. If she did take up Jen's offer of work, and nothing bad happened, maybe she could finally put her paranoia to rest. She pushed the competing thoughts from her mind and, without analysing it any further, dialled the number on the Post-it note she'd had tucked beneath her fern desk plant for the past week.

'Hi, can I speak with Jennifer Black, please?' Her voice shook.

She cleared her throat, and sat up straighter, waiting for the person on the end of the phone to speak. Connie hoped Jen was in the office; she wasn't sure if she'd have the nerve to call back again.

'Just a moment, I'll transfer you,' the voice said.

There was silence for what felt like minutes, then a click.

'Jennifer Black. How may I help?'

Jen's 'professional' voice was one they'd always mocked when Connie had worked at HMP Baymead. She always put on a posh voice to conceal her strong Plymothian accent when speaking on the phone. She'd moved from Plymouth to Torquay when she was a teenager, but never managed to fully escape the accent.

'You can drop the fake accent, Jen – it's just me.'

'Connie! Thank God. I didn't think you were going to return my call, you've taken so long. I hope this means—'

'Slow down, slow down. I'm calling to find out more details, that's all. Don't get too excited.'

'Oh, come on. You'll do it. You wouldn't have phoned otherwise.'

Connie shook her head. Damn this woman. Her abruptness,

her perceptiveness and her knack of getting to the point quickly was what made Jen one of the best managers the programmes department had ever had. You always knew where you stood with Jen.

'Seriously, Jen. I need to weigh up the pros and cons of doing this – coming back in after . . .'

'Pah! Water under the old bridge, Con. You know . . . *we* know, you did nothing wrong. You acted in line with every protocol. It was *you* who blamed yourself.'

'Er, I think you'll find it wasn't just me. I didn't see anyone else being dragged through the papers, and there wouldn't have been a capability hearing if the governor didn't think I'd messed up Hargreaves' risk report.' Merely talking about it again caused Connie's heart rate to increase and her armpits to tingle with sweat.

End the call. This isn't worth it.

'Look, I know things went downhill rapidly for you after Hargreaves, but you shouldn't let that stop you from coming in and completing a few assessments.'

'Are they high-risk prisoners?' Connie was immediately mad at herself for asking; it sounded as though she was seriously considering the offer.

'Not really. None are up for parole. It's their progression through the system we need to focus on. Some of the guys have been here a long time, and we have a fair few refusing to do any of the offending behaviour programmes. We're under pressure to get arses on seats so they can move forwards in their sentence plans, get them into a Cat-D establishment.'

'Nothing new there, then.'

'Exactly. Our group numbers are actually falling. Anyway, point is, you can come in, do the assessments, and get out. You can write the reports at home. That's the extent of your involvement. I wasn't kidding when I said it was easy money, Con.'

Connie exhaled loudly and sat back in her chair. Risk-wise, these prisoners weren't up for release, so her reports would only be used as evidence for the decision to move them to an open prison, or not – or recommend action, such as attending further offending behaviour programmes. An open prison would mean there was a chance of the prisoner absconding though, so she could still get a backlash if she wrote a favourable report and then something bad happened later down the road.

'And how many would I be assessing again?'

'Only three. We have another psychologist coming in as well, so between us all, we should catch up on the backlog. Might have to spread it over a few weeks though.'

Connie's shoulders sank. She'd been hoping, if she were to do it, that it would be over in a week. Realistically though, she'd known deep down it wasn't likely to be possible.

There was one other thing that was bothering her.

'I need to ask something.'

'Shoot,' Jen said.

'You don't have an Aiden Flynn at Baymead, do you?'

CHAPTER EIGHT

Deborah

She doesn't realise I know.

I sit here anyway, listening to her. I've made a pot of tea and I pour her a cup from the bone china teapot belonging to the set that once sat on my mother's oak sideboard – reserved for special occasions; people she wanted to impress. I don't know why I chose to dig it out from the back of the cupboard now. Or why I'm trying to impress this woman. I'm turning into my mother.

'That's a lovely picture of Sean,' she says, gesturing to the large silver-framed photo on the mantelpiece.

I take a deep breath.

'Yes.' I force a smile. 'Would you like a biscuit? I have chocolate digestives or rich tea.' I want to avoid talking about my son. Even though I know that's why she's here.

'Oh, um . . . chocolate, please. Although I really should be watching my waistline.' She pats her belly. There's no fat on the woman, but I refrain from remarking as I shake out some biscuits from the packet and offer them to her.

'Thanks for letting me come in,' she says as she dips the biscuit in her teacup. She leaves a trail of brown slush on its side. I look away. It's a bone china cup for God's sake, not a mug.

'Well, I couldn't leave you on the doorstep, could I?' Although that's exactly what I'd wanted to do at first – her babbling on about her son being at school with my Sean was irritating at best. My lips are tight; the smile harder to come this time. How polite should I be in this situation? A huge part of me doesn't want to be polite at all – it wants to shout in her face, tell her to get out of my house. But there's something about her – vulnerable, yet brave. It would be like kicking an inquisitive puppy. It must've taken some guts to turn up at my door, even though she's yet to come clean and tell me who she really is. Didn't she think I'd recognise her? I thought I'd hardened over the last few years, but the harsh words that spring into my mind – the ones telling this woman exactly what I think of her efforts to squirm her way into my life – evaporate before I can speak them.

Maybe it's curiosity.

I find myself wanting to know why she thinks it's a good idea for her to visit the mother of a murdered boy. He was only eighteen. Not even a man. He'd hardly lived, had so much to look forwards to.

She puts her cup and saucer down on the table, and I watch as her pale-blue eyes travel back to Sean's photograph.

'You must miss him terribly.' Her words are quiet, almost inaudible – her face directed away from mine.

My skin is suddenly cold, as though someone has placed a blanket of ice on me. Of *course* I miss him. He was my only child; my life, up until that terrible day. I've had to learn to live without him, carry on with everyday things, all the while knowing my life would never again have meaning. Not the same meaning, anyway. I'm no longer someone's mum. Tears come at this thought.

Perhaps I shouldn't have allowed this woman in. Curiosity is not good for me.

I wipe my eyes with my sleeve.

'Yes, it's like I have a part of me missing. A hole that will never be filled.' I can feel a bubble of anger. I should keep a cap on that.

'I'm sorry,' she says, simply.

'Oh, so am I. Sorry he ever encountered Kyle Mann. Sorry I wasn't able to protect him.' I must be careful, or years' worth of hatred will erupt in this lounge. Amongst my mother's bone china tea set. With the smiling face of my handsome Sean staring down at me.

'Maybe I shouldn't have . . .' She shifts awkwardly; she's flustered. It looks as though she's thinking about leaving.

'No. Maybe not. But you're here now,' I say firmly. We lock eyes.

'Yes, it's taken quite a while to pluck up the courage.' She gives a wavering smile.

'Right.' It's time to stop the pretence. 'So now that you're here, what exactly do you want, Alice?'

CHAPTER NINE

Connie

'Well, well. If it isn't the infamous Connie Moore!' The voice bellowed from behind the glass partition.

'Hey, Barry.' Connie kept her chin low, almost tucked into the collar of her blouse. She didn't want him to see her discomfort at being back inside the prison. Barry had been an operational support grade for as long as she could remember, and clearly, even given the time she'd been away, her reputation still stood. She'd contemplated giving them her new surname, Summers, which she started using when she set up her own practice to avoid any connections with the Hargreaves case. But she decided it would be a bad idea in this instance. She preferred to keep her prison life in a separate box.

'I saw you were on the list today. Says here I gotta give Verity a call and get her to come and fetch you, now you haven't got your own keys and ID. Take a seat, love. Won't be long.'

Connie turned on her heel and sat heavily on the leather-look bench seat that ran alongside the window of HMP Baymead's gatehouse and placed her coat beside her. She'd only ever sat here once before: the day she came for her interview, eight years ago. She pulled self-consciously at the cuffs of her sleeves. She even *felt* like she had all that time ago: nervous, uncertain – questioning

29

whether her skills were up to the job. She kept her eyes down, not wanting to catch a glimpse of anyone else she knew from her previous life there. She didn't want to face any awkward questions.

Why did I agree to this? Stupid, stupid woman.

Connie pushed her cuff up, checking her watch. It would take at least ten minutes for Verity to reach the gatehouse. Baymead was spread over a wide area, and the psychology block was on the far side of the grounds. She used to love the early morning walk to the office from the gatehouse, when the prisoners were yet to be unlocked. She could stroll along the tree-lined concrete paths, taking her time to let herself through the huge gates. The walk back after her day ended was never quite so pleasant. She'd often time it so her departure didn't coincide with prisoners going back to the wings after their activities, or work. But even then, if she was on her own, she couldn't help feeling vulnerable. And the times she'd happened to leave the office when the prisoners were on their way back to their living blocks were more stressful. She didn't miss that at all.

At least now, for the period she was going to spend here, she'd have someone accompanying her around the prison. She'd have to be let through each gate in the grounds, and have the living-block gates opened for her. She'd be collected from her interviews with the prisoners and taken back to the psychology block.

Connie consciously unclasped her hands, placing them loosely on her lap. This could be all right. It wasn't as though she was going to be spending enough time within the confines of the establishment to warrant anyone taking much notice of her. And it *was* almost two years since she'd last been here. Some staff were bound to know her, remember her, but it was unlikely many prisoners would. At least Aiden Flynn, the man responsible for the murder of Ricky Hargreaves last year, was not residing at Her Majesty's pleasure in Baymead. That had been one of her biggest fears. He was the last person she'd want to come into contact with.

Not only was he a cold-blooded murderer, but he also had a personal vendetta against Connie and had been determined to exact revenge on her because of something that her father had done twenty years previously. And he'd almost managed to accomplish his task: attacking Connie in her own home, beating her to the ground. If it wasn't for Lindsay . . . Connie shook the memory away. No, the most that would happen is she'd get some attention from being a 'new' female about the place. Whistles, some remarks shouted at her – the common response from a proportion of the men – those she could handle.

A whooshing noise alerted Connie to someone coming through the glass security doors. She jumped up as a young woman, who looked to be around twenty, walked towards her.

'Connie?'

'Yes.' Connie grabbed her coat and offered her hand. The woman limply shook it.

'I'm Verity, the new admin for the programmes department.' She smiled broadly, her small, round face appearing to almost split in two. 'I'll be your *key* person.' She laughed.

'Great, thanks, Verity. I appreciate it. Sorry you'll have to be dragged wherever I'm going though, not much fun for you.'

'No problem. It'll be a good excuse to get out of the office. It's manic in there at the moment.'

'Oh?' They both entered the glass box of the security pod and stood still, waiting for the operational support grade to close one door before he opened the other. Connie had always disliked the pod. Sometimes, if she'd timed it badly, she'd been stuffed inside there along with some twenty-odd people: admin staff, officers, service providers – all squished in, waiting at the mercy of the OSG on duty in the gate room to be quick with the release button for the other door. It was claustrophobic. Today though, it was only her and Verity, and the OSG didn't leave them too long before releasing the inner door.

Connie's tummy flipped as she left the pod and walked the

familiar corridor that led to the outside. Which was really *inside*. She put on her coat as they stood by the heavy door, waiting for the noise that would inform them it was open.

Click.

For a moment, Connie wobbled. She was dizzy.

Take deep breaths.

A waft of air hit her face as Verity opened the door and stood aside to let Connie through.

That sight. The grassed area, the large trees, the metal fences separating the living blocks beyond. She shivered, pulling the coat tighter around her. What was she doing? The old twinges of stress, worry – the unease – were suddenly back, swooping in at her from every angle.

This is a mistake.

'Are you okay?' Verity's concerned face turned towards Connie's. 'Jen said you might feel a bit, well . . . odd. Coming back.'

Odd? That didn't come close.

'No. All good. I'm fine.' Connie forced a smile, keeping her gaze forwards while quickening her pace. She was aware of Verity tripping along beside her, trying to keep up, chatting away as they walked. But she wasn't listening. She'd feel better once she was less exposed, safely inside the psychology portacabin.

They paused at each gate as Verity unlocked, then relocked them as they moved through – every clank of the locks sending a wave of familiarity through Connie's mind. Then goosebumps. It was a sound she had assumed she'd never hear again.

As they approached the psychology office, Connie's muscles finally relaxed. She rubbed at the back of her neck, at the knot of muscle – she hadn't realised she'd been hunching her shoulders. Verity ushered Connie in, then locked the door. The large whiteboard inside the entrance named everyone in the office: showed whether they were in or out, and if out, which block or room they'd gone to and an approximate time they were due back to the office.

Jen was ticked in. Connie took a slow intake of breath, holding it as she pushed through the inner door.

'Hey, mate! So pleased you decided to come and help us out.' Jen jumped up from her seat upon Connie's arrival, and arms outstretched, strode towards her, enveloping her in a hug that expelled her held breath.

'Good to see you, Jen.' Connie gently pulled back and gazed around the room. Very little had changed. A couple of people she didn't recognise were sitting at the desks, but that appeared to be the only difference.

'Yes, as you can see, things are just the same, bar a few new faces. I'll introduce you in a sec, but let's get the kettle on first.'

She was in there now. In the prison, in the office. She could hardly revoke her offer of helping with the reports. But a creeping uneasiness spread through her, like her blood was travelling around her body delivering tiny parcels of adrenaline.

Preparing her.

Fight or flight.

And Connie wasn't at all sure she had enough fight in her.

CHAPTER TEN

Alice

Things are moving along nicely now. I couldn't imagine being at this point before: feeling more positive than I have in years. I even feel a bit lighter. I noticed my reflection in the shop windows as I walked past this morning, and I'm standing taller too – not stooped as I had been. This is good. I want to mark this progression somehow.

I should share it.

As founder and leader of the group, it's my duty to give positive news to my members. Tell them about the steps forwards I've made. Of course, I'll have to be slightly economical with the truth – mould it to make it fit. But it will give them hope. Inspiration. Let them know we can all come through these terrible times, bit by bit. Moment by moment.

I'll finish washing the breakfast dishes, then I'll get on the laptop and go to the online support group page. Our next in-person meeting isn't for another eight days – the last Wednesday of the month. Maybe by then I'll have even more good news to share. More to celebrate.

My heart sinks a little as I gaze out of the kitchen window. Is it right to feel this way? Excited about a few minor steps in the right direction? There's still so much to do; such a long way to travel to get to the end. If there is an end. Oh, please God, let there be an ending to this. I make the sign of the cross on my chest. Before all of this happened, I'd go to church to pray; being in God's house made me feel as though I had a direct link with Him. After the murder, though, I was afraid. They'd know. I couldn't face being judged by the congregation. And, after all, my support group is giving me what the church once did, and God is everywhere – I don't have to be in a holy place to pray, to be listened to. So now, at times like this, I look to Heaven for help, wherever I am. Surely I deserve some help, some divine intervention.

I'm doing God's work here.

Once the dishes are neatly stacked on the drainer, I settle in the lounge, at the rectangular pine table on the far side, the one I eat my meals at – alone. I've angled the table so I can see the TV. It's my company these days. I also keep my laptop on this table.

The house is silent. I rarely get disturbed. I'm rarely needed.

I fire up the laptop and go to the only icon on the menu I regularly use.

Group support.

There are no members live. My shoulders slump, my back arching in disappointment. My initial excitement gives way to a darkness. Gloom.

Never mind, I can still leave a comment – I'll begin a new thread so it's the first thing people notice when they log in. I see Bill has been active over the past few hours. Poor man. His daughter, Isabella, has gone off the rails and he has no clue how to handle it. His wife, he says, is useless. Isabella's already been cautioned for drug possession, and now it seems she's disappearing every night and they don't know where she's going. The group have asked Bill why he doesn't stop her – prevent her from leaving the house. Lock her in her room. But I know these 'easy' steps are, in fact, incredibly difficult. Near to impossible sometimes. She will

35

find a way, because it's not like she's a child – she's in her early twenties. It's even more challenging with a boy, when you're a single parent – my strength was no match for his.

Before I compose my own, I write a supportive message on Bill's thread, encouraging him to attend the group meeting at the end of the month. I think he needs more help than we can offer him online. He needs to be with us, see us, speak to us in person. Share everything. It'll lighten the load. Plus, we need another man in the group.

I have another session with Connie Summers two days before the group meeting. She'd wanted me to see her weekly, but I'm struggling to get the money, so I explained I could only do fort-nightly. I didn't tell her it was due to lack of funds. I'm hoping to steer the next session where I want it to go. If I can gain some more insight, and helpful suggestions from her, I'll be able to share those with my members on Wednesday. It makes me sound more authoritative when I can spout jargon and give good advice.

I can't help smiling.

I am giving back to the community; I'm helping parents to cope with their unruly offspring. I'm offering a service.

That makes me a good person.

Doesn't it?

CHAPTER ELEVEN

Connie

The sound of men in the exercise yard behind the psychology portacabin filtered into Connie's consciousness. She was sitting at the desk closest to the window, but her back was to it. Wooden fencing panels separated the area from view, so even if she'd been facing the window she wouldn't have seen the prisoners. From the lower floor of the portacabin they were only visible if you were standing. Still, a sharp tingling sensation ran the length of her back. She'd never been bothered by her proximity to them before – in fact, she'd often stood and watched to see who was interacting with who, trying to pick up on the body language of the men she'd had in her group at that time, or those she was compiling reports for. It was good to get a different perspective, watch them when they were unaware of it, so their actions and behaviour were more natural than when they were sitting in front of her.

Now though, for a reason she couldn't pinpoint, she was uncomfortable.

Maybe it wasn't them – maybe it was her. Being out of the establishment for this long meant she'd lost some of that toughness – her invincibility – which was required in order to work in the prison environment. She wasn't the confident leader she had once been. This was no longer her territory, and it felt every bit as alien as she'd expected it would. That must be the reason she felt so out of her comfort zone. As she'd said countless times, there were good reasons why she'd left in the first place.

Coming back now was revisiting the past – the past she'd worked so hard to put behind her.

'How are you getting on with those files? Got everything you need?' Verity popped her head over the blue partition that divided the desks.

Yes, she must keep focussed. The quicker she read the files, the quicker she could get on with the job in hand.

'Fine, I think everything's here.' Connie slid out the bottom of the three files given to her and flicked through it. 'Actually, there doesn't appear to be a list of pre-cons for a . . . Michael Finch.' She looked up at Verity.

'I'll walk over to the offender manager unit, check his main file and photocopy it,' Verity said, immediately rising from her seat. 'I mostly only keep the psychology-related stuff in our filing room. The bulk is kept with the offender managers.' She was out in the corridor, her coat half on before Connie could say another word. It was a shame Verity hadn't been around when Connie worked here; having admin support would've really cut down her running-around time.

Connie returned her attention to the other files she had on the desk. The name Kyle Mann stared out at her. Connie leant back; what were the odds? It might be a conflict of interest to see him, compile his report now she was in a therapeutic relationship with his mother.

'Jen?' Connie stood, and then made her way over to Jen's desk. 'Not sure I can do this one.' She handed Jen the file.

'Oh, this is the guy you saw way back when he first came to Baymead. *The silent one.*' Jen made quote marks with her fingers.

'Yes, I remember that – those one-way conversations with him were so frustrating.' Connie raised her eyebrows at the recollection.

Jen's forehead wrinkled. 'Why can't you see him now?'

38

'Ethically. His mum is a client of mine.' The only reason she'd decided it wasn't unethical seeing Alice Mann was the fact Kyle had never spoken a word during any of Connie's previous encounters with him. It was ironic she was now concerned about seeing Kyle because of her sessions with his mum.

Jen sat up straighter, her mouth gaping. 'Oh! Um . . . well, to be honest, Con, I don't reckon it'll matter much. He still hasn't uttered a word to any of us. We need his report doing, but I'm not expecting any great things. It'll be compiled on what we already have in his file, and info from the wing records, his personal officer and whatnot. I mean, I could swap him for another, but we've all started the assessments on the other guys . . .'

Connie pursed her lips. If Kyle had not spoken to any of the psychology or programmes team before, he was unlikely to now. Maybe it wouldn't be unethical. She'd literally be going over old ground, things she'd already known before. She weighed it up in her mind. If he didn't speak, then it wouldn't take very much time to get his report done. That was a bonus – she could get out of the prison even more quickly than she'd hoped if she didn't have to start from scratch with a new prisoner with lots to say.

'His risk is going to remain high if he doesn't comply, doesn't commit to doing any offender behaviour work. He does know that, right?'

'Con, he's been informed many a time. There are a lot of refusers, he's not the only one, and it would appear they don't care whether it's keeping them from progressing through the system.'

'I bet he's the only one who's never spoken, though?'

'Yes, that's true. Four years of silence is some accomplishment. I just can't understand why he won't talk.'

Connie delved into her somewhat hazy memory of the case. 'Wasn't there a suspicion someone else was involved with the crime?'

'There was something like that.' Jen moved to her keyboard and opened the OASys database, which kept records and assessments of all the offenders in the establishment. She scanned through the various pages, searching for the details of the offence. 'Of course, this didn't come from Kyle Mann – it says here that police suggested due to the nature of the abduction and murder that it was improbable that a single individual was able to carry it out. The police pushed Kyle for details, but he went down the *no comment* line, and they didn't have any substantial proof, so . . .' Jen clicked on another page in OASys: 'the only hard evidence they had was all stacked against Kyle and it was enough to safely convict him of the murder of Sean Taylor.'

'He was only eighteen.' Connie frowned. 'Such a terrible crime for someone so young.'

'Poor bloody victim, though. Jesus, have you read the file?'

'I did originally, back when he first came to us, but haven't refamiliarised myself yet. When I saw the name, I thought it best I should mention it.'

Jen tapped her pen against her bottom lip. 'It's not like your client is the *victim's* mother – then I'd definitely say not to carry out his assessments and report. But I don't see a conflict of interest here. As long as you don't disclose anything of your work here to Kyle's mother, and vice versa, then there's nothing to worry about. And anyway, like I said, it's not like we're going to gain new information from him, is it?' Jen held the file up.

Connie took it from her. 'Okay. No problem, I'll get to work.'

CHAPTER TWELVE

Deborah

'Deborah.' I hear the voice, but somehow it sounds far away, like a distant echo, rather than directly behind me.

I carry on walking, entering the building.

'Hey, Deb!' It's more insistent. She knows I hate being called Deb. I guess I can't really ignore her now. It'll be obvious I've heard that harsh yell.

My muscles are all tense. What does she want?

I slow and, reluctantly, turn to face Marcie. My boss.

Her face is flushed, but otherwise she's the usual picture of perfection. She's half my age, practically, and runs the marketing business with her brother.

'Didn't think you were going to stop,' she says, her breathing rapid.

'Miles away, sorry. Just keen to get to work, you know me,' I say with a smile I know is disingenuous.

'I wanted to catch you before we reached the office. Have a quick chat.'

My pulse dips. This can't be good. This'll be a 'you're not pulling your weight' kind of chat. My mind has been preoccupied of late; I'm here in body, but my head has been AWOL. I've been in this job for seventeen years – I was here at the beginning, when her father, George, ran the place. I'd secured and managed some of the company's biggest client accounts. George had often told me I was indispensable. I'd loved the job back then – and although I can't say that with conviction now, I still need it; it's my home from home.

Before I realise what's happening, Marcie's arm is looped through mine and she's gently steering me back to the door, against the throng of people entering the foyer. I catch sight of Andrew and Marcus; they stare questioningly at us as we exit the building. This will set the office gossips going. They will be thinking I'm about to get the sack.

Oh, bloody hell. *Am* I about to get the sack?

I need this job. I can't do without it. Not only the money, but the time outside of my own head – when I can focus. It's what keeps me going.

I swallow the rising panic. Take a steadying breath.

'What's this all about, Marcie?' I say as she guides me into the Costa a few feet away.

'Coffee and a heart-to-heart.' She grins. Her teeth are a perfect line of white squares. She gets them whitened. Everything on this woman is falsely enhanced: teeth, eyelashes, eyebrows, hair, boobs, the lot. I suddenly feel old and ugly in her presence.

But at least I'm real.

And a cosy heart-to-heart with this young, business-driven woman is really not what I need right now. I still remember her prior attempts to get me to open up. I easily brushed aside her offers to chat. But now – almost four years later – she's actually managed to 'trap' me. It's futile, though. This chat. How is she likely to understand what I went through? What I'm still going through? Every single day is a struggle. A struggle to stay in this life.

I sit at a table at the back of the coffee house, waiting for her to bring the drink I don't want. I used to love people-watching. It was one of my favourite pastimes. Not any longer. I don't care enough about them to watch. Their lives are of no interest to me.

I watch as Marcie heads towards me with two lattes on a tray. I don't even like coffee.

I can hear my own heartbeat.

I lean my elbows on the table, clasping my hands together to stop them shaking.

'Thank you,' I say as she places the drink in front of me.

'Right. So, Deborah, how are things for you at the moment?'

'Great,' I hear myself saying.

'Really?' she says. Her head tilts to one side.

Christ. She's giving me a sympathetic smile to boot. How condescending.

How can I veer the conversation in a different direction?

'Yes, really, Marcie. I'm good. Getting stuck into work helps, but you know that. After your dad died you did the same, didn't you?'

I see the flinch in her face, the flicker of her eyes as I bring the conversation back to her. See how she likes it.

Over to you.

'I guess so.' She takes a sip of her drink. 'But I had little choice. Me and Alexander had to get stuck in, keep the business Dad had built afloat. We owed it to him. Not to mention that we had to ensure everyone, like you, kept their jobs.' She smiles.

Back to me.

'That must have been a challenging time. No opportunity to grieve for your father.' Now I put *my* head to one side.

Over to you.

'It was challenging at times, yes. But I mourned in private. And I tried to keep my private life separate from work, you know? I think that's important.' Her eyes are fully on mine as she places her cup down and props her elbows on the table.

Back to me.

Now I'm aware of where this 'chat' is going, I drop the pretence – the personal game I'm playing – and get to the point.

43

'You're trying, in your roundabout fashion, to tell me I'm not keeping my private life separate from my work life.' My irritation oozes out in my tone.

She exhales dramatically and looks away from me for a moment. Then faces me and begins to deliver her speech, the one she'd probably rehearsed all night.

'I'm . . . *we're* . . . worried about you, Deborah. It's been four years, yet you still appear to be in mourning. It was a shocking, terrible, event—'

'Event!' My shrillness pierces the room, other people stop their conversations to look at me. 'Event, Marcie?' I lower my voice to a harsh whisper. 'My son was *murdered*. I lost my only child.' The tears are escaping my stinging eyes. I didn't want to show my emotion in this way. It's not helping my cause.

'I know, and I'm so sorry – I can't even begin to imagine . . .'

'No. Of course you can't.' I look down at my lap. Wait for her next shot.

'You didn't take a lot of time off work when it happened. I thought that was a mistake at the time, now I definitely do. Take some time right now, Deborah.'

I look up sharply. 'No. No, I don't need to take time off. I need to be in work, with other people.'

'But, Deborah, you don't even speak to your colleagues. I mean, unless you absolutely have to for your role. You are falling behind on your workload, and most of the time you don't appear to be *with* us at all. Things are getting missed, others are having to carry you.' She leans forwards, takes my hands.

This is it. She's letting me go.

'You've been part of this company since its birth. I want you to continue to be part of it. But I'm seriously concerned for your welfare, and with that in mind, I'm *telling* you to take some time – with full pay to start with, of course. Two months, maybe three, that's all. To get your head together.'

I'm defeated. I can't even think of an argument to strengthen my case to stay. The words 'to start with' echo in my ears. It won't be just two or three months – she'll keep stretching it out, make sure I don't return at all.

'What will I do, Marcie?' I hate the sound of my own desperation.

'That's the problem, isn't it? Outside of work you have nothing. Maybe you need a hobby.'

And we're back to being condescending. Even more so.

I *do* have a husband – has she forgotten that?

'Fine.'

I push my chair back, the loud screech hurting my ears. I don't look at her again. I take my bag and walk, head down, out of Costa. Out of my job.

What the hell am I going to tell Nathan?

Marcie demanding I take time off work is a mistake.

Me, alone with my thoughts, is going to be an even bigger one.

CHAPTER THIRTEEN

Connie

The chill of the wind caught Connie across her face and made her eyes water. She touched the back of a hand to her right cheek and winced.

'Shall we make our way back down to the car park?' Lindsay's arm reached out, giving Connie's a tug.

'Sorry. This outdoor life's still taking some getting used to.'

Lindsay shook her head – a gentle mocking of Connie's fragility.

'Yes, your ability to survive on the moor in adverse conditions is questionable. But you'll become hardy, eventually.'

'If you've got anything to do with it. Even if it kills me.' Connie slumped against a large rock, catching her breath. Her walking boots were heavy, clogged with mud, making her feel a stone heavier when she walked. On the plus side, she thought her thighs had started looking less chunky. But today was a bit much. They'd walked further than they'd done before and the weather was bitterly cold on the high ground. Dartmoor was one of the most beautiful places she knew. It was Lindsay's idea to spend more quality time there, despite it being an area her professional life had brought her to on a few horrible occasions. She wanted to make good memories on the moor. Replace the bad ones. Or at least, diminish them.

'Ready to go back down?' Lindsay offered an arm.

'Oh, yes. I'm ready.' Connie gave a grateful smile.

Connie sat in the passenger seat and shivered, the North Face jacket Lindsay had lent her rustling with the small, jerky movements.

Lindsay poured a coffee from the flask, and handed it to her.

'That'll have you warmed up in no time,' Lindsay said. She poured herself a plastic cupful as well and leant back in the driver's seat. 'What do you reckon to eating out tonight, save either of us having to cook?'

Connie shrugged. 'Sure, I'm up for that. Where do you fancy?'

'I thought maybe the Italian in town, we could walk there?'

'More *walking*?' Connie raised her eyebrows, but smiled. 'Sounds good. We've not been out for ages.' She drained the cup of the warm liquid.

With Lindsay's recent work pattern being so erratic, they hadn't seen a great deal of each other in the evenings. Often, Connie spent the hours of darkness alone. Her previous irresponsible, single-life antics had all but ceased weeks before she'd met Lindsay, so she'd got used to the quiet, lonely evenings prior to her moving in. But then she'd had a period of time with Lindsay being home with her more, her hours almost sociable. It'd been comforting; she enjoyed Lindsay's company – her friendship had become important to her. Now, again, she was having to accustom herself to it being just her and Amber, her ragdoll cat, most evenings. This weekend had been a rarity – they'd spent the entire time together, uninterrupted by work.

Connie knew it was likely to be a one-off. Something was bound to crop up – some big case that would take all of Lindsay's focus; her time, even at weekends. For now, though, Connie would make the most of it.

She followed Lindsay's gaze – her eyes were intense, focussed on the rocks of Haytor looming in front of them.

'You okay?'

Lindsay didn't take her eyes from the tor. 'Still plays on my mind. This place.' She sighed.

'I can imagine.' Connie placed her hand on Lindsay's arm. Even she had bad thoughts about Haytor: of Steph, one of her clients last year, and her son – but she hadn't had to witness it first-hand like Lindsay had; the broken bodies at the foot of the rock, the shock of seeing an innocent child taken to his death by his own mother in what was, as far as the police were concerned, a terrible suicide. Connie took some comfort in the fact that she wasn't the only person troubled by her past and wanted to support her friend just as she'd been supported herself. 'New memories, though – remember? We both need to attach positive feelings to this place, I think it's the only way we can move on.'

'Yep. Absolutely. Thanks, Connie.'

'You don't have to thank me. That's what friends are for.'

'That, and half-killing them in the name of fitness,' Lindsay laughed.

'Yeah, don't push it. Friendships can turn nasty, you know.'

CHAPTER FOURTEEN

Alice

It was hard to get out of the house this morning. Every time I was about to leave, something dragged me back.

One more chore.

One more check.

One more problem.

I'm out now, though, and I'm trying to stop my mind wandering as I walk to the bus stop. I want to be thinking about what's ahead, but what's behind me appears to be dragging me back. I need to talk myself out of it – keep my goal firmly in my mind's eye.

I concentrate my thoughts on her. I know where she lives, and now I've found out where she works. It didn't take much. The internet is both a curse and a blessing. It's so easy to find out details with a few clicks, some clever searches using key words. Most people would think I'm mad, given how the internet brought my life crashing down. But it's like most things, there is good and bad in everything. You just have to be careful – treat it with respect.

As I approach the bus stop at The Plains, opposite the Seven Stars Hotel, pain in my palms alerts me to my clenched fists. My nails have left crescent-shaped imprints where they've dug in. I can't believe she's still working. I wonder how she's managed that when I was barely able to drag myself out of bed – the amount of sedatives I was taking for my anxiety, together with the drinking, turned me from a bubbly, chatty customer assistant at Marks & Spencer into a drowsy zombie not fit to be employed. A small part of me is jealous she's continued with her life. She's kept her job. I lost mine. She's kept her husband. I lost mine.

But our sons. They're a different story.

She won't agree we've both lost them.

Maybe she doesn't have to agree on that point. There is a truth in her denial. But we've both suffered, and I need to show her that. I can help her to come to terms with what happened. She'll realise I am like her, that we can both support each other. I must help her. Then, in return, she'll help me achieve my goal.

It's the only way I can be free.

I cross the road quickly as the bus is there already. I pay my fare and take a seat halfway up – a window seat. The glass is smeared. Dirty. I don't want to contemplate what with. I shuffle into the aisle seat. I don't need to see where I'm going anyway. I hate having to use public transport, but I can't afford a taxi to Coleton, my destination. The only destination I've ventured to this past month. I'm lucky no one has sat with me. Nothing worse than being squashed next to another body, a stranger who typically feels the need to speak – make polite, yet utterly useless, boring conversation. Small mercies.

Every now and then I check where we are – counting down the minutes until I arrive. Not long now. We've just passed the huge grey monstrosity that is the multi-storey car park. Another minute and I'll be there.

A tall, narrow-looking building comes into view. My heart flutters nervously. I'm not sure what I'm going to do once I get off the bus. I don't want to draw attention by hanging around the entrance to her workplace.

I press the bell. The bus slows and I stand, gradually making my way to the front. The bus stop is opposite the building, so once I step out, I stand for a few moments to gather my thoughts. I stare at the rows and columns of windows. Which one is hers?

I'm buffeted by someone walking past. I didn't realise I was in the middle of the pavement, getting in the way. I back up, pressing myself against the wall of the hairdresser's to allow the shoppers, the random people, to go about their business. Despite having been thinking about this for days, now I'm here I have no idea of how to progress. Should I wait for her to come out? Or make an excuse to enter the building, ask to speak with her. I'm not certain how she would react to my presence here, she could make a scene. I can't risk that.

I'll have to go into the building, though, as I've no idea which level she works on. I could do a recce of the place, then sit somewhere out here. I glance around me to see where would work. Yes, I could sit on one of the benches along from the building, near the river. Maybe she'll leave at lunchtime, and I can catch up with her then, save me going inside. Whatever happens today though, I can't wait past three o'clock. I've got my appointment with Connie at four, so I have to get the 3.10 bus back to Totnes to get there on time. I probably should've waited to do this until tomorrow rather than have two things to worry about in one day. But once I decided I was going to do it, it had to be attempted right away. No putting it off.

'Hello, Alice.' The voice, though soft and unassuming, sends a jolt of electricity through my body. I take a steadying breath as I realise it's only Wendy, from my support group. Not great timing, and I could certainly do without her here, but it could be worse.

'Lovely to see you, Wendy,' I trill, twisting my lips into a forced smile. Now, how to get rid of her quickly without appearing rude. 'Not long until our group session now – will be great to catch up on Wednesday, see how we've all done these past few weeks.'

'Yes, I'm actually looking forwards to it.' She lowers her dark eyes, looking to the ground. She carries on talking, and while I *am* listening to Wendy, and trying hard to appear interested in whatever she's talking about, my eyes keep flitting around her bulky frame. I want to keep my focus on the entrance, in case she walks out.

Then the situation worsens.

A familiar face stands out from the crowd of people walking alongside the building.

What's *he* doing here?

How?

I turn quickly, snapping my head around to face the wall I'd been leaning against prior to Wendy turning up.

Please, God, don't let him see me.

I forget Wendy's here, next to me. I take her arm, and gently pull her towards me. I whisper conspiratorially in her ear: 'Don't look behind, but my ex-husband is over there and I can't handle him today. Just keep facing this way.' I keep my grasp on her arm, so she knows I'm serious.

Her eyes are wide as she stares at me, saying nothing.

If he hasn't seen me, it'll be all right. If he has . . .

I use Wendy as a shield as I twist my head slightly to look over her shoulder to the building opposite. It's clear. He's gone.

For now, at least. But that was too close. And with Wendy here too. It could've been disastrous.

I relax my grip on her and give a brief explanation of how awfully things had ended between us when Kyle was convicted of murder.

She needn't ever know it's a lie.

CHAPTER FIFTEEN

Deborah

Marcie's words played over in my mind all weekend. They wouldn't stop. I've flipped between full-on anger and complete helplessness and now, standing at the top of Berry Head, I just feel utterly lost. This seemed the best place to come – something drew me here.

The waves smash loudly against the rocks below. I watch the tiny droplets of water as they fly upwards, but I can't feel the spray on my face as I'm too far above. Must be a two-hundred-foot drop.

Enough to kill me.

Put me out of this misery.

Nathan would be all right. He's got *his* job, his overbearing mother, his precious golf buddies. I'm fairly sure he has a mistress, too. He'd do fine without me.

I teeter on the edge; the grass is slippery with dew. The intermittent gusts of wind shake my body – push me ever closer to the sheer drop. It really wouldn't take much.

The nerve of that woman. Sitting there, spouting on about how she misses her son. The nerve of Marcie, making me take time off work. The pity in her perfectly line-free face. Why now? I know I've been a bit more distracted recently – it is coming up to the anniversary. However, it's nothing she, or any of my colleagues, *should* take issue with. Others are worse. Colin, now he is one lazy shit – he's the one they should be telling to have time off. He's the one who delegates all his work to others while he wanks off in the loos in a vain attempt to compensate for his marriage break-up a year ago. Why isn't anyone bringing *that* to Marcie's attention? They're ganging up on me, picking faults, trying to get enough on me to get rid of me permanently. What have I done that's so wrong?

Surely it's enough that I lost my son. I don't think I should be punished further. Not me. I'm not the one needing punishment.

I catch my breath. The clarity of that thought hits me, like a short, sharp punch to the stomach.

I look down. I don't deserve those rocks, the crashing waves, the deep, dark, cold water as my grave. I shouldn't be the one to suffer that fate.

I take a step back.

I shouldn't be the one to suffer at all.

Maybe it was a blessing, Marcie forcing me to take leave. I have time now.

Time to put a few things straight.

CHAPTER SIXTEEN

Connie

The Alice standing opposite Connie was not the same calm and collected Alice she'd seen two weeks ago. She was now red-faced, flustered, and appeared agitated.

'So sorry I'm late,' she said, her breathing laboured. 'I had to . . . practically run . . . up the hill.'

'Please, Alice, don't worry. Take your time, there's no rush – you're my last client of the day.'

She took some deep breaths, then slumped, relaxing into the chair. Connie took her seat and waited for her to recover. After a few minutes, her colour had returned to normal.

'How have you been since our last meeting, Alice?'

Connie noted Alice's rapid blinking and how she was rubbing her hands together, and wondered what had happened to alter her demeanour. She waited for a response, but Alice remained silent.

'Maybe you could begin by telling me something you felt was positive?' Connie coaxed.

Alice's face broke into a wide smile. Connie gave an inward sigh of relief. At least there was something good to give her a starting point for this session.

'Positive, yes – there have been some good things since I last saw you. Some progression.'

'That's excellent, Alice. Let's begin with that then, shall we?'

'I found someone like me, someone who's going through the same issues as me. It's given me a purpose; some motivation.'

'It can be very helpful to know others have experienced similar situations to yourself, showing you that you're not alone in your struggles. Is it someone from your support group?'

Alice's mouth twitched; she took a while before she nodded.

'And you began the group, didn't you?'

'Yes. It was just online at first, but I decided it was more important to have proper face-to-face meetings.'

'That's such a positive step, and a really good outcome that you've bonded with someone else so early on in the group sessions. You must feel proud of your achievement?'

'I do, actually. The group is the best thing I've ever done,' Alice said, her face glowing. 'I feel as though I've met a kindred spirit.'

'Ah, that's great,' Connie said, nodding her head encouragingly. 'How has it helped you, in your everyday life?'

'It's given me hope. A focus. The group as a whole has obviously helped, but this one person is the key, I think.'

'The key? To what?'

'To me forgiving myself,' Alice said, her voice soft, almost a whisper.

Guilt was one of the biggest obstacles Connie had picked up on during her sessions with Alice. The fact she recognised she needed to forgive herself was a huge step. But that being said, Connie had a niggling feeling about Alice's part in all of this. Maybe she had good reason to blame herself. But that wasn't really Connie's role – to apportion blame, dig into someone's life and play detective. That was Lindsay's area of expertise. If she did unpick Alice's reason for guilt, and she *was* somehow to blame, Connie had to deal with it in a totally different way. Alice was her client. She had to help Alice. It was her job.

Now Connie had found out some of the positive things, she wanted to explore the reason for her earlier agitation.

'When you arrived today, it seemed like you were flustered. I know you were late and had rushed, but there was something else. What caused that?'

'Oh, it was nothing much. Stupid, really.' She flicked her hand dismissively.

'It didn't appear to be nothing, and I'm sure it wasn't stupid.'

Alice dropped her head, then snapped it back up, her intense eyes boring into Connie's.

'I had a shock, is all. Saw my ex-husband in town when I wasn't expecting it. I suppose it rattled me, made me panic.'

'Why would seeing him cause you to panic?'

'He's not a very nice man, Connie. Not someone I would want to have confronting me, especially as I was with someone from the group, too – and I didn't want her to see him. Meet him.'

'The woman you were talking about? The one you feel you have a lot in common with?'

'Um . . .' Alice looked confused for a moment, then nodded. 'Yes, yes – that one.'

'If you felt a connection with her, had things in common, maybe she would've understood if you'd confided in her?'

'Maybe. But I couldn't take the chance. I didn't want to expose her to him. Didn't want him knowing what I'm doing, who I'm friends with. He'd ruin it, put a stop to it. He doesn't like me talking to people about, you know, what happened. About Kyle.'

'I see.' Connie thought about this new information. It sounded as though Alice feared her ex-husband, and coupled with what she'd told her in the last session about how her son had taken over where her husband had left off, Connie suspected that Alice Mann had experienced a lot of trauma in her past – possibly abuse from both of them.

'I'm really sorry he made . . . *makes* you feel that way, Alice. I'm sure it must cause difficulties, and means it's challenging for you to move forwards.'

57

'He prevents me moving forwards, yes. I have to do my best *despite* him; pretend he's not here. I suppose I pretend a lot.'

'You shouldn't have to pretend. I can help you work through these challenges, help with coping strategies. If your ex-husband is threatening you, causing you fear, there are people who can assist with that too – not only the police, but services who can offer practical support.'

'No!' Alice jumped up. 'No, Connie. Thank you, but that won't be necessary. I'm sorry. This wasn't what I wanted to talk to you about, not what I wanted help with.'

'Okay, I'm sorry, Alice. Please sit back down.' Connie got to her feet and reached out to touch Alice's arm, but the damage seemed to have been done.

Alice turned her back and walked towards the consulting room door. She stopped in the doorway, looking back over her shoulder.

'I'm wasting your time, I'm sorry.'

The door slammed behind her.

Connie screwed her eyes up. *Damn.* She must have gone too far.

She had pushed Alice away.

CHAPTER SEVENTEEN

Connie

'Yes, Mum, I promise I'll be careful.' Connie's ear was hot from pressing the phone to it for so long.

'I feel it's a mistake, I can't help it, love. You shouldn't be going backwards, you should be concentrating on the future, moving forwards in your life. No good can come of this – your practice should be your focus, not those *degenerates.*'

'I know, I know.' Connie rolled her neck, attempting to release some of the tension stored there. Her mum had repeated this advice at least four times in the one call. 'This will be the one and only time, I swear. I've done one session, I'm there tomorrow, then perhaps two more days next week, that's it.'

'Yes, you already said, dear.'

Connie closed her eyes and shook her head, suppressing the urge to say, *it must be catching*, saying instead: 'Well, I thought I'd reiterate it.'

'I don't want any harm to come to you. That's not a bad thing, is it?'

'No. Of course not,' Connie said.

There was a silence at the end of the line. Connie knew why. It wasn't only the last few years she was alluding to. When Connie was fifteen, her mum had feared for her well-being, had told her she was making mistakes – but her words had gone unheeded. Connie dropped her hand to her stomach, thinking about how her behaviour back then had led to one of the worst things that had happened to her. It was no wonder her mum was always worrying about her. But in some ways, Connie could understand that. While she wasn't a mother herself, she knew exactly how it felt to *need* to protect someone.

Because Connie was keeping the biggest secret of all from her mum – one that had come crashing into her own life last year, and that she'd worried about every day since. Twenty-one years ago, Connie's older brother Luke was stabbed to death. And just eight months ago, Connie discovered that his injury had not, as they'd all been led to believe, been fatal. As a result of her involvement in the Hargreaves murder inquiry, her father's lies had been spilled, their abhorrent nature made clear. Luke's death had been faked to protect him from their father's toxic business dealings, dealings that ensured Manchester gangs were out for blood. His, or his family's. After Luke's supposed death, Connie had spent years feeling she was the one her father would've rather lost. *Anyone but his precious son.* She'd fought for his approval throughout her life, even when he moved back to Manchester, leaving her and her mum in Devon. Connie strived to make him proud of her, to the point she began to hate him, or maybe even herself, for the way she allowed him to make her feel. And then she'd discovered that the bulk of her life was built on a lie. At the time of the revelation, Connie had been absolutely convinced she should go straight to her mum and tell her everything she'd learned. She'd wanted to resist her father's control, his warped sense of protection over them.

It'll kill her if she found out now. Don't do it, Connie, he'd begged.

It's killing her anyway, Connie had argued.

She would never forgive her father, but for her mother's sake, as well as for fear of putting Luke and her family in further jeopardy, Connie continued pretending that none of it had resurfaced – that Luke was still buried.

60

'So,' her mum's voice cut into her thoughts, 'are you free to come over for a bite to eat on Saturday? I'd quite like some company . . .'

Connie drew in a large lungful of air. It was Luke's birthday on Saturday. Her brother would've been forty-one if he hadn't been taken from them at seventeen. Connie quickly shook away the thought. He is *going* to be forty-one.

'Yeah, of course, Mum. Do you want me to bring anything? Wine? Pudding?'

'Just yourself, dear . . . and your friend, if you like?'

That would make things easier. Lindsay would help with conversation, prevent it from slipping into the dangerous territory of family secrets.

'If you're okay with that, then yes. Lindsay would love to meet you properly.'

'It's a date, then.'

Connie could hear in her mum's tone she was smiling. Maybe the fact Connie was keeping this huge secret from her *was* the right thing to do.

CHAPTER EIGHTEEN

Deborah

A chill ripples inside my body, shaking my foundation like a gust of wind through a tree threatening to shed its leaves. My fingers tremble as I flatten the yellowing newspaper page. I hide the tin full of cuttings from Nathan. He doesn't think it's good to brood over the past. Now, seeing the headlines again, I relive it all with frightening clarity.

I am there. Back on that day. I can feel all I felt then, only now it's even worse. Because I know more now than I did when I was first told of my son's death. His murder. I know far too much about Kyle Mann. I swallow the rising hatred.

Why does the media insist on displaying the faces of those who have committed such hideous crimes, name them, talk about them, dissect every area of their lives? Why give them the space, the attention? I can't stand it. It's the victims who should be the focus. I don't want to read about how this murdering bastard had a hard life; a difficult upbringing. So what?

I had many of these thoughts back then. I told anyone who was willing to listen. Even those who weren't. Looking at these articles again now, I'm aware my anger hasn't subsided. I've just done a good job of distracting myself from it.

But now that distraction has gone, thanks to Marcie.

The driveway gravel crunches beneath a car. I jump up, place the cuttings back inside the old biscuit tin and push it under the pile of my jumpers on the shelf in the walk-in wardrobe. Nathan's home. I haven't told him I'm on 'gardening leave' yet. Not sure whether I should. Maybe I can keep it to myself, for a while at least.

He won't know that I'm not leaving for work. He always leaves the house before me, and I'm home before him. I can keep up the facade easily. After all, I'm well-practised.

CHAPTER NINETEEN

Alice

I'm sitting waiting.

The last Wednesday of February seems to have taken an age to come around, and now it's here, I'm consumed with impatience for my group to arrive. I got here nice and early to ensure I had plenty of time to set up the room. I've brought supplies for a tea break too this time. We can all have a relaxed chat while we refuel.

It's cold today. The air in the large, high-ceilinged church room envelops me in its cool cocoon. I do up the buttons of my cardigan, but it won't be enough to stop the shivers. Maybe I should bring my electric blower heater next time. Although, looking around me, I can see there are radiators. I'll ask the caretaker why they aren't on. Perhaps he doesn't think a small group like mine deserves to have money spent on it. It must cost a lot to heat this huge space.

Half an hour to go.

I'm regretting arriving here quite so early. This last thirty minutes is dragging. What if no one turns up this time? The first session went well, I thought – and Wendy *did* say she was looking forwards to it.

Relax. They will come.

I get up, and begin to pace the wooden floor. I need to try to warm up.

My mind goes back to my session with Connie. I've gone over it again and again. It hadn't progressed the way I wanted it to. She'd been clever, picked up on something I didn't really want to talk about, and directed the session her way. Towards her agenda, not mine. I hadn't had a chance to ask the questions I'd planned; ones that would've been useful for today's group meeting. The next counselling session could be awkward, she might continue down the abused wife route. I'll have to think of something to start off the session differently. A big disclosure to knock her sideways, steer it in the opposite direction to what I know she wants.

Actually, maybe I have just the thing . . .

No time to think about it now – I hear the outer door bang.

'Thank you, God.' I look up to the Lord, crossing my chest. At least someone has turned up.

It's Wendy. She was first here last time too.

My heart dips a little. I hope some others come early as well. I don't want too much time alone with her – I don't want her to bring up the episode with my 'ex-husband'. I've got a little story planned, though, just in case. I have to cover all bases, be prepared.

As I'm welcoming her, a few others follow.

Warmth replaces the cold I'd been feeling.

Finally, when everyone has filtered in, I notice that my group has grown by two people. Once we're all settled in the circle, we do another brief round of introductions, welcoming the new members. And I'm thrilled to find one of them is Bill.

I smile widely, feeling my face glow. Excellent. I've been successful in getting him to the group – my comment on the online support group obviously did the trick. It feels good to know I have *some* powers of persuasion.

CHAPTER TWENTY

Connie

'Any men on the scene, Connie, love?'

Connie slumped against the high back of the dining chair. She'd been waiting for something like this all evening; her mother's idea of small talk at the dinner table.

'No, Mum. It's been a while since I've been on the dating scene – no time for all that.' It was the easiest and quickest way to shut that particular conversation down. She'd had issues trusting men ever since her teenage trauma – 'That Night' at the party where things had gone terribly wrong and she was taken advantage of. It was a time in her life Connie didn't like to dwell on, or revisit.

'Oh, that's a shame. You're not getting any younger – I suppose I'm not going to be a grandma anytime soon then.'

Connie's face flushed.

'What about you, dear, anyone special?' She directed her probing question to Lindsay.

'About the same, I'm afraid, Bev.' Lindsay took a large gulp of red wine. 'My divorce came through a few months ago.'

'Ahh, I'm sorry. Is that why you've got a room in Connie's house?'

'That, and it made sense financially and geographically. I was travelling to Coleton every day from Plymouth, it was a long trek.

After Connie's . . . experience . . . last year, we decided it would work well for both of us. And it does.' Lindsay turned to Connie and smiled as she raised her glass in a toast.

Connie noted that her mum had inched forwards in her seat, clearly itching to interject. She certainly didn't waste any time.

'So, tell me, Lindsay, what big case are you working on right now? The missing girl I heard about on the news?'

'You can't ask that, Mum! Lindsay can't talk about cases outside of her work.'

'I'm sure she talks to you about it though, doesn't she?' Her mum gave a cringeworthy wink as she passed Lindsay the dish of vegetables. Connie threw an apologetic smile at Lindsay.

'It's okay.' Lindsay slyly jabbed her elbow in Connie's side and widened her eyes at her before turning back to her mum. 'If I don't divulge anything that could compromise any ongoing investigations, I can talk about them. You know, in general.' She smiled. 'I don't tell Connie very much, actually.' Lindsay pushed the serving dish towards Connie.

Connie took it and dolloped a small spoonful of veg on her plate. Her appetite had waned the minute Lindsay had turned off the main Teignmouth road and crossed the bridge into Shaldon. As soon as Connie had walked through the front door of her mum's terraced house, her gut had twisted into a painful knot and hadn't relaxed since. At least the emphasis so far had been on Lindsay and her role as detective inspector. She hoped she didn't feel uncomfortable with her mum's questions. Judging by the dig she'd been given in the ribs, she guessed she must be fine with it. She should try to relax a little.

'See, Connie, Lindsay doesn't mind.' She smirked teasingly at Connie and then took a mouthful of food.

'I am involved in the missing person case, yes,' Lindsay said.

Connie looked up sharply. 'Are you? I didn't realise.'

Lindsay had worked long hours the last couple of days, but hadn't told Connie why. She should've guessed it was on the missing twenty-one-year-old's case, which had been widely reported since Wednesday evening.

'See, Bev, I don't tell her everything.' Lindsay laughed.

'Terrible business. That poor family. I do hope it's a happy ending. Do you think it will be, Lindsay?' Connie watched as her mother's eyes darkened. This topic of conversation wasn't a good idea; her mum would be thinking about Luke, especially given today was his birthday, and how she'd lost her son under such tragic circumstances. It would make it difficult for Connie, knowing what she now knew. She'd tried so hard not to think about Luke, not to contemplate the hows, whys and whens. Tried hard not to spill everything to her mum, often wrestling with her decision not to disclose the details.

Lindsay placed her knife and fork on her plate and leant back, exhaling loudly. 'If I'm honest, Bev, it doesn't look very hopeful. In this kind of case we're searching for proof of life. It's been over forty-eight hours and we haven't found any evidence of that yet. Those first hours are critical.'

'But maybe she's gone off with friends without telling anyone?' Her mother's voice was filled with a hope that made Connie's heart ache.

'It's a possibility,' Lindsay said, 'but she hasn't accessed her bank account, her mobile phone hasn't been used, so . . .'

'Must be a hard job, dealing with something so awful – having to be the sole hope for her family.'

'Yes, it is. You never really get used to it, although you do learn to manage. All my major cases have been challenging, each one for different reasons.'

'You must be very strong, Lindsay. I'm glad there are people like you who work for the victims, their family. Get justice.' Tears sparkled in her eyes.

Connie looked down at her plate, not wanting to witness her mum's pain.

'I try to be strong. You have to be, really, to keep on doing the job. We don't always serve justice though, I'm afraid. Not every case results in a conviction.'

'No. I know. We never got justice for our Luke.'

Connie's stomach flipped. She shut her eyes tightly, not trusting herself to look into her mother's eyes. The silence stretched.

'I'm really sorry about your son, Bev. I'm sorry closure wasn't gained.'

Connie felt a hand on hers and opened her eyes. Lindsay had her other hand on her mum's. Connie wondered if Lindsay felt guilty too. She had confided in her, and so she also knew about Luke being alive and well. Not dead.

The weight of the lie dragged Connie down; made her heavy. Almost twelve months of keeping this huge secret. How had her father done it for twenty-two years? Unbelievable.

'You are back working in the prison on Monday then, Connie.' Her mum's sudden change in direction was both welcome and unwanted. At least she wasn't talking about Luke. It wasn't long ago that she'd wanted to hear her mum talk about her brother, encouraged her – manipulated situations in order to *make* her talk about him. Now she was quashing her attempts, changing the subject and avoiding any talk of him. It was unfair. Cruel.

She hated her father. For lying in the first place, for hiding the truth for so long. And for dragging Connie into his deceit, making her a co-conspirator. A liar.

At the same time, she didn't want to discuss her decision to go back to HMP Baymead, to go over her mother's fears yet again. Didn't she have enough to feel guilty for?

'Yes, Mum. It's going okay, actually. It's not the same as before.' She smiled at her mum. 'Honestly.'

'Good. I'm glad. They won't keep asking you to do these . . . report things, will they?'

'Oh, don't worry. I've made it perfectly clear this is a one-off. Even if they ask again, I'll say no . . .'

'No you won't, Connie. You're like your dad in that way.' Her voice was flat, monotone.

Connie's heartbeat jolted. *Like your dad.* The words cut deep. But there was a truth in them that Connie couldn't deny.

CHAPTER TWENTY-ONE

Connie

'I'm Connie. I don't know if you remember me – I saw you when you first arrived at Baymead two years ago . . .'

Kyle Mann's eyes were cloudy, red-rimmed. He looked as though he'd just woken up after a heavy drinking session. Or, as was more likely in prison, he'd taken drugs. The mass of blond curls he'd had when Connie first met him were gone: a shaved scalp now replaced them, giving his features a harder edge. He looked more like the criminal he was than the younger butter-wouldn't-melt appearance he'd entered the prison system with.

Connie tilted her head in the direction of his gaze, seeking his attention. He didn't give any sign he'd heard her, or that he was even aware of her presence. He was sitting opposite her, a table separating them, with Connie closest to the door. And the alarm. He appeared relaxed: his legs loosely positioned, knees splayed – very close to Connie's – and hands resting on the table.

Jen had said that he hadn't spoken a word to any of the staff since his imprisonment. She wondered if he kept this vow of silence with other inmates. She'd get Verity to take her to the wing later so she could speak to his personal officer to find out who he associated with, and if they'd had any evidence of him communicating in any way.

'I am a forensic psychologist. I'm here today to carry out an assessment that will be used together with a number of other reports and will be compiled for the parole board in relation to your progression through the system. Do you understand, Kyle?'

Nothing.

Jen was right; it was unlikely he would start talking now, not after all this time. Connie needn't have worried about a conflict of interest, any ethical dilemma in working with Alice. She'd have to carry on with this meeting regardless though, get what she needed, and then call for Verity to come back and escort her to the psychology office.

'I'm an independent psychologist, which means I don't work in the prison, or for the prison service. My role is to work with you, talk to you about your offence, your risk factors, and give recommendations for rehabilitation programmes. I'll do a written report, which will be provided to the parole board. Okay?'

Connie thought she saw a flicker in Kyle's eyes. A quick glance in her direction. But still she was faced with the wall of silence. She moved her chair along slightly, lining it up so that she was in his direct line of vision. He lowered his head, purposely avoiding catching her eye. So, he did know she was there. He was well aware of why she was there, she felt sure.

'Right, well, I'm going to read through some of these notes I have here,' Connie said as she placed his file on the table and opened it. 'And you jump in whenever you want. Tell me if there's anything you want to clarify, or add. Anything you don't agree with.'

Connie started to read out the description of his offence. Every now and then she paused, looking up to observe his body language, to see if his expression had altered. He remained closed. He'd had a few years to perfect this routine. He was good at it. It was highly improbable Connie would crack him without something new, something to give him cause to wobble – a reason to speak.

During her last visit to the prison, when she'd studied the files of the men she'd be assessing, Connie had reread the police transcript of their interview with Kyle prior to him being charged with murder. He'd been incredibly vague, often giving one-word responses, but *had* spoken. However, as soon as they charged him, further interviews had been 'no comment' ones or he'd simply remained quiet – supposedly at the advice of his solicitor. She'd also read the lengthy transcript of the interview with Kyle's parents. With Alice, and her husband, Edward. How they'd been so certain their son would not have committed this crime without serious coercion. His mother in particular had been totally convinced he'd been targeted, manipulated and groomed by someone. She'd said he was an easy target because of his behavioural difficulties. She'd said he suffered with mild Asperger's and had some learning difficulties growing up. None of this could be substantiated in court later – there was simply no hard evidence to back up her claims. No assessments, no input from services, school, or any doctors able to confirm anything Alice Mann had asserted.

As Connie began reading from the notes she'd taken from the transcript, Kyle's eyes closed, and she noticed his knuckles turning white as he clenched his hands into fists.

Just talking about what his mum had said to the police had touched a nerve.

'Your mum really believes in you. You know that, don't you?'

There was a scraping sound as Kyle drew in his legs, tucking them under the chair.

'You know she doesn't believe you would be capable of such a crime. Of murder.' Connie was on a roll. Her passion for forensic psychology was reignited in that moment; she wanted to do a good job, like she always felt she had prior to the Hargreaves incident. Looking at Kyle now, she was suddenly eager to get something from him. A reaction. Even if she couldn't get him to speak. She picked up a piece of paper containing her scribbled notes and, holding it so she could see it and Kyle's face easily above the paper, began reading:

'Kyle wouldn't purposely hurt anyone. He's always been a kind, considerate boy, but he was used. People took advantage of him, of his vulnerability. He couldn't have done this on his own. It's impossible.' Connie read the words loudly, leaning in towards Kyle's face. She was pushing it, she knew – but something made her feel safe; she didn't sense he was a risk to her.

Kyle's breathing rate increased; Connie could hear the flow of air as it pushed through his nostrils and was quickly drawn back in again.

This was the most reaction she'd ever known Kyle Mann give. His mum was the key. The way she could get him to speak, she was convinced of that now.

Without much thought of the consequences, Connie played her trump card.

'I know your mum feels incredible guilt about you being here. She believes she's let you down, that she could've done something to prevent it.'

His eyes were wide now. Focussed on Connie for the first time.

She continued. 'I know this, Kyle, because she told me. The other day in fact, when she came to see me for my help.'

Kyle lurched forwards. Connie's pulse banged in her neck.

'You're lying,' he shouted, before slamming his back against his chair, the plastic bouncing with the force.

Connie's mouth slackened. She'd done it. Made him utter actual words.

She stalled in her shock, but quickly recovered; she had to keep it going now she'd made a breakthrough.

'I wouldn't lie to you, Kyle. I think you should know what your mother is going through.'

A pang of guilt struck her. She shouldn't have told him, she'd really compromised herself now. In her eagerness to get Kyle to speak, she'd broken the code of conduct.

Dammit.

What if Kyle's stony silence didn't stretch as far as his mum?

He could call Alice, tell her what Connie had said. She'd be in all kinds of trouble. Again. But she'd done what no one else had been able to: she'd made Kyle Mann talk. She may only have this one chance. She had to continue – and deal with the consequences later.

'She's not the only one who thinks you didn't act alone, is she? The police also suspected you were with someone else that day. That another person was as responsible, if not more so than you, for the murder of Sean Taylor.'

'They're wrong.' His voice was a quiet rasp, as though not speaking for all this time had dried his vocal cords and stringing a whole sentence together was challenging.

'Are they, Kyle? Even your mum?'

'Especially my mum. I'm not the son she thinks I am.'

Connie sat back, turning over in her mind what Alice had revealed so far about Kyle during her sessions. The aggressive, almost bullying nature she'd described as part of the behaviour she'd endured from Kyle at home, prior to his offence, was not the same picture Alice had painted at the time of his arrest. Didn't sound like the Kyle she'd spoken of in the transcript Connie had read. Had Alice lied in the interview with the police in an attempt to protect him?

'I would really like to hear an account of what happened in the lead-up to Sean Taylor's death. How did the day begin for you, Kyle?'

He snorted and shook his head. 'I've done all this.'

'Well, actually you haven't. If your records are correct, you gave "no comment" interviews. Where did you spend the day, Kyle?' Connie laid her notes down and rested her elbows on the table.

Kyle shrugged his shoulders. Had he verbally communicated all he was willing to? An unexpected sense of disappointment swept through her.

'Who else did you see that day? Did you meet up with someone?'

He averted his eyes from Connie's. She was losing him.

'Who was it? Someone you used to game with online?' Connie immediately regretted her question. She was using things arising from Alice's session as a way of forcing Kyle to speak. It was so unethical, she felt her face grow hot with the knowledge of what she was doing.

Kyle's own face flushed, his eyes growing wider, darker; his pupils dilating.

Connie swallowed hard as he pushed violently up from his chair.

He left the room without saying another word.

Someone else had been involved with Sean's murder, she felt sure now. The one that got away. And for some reason, Kyle was protecting him.

CHAPTER TWENTY-TWO

Tom

The house was even quieter than usual. He knew he must be alone. He was glad. At least he didn't have to worry about being caught; he was getting fed up of having to deal with endless questions. He could talk online uninterrupted. His sessions had increased again. The time it'd taken to organise the gaming site had taken far more effort; it was time-consuming getting the right people involved. Keeping them on his domain, even more challenging. Everyone thought they were a gamer these days. Most didn't know the skill it took. Most didn't realise the thrills would diminish later down the line. When they'd played as long as he had, they'd come to the same conclusion: online slaughter isn't enough. Once you reach a certain level it's more difficult to get the adrenaline going, more difficult to feel alive.

When you're at my level, things have got to get real.

He'd lasted four whole years. He'd tried to recreate the thrills online only. But now the urge was too strong, he needed more.

He'd obviously got away with the last one, so he should be fine. It was time.

He needed another kill – and he'd found the perfect player.

CHAPTER TWENTY-THREE

Deborah

I lie still, watching as Nathan dresses in his charcoal-grey suit. He's still attractive – he's aged exceptionally well. He doesn't even have any visible grey in his hair, and is not receding, or balding like a lot of men his age. He keeps himself trim, weekly visits to the gym, plus running and golf at the weekend. I can see why he gains female attention at work. There seem to be a lot of women employees at the district council offices. When I used to pop in to see Nathan on my lunch breaks, I'd noticed how the reception desk was manned by dolled-up, pretty women. Back when I really cared, it would bother me, how they tripped over themselves to speak to him, almost scrambling to get his attention. Even if I was standing with him, they would openly flirt, as if I wasn't there.

I wonder who he's shagging.

'Come on, lazybones, you're going to be late for work,' he says as he bends to plant a kiss on my head.

'Five more minutes.' I stretch and make out I'm still tired. I am tired, as it happens. I lay awake for long periods in the night, thinking. About work. Or lack of it – and how I'm going to fill the endless hours each day. And thinking about Alice. How I might pay *her* a visit. The newspapers didn't say much about her at the time of Kyle Mann's arrest and subsequent trial; her husband,

Edward, was the focus. The troubled father-son relationship, often speculative and also told through the subjectivity of neighbours, was what gained column inches; sold papers. It would perhaps be interesting to find out what part Alice herself played in her son's delinquent behaviour; his ultimate ability to take another's life.

'I might be a bit late tonight, sorry. There's a planning meeting at six, discussing the new project, remember – the expansion of a small industrial estate to incorporate a supermarket?'

He'd not spoken of it since the last meeting he'd had that had run over time. By two hours. 'Oh yes, right. I'll cook late then, for eight?' I push my lips into a smile.

'Oh, I would just put something back for me. You can never tell how long these meetings are going to take. No doubt Phil will have countless questions to ask right at the end – always does.' Nathan doesn't look me in the eye. It's the first time I really *feel* it – the disloyalty. I'm not sure whether to be angry or sad, or thankful that at least someone's giving him what he needs. How can I blame him for grasping any ounce of happiness that comes his way? Life has been such a struggle for us since losing Sean. If I had the inclination, I could probably stop him from straying. But I don't, not at the moment. Plus, if his attention is elsewhere, I'll be more likely to get away with my own indiscretion.

I wait until the front door bangs closed, listen to the car wheels noisily spewing small stone chippings as Nathan leaves the driveway, before I swing my legs from the bed. I shower and dress as I would for a normal workday.

Only, today isn't normal.

Today is the first day of living a lie.

Or is it? Maybe that's what I've already been doing up *until* today.

A change is as good as a rest, my mum would've said. Having no job to go to is certainly a change.

I don't know where to find Alice. She didn't say where she lived and I only gleaned a few things from her nervous chatter – like she works, or worked, part-time somewhere – but I can't remember much, as I wasn't taking it in. I didn't ask any questions about her, or her life. I wasn't interested before now.

I have a strong suspicion I won't have to find her, though – she'll come to me.

CHAPTER TWENTY-FOUR

Alice

I haven't stopped thinking about last Wednesday's group session. Even now as I watch the TV, and the unfolding drama on *Jeremy Kyle*, snippets of it pop into my mind. It went so well. I always hoped it would, of course, but it exceeded my expectations. Listening to how the others opened up – spoke without fear of judgement – filled me with such pride.

I've done this; *I've* made it happen. I'm helping others.

Bill is an asset, too. I knew he would be. I'm so pleased I managed to convince him to meet with us all in person. For at least half the session the focus was on him, his daughter Isabella, and the situation tearing his family apart. He held the group in the palm of his hand, every one of them enthralled by his words, his emotions laid bare for all to witness, to share. He showed us a photo of Isabella, passed it around the circle, lapping up the group's comments on how beautiful she is. I saw how his face lit up with love for her, then crumpled as he spoke of his worry about her behaviour. Everyone seemed shocked at how the stunning young woman in the photo could be the cause of so much anxiety, pain. But not me.

I wipe a tear away. Broken families. I can relate to that.

Bill is strong, though. Far stronger than I am. Not only

physically – which is plain to see as he's around six foot and his biceps are well defined – but mentally, too. I noted a fight in his hazel-brown eyes, a steely determination to keep his daughter safe from harm. The love he has for Isabella is unconditional, limitless – her behaviour, her frequent arrests are, as Bill told us, a cry for help. It's his responsibility to ensure she gets that help, he'd said. His wife, on the other hand, sounds like a wet blanket – unable, or unwilling, to step in or make waves in fear of the repercussions from Isabella. He's strong. She's weak. The similarities are not lost on me.

Bill and I would make a strong team; we could face anything. If I'd had such a man, things might've been different.

Jeremy's condescending voice screams out of the TV, then the programme cuts to a commercial break. The words *The Jeremy Kyle Show* are displayed momentarily on the screen. Kyle. There's no escaping the name.

It seems like a huge gap again before the next support meeting. A whole month to ruminate. I do have things I can fill my time with at least – not just mindless television programmes. I may not be needed as much, or in the same way as my group members need me, but I can still be of help to *someone*. Even if she doesn't see it herself yet. I'm sure she *will* see it, once I confide in her. I think I'll have to share a bit more than I planned though, to gain her trust. She won't accept the similarities, the fact I can help her, if she doesn't trust me. And I need that. I have to help her, so in return she can get me closer to my goal of redemption. But I'm not sure I should try her workplace again. After the last failed trip, and almost getting caught out, it would be far easier, and safer, to visit her house.

Of course, at her house she has more control; the upper hand. Can refuse to open the door to me. I need her to *invite* me in rather than me just turn up out of the blue again. I wonder where she does her shopping? Does she do it daily, weekly? At weekends, evenings? If I could find that out, I might be able to bump into her, get chatting and somehow manipulate the situation so she invites me into hers.

A sudden crashing noise stops my thoughts. I quickly jab the remote control to mute the volume of the TV and hold my breath so I can hear properly. Was it outside, or inside?

I hear the hum of the fridge-freezer in the kitchen, the ticking of the wall clock above the mantle.

I hear a squeaking. The door handle?

I shrink down a little, my shoulders slumping.

CHAPTER TWENTY-FIVE

Connie

The day had stretched once Connie returned to the psychology portacabin following her interview with Kyle Mann. She'd been part thrilled and part scared to tell Jen she'd finally got The Silent One to utter words. She'd dared not mention *how* she'd accomplished it. The shock of her revelation was clear to see on Jen's face. The shock, however, was quickly turned back on Connie when Jen told her it would be good if she visited him again, seeing as she'd been the one to break the silence. Getting herself in deeper was not in her game plan. In and out had been the intention. Not making herself desirable to the psychology team and therefore ensuring more days within the prison walls. She'd been vague when Jen asked when she would next be in. Connie needed some time to figure out how to get out of seeing Kyle again.

The relief of finally walking through her front door washed over her. Connie grabbed Amber and snuggled her face into the warm, fluffy white fur. There was no sign of Lindsay and she hadn't received any texts from her during the day, no communications on her phone when she'd got back to her car and checked it. She resigned herself to another evening meal alone.

*　*　*

Having eaten leftover cottage pie, Connie stood at the window, eyes searching the road for the appearance of Lindsay's dark blue Volvo. The TV played to itself behind her. She'd watched the six o'clock news, listened as the family of the missing young woman appealed for information. Connie hoped that despite what Lindsay had said the other night, there could still be a positive outcome. She'd left the TV on so there was some sound in the house, a semblance of company.

The world outside the window darkened as black clouds converged, blanketing the sky completely and plunging the houses opposite into shadow.

Finally, Connie spotted Lindsay's car. She smiled as her friend's red-haired head came into view and she pulled up outside. Her movements were slow as she got out and made her way into the house. Even from the window and in the relative darkness, Connie could see the tiredness etched on her pale face.

'Hiya,' Lindsay said, throwing her coat over the bannister as she came in.

'Hey! How's your day been?' Connie tried to make her tone light; upbeat, but from Lindsay's expression it'd obviously been a long, hard one.

Lindsay rubbed her eyes with her fingertips, then dragged her splayed fingers down over her face and neck. 'Ugh. I don't think I've the energy to tell you about it.'

'That sounds bad.' Connie followed Lindsay into the lounge. 'Have you eaten?'

'Mack brought us some fabulously healthy Maccies to keep us going.'

'Maybe just as well. There's not much food left here until I get around to shopping.'

'Ah, sorry – I don't even know what day I'm on, haven't even thought about food shopping.' Lindsay threw herself onto the sofa.

'No, don't worry, I'll do it tomorrow after work.' Connie perched on the edge of the sofa, next to her. 'Look, I need to say sorry for the third degree from my mother the other night. I haven't really seen you since . . .'

'Hah! Really, it's fine. Interesting being on the receiving end of an interrogation for a change.'

'Hopefully it's out of her system now. Next time you're in her company, she'll be less inquisitive.'

'It's actually quite nice having someone pay an interest in my work.'

'Oh, I see. Meaning I don't . . .' Connie gave her a gentle push.

'Oi! You know I didn't mean that.' Lindsay managed a smile, although even that looked as though it took a lot of effort. 'Right, I'm done in, Connie. Off to bed for me, early start tomorrow.'

'Yes, this missing person's case? Sorry, I didn't realise you were dealing with that.'

'There's so much more to it, I think. Not a straightforward misper.'

'Oh, sounds bad. Poor girl.'

'Tomorrow will be the turning point.' Lindsay gave Connie's shoulder a squeeze then turned, leaving the lounge and heading upstairs without expanding on her comment.

After her day at the prison, Connie's mind was too full – there was no way she'd be able to go to bed at this time. It was only 8 p.m. She kicked off her shoes and went to the fridge, pouring herself a large glass of Pinot Grigio. She'd wondered whether to confide in Lindsay, tell her about the meeting with Kyle Mann. Maybe even explain how she'd pushed ethical boundaries. But seeing how exhausted Lindsay was, and then her going to bed so early, meant the opportunity was lost anyway.

For now, she'd have to keep it to herself.

Connie took a gulp of wine.

Another secret to add to the list.

CHAPTER TWENTY-SIX

Alice

I'm so tired.

I dot some concealer, then foundation to cover the dark bags under my eyes. The once-firm skin crumples and puckers underneath my fingertips. I wince as I spread double the amount over my right cheekbone.

I have to get out of this house today. Do something positive, something to make progress. I fear time is running out. I've decided I should go into Coleton every day for the rest of this week, either to her home or work. One way or another, by Friday, she will have invited me to become her friend, her ally. I feel sure.

I don't hang around once I go downstairs; no breakfast for me this morning. No dallying – watching TV, checking the online support group or tidying. I grab my coat and bag and leave quickly without a backward glance. I'm a woman on a mission.

The ground is damp from overnight rain, remnants of it puddling in the dips in the pavements and potholes in the road. The sky is clearer now, thankfully. I don't want to be stuck outside in bad weather while I wait for her to emerge from her house. Supposing she even leaves her house today. I do hope so, I could do with a spot of luck following the failed attempt to see her at her workplace. Yesterday I'd braved a call, making up a random query and asking to speak with her. They'd said she was unavailable, and when I mentioned calling back the following day, I'd been informed she wouldn't be in. I wondered if they were lying, but then questioned why they'd need to. If God is on my side, she won't have left home this early even if she has plans, and I will therefore see her when she does.

The bus driver looks me straight in the eye and gives a courteous nod as I climb the steps. He recognises me. I'm a regular now. I'm hoping that's why he gives the nod anyway, not because he knows my face from before. I push the thought aside as I take my seat and the bus rumbles off.

I need to be careful where I position myself; I can't wait directly outside her house because obviously I'll raise suspicion. Plus, if she sees me she might cause a scene, ask me to leave. No, I must play this carefully. I carry on past her house without looking up. The road is long, with a small shop at one end and a newsagent next to it. If I lived here, I'd use these amenities often. So maybe she does too. That would be good, and easier than trying to find out which supermarket she goes to. Although, the downside is it will be far more difficult to make it seem like an accidental meeting. I don't think she knows where *I* live, though, so in theory, bumping into her here could be put down to coincidence.

I must perfect my brief-but-convincing story of why I happen to be in the same place as her. But I can't really hang around here for hours waiting for an appearance, it would look odd.

I amble up and down the four aisles of the shop. It's one of those corner shops that has all sorts in it. I pick up random items, stare at the labels intently for ages before replacing them. Then I move a few steps forwards and repeat the process.

After doing this for what feels like an hour, I decide I should buy something, or I'm likely to be suspected of shoplifting.

I opt for a bottle of water and a Mars bar. The sugar hit will keep me going. This could be a long day. I'll come back a bit later for a sandwich.

Back outside, I stop and read the notices on the huge corkboard in the window of the newsagent next door, each 'lost' poster and every 'for sale' post.

I check my watch. Ten o'clock. I've passed an hour, that's all. I sigh, looking up and down the street.

There she is.

I can't believe it. She's heading this way.

I dart inside the newsagent's, heart galloping, the blood whooshing through my veins. I cross my heart – *Thank you, God.* I pray she doesn't walk on by.

The door clangs as it opens. I turn away quickly when I see it's her who comes in, so she doesn't notice me straight away. My heart needs to settle before I make my move. I pull a newspaper from the white, plastic rack and hold it in front of my face, lowering it enough to see her. She approaches the post office kiosk, a large white envelope in one hand. I should be able to time it so I walk in front of her as she's going back to the door. I'll take this newspaper to the counter at the same time and bump into her.

Perfect.

She glances over in my direction, so I raise the paper again and, for the first time, I look properly at the front page.

My heart jolts as I take in the headline.

Still No Leads As Missing Isabella's Dad Makes Emotional Plea.

The photo, immediately below the words now floating in and out of focus, is Bill's daughter. I take a sharp intake of breath. Oh, my dear God. I can't read the article; my eyes are too bleary.

I throw the paper back in the rack, holding onto the A-framed structure for support. How has this happened? When? I only saw Bill on Wednesday. I need to know the details, yet I also need to keep to my plan. I take a deep breath, and make to move off. The woman behind the counter is casting me a worried look. She probably thinks I'm about to keel over, have a heart attack. I may well do. The shock of this could bring one on, and together with my other stressors, I could be six feet under before I know it. I must get a hold of myself. Concentrate on what I'm meant to be doing. I look around.

She's no longer in the queue.

During the time of my brief distraction, she's sent her post and left. She's nowhere else in the newsagent's. I curse under my breath and head to the door. I can't be far behind her. I walk outside on shaky legs – if they don't stop shaking, it's going to make catching her up very problematic. I can only just make her out ahead of me. She's gained so much ground. She must be late for something, the speed at which she's walking.

She walks in the opposite direction of her house for a fair distance, maybe half a mile or so, before I see her slow, then stop. She disappears from my view, presumably into a house. I am too far behind her to be sure. The opportunity to bump into her accidentally, as I'd planned, has seemingly passed. But I'm nothing if not patient. I'll have to adapt my plan now, think quickly on my feet if I still want to get into her house today.

CHAPTER TWENTY-SEVEN

Tom

After checking the coast was clear, Tom climbed the stairs from the basement and grabbed a bowl and the nearest cereal box from the kitchen cupboard. He poured milk over the cornflakes until the bowl was brimming, then stood looking outside the back window while he spooned the food into his mouth. He was starving – couldn't remember when he'd last eaten, as he'd been so busy meticulously planning his strategy. A few unexpected things had cropped up, meaning he'd had to alter some stuff – add in another level before he could make his kill.

That was okay. It made the game more interesting. A higher level of difficulty.

They'd see how good he really was now.

His player was in place. Safe and secure – away from prying eyes and those who could ruin the plan. Waiting for his command.

He hadn't been totally convinced about using a girl this time. But she was a good gamer, and out of the ones in his online gaming group, she'd proved herself the best candidate to take it to the next level – reality. He hadn't had as long to work on her as he'd had with Kyle, though. And she was more intelligent than Kyle, so there *was* a bigger risk. She might not keep him out of it if she got caught carrying out his instructions. Would she break and give him up? Kyle never had. That was his strength – he might not be the sharpest tool in the box, but he was loyal. He could use drugs against her, he reasoned; she seemed willing to do most things for easy access to ecstasy tabs – her drug of choice. In addition, he'd done a stellar job of convincing her that her parents were useless, didn't care about her and shouldn't be trusted. It'd been the ace up his sleeve and he was chuffed he'd manipulated the situation so well. She was certainly keen to make them suffer now; she'd already made her first move.

Whether or not he'd made the right choice wasn't something he could afford to brood on, though. Not now things had escalated. There wasn't the luxury of time any more. He had to get going now.

But he still had a couple of other things to take care of before he was ready to go to her.

Then, and only then, could he hit the 'start' button.

CHAPTER TWENTY-EIGHT

Connie

Connie's phone alarm woke her with a start. She bolted upright and attempted to rub the lingering dream away with the palms of her hands. Another mash-up of dark images, this time with Kyle and Alice as the stars. Her unconscious was filled with guilt, and now worry. It clearly knew she'd done wrong, using unethical tactics to get Kyle to talk.

She stumbled into the silent kitchen and flicked on the kettle. As she was about to open the fridge to retrieve the milk, she saw a note under the Mulder and Scully *X-Files* fridge magnet. Connie had jokingly begun using this as a way of communicating after complaining to Lindsay that she never checked her phone for texts, but it had stuck and now they both used it. She huffed as she read: *Sorry, left early, didn't want to disturb you – not sure what time I'll be home. Have a good day, L xx*

She'd wanted to have a chat with Lindsay before she left for the prison today. Ask her advice about how to get out of the predicament she'd got herself in. When Connie had discussed going back, doing these assessments for the prison and said she couldn't face it, Lindsay had encouraged her, said it wouldn't be like before, because now she had Lindsay. She didn't need to go through it alone.

Connie slammed the fridge door. Alone was exactly how she was going through this. She spent most of her time listening to other peoples' anxieties, helping them manage their problems, now she wanted someone to do the same for her. If Connie had known that Lindsay would hardly be around, wouldn't be in a position to offer the support she'd need, she most definitely wouldn't have agreed to do the stupid psychology reports.

Hopefully today would be the last of them, though. Her final day going through those gates. She'd almost finished gathering all the information she needed to enable her to compile the reports at home. One big push today and that would be the end of it. The thought spurred her on; she made and ate some porridge, downed two cups of coffee, then jumped in the shower.

'Well you've got the office buzzing.' Verity's words of greeting, along with her big smile, immediately set Connie on edge as she was collected from the main gate. She didn't need to ask why.

'I obviously have good timing – Kyle was ready to talk,' Connie said and she shrugged her shoulders as if to back up the statement.

'That's not what Jen said. She said you have a knack, a flare with the men.' Verity's voice was bright, cheery, and her eyes sparkled with what seemed to be admiration. If only she knew.

'A flare with the men, eh? Sounds bad.' Connie gave a laugh she knew seemed awkward. She was trying to come across as jokey to hide her growing anxiety. But her stomach griped painfully, letting her know it was getting into flight mode.

'So, you're The One now,' Verity said enthusiastically as she opened the last gate and let Connie through. 'You know, like in *The Matrix*?' She paused, waiting for a response.

Connie felt sick. She didn't *want* to be The One. Shit. Making this her last day within the prison walls might well be problematic now. Unsure how to respond, she smiled and walked ahead of Verity without saying anything.

94

CHAPTER TWENTY-NINE

Deborah

It's not like I can get to him. Kyle Mann. The one who took my Sean away. He's locked away, doing his time. Justice was served. To a degree, at least. So why don't I feel better? Why, when faced with the wide-eyed eager face of his mother, do I feel so wretched? So bloody angry?

Even her voice, the sickly, treacle-covered sweetness of it, sets my teeth on edge. What began as curiosity has grown, nurtured by a deeply ingrained sense of being cheated, into full-blown obsession. I need to find out more about her. Need to make this woman see *she* is responsible for what her son did. What she *allowed* her son to do. You can't tell me she had no idea. She must've thought something was very wrong for him to spend hours and hours shut away in his room playing violent games. In court, it was said 'he was left to his own devices from a young age'.

It's down to her then. She created a monster.

And now Alice has shoehorned herself into my life. For reasons my mind is blocking from conscious thought, I've allowed her to. I know she often stands outside my house, waiting for an opportunity to pounce. She's a fucking predator. Like mother, like son? I think she has a screw loose. Her need to have me as a friend, some kind of ally in our shared grief, as she's currently describing it to me, is sick. Her son is alive. Mine is dead. How can *she* be grieving?

You can go and visit your murdering bastard of a son in prison.

Somehow, despite their potency, those words don't make it from my mind to my mouth. My lips seal them inside.

Just.

She sits, my bone china teacup rattling in its saucer as she balances it precariously upon her knee, watching me. Waiting for my response to her question.

The pressure builds inside of me. It makes it hard to remember what she asked. Makes it hard to stay calm; serene.

'Sorry,' I shake my head, 'I've forgotten what you asked me.'

Alice gives a nervous giggle. 'I was asking about how you manage. I know I get days where I struggle to get out of bed.' She reaches forwards with her drink, slopping some tea into the saucer as she places it on the table. 'Although, I suppose you have your husband to help.' She quickly lowers her gaze – maybe because she catches the expression that must be on my face, or because she knows the absurdity of the question. How does she want me to respond?

The urge to launch myself at her, pull her hair out, is strong.

She honestly thinks she is the victim in all of this.

I take a moment to compose myself, and suddenly I know what to do – how to continue this bizarre interaction, now and in the future. Because she *will* keep coming; she'll be there at every turn until I give her what she's after. Yes, the only way forwards is to tell Alice what she wants to hear. Make her think she's bringing me around to her way of thinking, allow her to believe we *are* alike, that we are both going through the same thing – both traumatised at the loss of our sons.

Make her believe she is forgiven.

Then, when she least expects it, I can deliver the truth.

I want her to hurt as much as I do.

CHAPTER THIRTY

Alice

I let myself in the front door, then rush to the kitchen. Disregarding the dirty dishes accumulating in the sink and on the worktop, I grab a clean glass and turn on the tap. I gulp down the water, then refill it and drink another, swallowing two paracetamols with it. Pain is splitting my head in two. It's the stress. I've had a long day, my feelings swinging first in one direction, then the other. I think I must be shell-shocked. How can the same day hold such wild emotions?

I grab on to the worktop as a dizzy sensation takes over me. I need to log onto the support group, contact Bill. I can't believe this has happened. How did I miss this appalling news? There's a hard ball in the pit of my stomach, the water inside it churns over and over. My mind *has* been otherwise occupied these last few days, but it's no excuse. I'm the leader. I should've been there for Bill. I bet there are a lot of messages, appeals for help and support from his fellow members. He must think I'm awful, *heartless*. But then, I haven't had any notifications pop up. I would've been sure to log into the group page if I had – I always respond as swiftly as possible when I see there've been new messages.

Poor Bill. This will set him back, he'll be feeling terrible. I wonder what's happened to Isabella. I didn't have a chance to read more than the headline and first few lines before I had to run out, and then I was too busy to give more thought to it. I didn't have much time to dwell. Now I'm back, though, it's all I can think about. I'm scared to turn the TV on. What if she's dead?

If she is, he won't come to group anymore. Not mine, anyway.

The dizzy spell passes and I cautiously move to the lounge. I do turn on the TV, but it's more important I get online – I'll keep the volume up so I can hear the news when it comes on. Sitting at my usual chair at the table, I reach across to get my laptop. It's been a while since I used it, but it's normally right there in the space in front of my chair, not across the other side.

I turn on the power, willing it to hurry up. It seems to take an age to whir into life.

'That's odd.' My fingers shake. My eyes roll over the home screen. I can't find the support group icon. It's always on my homepage – as soon as I fire up the laptop, it is there. Now it's gone. I've obviously unpinned it by mistake. My heart flutters wildly as I type in the web address for the group and wait for it to appear.

Please, God, let it be good news.

It's not. And there *are* messages from Bill – from last Friday. Four days ago! I feel sick. He'll assume I've abandoned him. A quick glance on the thread shows me every other group member has written a message – offers of practical help, emotional support, prayers – everything. But not me. I cross my chest – dear God, what a terrible mess. I should've got so many notifications with this much activity in the group – did I switch them off?

'Stupid woman!'

I take a deep breath. I need to calm down – I'll have to sort the issue out later, for now I must concentrate. Focus. Bill is my main priority. I see he hasn't left another message, no updates since Sunday. I read the first post, my mouth drying despite the water I've had. The message is full of desperation. I can feel the pain oozing through the words. Further down the thread he has written how Isabella is still missing and the hope is fading for her safe return.

That had been the last thing Bill wrote.

I pace the lounge for over half an hour, my mind running wild trying to create the best message I can, given the circumstances. Once I feel it's right, I take my time to type it out. I have to double-check I've worded it well and to ensure it comes across as supportive, yet apologetic that I haven't sent it sooner.

My finger floats over the key that will 'publish comment'.

There's a niggling in my gut – is it somehow my fault? Did I give him advice which caused Isabella to leave? No, I'm sure I've been careful, haven't spoken out of turn, or against what any of the other members advised him.

But it's the timing. Something in the timing of Isabella's disappearance is ringing alarm bells.

Or is it simply a coincidence?

I tap the publish button before I can analyse it any further, then close the laptop. I listen for sounds in the silence as my mind races. Something has shifted today, and I have the awful sensation of impending doom.

CHAPTER THIRTY-ONE

Connie

Kyle's posture was upright, stiff. Tense. Connie imagined she looked much the same. Her muscles certainly felt rigid, her nerves on edge. It felt like they were mirror images of each other's anxiety.

She'd reluctantly agreed to come in today to do the extra session. As she'd anticipated, Jen had said that Kyle now appeared willing to talk, and to Connie, it would be detrimental to his rehabilitation if a further assessment wasn't completed. Connie had been unable to give a good, solid reason as to why she couldn't be the person to undertake it.

So, on this dull Thursday morning, here she was.

If she could get Kyle to talk about the offence, about his responsibility for it, together with his risk factors, then they might be able to get him to do an offending behaviour programme like the Thinking Skills Programme, and perhaps Connie's name might be remembered for something *other* than the Hargreaves incident. This could work in her favour. That's the positive spin she'd put on it, anyway.

Her plan was to avoid any mention of Alice, but she feared it would be impossible given she'd used that fact in the previous session and it's what got Kyle talking to begin with. He'd undoubtedly remember this, and surely if he was going to talk, he would bring that up. Furthermore, if they were to discuss his offence and his related risk factors for offending, along with his protective factors, then his mum was likely to feature. Connie would have to keep it professional. Try not to colour outside the lines.

'As you're aware, Kyle, the parole board stipulated you needed to attend various sessions and courses to address your offending before any progression towards release could be made.' Connie paused. Kyle's hands drummed on the table, the noise escalating with each of Connie's words. Was he going to revert to non-cooperation, and not speaking? 'Kyle? What's wrong?'

His hands stilled. 'Why is my mum seeing you?' He squinted.

'We aren't here to discuss your mum. We need to concentrate on you today.' Connie felt her right eye twitching and wondered if he could see it.

'I can't . . .' Kyle repositioned himself. 'I can't concentrate. Not until you tell me. You were keen enough the other day to tell me.' Connie noted the strength to his voice – it didn't sound as croaky, as unused as it had done the first time. And he made a good point – she *had* been keen to tell him about Alice the other day. She'd slept on it since then. God, how had she managed to put herself in this position?

'I'm sorry. I shouldn't have said what I did.'

'So, you did lie then.' He shook his head. 'I knew it.'

She could leave it at that. Letting him assume she lied would let her off the hook in some ways. Maybe he wouldn't pass on her indiscretion, or mention it to Alice if he spoke to her. But Connie needed him to trust her to enable her to get what she needed for his report. And to trust her, she had to be truthful, no matter the consequences for her personally. She should've thought about that before she opened her mouth the other day.

'No. I meant I shouldn't have used that in order to get you to talk. It was wrong of me, I apologise. Now, let's get back—'

'No. No way. You have to tell me what she has told you. Has she talked about me?' Kyle rocked on his chair.

101

'I can't really tell you, Kyle. I'm sorry. But you know from what I've already said that she worries about you. And I guess she feels guilty she didn't know what you were up to. That all the while she left you playing games in your room, you were getting deeper into the online gaming world, talking to people she felt were taking advantage of you.'

'Everyone was harping on about that, I remember. Mum kept saying it during the trial. Do you think the same?'

The question threw Connie for a moment.

'I only know what the files say. Obviously, as you haven't spoken before now, it's been difficult for anyone else to make their own judgement.'

Connie studied him, his pale skin, his stubble of fair hair, sharp-blue eyes. He spoke well, used appropriate language, knew the right words to use. He didn't immediately come across as having psychological difficulties, which Alice had stressed was the case in the police interview transcript. But there did seem to be a vulnerability. Connie couldn't quite fathom what at this stage, but she wondered if there was something else – not educationally vulnerable, but perhaps socially. Someone – a teenager – who spent a huge part of their life online, not interacting with others in the real world, must suffer adversely. It would impact on their social skills. If Kyle *had* made a friend online, as Alice and others had suspected, and they appeared to have the same interests – couldn't there be a possibility he had clung onto this new friend? Done what the friend wanted, just to keep the friendship, something he hadn't experienced before? Connie was all too aware there were people – criminals – out there who knew what to look for when choosing their victims, knew how to manipulate others for their own gains. There was a strong possibility Kyle was such a person; a targeted victim, easy to influence.

'Do you think you are vulnerable, Kyle?'

He shrugged and lowered his head.

'How many friends do you have?' Connie continued.

'Not many.'

'How easy do you find it to make new friends?'

Kyle remained with his head bowed; Connie could see his bottom lip protruding, like a sulking child.

'My mum didn't really like friends coming over, so online was all I had.' His voice was muffled, his chin lowered onto his chest.

'Kyle, look at me a moment.' Connie waited for him to respond. 'That's better. Did you play the online games with someone in particular? One person more than others?'

'I mostly played on one person's server. There were a lot of gamers who wanted to be in this guy's group. It was one of the best – we were all top players, but he was even better. He was big in the gaming world – was important.'

'Really? How did you know that?' Connie felt her body shift forwards in anticipation. Was she getting somewhere?

Kyle shrugged again. 'Cos he told me.'

'Okay, and you believed him?'

'Why wouldn't I? He had no reason to lie.'

Connie's pulse skipped. Kyle trusted this guy at his word. Maybe it'd been his downfall. Perhaps being too trusting was his vulnerability. Could this other gamer be the one everyone thought was involved in Sean Taylor's murder?

'Did you tell anyone about your friend?'

'No, not really. My mum knew I was talking to other gamers, but he said it would be better if I didn't talk about him. He said my mother was nosey enough and would stop us from chatting.'

'So, you spoke about your mum with . . . what was his name?' Connie tried to be nonchalant, slip in the question in the hope Kyle would automatically say his name.

He stared at her, then gave a wry smile.

'I can't tell you. But yes, I talked about my mum. How she didn't know what to do with me, how to *cope* with me.' He looked thoughtful, his gaze wandering to the window. 'I feel bad. She was always worrying about me and all I did was tell her to leave me

103

alone. She'd make excuses to come into my room, listen to what I was saying – she even tried to join in the conversation I was having with my mate. It was embarrassing. I had to pretend I'd stopped gaming at one point because she was interfering so much. We couldn't talk properly.'

'You and this one mate?'

Kyle's face flushed red. 'I . . . I shouldn't be telling you.'

'It's good you are talking, Kyle. Better for you.'

'Not better for my mum, though.'

'It will be, Kyle. She'll be delighted you're making some progress.'

'That's not what I meant. Look, thanks for being so nice, but I can't say any more. Can I go now, please?' His eyes shone with tears.

Someone had done a good job on this young man.

Had Kyle Mann's silence been protective – of his mum?

CHAPTER THIRTY-TWO

Connie

The week had seemed never-ending, but finally it was Friday, and Connie was looking forward to a relaxing weekend ahead. She yawned and stretched back in her chair. She'd caught up with the admin she'd neglected due to the prison visits and now a tiredness crept up on her. Yesterday's interview with Kyle had taken it out of her mentally and emotionally; she felt drained. The write-up of the session had taken her two hours. Hours spent inside the psychology portacabin when she'd really planned on taking the report home to complete. Jen had had other ideas – she'd wanted the low-down and to read Connie's session notes there and then. And she'd asked Connie to do a further interview with Kyle Mann.

Despite dreading the prospect of yet more time inside the prison walls, Connie was strangely keen to continue. Jen gained the governor's permission to extend Connie's temporary position as independent psychologist, and it was agreed she would go back next week. Her professional curiosity, and something else she couldn't put her finger on, were compelling her. She wanted to get to the truth. Kyle's truth.

If she managed to help Alice in the process, that would be a huge bonus. She'd perhaps be able to use some of what Kyle had said in her next counselling session with Alice – indirectly, at least. But, she'd have to make damn sure she didn't disclose the fact she'd been visiting Kyle. She hoped Kyle would also refrain from speaking to Alice about *her*. She'd found out Kyle didn't get any visitors – according to Jamie, he never sent out any visiting orders. But just because he didn't want his mother visiting him, that didn't mean he never called her or sent a letter.

Connie gathered the paperwork together and filed it away in her desk drawer. She got her coat and bag, and made her way out of the office. She'd be able to get the earlier train and be home by 5 p.m. She really hoped Lindsay would be home in time for them to eat together. Another night with only Amber and her own thoughts for company didn't seem at all appealing.

Connie drew the heavy, beige lounge curtains to block everything outside from view, and to prevent anyone looking in at her. A tingling sensation trickled over her skin as if an army of ants were crawling across it. She rubbed violently at her arms to rid herself of the feeling.

Was she being paranoid, or was someone watching her? She'd first experienced the uneasiness as she disembarked the train at Coleton station. There was a sense of déjà vu about it. Maybe that's *all* it was. But as she'd rushed inside her house, closing and locking the door, her nerves hadn't settled.

It might even be Luke.

She dismissed the thought. Her brother wouldn't dare risk being here, and no doubt her father had seen to it he didn't come within a hundred miles of Coleton. It was more likely that her involvement with Kyle Mann had somehow triggered her reaction. He was clearly afraid of the repercussions of talking, giving the other person away – so much so, he'd seemed afraid for his mother's safety. Should Connie be worried for her own?

Connie wished Lindsay would get home now. She checked her phone. No messages. She went to the kitchen fridge, grabbing a bottle of white wine from the rack. The year had begun so positively, how could it have changed so quickly?

A car door banged. Lindsay was home.

Connie ran to unlock the deadbolt on the front door. Her heart plummeted as she saw a man unfold himself from the passenger side of the car and pull up to his full six-foot five-inch height.

Dammit. She'd brought Mack, her DS, with her. Lindsay got to the door first, and Connie gave her a stern look as she stepped aside.

'Sorry, Connie,' Lindsay said. 'If I didn't bring the work home, I'd never have left tonight.'

'It's fine.' Connie gave Mack a tight smile as he approached the doorway.

'Hey, Connie. Good to see you,' Mack said, not quite making eye contact.

Connie had briefly been involved with Mack's son, Gary. It was a very short-lived affair eighteen months ago, which hadn't ended well for either of them. Connie and Mack were civil now, but not exactly friends. Lindsay had done her best to build bridges, but they were both too stubborn.

'You too, Mack.' Connie closed the door behind him, locking it again.

'Everything okay?' Lindsay's brow furrowed as she observed Connie locking the door.

'Well, actually, I could do with a chat. Privately.'

'Ah. Sorry, can it wait a bit? We've got to go over some work stuff.'

Before Connie could respond, Lindsay ushered Mack into the lounge.

'You don't mind, do you?' Lindsay smiled as she made a move to close the lounge door, leaving Connie standing in the hallway. 'We've got a new lead in the misper case to discuss.'

Connie threw up a hand, slapping it against the door to prevent it from closing. 'Really? You're keeping me out of my own lounge?'

'I didn't think you'd mind, as it's so important. Once we're done, I'll come and get you. Perhaps we could order a takeaway after?' Her tone was bright, an attempt to bring Connie around.

'Well, I do mind. Actually.' A lump formed in the back of Connie's throat. She was being pushed out. And at a time when she needed support. 'You said you'd be here for me if I needed to talk.'

Lindsay relaxed her grip on the door and put out her other hand, laying it on Connie's shoulder. 'I won't be very long,' she said, her eyes, heavy and tired-looking, squinting at Connie. 'Unless . . . I mean, if you really need to talk *right now*, I guess we could put this on hold for a while . . .' Lindsay turned away from Connie and gave a shrug towards Mack.

Connie's face grew hot. She suddenly felt silly and needy, and the way Lindsay was looking to Mack like they were both attempting to calm a stroppy child, made it all the worse. Tears were threatening.

'No, no need . . .' Connie looked down at her shuffling feet. 'It's just that you said I wouldn't have to go through it on my own this time – taking the job in the prison would be fine, you said. I need to get things off my chest, Linds . . .' Connie looked back up at Lindsay. She *did* want to talk right now, but she could sense that she was making Lindsay uncomfortable. 'But it can wait,' she heard herself saying.

Lindsay took a step back. 'Okay, great.' And she closed the door without further discussion. The thud echoed in Connie's ears.

Connie blinked in shock. That was a pretty quick brush-off. Clearly, Connie was low on her list of priorities, despite her promises of being there for her. Part of her wished she'd never opened up to Lindsay in the first place. Connie might not have dealt with her past problems brilliantly, but at least she could count on herself. It had taken a lot for her to trust someone else, confide in them, *lean* on them. And this is what she got in return? It'd been that way before though – the minute she used to turn to someone else for support, they let her down. It'd happened when she was young, and it had happened when things got rough in her prison psychologist role. Why would it change now?

She grabbed her coat from the bannister and, not caring now if there was someone watching her, unlocked the front door. She stormed out, slamming it behind her. She didn't know where she was going, but there was no way she was waiting in the kitchen or her bedroom for Lindsay and Mack to finish their little meeting, in *her* house.

For the first time in a while, Connie felt totally alone.

CHAPTER THIRTY-THREE

Alice

Connie Summers' complexion is even paler than usual. Her green eyes – normally bright and sparkly – are dull. I want to ask her if everything is all right, but catch myself in time. I'm not here to talk about her. We all have our problems, and although I'm curious as to what hers are, I'm the paying client. Maybe after my session I'll drop in a concerned question, see if she tells me why she looks so dreadful. I wait for her opening line, the one I've come to expect.

'How have you been over the last two weeks, Alice?'

There it is.

I take some time to consider my response; I don't want to say the wrong thing. I've thought about how to approach this session, I want to get her thoughts on my plan – but in an indirect way. Coming straight out with what I've been up to and what I *will* be doing soon, will, no doubt, have her reaching for the phone to call the men in white coats. But I can be selective in what I say, twist the truth a little. I'm getting used to that.

'It's been a mixed few weeks if I'm honest, Connie,' I say.

'Go on.' Connie widens her eyes to me in encouragement.

I let the session amble along for a while. When Connie asks something I'm not willing, or able, to talk about, I steer the conversation around to my comfortable topics. She's quite easily led. Finally, she asks about my support group and I sit up a little straighter.

'The last group support meeting was extremely successful; the numbers have grown too. I'm thrilled.' I beam at her. I still feel proud of my achievement, although it's tinged with sadness, with guilt now Isabella is missing. I don't tell her about this terrible development. It'll detract from my purpose.

'Excellent. You're really making progress. It must be rewarding, as well as helpful to you. Do you feel any less guilty when you listen to others telling their stories?'

That seems a funny question to ask. Is she suggesting I'm using these other poor souls' misfortunes to make myself feel better? To lessen my guilt by realising everyone has difficulties with their offspring?

'I'm not sure I know what you're getting at.' I am aware my voice has risen. I sound defensive. 'I haven't set up this group so I can feel less guilty about my son taking another's life, Connie. I did it to help other people – to give something back, I suppose.'

But it's not the only reason, is it? She must see that, which is why she's asking this. I need to get back on track.

'I need to help others now, that's my purpose. Do all I can to make things right. Which is why I've decided I'm going to visit the boy's mother . . .'

Connie sits forwards abruptly. 'Sorry, what boy's mother?'

She knows exactly who I mean. 'The mother of Sean Taylor.' I smile.

Her jaw slackens, only slightly, but I notice it. I wonder what's going through her mind right now.

'I really don't suggest you do that, Alice—'

'Oh, it's only a thought at this stage,' I say, lying. I am testing the waters, curious to know what a psychologist would make of it. By her expression, and her immediate advice to not do it, I think it's safe to say she doesn't think it's a good idea.

111

'You have the support group, and me. I think it wise you stick with that, don't you?'

'I do think it's important to face her, tell her I'm sorry for her loss. I am sure she'd appreciate that.'

Connie is silent for a moment. Her brow is knitted in contemplation. 'How would you feel, if your son had been murdered, and the mother of one of those involved came to visit you?'

I sit up sharply. 'The mother of *one* of those involved?'

'Yes. You said you were sure that . . .' She stops. The skin of her décolletage flushes a deep red, it spreads up her neck.

I have never said to Connie I believed Kyle was one of two involved with the murder. Has Connie been doing some research into the case? I hadn't considered she might do that, wouldn't have thought there was any need. I wonder how much she's found out. I recover enough to answer – ignoring her unfinished sentence.

'I'd think it courageous of the woman. I'd want to get to know her. After all, we've both lost our sons.'

Connie leans her elbows on the arms of the chair and steeples her fingers. Her frown deepens, and she sighs. She's making a real meal of this.

'We need to talk about this some more, Alice. I wouldn't attempt to see the mother at this point; it could be a bad outcome for both of you.'

Connie Summers doesn't know everything. She's wrong in this case.

I know best.

'I could do with an extra session, actually, next week if you can fit me in,' I tell her. It'll help if she thinks she can talk about this again soon, even though I have no intention of listening to her advice.

'Oh, yes – I'm sure I can do Wednesday—'

'I need Monday,' I say quickly. 'It's important. It's to cope with the anniversary of Kyle's conviction – I always find it difficult.'

'Monday the nineteenth . . .' Connie studies me for a moment,

112

then slides her chair over to her computer. 'Yes . . . should be fine. It will have to be an afternoon appointment though – is 3 p.m. suitable?' She looks to me, her hands hovering over her keyboard.

'Yes, that'll do. Thank you.'

Her fingertips click on the keys.

'We still have more time today, Alice,' she says as she checks her watch.

I glance at the clock on the wall to Connie's right. Ten more minutes today. But I'm not sure now how much time I have overall.

The clock ticks life away.

CHAPTER THIRTY-FOUR

Tom

The whispered phone call in the early hours of the morning from Kyle's smuggled mobile, unexpected, with few words spoken, had angered him.

What the fuck was she up to? Did she know something? He believed it when Kyle was adamant he'd not said a word. He wouldn't grass, he was sure – as far as Tom knew he'd kept his vow of silence, as promised, while in custody. The fact Kyle'd told him about his mum meant he'd been prioritised over her. Kyle would've known by telling him the information it would put his own mother at risk.

I mean more to him. He wants me to be safe. Free.

He'd told Kyle everything would be okay – he'd got someone who could sort it. No harm would come to her. Not permanently, anyway. He'd only need to give her a shock, a warning. Of course, this was what he knew Kyle wanted to hear; needed to hear. Tom didn't want to reveal his true intentions, that would be too risky.

He couldn't afford for Alice Mann to dig around. She had to stay away from the shrink. Stop talking.

What was it with mothers? Interfering fucking busybodies.

For Kyle's mum, the player was ready in the wings. She'd be able to sort her. After all, she was eager to prove to Tom that she was a serious player. She'd have her chance now. Everything would work out. Tom was in control.

CHAPTER THIRTY-FIVE

Deborah

There's someone standing close to Alice's house – part obscured by a large privet hedge. I'm too far away to see who it is, whether it's male or female even; from my position all I can see is a hunched figure.

What are they doing?

A car drives past me at high speed and it seems to startle whoever it is, because they suddenly move on, disappearing around the corner. I lock my car and cross the road. I'm strangely nervous. My legs shake; a fluttery sensation consumes my stomach as I approach the front door.

Is this how she feels when she's outside *my* house?

She gave me her address. She's so trusting for someone who's been treated to angry outbursts from random people for the best part of four years. Those who felt they had reason to abuse her when really it was an excuse to direct their outrage at her because the real focus of their hatred was locked away. She was the closest thing, the next best target. How does she know I won't use this knowledge? I could post her address and identity on the internet and her life would become intolerable again.

She's stupid to trust me, because I don't even trust myself.

116

The house is standard, nondescript – like most others in the newer estates. Void of personality.

The reality hits me. I am standing outside the house of my son's murderer.

My mind flashes back to the court case – a replay of the description of how Kyle Mann stabbed Sean. He delivered a single, horrific wound to the back of his neck. And then he walked away, leaving him to die, slowly. He didn't even give a reason why he chose Sean. No motive. My poor boy, he must've been so frightened. It's unbearable to imagine what went through his mind as he lay alone, his life ebbing away. Visions haunt me in my waking hours and follow me into my dreams. Not only visually, but aurally – I hear his voice, raspy and weak, asking for me, for 'Mum'.

I don't think a knife through my heart would hurt as much as me knowing he was in pain and might've been asking for me. You never want your child to hurt, ever. It's inevitable of course, during certain times in their lives, and you can't prevent all of it. But you can be there, support them, hold them, comfort them. Even when Sean had chickenpox, I longed to take it away from him, have it myself to stop his pain. I'd have done anything to be in his place, that day – my life for his.

But I didn't have that opportunity.

I did not protect my son.

Maybe my anger is misdirected. Is it Alice's fault, or my own, for not seeing what was going on? For not intervening before it was too late.

A heat begins to build inside of me, like a pressure cooker with its steam trapped.

If she's home, she'll invite me inside. What if I can't handle it and I snap? Even before I go in, there's a risk of me losing my self-control. I hate this woman for her son taking mine away. Why on earth am I putting myself through this?

I could walk away now, call the police and tell them I'm being harassed by her, and then try to get on with my life – as pathetic as it is.

My feet are planted, though. I can't turn back now. I'm compelled to see it through.

With a huge intake of air, I force my feet to move forwards. Gravel chippings, similar to mine, scatter the path. I swipe them off with the side of my shoe and continue to her front doorstep.

CHAPTER THIRTY-SIX

Connie

That had been close.

Connie typed up her notes from Alice's session into her file on the computer. She didn't, however, write about the fact she'd almost fucked up: she had begun to forget who had said what. She realised she'd been mixing up things she'd read in Kyle's psychology file and what Kyle had talked about, with what she thought Alice had told her. She'd thought she could use knowledge gained from her prison role to her advantage in her work with Alice, but at this rate she was only going to do more damage.

It hadn't helped being so tired from lack of sleep over the weekend, the remnants of the flare-up with Lindsay still strewn in her mind like dark clouds. She knew her outburst on Friday evening, her behaviour towards Lindsay in front of Mack, had been childish. But she'd wanted to know she wasn't alone. Flouncing out of the house had served only to make her feel worse, more isolated. She'd thought Lindsay would come after her. She didn't. Like a sulking child, Connie had returned to the house less than half an hour later, having slowly walked around the perimeter of the park down from her house, afraid to venture too far – her earlier thoughts of someone watching her setting her nerves on edge again.

Lindsay had still been in the lounge with Mack, their muffled voices penetrating the door as Connie walked past to the kitchen. After another hour, Mack left, his head bowed so as not to catch Connie's eyes. Connie and Lindsay had spent the rest of the evening talking, each laboriously attempting to make the other understand their point of view. The weekend had been long – Connie at home, Lindsay mostly at work – and when she *had* seen Lindsay, it'd been awkward between them. It felt as if Lindsay had returned to the hostile, stern detective inspector she'd first met last year. So much so, Connie had held off sharing any of her concerns about Kyle, and about Alice. It hadn't been the right time.

Connie sighed and walked to the window. Arms crossed, she gazed out over Totnes market square. Had she put all her eggs in one basket? She had to acknowledge it was unfair to lay the onus on Lindsay to be the one to support her. It wasn't Lindsay's fault Connie had burned all her bridges. Her mum had asked if there was a man in her life, and she'd categorically said she didn't have time for one. Connie told herself she didn't *need* one, although really it was because she didn't want to trust another man after she'd felt so used by men in the past. But perhaps it was time to get back on the dating scene, after all. She could do with a distraction.

Connie turned back to her desk. She'd agreed to the Monday session for Alice even though it was the same day she'd arranged to see Kyle. If she altered Kyle's time slot she could probably fit them both in: she'd booked Alice's appointment for three, giving her time to complete her session with Kyle and get the train back to Totnes. The anniversary was bound to be a challenging time for her client, and so it was important to offer the extra support. Connie made a call to HMP Baymead and asked Jen if she'd swap the appointment time with Kyle to early Monday morning and send out a fresh movement slip to the wing for him to attend at 9 a.m.

She'd have to be more careful next week, make sure she was

fresh, on top of things – it would be extra challenging to see mother and son in one day. And she must keep to what Alice was actually telling her in future, not what she knew from other sources – although she could still use information gained from elsewhere to ask the relevant questions, to point Alice in the right direction. In particular, Connie would have to work on Alice's warped idea of seeing the dead boy's mother – enable her to realise her feelings of guilt needed to be addressed *without* involving the victim's family.

She really couldn't see a happy ending with that.

CHAPTER THIRTY-SEVEN

Connie

Connie took in her appearance in the full-length mirror. She'd not been out in the evening without Lindsay since she'd moved in last year. The confidence she'd once had, prior to the Hargreaves incident and her subsequent exit from her prison job, was finally beginning to return. Her straight black hair – a longer-styled bob in comparison to how she'd worn it last year – had a lovely, healthy sheen to it. She looked good in the skinny black jeans and figure-hugging, low-cut top. She *felt* good.

The taxi was booked for 8 p.m. Connie hoped Lindsay would come home before she left, so she could see Connie was going out for the night. She wanted her to know she wasn't going to sit around the house forever waiting for Lindsay to return. She needed something more. Her plan was to head to The Farmer in the centre of Coleton. It tended to be relatively quiet in there until much later, but that would give her chance to find a table and down a few drinks to relax. With luck, she'd see some familiar faces, regulars who might recognise her too, despite the fact she hadn't been on the scene for quite some time.

As 8 p.m. approached, there was still no sign of Lindsay. Connie scribbled a note on a Post-it and put in under the *X-Files* fridge magnet for Lindsay to see – if she even bothered to check for a note. The taxi blared its horn. Connie gave Amber a quick cuddle, then grabbed her bag and jacket.

Walking into places alone had never fazed her. It'd been her life for a while after leaving Baymead, when she'd been on the pull every weekend. She'd frequented all the local pubs on her own, only meeting up with men once inside. Because it wasn't a weekend, she held little hope of meeting someone of interest tonight, but company of any sort would do right now. And even if that failed, she could do with having a drink anyway.

After buying a large white wine, Connie found a table halfway between the bar and the entrance – a spot to give her the best visibility. The only thing with being on her own was acting naturally – knowing what to do, how to 'be'. She twisted the stem of the glass with one hand, the other lay on her lap. She'd give it a few minutes then get her mobile phone out. It was acceptable these days – people didn't think you were Billy-no-mates if you were scrolling through your phone. The music was loud, or maybe it was the fact it was her only focus. Or was she getting old? There was no live band tonight, so she thought she might come back at the weekend – The Farmer's live music generally drew quite a crowd.

She cast her eyes around the pub. Apart from four people, two couples by the look of it, standing with their drinks at the bar, the place was deserted. Eight o'clock was probably *too* early. Yes, she'd got herself a table, but would she be able to sit here for hours waiting for someone remotely interesting to talk to? Connie took a large gulp of wine. Then another. Tonight might just be for getting plain drunk. Alone.

Connie got her phone from her bag. She had two missed calls. Typically, she'd left it on silent. Her heart dipped when she noted they were both from her mother. Probably checking up on her again, making sure she was all right after her days working in the prison. At least *someone* was bothered. She drained what was left of the glass of wine and went to the bar to get another.

'Not seen you in here for a long time,' the twenty-something asked as he took her money. 'You been away?'

'Something like that,' Connie said.

'You're looking well.' He grinned, his eyes fully on hers. Was he trying to chat her up? She was so over younger men – had been there, done that. Mack's son, Gary, being the last. Ever.

'Thanks.' Connie took her drink and retreated to her table, avoiding further conversation. In her peripheral vision, she caught sight of him as he walked along his side of the bar, then through the gap over to the customer's side. He was going to come and talk to her. As much as she'd thought any company would do, she wasn't in the mood for a jumped-up youngster who likely assumed she was a middle-aged woman desperate for attention. She laughed in spite of herself. Wasn't attention precisely what she was after? Although, at thirty-nine, she didn't class herself middle-aged. Not far off forty. A frightening thought. No wonder her mum was beginning to panic that she wasn't going to have any grandchildren. It didn't help that all the pressure was on Connie with Luke not around.

Connie pretended to make a call as the bartender lingered behind her. She was saved by a group of men bursting through the pub door, so he had to head back to his position at the bar. Connie ended the fake call. These men were more promising. Although they were roughly in their early thirties, so not quite as mature as she would like, it was probably the best she could hope for on a Wednesday evening. They looked as though they'd not long finished work – messy work if their clothes were anything to go by. Men not afraid of getting their hands dirty.

One in particular caught her attention as he ordered a drink – his voice deep, smooth. Yes, finally – someone of interest.

CHAPTER THIRTY-EIGHT

Alice

My positivity wanes; my self-belief swings in the balance. I'm no longer sure I'll achieve my goal. Too many things have suddenly leapt from the shadows and created doubt. Fear, even. Connie said I shouldn't visit Sean's mother. How can she think it's wrong of me to try to make things right? She wanted me to see things from her perspective. Has anyone ever attempted the same for me?

No. But then, why would they? I'm just the mother of a murderer.

I unscrew the cap of the vodka I bought after I'd walked around Totnes most of the day to avoid coming back here, and pour myself a small glass. A clear, harmless-looking liquid. I stare at it. I haven't had a drink in four years. I'm being weak, I know. But one will take the edge off.

It burns my throat and I immediately feel nauseous.

I pour another.

Damn Connie Summers. She's been useful, of sorts, and I suppose I didn't ever really expect her to think my plan was a good one. What did I want from her – permission? It might have been what I was seeking, in the beginning. Not now, though – I know my path. I've started the ball rolling and I must see it through. With or without her blessing.

Even one small glass of vodka has made my head woozy. It's a sensation I'd forgotten. I'll check the support group page, then I should go and sleep it off.

CHAPTER THIRTY-NINE

Deborah

Nathan has been pushing his food around his plate with the fork without taking a single mouthful for the past ten minutes. I watch: part curious, part worried. Clearly something is on his mind and I'm not sure if he's waiting for me to ask before he lets the dam break, or if he doesn't want to speak to me at all. His mood, his behaviour, could be work-related, or due to his mistress – or, it could be he has found out I haven't been going to work; that I've been given leave. Possibly permanent. Has he spotted me out and about? Found out what I've been up to? I close my eyes. I can't bear to watch him anymore.

'How's work?'

I snap my eyes open. Christ. He must know.

I take a mouthful of lasagne, chew for a bit, considering how best to play this. Then I decide. 'I've not been in this week. Holiday.' That's pretty much the truth, after all.

'You never mentioned it.' His voice is monotone, his eyes remain on his plate.

'No? Well, I haven't really seen you much of late. How's the big project going?' I need to push the topic back to him. I put my knife and fork down and place my elbows on the table, giving him my full attention. Finally, he looks up. A cold tingling branches throughout my insides as I catch the look in his eyes. They seem almost manic – wide, red.

Whatever is wrong, it isn't about my job.

'I . . . I—'

'Nathan, what on earth is it?' He's scaring me now. I haven't seen him so distressed since Sean, but there's nothing that can be as bad as that.

'I can't. Shit, Deborah. I'm sorry.' The clatter of the fork on the plate rings out. Nathan pushes back from the table and bolts from the dining room, leaving me sitting, stunned. I'm lost. I should go after him, but I'm afraid to find out what he's sorry about. Is he planning on leaving me for this other woman? Surely he wouldn't do that to me. Not after everything we've been through. My heart thuds against its cage.

Taking tentative steps, I make my way to the foot of the stairs. I can hear Nathan in our bedroom. Can hear the wardrobe doors, the squeaking of the clothes hangers. With a surge of adrenaline, I take two steps at a time and race into the bedroom.

'What are you doing?' I ask, even though it's obvious. The large holdall he often uses as an overnight bag is unzipped on the bed, and he's shovelling items of clothing into it. My chest tightens, my breath is coming in short, shallow bursts.

'I'm sorry, Deborah.' He doesn't look at me, but carries on pulling things from his side of the wardrobe. I plunge towards him, putting my body between him and the wardrobe.

'Stop saying that. Stop saying sorry and tell me what is going on!'

'I can't. I can't do this . . . anymore.' He is sobbing now. 'I'm so sorry.' Tears streak his face.

I shake my head. This can't be right.

'Are you leaving me?'

Nathan places his hands either side of my face and closes his eyes tight.

'For now, yes.'

I feel his hands leave my face. He turns, collects his bag and walks out the room.

Down the stairs. Out the front door.

Leaves me.

I collapse onto the bed and bury my head into his pillow. It muffles my screams.

Why is everything suddenly falling apart?

It's since Alice came onto the scene.

She's the one who's upset the equilibrium. I can't let Alice ruin things this time around.

CHAPTER FORTY

Connie

The dryness in her mouth woke Connie. She reached for the glass of water – it was warm from the night before, but anything would do. She lay back, resting her head on the pillow. A dull ache consumed her skull. Any sudden movement would make her dehydrated brain feel like it had been hit against a wall. Slow was the way forwards.

The man lying beside her grumbled and reached an arm across her middle. Scott – the man from The Farmer – had made a move on Connie not long after entering the pub. She wasn't sure if it was his tentative approach, his unconfident humour, his eyes – a sharp blue that popped against his olive complexion – his full lips, or the way he sat in silence as Connie talked non-stop for over half an hour, that made her ask him home. Or maybe it was simply because she wanted someone else there, if only for one night.

Connie gently pushed his arm from her and checked her phone. She was going to be late getting into Totnes this morning – she hoped she'd make it to her office before her first client. Going out on a school night really wasn't her best idea.

As she got in the shower, her head heavy and fuzzy, she wondered if Lindsay had already left for work. Or if she'd even come home last night. She couldn't remember seeing her when she returned home with Scott – although, if she recalled correctly, they had gone straight upstairs.

She blasted her hair dry on the highest heat – which would undoubtedly make it frizzy for the rest of the day – gave Scott a gentle nudge, telling him he had to leave, then watched him dress sheepishly before escorting him down the stairs. At the door, he turned to kiss her.

'You're going to miss your train.' Lindsay was leaning against the frame of the kitchen door, a bowl of cereal in one hand, spoon in the other.

Connie pulled away from Scott and mumbled a promise to call him, then ushered him out.

'Yes. I likely will.' Connie closed the front door and remained facing it, not Lindsay.

'You want a lift into Totnes? I can afford to be half an hour late.'

'Can you?' Connie turned. 'I wouldn't have thought so, given how many hours you've been putting in lately – in fact, I can't believe you're still here.' She swept past Lindsay into the kitchen. 'Anyway, I need coffee before I go anywhere, so you go ahead. I'm sure the next train will get me there before my first client's due.' Connie refilled the kettle.

Lindsay sighed. 'How long are you going to give me the cold shoulder for?'

'I'm not giving you anything of the sort.' Connie knew her denial sounded unconvincing.

'Yep. You are. I know how this goes, Connie. I remember it well from how Tony ended up treating me. Distancing himself, abrupt communications. I get it. My work always comes first, I lose sight of other important things in my life. I really don't want to alienate you, Connie.'

'Then be around for me a bit more! I'm not asking for a lot. Just what you promised.'

'I know. It is *such* bad timing this poor girl went missing the same week you began the work at the prison. But I am here for

131

you. Granted, I'm not here physically very much at the moment, but it doesn't mean you can't tell me what's going on.'

'Lindsay. You're barely here at all, and even when you are, you're tired and going off to bed early, or bringing your work – and Mack – home with you.' Connie cringed at the whine in her tone. Even though she knew she was coming across as self-centred, she couldn't seem to stop herself.

'Look,' Lindsay said as she put her bowl into the dishwasher, 'get ready and let me drive you to work, we can at least chat then. Don't cut your nose off to spite your face just because you're angry with me.'

Connie opened her mouth to argue, then stopped. Lindsay was right. If she declined the lift it would be a ridiculously pointless protest. And she'd come off worse. Plus, a lift would certainly be better than the train. 'Fine. Give me ten minutes.'

'The misper case is still ongoing then?' Connie opened the conversation as soon as Lindsay drove away from the house. She had to pack as much into the twenty-minute journey as she could – best to start with something relating to Lindsay, so she didn't come across as selfish and needy.

'Yep. Every time we think we're getting close, getting a positive sighting of Isabella, we follow it up and they turn out to be dead ends. So frustrating.'

'Must be. You said before that you thought there was more to it – like, bad stuff?'

'Bad enough, I think. Some interesting things were found on her computer; she was part of a gaming community, and it seemed to go beyond online interactions. Her father said she was spending more time out of the house, becoming very secretive. We're looking into whether the two are linked.'

'God, do you think she's been murdered? Some weird game gone wrong?'

'It's a thought. Sadly, because we've found no proof of life . . . well . . .' Lindsay's sentence trailed, then she changed the subject.

'Anyway, let's concentrate on you for a moment. Clearly, you're pissed off with me. Bringing some random bloke home. I know I've not been the support I said I would be and I'm really sorry. But talk now, maybe it will help.'

'He isn't some *random* bloke. His name is Scott.' Connie shot Lindsay her best hoity look. 'And it's not that I'm pissed off with you, just that I've had some concerns of my own that I'd have liked to discuss with you. It's kind of complicated.'

'Go on,' Lindsay said, her eyebrows raised.

'It's about a mother and son, whose lives were ruined by what he did.'

'Oh, really? What happened, and how are you involved?'

'Long story short, my new client is the mother of a boy who, at eighteen, stabbed and killed another boy. The details were never really clear in terms of motive, but there was enough evidence to convict him. And I'm now seeing the son at HMP Baymead – he's one of the assessments that Jen brought me in to do.'

'Shit!' Lindsay lengthened the word as she spoke it.

'I know. Shit, indeed.'

'When was this?'

'He was convicted four years ago, I'm assuming you won't know about it – you weren't Devon and Cornwall back then. Anyway, point is, initially he never spoke a word, hadn't done for years, but then decided he would speak to me. Which is my fault . . .' Connie lowered her gaze, not wanting Lindsay to see the guilt in her eyes. But Lindsay knew her too well.

'Ahh, Connie. What did you do?'

'I thought I could use the fact I was seeing his mother to coax him into talking.'

'So, you coerced and manipulated a *prisoner*?' Lindsay took her eyes off the road, her head turning sharply to face Connie.

'Shit.' Connie put her head in her hands. 'When you put it like that . . .'

'Wow, that's a turn-up for the books. Isn't it meant to be the other way around?'

133

'I'm not sure why I did it. It got him talking, though.' Connie shrugged. 'But now I have to continue seeing him until I can get the full assessment done.'

'Hmmm. Didn't think those consequences through, did you?'

'No. And now I'm getting into deep shit as I need to keep the fact I'm seeing him from his mother, but I accidentally mentioned to her something *he* told me, thinking it was what *she'd* told me.'

'That's quite a pickle you've got yourself in.'

'Thanks for the "in a nutshell" summary.' Connie sighed. On the one hand she felt relieved to be finally talking about it, but on the other, saying it out loud confirmed her actions as imprudent.

'How many more sessions with each?'

'Hopefully only one with him, but more with her. She asked for an extra one on Monday, too, to help her cope with the anniversary of Kyle's conviction. So, I'll be seeing him in the morning and her in the afternoon.'

Lindsay was at the roundabout at The Seven Stars, it was only a minute or so before Connie would have to jump out.

'Christ. Okay, well, I'd concentrate on the anniversary with her and let her do as much of the talking as poss. Only focus on what she's telling you in that session, don't bring anything up from previous ones. You can't say something you shouldn't then.'

'But what if he's told her he's seeing me too? And it comes out about me informing him that his mum has been talking to me?'

'Then I think you're going to have to start being a lot more careful, Connie. It's not just a case of you making things awkward if they find out, you're putting yourself in a compromising position – and not a safe one. Remember your track record . . .'

Connie opened her mouth to say something, but thought better of it. There wasn't much she *could* say to that. She thanked Lindsay for the lift and, her mind brimming with concern, got out of the car. At least she had a few days before seeing them both to try to get her head straight.

CHAPTER FORTY-ONE

Connie

Let this be the last session, please let it be the last, Connie thought as she walked towards the wing with Verity at her side. Since her brief discussion with Lindsay on Thursday, her warning to Connie had been in the forefront of her mind. Now she was back inside the prison walls, Lindsay's words 'you need to be careful' were repeating on a loop in her head. Connie couldn't afford to make a slip again.

Verity was uncharacteristically quiet, no friendly chit-chat as they walked, no questions, no conversation about what she'd got up to at the weekend. Connie was afraid to ask what was wrong. Verity was even walking more slowly, and despite Connie waiting at each gate for her to lock it again after they'd passed through, Verity still kept dropping behind. As they approached living block 3, Connie couldn't help herself – she had to at least ask. She stopped and waited for Verity to catch up.

'Did you have a good weekend, Verity?'

'Yeah, it was good, thanks,' she said, her gaze trailing the ground.

'That's good. And everything here is okay?'

She shrugged. 'Yeah, I guess.'

Connie laughed. 'Now, that doesn't sound at all convincing, come on – spill.'

They were at the block. Verity unlocked the door and as they walked onto the wing, she held the door for Connie. She didn't answer the question. Very odd. Something definitely wasn't quite right.

'Morning ladies,' Jamie said as he disappeared into the wing office with two mugs. 'If I'd known you were coming I'd have made you a cuppa.'

'No, you wouldn't,' Connie said as she followed him in. 'And you *did* know we were coming. You've always been tight with your cups of tea, Jamie.' Connie smiled as she put her name on the board to let everyone know she was on the wing and going to be using the interview room. Being on the wing, with officers nearby, was a more reassuring environment than when she carried out interviews in the more secluded portacabin. She was about to put Verity's name on, but as she turned she realised she'd already left. Connie looked out the office window in time to see her skulking down the path.

'What's up with your mate today, then?' Jamie's eyes followed Connie's.

'Must've been annoyed you didn't make her a drink,' Connie said, trying to hide how Verity's demeanour had unsettled her. 'Right, work to do. I'm seeing Kyle Mann in the interview room next door. How's he been on the wing over the weekend?'

'Good as gold, mate. Never no trouble, that one.'

'Does he speak to the other inmates?'

'Not that I've witnessed. But he has been making phone calls, which is a new thing. Not sure if it's a good sign or not – but at least he's talking to someone.'

Connie's heart rate picked up a little. Phone calls to who? Had he been speaking to Alice? She'd probably find out soon enough. The hard way.

'Okay, thanks, Jamie.' Connie straightened, smiling widely to conceal her anxiety. 'I'll only be an hour or so.'

Connie left the wing office and settled in the room along the corridor. She'd just put her folder on the table when there was a knock.

'Come on in, Kyle. Take a seat.'

'Morning, Miss.' He sat down, his eyes lowered, arms crossed.

'How have you been since I last saw you?'

'All right, I guess. You?'

'Good, thanks. Right, I want to finish the interview today so I can complete your assessment. I want to concentrate on the day of the offence, and for you to talk me through what happened.'

Kyle spoke with no hesitation. It was as though now he'd begun talking, a dam had burst, and he wanted to tell her his story. His voice was monotone as he described what he did. How he forced Sean Taylor to his knees, tied his hands behind his back, made him lower his head. How he sunk the blade into Sean's neck, left it, handle sticking out, and walked away without a thought about the incoming tide. Connie had heard a lot of bad things – descriptions of crimes, hideous acts of violence – and Kyle's story wasn't particularly unique in that way. But what did strike Connie was the disparity between what she was hearing now and how Kyle had come across to her since their first meeting – his quiet persona, his vulnerability.

'Was he drugged?' she asked.

'What, Sean? Not that I knew.'

'You didn't give him anything yourself?'

'No.'

'Then how did you overpower him, get him to submit the way you describe?'

Kyle stared at her for a while before answering. 'He did what I asked him to. That was it.'

'Why did you do it, Kyle?' Her brow creased as she asked this. She really did feel confusion as she fought to reconcile what he'd told her with what his family had said, with the picture she had built up of this young man in her own mind. If she was honest, like Alice, she too didn't want to believe him capable of such an act, not without some serious manipulation in any case.

'Always wanted to know how it felt, putting a knife in for real.

Not just in a game.' Kyle shrugged, his words spoken matter-of-factly. It was as though he was talking about something far removed from himself, from reality.

'Why did you choose Sean?'

He lifted his shoulders, kept them there for a few seconds before dropping them. 'Dunno, really.'

'Was he someone you knew from the online gaming?'

'Yeah, that's it.' He shuffled in his seat. 'Yes, a gamer, like us.'

'Us?' Connie immediately latched onto his use of words. Had he slipped up?

'Me. Like me,' he corrected himself. But it was obvious to Connie he meant he hadn't acted alone.

'I realise you don't want to tell me about the other person or even people involved, but this session isn't being recorded, you know – it's only me and you.'

'I am not a grass. My mum might be telling you some bollocks about me, but *I'm* not a grass.'

Connie didn't want to get side-tracked by the subject of his mother now. She wanted to press him further about who else might've been involved in the murder.

'You feel the need to protect this other person. Do you owe them?'

'I don't want to talk any more.'

'Why are you afraid of them?' She was so close, she was determined not to let this go.

'I'm not afraid of anyone.' He spoke assertively, looking right into Connie's eyes for a moment before turning away sharply. 'I wish I'd not started talking to you. I've made everything worse.' He propelled his feet forwards, knocking the table leg and sending it shuddering a few inches across the floor.

'I'm sorry you feel that way, Kyle,' Connie said, ignoring what he'd done. 'But worse for who?' Despite Kyle's apparent discomfort for this line of conversation, Connie felt compelled to forge ahead.

'For everyone.' Kyle's eyes glared.

'So, this guy on the outside, the one who's got away with murder – he's going to do what, precisely? Kill again?' Connie knew she might be pushing it, but everything was pointing to there being someone else involved, maybe even responsible for Sean's murder. She wanted Kyle to admit it. 'Don't you think you owe it to others to do something before he does more harm, ruins others' lives?'

'Stop!' Kyle banged his fists down on the table. 'Shut up now.'

'I don't understand why you're the one in here, and he's free out there.' Connie waved her arm, alluding to the outside world, free of bars.

Kyle shook his head, sighing loudly. But he remained in his chair. He hadn't stormed off yet, at least.

'Is it because this guy was the only male figure you had in your life, the only role model because your dad left you?'

Kyle frowned. 'My dad wasn't great, but he was around.'

'But he left the house, your mum – he didn't live with you. It must have had an impact.'

'Look, I don't know what my mum's been telling you, but my dad never left us. He went on and on at me, said I was wasting my life, and I rebelled against him. We had our arguments, but no more than most families. I don't think they had a clue what was going on with me. *I* didn't most of the time.'

Connie took notes as Kyle spoke. It was interesting that he was giving a different story about his home life to Alice's. Connie had no reason to doubt what Kyle was telling her was true. But Alice – did *she* have a reason to manipulate the truth?

'Your dad, where is he now?'

'I assume he's still at home, with my mum. Why?'

'Was there abuse when you were growing up, Kyle?'

'Abuse?' He sat forwards. 'Jesus. No. Why are you asking this?'

'Sorry, it's the picture your mum . . .'

He got up. 'This is bullshit, she has to be called out on this.' He shook his head, turned and left the room.

139

CHAPTER FORTY-TWO

Tom

He couldn't stop fidgeting; the excitement had built to an obscene level. A few calls, some last-minute alterations, and he was good to go. She'd played her part well so far; he was impressed with her commitment and ability to stay below the radar, keeping out of sight while waiting for the right time. She had even more patience than him. He'd formed a good, strong, tight team. Nothing could go wrong, no one could stop him. He was the top player – The Boss – no one could beat him.

He gave her the signal.

CHAPTER FORTY-THREE

Connie

Rather than chance being a bit late and Alice not waiting, Connie had ordered a taxi to take her back to Totnes. It dropped her right outside her consultancy, and now, coffee next to her, Connie retrieved Alice's therapy file from her computer and sat rereading the notes she'd made so far.

It could be possible Alice felt responsible for Kyle's behaviour, had internalised it, and made it her own failure. But maybe when speaking of it, she felt the need to protect herself, her self-worth, by fabricating the actions of others – in this case her husband – thus allowing the blame to be directed away from her. Basically, she could be using self-deception as a coping mechanism, by not confronting a truth about herself she found too terrible. Connie also wondered if Alice was planning on seeking out Sean Taylor's mum as an abstract attempt to diminish her own feelings of guilt.

Alice was certainly becoming a more complex client than Connie had first thought. In a moment, that complexity might be even further added to. If Kyle had immediately called Alice after leaving the interview room, then this session was going to be challenging. As Lindsay had quite rightly pointed out, she was compromising her position, and no good was going to come of it.

Connie paced from one end of her room to the other, the heels of her shoes making lines in the pile of the beige carpet. She wanted this over with. She checked her watch. Alice was late. Opening the window, Connie hung her head and shoulders out clear of the frame, checking up and down the street. Alice wasn't in sight in either direction.

Was she late, or not coming?

If it wasn't for this morning, Connie would think it very strange Alice would miss a session she herself had asked for – had stated she *needed* for extra support. Not today of all days. But given the fact Kyle might have put her off, told her not to come, then perhaps it should be of no surprise.

Despite doing it for the best intentions – to encourage Kyle to speak out and stop protecting the other person – Connie had crossed the line. If Kyle had spoken to his mother, then she too would know that now. She wouldn't trust Connie enough to carry on her sessions.

The time passed slowly, Connie clock-watching and periodically checking the road outside. She slammed her hands on the desk. 'Stupid woman.'

She'd compromised her professional duty, broken the code of conduct. Now she'd probably lost a client, *and* done untold damage in the process.

Connie snatched up her bag, took her coat from the stand and left. She was going to see Lindsay.

Connie approached the entrance to the police station, hesitating before pushing through the huge glass doors. While it was the only possibility of seeing Lindsay these days, she wasn't sure what kind of reception she'd get, particularly from Mack. If, of course, they were both in the station and not out on a job.

The man at the front counter made a call and a few moments later Connie heard familiar footsteps behind her.

'Business or pleasure?'

'Neither,' Connie said.

'Hmm.' Lindsay pressed her lips together and raised her eyebrows. 'Okay, sounds like a cup of coffee and a chat material. Follow me.' Lindsay turned tail and disappeared up the stairs. Connie hurried after her.

The whiteboard at the end of the incident room brought a sudden, sharp memory back to Connie as she followed Lindsay through to the coffee machine. Connie's own photo had been on the very same board last year. She shuddered. Now, though, it was filled with things relating to Isabella Bond. Connie had a twinge of uncertainty about showing up, creating an unwelcomed interruption for Lindsay. The room was a buzz of activity: phones ringing, officers all talking at once. A very different environment from her own work. She'd enjoyed being part of the team last year, when she'd been asked to consult on the Hargreaves case. She hadn't realised how much she missed teamwork and company until she'd been catapulted back into it.

'So, what's up?' Lindsay asked as she handed Connie a polystyrene cup of unidentified deep-brown liquid. Could be tea, could be coffee – she probably wouldn't be any the wiser when she took a sip.

'After our talk about how to handle seeing my client and her son in the same day—'

'Oh, God. It hit the fan?'

'No. Well, not yet, anyway. I saw Kyle this morning, but she didn't turn up this afternoon. I think he's told her and now she's pissed off with me.'

'She would have every right to feel that way if she believes you've been keeping the fact you're seeing Kyle from her,' Lindsay said. She was always straight-talking, never sugar-coating anything.

'Yes, and I'm worried about her.'

'Did you try calling?'

'Of course.' Connie took a tentative sip of her drink. 'When I was waiting at the train station. I got a disconnected tone, which is worrying given that it's the main contact number she supplied at her initial consultation.'

'Ah, well, perhaps she doesn't want you to get hold of her. You might have to wait it out, see if she comes to you.'

'You can't . . . you know, check—'

'Sorry to disturb you, Boss. We need you a sec.' DC Clarke walked in between her and Lindsay. Connie recognised him; she'd had dealings with him last year.

'Sorry, Connie. Hang on if you want.' She moved off towards the team who were all congregated around Lindsay's desk.

Connie could hear parts of what was being said. There'd been a violent assault, a woman seriously injured in her own home. Something about a head injury. A hate crime. The words were distorted; Connie's ears hummed. As the team began to disperse and some headed for the door, Lindsay rushed over to Connie. 'Sorry, have to go. Catch you at home later?'

'Sounds like a serious one; I doubt I'll see you later,' Connie said, forcing a smile to prevent coming across as critical. 'I overheard parts. Something about a woman being attacked, possibly a hate crime?'

'Yes, doesn't sound good. Left for dead, so could be looking at attempted murder.'

Connie grabbed Lindsay's arm before she ran off. 'I've got a bad feeling.'

'About this?' Lindsay asked.

'Maybe it's just a coincidence, but the timing . . .'

'You think this might be your client because she failed to attend her session with you? Come on, I'm sure there's a reasonable explanation for that – you know, like she's found out about you visiting her son.'

'Yeah, thanks.' Connie rolled her eyes. 'But, you're probably right.'

Connie stood a while after Lindsay and the team had left, not quite able to shake the feeling in her gut; the nagging suspicion that she knew the victim was going to be Alice Mann.

CHAPTER FORTY-FOUR

Connie

Connie was sitting on the sofa, her laptop balanced on her knees. She trawled the internet for news of the attack. It was unlikely she'd find anything – it had only been a few hours since Lindsay and Mack rushed off to the victim's home. She'd checked her texts and emails every few minutes in the hope of seeing one from Alice. The only messages on her mobile were from Scott. She frowned. Had she given him her number? She thought she'd taken his. Damn, she must've drunkenly allowed the 'I'll call you now and then you'll have my number' trick. She scrolled past his texts, tutting to herself; she'd have to respond to those at some point later. For the tenth time, Connie tried the mobile number Alice had given in her initial consultation. It was still not connecting.

The bang of the front door made Connie jump. She flung the laptop on the coffee table and ran out to the hallway, bumping into Lindsay coming the other way.

'Shit, Lindsay. Didn't hear your car.'

'No, I'm parked down a bit. I'm only popping in quickly, then I'm going to the station. Will probably be a late one.'

The fact Lindsay was popping in instead of going straight to the station rang an alarm. Connie was almost afraid to ask. 'So?'

'So, it appears the victim was the target. It wasn't a burglary gone wrong or anything. She sustained head injuries and has been put into an induced coma.'

'God, how terrible. Was it a hate crime, like you thought?'

'The graffiti painted on the wall inside the house certainly points to a hate crime, or some kind of revenge attack, yes.'

Connie's mouth dried. 'What's the victim's name, Lindsay?'

'It's not been released yet, we need to contact her family.'

'You can tell me, though. It's not like I'm going to put it on Twitter.' Her voice had raised an octave, the dread of the answer pressing on her vocal cords. Lindsay pursed her lips, clearly contemplating whether she should release this information. 'Please, I'm driving myself mad here. If you tell me her name, I can get on with my evening and worry about how I'm going to make it up with my client instead.'

Lindsay closed her eyes for a moment, then said, 'You tell me your client's name, and I'll give you a yes or no.'

'Okay.' Connie took a deep breath. 'Her name is Alice Mann.'

Lindsay's eyes widened. She didn't need to speak, Connie could see the answer in her shocked expression. She stumbled backwards, her back hitting against the staircase.

'Fuck.'

Lindsay dragged both of her hands down her face. 'It's your client. I can't believe it. How do you keep getting involved in stuff like this?'

'Hey, what's that supposed to mean?'

'Well, shit, Connie. First the Hargreaves case, now Alice Mann?'

'I'm not trying to get involved in anything! She sought *me* out.'

'But you're the one who's seeing her son, *the murdering bastard*, as was written in red on Alice's wall.' Lindsay's eyes were wide, her pale freckled skin flushed red, matching her hair.

'It wasn't written in blood, was it?'

Lindsay shook her head, clearly exasperated. 'That's yet to be confirmed. But my point is, yet again you are involved, however indirectly.'

146

'I don't know how this happens to me.' Connie slid down, and crouched with her knees bent, elbows leaning on them, with her head in her hands.

'No, neither do I,' Lindsay said.

Connie looked up sharply. 'If *you* hadn't convinced me it was a good idea to take Jen up on her offer of doing those prison assessments . . . well, then I wouldn't be involved, would I?'

'I didn't suggest you should agree to assess your client's son though, did I? And even if you hadn't taken the prison job, you'd still be involved because you were seeing Alice Mann!'

'Okay, okay.' Connie held her hands up. This wasn't helping matters and was detracting them from the very serious issue of Alice Mann's attack. 'No point getting annoyed with each other. What's going to happen now?'

'I'm going to do my job, Connie. Which means soon I will probably be paying you a visit. Or, rather, Mack will.'

'Oh, fantastic. Can't wait.' Connie pushed herself back up and stood in front of Lindsay, whose hands were now firmly placed on her hips. She looked like a stern headmistress. 'Seriously, does it have to be Mack? Can't you send Clarke?'

'I'll see who's available,' Lindsay said, her voice softening. 'You can always start praying that, *one*, Alice Mann doesn't remain in an induced coma for long and can tell us herself who attacked her, or *two*, we can ascertain who's responsible ourselves using our first-class detective skills and don't have to involve you at all.'

'That would be good. If you could arrange for one or two . . . or both would be better, then I'd be forever grateful.' Connie moved forwards, giving Lindsay a gentle hug. After what felt like minutes, Connie felt Lindsay's posture relax; she responded by squeezing her own arms tightly around Connie.

'Here's hoping,' she said, releasing her and turning around, leaving Connie on the threshold of her house, deflated and consumed by anxiety.

CHAPTER FORTY-FIVE

Connie

Connie paced – a nervous energy flowing through her, compelling her to keep moving. There was no way she could sit still now, knowing what she knew. Was this her fault? She'd somehow started a chain reaction by forcing Kyle to speak to her, and now something bad had happened to his mum. She'd had the suspicion he'd been keeping silent to protect her from the *one that got away* – had this person now attacked Alice to get to Kyle – stop him from talking any further to the professionals? Was he afraid of being grassed up by Kyle – identified as the other killer? Connie's mind whirred. She had a vision of Alice, battered and bruised, lying motionless in a hospital bed, wires and machines attached to her, keeping her breathing; keeping her alive.

Blinking the image away, Connie decided she couldn't wait around uselessly doing nothing.

Taking her bag and coat from the hallway, she left the house. She had to see Alice for herself.

Connie stood in the doorway, afraid to enter the hospital room. All she could see were black, purple and red patches interspersed with bandages and numerous monitors. An intubation tube jutted from Alice's mouth: a machine was doing her breathing for her. A pump made hissing and whooshing noises, the monitors bleeping incessantly. Connie could see from where she was standing that Alice's ash-blonde hair was matted, a dark red staining the loose curls. The woman was unrecognisable as the Alice Mann she knew. Connie gripped the frame harder. Someone came up close behind her.

'What are you doing here?' Lindsay's tone was hushed, but severe.

'I had to see her. Sorry, but I . . .'

'Well, now you have, please can you go and wait in the ward's day room. I'll come and see you in a minute.' Lindsay tugged Connie backwards, away from the room. 'Go please, Connie.' She did as instructed, her legs unsteadily carrying her down the corridor.

The view from the day room was of the main road leading into Torquay, of the housing estates that had sprung up during the '90s. Connie watched the cars zooming along the road, but didn't *see*, her eyes unable to focus on anything. Poor Alice. Already suffering for her son's act, she was having to face a new kind of suffering – more pain. Only now it was physical, as well as mental. Who would want to inflict such an attack on an innocent woman? Connie swallowed the hard lump in her throat. Was she to blame?

'Right, Connie.' Lindsay strode into the room, her face set. 'Now you're here, you may as well see if you can be useful.'

'Sure, whatever I can do,' Connie said, moving away from the window. She sat at the table where Lindsay had placed a file. Lindsay remained standing as she spread some photos out.

'How much do you know about Alice Mann?'

Connie gazed at the photos of a house, the exterior and interior, the hateful words daubed in what she assumed now to be Alice's blood on the wall. The crime scene. Blood splatters on the wooden floor. She turned away.

'I know she's the mother of Kyle Mann who was sentenced four years ago for the murder of Sean Taylor. I know she seemed afraid of her ex-husband – I got the impression he'd been abusive towards her and her son.' Connie paused, sucking in a big breath of air. 'I know I used the fact I was seeing her to make Kyle talk. And I think I started something by doing that. God, I'm so sorry.'

'So you believe Kyle may have told someone on the outside about Alice seeing you?'

'Yes. I don't think Kyle acted alone in the murder of Sean Taylor. He had help, or he was manipulated into helping someone else commit the murder. He's hiding something, protecting someone. During one of our sessions, when I told him that by talking about what happened he would help himself, he replied, *but it won't help my mother*. It struck me that it was possible he wasn't only protecting the other perpetrator, but his mum too. I wonder if this other guy was threatening to hurt Alice if Kyle spoke out?'

'Okay. That gives us a fair bit to go on. Thanks, Connie.' Lindsay gathered the photos and popped the file under her arm. 'Now go home. Please. I'll see you later.'

Connie had wanted to wait for Lindsay to come home, so she'd settled on the sofa and put on a film. She'd tried hard to stay awake, but sleep had finally taken her. She lay with a blanket draped over her, Amber nestled into the crook of her bent knees. Now, she was being gently nudged awake.

'Hey, sleepyhead,' Lindsay whispered. 'Don't you want to go to bed?'

'What time is it?' Connie rubbed the sleep from her eyes.

'Three in the morning.'

'Wow, another late one for you.'

'Two big cases, it's mad at the moment.'

'Sure is. Any developments?'

'Sort of.'

Connie sat upright, all remnants of sleepiness jolted from her. 'Oh? Good news?'

'Leads rather than good news. I know you're not really fully awake, but you mentioned an ex-husband, how Alice had talked about an abusive relationship?'

'Yes, she was very shady about it, didn't really want to talk about it when pushed.'

'Hmm.'

'Why?'

'Well, we obviously followed it up, questioned the husband. It appears he is her husband – like, current, not an ex. He'd been away for the weekend, visiting a military event in London. It checks out.'

'Weird. Kyle also queried why she would have said they were separated. Why would Alice have made out that she was divorced?'

'I don't know. Mr Mann certainly gave the impression they were happily married – said they had their "difficulties" due to their son's conviction, but he came across as genuine. He was visibly shaken and upset about Alice being attacked.'

'He could've got home from the weekend early Monday and—'

'He did get home on Monday. He was the one who called the ambulance and police. But it's clear Alice was attacked prior to his return – and left for dead.'

'Oh?'

'We've got accounts from Alice's neighbours, most saying there had been some coming and going – people spotted hanging around Alice's house. It appears there are a few people who had the opportunity to get inside, attack her.'

'And so it's a possibility one of those people was the other killer of Sean Taylor.'

'Yes. It's a possibility.'

'Tying up loose ends,' Connie said, more to herself than to Lindsay.

'You might know more than you realise, Connie. Get some sleep, we need to talk more later.'

Connie gently pushed Amber along the sofa and swung her legs off, stretching her back until it clicked.

Yes, she might well know more. From the beginning, a niggling suspicion had troubled Connie. Alice Mann was hiding something from her. Now she had to find out what it was – and why she'd bothered to lie to her in the first place.

151

CHAPTER FORTY-SIX

Deborah

Had I been seen skulking about like a common criminal outside Alice's house? Did her neighbours hear my rage?

The newspaper lies open on my kitchen table, the bold headline screaming out like an accusation.

Convicted Murderer's Mother Left For Dead!

My head is splitting. I've taken four tablets already this morning. I turn the unopened blue paracetamol box over and over in my hand. There are more boxes in the medicine cabinet. Maybe I should take them all. Nathan hasn't bothered to call me to find out how I am. It would be the police who'd find me, eventually, not him.

I pierce the foil packet with my thumbnail, taking out two tablets. Then another two. I repeat this until the blister packs are empty. I pile the tablets on the newspaper – the small mound of white capsules mounting higher until they collapse, sliding and spreading out across the article.

Alice's face is obliterated with pills.

What did I do?

CHAPTER FORTY-SEVEN

Connie

'Did you sleep at all?' Lindsay handed Connie a mug of coffee as she entered the kitchen.

'Not much. My mind wouldn't shut off.' Connie leant against the worktop. 'Kept going over in my head what I should have done, what I shouldn't have.'

'Try not to beat yourself up too much, I have a feeling this would've happened at some point soon anyway.'

'Really? I don't know. Even if you're right though, it's me, *my* input, that probably caused this to happen now. If I hadn't told Kyle . . .' Connie took a sip of coffee and almost spat it out. 'Did you put sugar in this?'

'Thought you might need it,' Lindsay said, giving a brief shrug.

Connie recalled the moment in the morgue last year when she'd had to identify the bodies of her client and her son. Lindsay had given her sweetened tea then, to help the shock, supposedly. Was she being prepared for a similar outcome now? A shudder passed through her.

'Have you contacted the prison, let Kyle know about the attack?'

'Yes, they are going to get the prison chaplain to talk to Kyle. Support him.'

'Aren't you going to question him? He probably knows who did this to Alice.'

'Let us deal with it, Connie. We know what we're doing.' Lindsay placed an arm on Connie's. 'Are you taking the day off today?'

She shook her head. 'No. I should go in. I've got clients booked in – I'm not going to let them down.'

'Well, take it easy. You've had a shock.' Lindsay placed her mug and bowl in the dishwasher. 'I've got to dash off, but call if you need me, yes?'

'Will do,' Connie said absently.

Having passed through the barrier, Connie walked casually along Coleton station platform. Being half an hour later than normal, she seemed to have missed the morning rush and there were just a few people waiting for the Plymouth train. The live departure board informed her there was a fifteen-minute delay though. Typical. Connie headed for the Pumpkin Café. An *un*sweetened coffee wouldn't go amiss.

As she passed by the rows of newspapers to reach the counter, the headline on the *Herald Express* caught her attention. A fresh surge of guilt and uneasiness shook her stomach. Curiosity won out though, and she grabbed a copy and took it to the counter. When she'd paid for both, she went back outside to sit at the metal table and await the delayed train.

Connie set the coffee down and spread out the paper. A photo of Kyle Mann adorned the cover. Even in the local paper, attention-grabbing headlines and a flourish of drama were common. The story of Alice's unprovoked attack began with the background details – and the dramatic ones – of Kyle's conviction for the brutal and 'assassination-like' murder of Sean Taylor. Alice's story continued inside. It was clearly a big scoop for the local paper. Connie turned to the inner pages.

Her breath caught, her chest tightened. The photo they'd printed was of Alice. Underneath it stated: *Alice Mann during her son's trial, Exeter Crown Court, 2014.*

Despite the photo being four years old, and slightly grainy – one thing was clear.

It was *not* Alice Mann.

CHAPTER FORTY-EIGHT

Tom

She must know now.

He climbed the stairs from the basement, unlocked the door at the top and entered the main part of the house. He rarely left his room, only when his food supplies ran low, or his cutlery and crockery needed washing. Then he dumped them on the worktop for her to sort. He knew he was lazy, but there was little point in carrying out such chores when she had nothing better to do with her sorry little life.

She'd seen him out and about a couple of times, not that it mattered. It was more likely to help him if she thought she was being followed, watched. It would keep her in check. Why, though, was everyone suddenly taking it upon themselves to try to ruin his game? One kill. That's all he was after. Not much to ask.

He was still one step ahead though, he reminded himself. He was confident he now had enough time and space to carry on.

Now some of the loose cannons had been taken care of, he should be able to concentrate on the target he'd spent months carefully priming online – the one who was a bit of a loser, like Sean had been. Someone who wasn't a great loss to the world, but who Tom would have fun building up to smash back down. Easy prey.

PART TWO

I created a monster.

It's taken me a long time to understand. To even think it, let alone say it.

You don't expect that something so amazing, brilliant, miraculous – something you grew inside your own body and nurtured, letting it take what it needed from you – could transform into something so evil.

We shared a connection – the physicality of the umbilical cord at first, then the emotional bond. I nursed him, allowed him to suck the goodness from my breasts.

That which ties us cannot be broken. We are inextricably linked. Forever.

That he is a murderer doesn't alter this.

Yes, I created a monster.

But I wasn't the only one.

CHAPTER FORTY-NINE

Alice

Angela

I'm in limbo, unable to go forwards, no chance of peddling backwards. Where can I go from here? The *Herald Express* lies open on the coffee table, her picture spread across the page. My stomach feels like a hard rock, and I swallow repeatedly to prevent bile from rising. I daren't open the laptop, cannot bear to see the fallout of my deception. Will they know I did this with the best intentions – or will they hate me? It was just one little lie. I was trying to make things right.

I'm *still* going to make things right.

'Hatred stirs up conflict, but love covers over all wrongs.' My voice cracks.

But I'm right, aren't I? It's not the end – I *can* carry on despite this setback, as major as it is. I can make amends for him. For me. It seems I'm going to have to bypass Alice Mann now though. I can't believe I'd been so close to meeting Alice and then messed it all up. Twice! I was so cowardly – outside her house on several occasions and never making it past the front door. Now it's too late. I take a deep breath. I can do this. I'll just have to go straight to Deborah on my own instead. It would've been so much better if I could have met Alice, got her onside, then we could've seen Deborah together; put on a stronger, unified front. Alice is the same as me. We're in the same boat. I wouldn't have felt as alone in seeking Deborah's forgiveness if I had her by my side.

But Alice had beaten me to it. *She'd* been seeing Deborah. I'd figured out it was Deborah's house I'd followed Alice to after she left the post office. I shouldn't have been surprised she'd wanted to meet Deborah – maybe we both had the same burning need for forgiveness. Only Alice had been braver than me. She'd gone there alone.

I've spent so many months being Alice, feeling as though I was living her life, taking responsibility for my actions as her – even talking about her son with a psychologist, as if he was mine. Showing remorse while pretending to be her was the best opportunity I had to gain redemption publicly without risking losing my son. It's what I needed. And I liked *being* needed too. Being Alice gave that to me.

I've been Alice for so long now that I'm not sure how to be me.

But I am Angela Killion again now. And I am still desperate to meet Deborah and make things right. It's going to be harder now. But one way or another, I must make it happen.

CHAPTER FIFTY

Connie

'Lindsay, it's not my Alice.' Connie raised her voice above the noise of the train.

'What? What do you mean?'

'I've just seen the photo of Alice Mann in the paper, and it's not my client. Her face was so bruised and swollen when I saw her in the hospital, I didn't realise it then. But apart from similar hair, it's definitely a different woman.'

'So, who is the Alice Mann you've been counselling?' The shrillness of Lindsay's voice indicated she was as shocked as Connie at this strange turn of events.

'I've no idea. I don't understand.' Connie held the paper up, looking at the photo again. It didn't make any sense. 'Have you got the right Alice Mann? I mean, is it Kyle's mum lying in the hospital bed?'

'Yes, definitely. Her husband has been with her. We've spoken about the fact she was probably targeted as a direct result of Kyle's murderer status – they'd apparently been having issues ever since he was convicted. There's no doubt, it's *the* Alice.'

Whoever Connie had been counselling, she wasn't Kyle's mother. Yet she'd spoken about Kyle, what he'd done, how she felt responsible. Why go to those lengths? It explained the discrepancies between her and Kyle's accounts, but not why she was pretending to be someone she wasn't. Who the hell *was* she?

Connie's stomach lurched along with the train as it hurtled around a bend, the reality hitting her hard: Connie had used false information to get Kyle to talk. And it had started a chain reaction resulting in the real Alice being beaten and left in an induced coma.

Did the fake Alice know what had happened? Is that the reason she didn't show up for her session on Monday, because her cover had been blown? But how did she know? Alice's attack wasn't even public then. Unless this woman – this imposter – was personally involved, she couldn't have known.

Which begged the question, was *she* the one who attacked Alice Mann?

Connie's mind filled with questions and half-formed hypotheses of why she would seek out counselling under the guise of another woman – a murderer's mother at that. Connie remembered Alice's plan of meeting with Sean Taylor's mum, and how she wanted to convince her they'd both suffered a loss – how they were sharing their grief at losing a son. Connie had rebuffed her idea, but if her client was as desperate as she seemed to be, she might well have carried out her plan despite its risks. Maybe the fake Alice really had lost a son and she'd become obsessed with the story about Kyle Mann killing Sean Taylor and was now somehow relating her own experience, her feelings of grief, to Alice's and Deborah's, to the point of deluding even herself.

Connie stepped off the train at Totnes, her body on autopilot. Her legs took her out the exit and along Station Road into town, up the hill and across the street. After she passed East Gate Arch she rummaged in her bag for the consultancy door key and let herself in. Halfway up the stairs she stopped. The security camera. She might be able to get a good still picture of the Alice who'd been coming for counselling and give it to Lindsay to enhance. They'd have a fair chance of someone recognising the

Alice imposter if they had a photo to distribute. She'd retrieve the SD memory card from the camera at the end of the day.

The sudden sound of the buzzer made her jump.

Her client was here already. At least, that's who Connie hoped it was. The sudden realisation that she knew nothing about this fake Alice woman, her background, her motivations or her intentions, made her shiver. What if she was watching? Waiting for Connie to be alone. She checked it was who she was expecting, then with palpable relief, pressed the button to release the front door.

What felt like an age later, her first client of the day, Alistair, sloped in, his arms loose at his sides, head bent. He reminded Connie of an orang-utan, guileless and gentle. This would be his fourth session, but, as yet, Connie didn't feel she'd helped him make significant progress in challenging his misconceptions about his role in the suicide of a friend who'd been the target of online bullying. She gathered her strength and focussed. She hoped today might be a turning point.

As Alistair left, Connie heard muffled deep voices, then a clambering on the stairs. She shot up from her chair. The point of the buzzer system was to only let in people she knew, who had appointments. She'd been burned before when Aiden Flynn had managed to get in when the doormat lodged itself in the way of the door closing. Connie'd sorted that issue, and then had the camera installed. But it was pointless if her clients held the door open for someone else. Her face was hot with annoyance as she flung the door open to face the uninvited guest.

Connie tutted loudly. 'Oh, it's you. Why didn't you buzz?' She didn't know whether to be relieved or angry. Mack knew the importance of her buzzer system.

'Lovely greeting as usual,' he said as he squeezed his large frame past Connie and settled himself in the chair Alistair had just vacated.

'Oh, please do sit down.' Connie didn't bother to disguise her sarcasm. She and Mack knew where they stood with each other; sarcastic comments were the norm.

'Lindsay tells me that the woman you *thought* was Alice Mann is not the Alice Mann currently in intensive care in Torbay Hospital.' He obviously wasn't planning on any small talk as he pulled out his black pocket notebook and poised his pen.

Connie took her seat opposite Mack. She had the feeling this was going to be a long, and probably strange, conversation.

CHAPTER FIFTY-ONE

Deborah

What have I accomplished? The woman who was sitting in my lounge, drinking from my bone china and telling me about her son, is now in a coma. Is that justice? Is it what I wanted? If it is, then why am I not feeling *justified*? I don't feel any sense of relief, nor do I have closure. Where has my hatred got me?

I have no son, no job, and my husband has abandoned me. I thought I wanted to punish someone else, someone who deserved it. But I'm left empty, deflated – like a breast once engorged with milk, depleted. A useless, empty sack.

The paracetamol pile on the newspaper – Alice's eye peeking through a gap in the tablets – beckons. It's been there since yesterday, mocking me. I haven't the strength to swallow them, but equally I don't have the strength to put them away, remove them from my sight and temptation.

I stare at them and wonder if I have the guts.

Something holds me back. Fear? Cowardice? Maybe it's the primitive part of my brain preventing me from carrying out this act – a last-ditch attempt to preserve life. Apparently, in the throes of death, you instinctively fight to survive. Regardless of any other factors.

I turn away from the death pile, for now at least. I want to call

Nathan, tell him what's happened. Share this with someone. I sit on the edge of the sofa, holding the phone loosely in my hand. I stare at Nathan's name on the screen. My heart drums in my chest as I press the button.

It rings.

He'll see my name pop up and reject the call. He won't want to speak with me, even though I have no idea what I did wrong, why he left so abruptly the other night and hasn't contacted me since. Is he with the other woman? That surely must be the reason he packed up and left.

It's rung three times now. Shit, will *she* answer? I'm about to cut the call when I hear his voice. For a moment, my stomach drops; I have a wave of nausea. Tears are pricking my eyes. I didn't realise how much I'd missed him until his velvety voice hit my ears.

'Deborah, are you okay?'

There is concern in his tone. And something else – guilt probably.

'I didn't think you'd answer. You haven't returned any of my texts or voicemails,' I say flatly.

'I don't know what to say to you,' he says.

'You could start with answering *why*?'

I think I hear a sigh. I strain to make out another voice in the background, a hint to where he is. 'You cut me out a long time ago. We weren't really communicating. Without Sean—' His voice catches and he clears his throat with a cough. 'Without him, it was like we had nothing in common anymore.'

I can almost feel my heart split. His words cause a stabbing pain, because I know he's right. With Sean gone, we are merely two people who lost their roles in life; who were once lovers, but lost their passion. Sean was the glue holding us together and now the cracks have been left with no support, and no reason to be fixed. Our marriage is a discarded has-been.

Can we still do something about it? Isn't it worth trying to find something else to bind us? Nathan obviously doesn't think so.

'Is there someone else, Nathan?' I need to know, but at the same time don't want to hear the answer if it's *yes*. I hold my breath and wait for what might be the end.

'I – I . . .' he stutters. This tells me enough. I have a sudden bubble of anger rise inside of me.

'Yes? Go on, tell me! You cheating son of a bitch.' My breaths are shallow and rapid, but in a way, it's good. At least I'm feeling *something*.

'Deborah,' he says softly, calmly. 'Please. I'm so sorry. I have struggled, wrestled with myself over this. I didn't take this decision lightly.'

'You haven't answered the question, Nathan. Are you with another woman?' I say more forcefully this time. My voice has found its power.

'I could be.'

'What the hell does that mean?'

'It means if I wanted to, I could be with another woman – the opportunity is there,' he says, adding quickly, 'but nothing has happened. Although, if I'm honest, Deborah, it's not because I don't want it to. That's one of the reasons why I left. I can't bear to break our wedding vows. I don't want to be the cheating son of a bitch you accuse me of being. I don't want to hurt you. Or me. We both deserve to be happy again.'

'Have you finished?' The tears are free-falling now, they drip down my chin and throat. How can I ever be happy? That fundamental human goal was robbed from me when Sean's life was taken.

'I don't know.'

It sounds finished to me. I'm not sure whether I want to fight for him or not. But what do I really want? The easy way out with the pills – or a chance at achieving some happiness in my life? Is Nathan likely to be that chance at happiness, or should I cut my losses, see what else is out there?

'I don't know either. Where would you like to go from here, Nathan?'

169

The silence is a death warrant waiting to be signed.

'Can we have some time to think things through, then meet in a while to discuss?'

I'm surprised by his response. Maybe there's hope after all.

'Yes, I'd like that.'

I end the call and place the phone on the coffee table. I walk on wobbly legs to the kitchen and scoop the tablet pile from the newspaper, revealing Alice's face beneath. My eyes flick from her to the pills in my hand, a palmful of lost hope and sadness.

I press my foot down on the pedal and the lid pops up. I stare at the contents for a moment before letting the white capsules slide from my hand. They fall into the metal bin, a rain of clinking sounds sealing their fate, not mine.

CHAPTER FIFTY-TWO

Angela

I press my ear to the door. He always has it locked now so I can't interfere, can't sneak up on him to see what he's doing on his precious computer. I can't hear anything. It's the soundproofing he's used – a better quality than what he'd had before. I rarely even think of him being here, in my house – hidden away in the basement. It's not even a proper basement – Tom worked on it until it was how he wanted it. Or needed it, as he said, back when we first moved in.

I'd hoped for something different in this new house. A fresh start for both of us. He didn't waste any time though, getting straight back into gaming, building up his network. It was true, what I told Connie. That I'd taken his door off, tried to encourage him to get out and meet people in real life; to get a job. He'd been to college, completing a computer course, then wallowed in the house, not attempting to find work. But that was then, back in the old house in Coleton. Here in Totnes, I've not mentioned it. I've given him space, done everything he asked of me. For a quiet life.

That quiet life is about to be blown wide open, it's going to become noisy and unbearable again. I can feel it in my gut. He's done another bad thing.

And I have a nasty suspicion I've helped him.

I tiptoe away from the understairs door leading to the basement. I don't know why – it's not like he could possibly hear me loitering. I seem to have grown accustomed to the fear, acting in a way that minimises the likelihood of him being angry with me. Hitting me like he did a couple of weeks ago. It had been difficult hiding the bruises from Connie, and from my group.

My group.

I make the sign of the cross on my chest. Can I claw it back? Somehow carry on being the leader of the support group? What will they be saying? I'm guessing at least one of them will have seen the news about Alice, and now know I'm not her. Not who I said I was. My stomach twists with pain – a deep anguish. I need to sit down.

The laptop on the table has been untouched for days. I feel sick with nerves even considering opening it, clicking on the icon that will take me to the forum where everyone will be writing about their shock, disappointment. Betrayal. I've let everyone down. What must Connie think? I'm tempted to call her, have a session to discuss everything, explain why I did it. She could still help me.

There are two reasons why I can't chance talking to her, though. One – she won't trust me and she'll be angry that I deceived her. And two – the most important – is that she could find out about Tom.

I must protect him. If it comes out now – what he did, what he might've done again – he'll be taken away from me.

He's my son. A mother should protect her children no matter what, shouldn't they? I know I failed him early on. My conscience will never be clear of that knowledge. What his father did; what I allowed to happen. I didn't keep him safe then, so now I must. It's my duty.

I think I can still right his wrongs. I can't bring Sean Taylor back, but I can help his mother, Deborah. My plan can still go ahead without Alice. I can't believe I came so close to speaking

172

with her, but bottled it at the last moment. Standing outside her house, hanging around where she worked – yet when the time came, I wasn't brave enough. Each time I saw her, I thought: '*Next time I'll talk to her*'. It was the fear holding me back. In my head I knew what I was doing, how it would play out – but, in reality, what was I going to say to Alice? How could I have got her onside without telling her who I was, that *my* son had been with hers, had killed Sean Taylor, too? I would've compromised Tom. It was my ultimate goal that had kept me trying. Now though, what makes me think I'll be able to face Deborah without an ally? The whole point was to befriend Alice first, then go to Sean's mum, together. We'd have helped her, somehow. Made up for what our sons did.

But I can still put it right. I *will* make amends. God will give me the extra strength I need. I look up to Heaven.

'Hatred stirs up conflict, but love covers over all wrongs.'

But first, I need to find out what Tom has done with Isabella.

173

CHAPTER FIFTY-THREE

Connie

Mack seemed more relaxed in her company than ever before. The three of them were sitting casually in the lounge: Connie and Mack side by side on the sofa and Lindsay on the floor, leaning against the armchair. It was approaching midnight and they'd been going over the two cases for the past three hours. Mack's tie was thrown over the arm of the sofa, his top few shirt buttons undone, revealing a patch of coarse, dark hair.

'Anyone for a drink now we're winding down?' Connie asked.

Mack rubbed the back of his neck and pulled his shoulders back in a stretch. 'Unless it's a sleepover, I'll have a decaf coffee, please.'

'And if it *is* a sleepover?' Lindsay smiled.

'Then lager. Or, sod it, whisky.'

Connie got up. 'I guess it's a sleepover then. I don't have whisky though, sorry. But there are most definitely a few cold lagers on offer.'

'I'll take that. I assume I'm not drinking alone?'

'Absolutely not,' Lindsay said. 'I could never let you do such a thing.'

Connie returned with three cans, the snapping of the ring pulls a heartening sound. They continued to look over photos and talk through theories. Connie realised she was in a privileged position, hearing the details of the misper case as well as the assault on Alice Mann. Lindsay had confided in Connie, saying she thought there was more to Isabella Bond's disappearance, how it was more complicated – and now, piecing together the known with the suspected, it was beginning to look like she'd been right. With Connie having finally taken the opportunity to share what Kyle had told her about the gaming world too, they'd begun to join some dots.

Data retrieved from Isabella's laptop pointed to her being involved in an online gaming site, as well as revealing details about some people she'd been meeting up with in real life. One message between Isabella and a person known online as 'The Boss' had set everyone's adrenaline going. It was cryptic, but hinted towards something big happening – a chance to 'put her skills to the ultimate test'. There were other messages too, referring to lying low until the signal. It was possible that Isabella's disappearance and Alice's attack were connected.

'We're going to have to pay Kyle Mann a visit, I think,' Lindsay said, her eyes on her can of lager.

Connie nodded slowly. 'I knew you'd have to. You're going to have to drag me into this, aren't you?'

'I wouldn't call it dragging. You were already knee-deep before our involvement. But yes, we will need to talk about your interviews, about what he said to you. What you said to him . . .'

'Great. I'll look forwards to the fallout.' Connie raised her lager. 'Cheers. Here's to another fine mess I've got myself into.'

Mack laughed. 'You are good at it, I'll give you that.'

'I'll be sure to add it to my CV.'

'Right, I think we're done for the night,' Lindsay said as she pushed herself up off the floor. 'I'll get you a pillow and blanket, Mack. You'll be fine on the sofa for a few hours, won't you?'

'Sure. I can sleep just about anywhere . . . Like you, Connie.'

Connie drew in a sharp intake of air. She'd obviously been

foolish to have thought Mack was over the fact she'd slept with his son. But Mack jumped in before she could respond.

'Shit.' He placed the palms of his hands on either side of his head. 'I'm sorry, that was meant to be a joke – it didn't sound like it, but it was.'

'Right. Well, I'm too tired to have an argument, Mack, so I'll leave you to sleep.' Connie started towards the lounge door.

'Wait. Connie, please . . .' Mack rose from the sofa and took hold of her arm. 'I really am sorry. It's not even an issue anymore; Gary's moved on and so have you. It was none of my business really, I was only looking out for my son. And, as it turns out, you're all right.'

'I'm all right?' Connie frowned.

'Yes. You know, you're all right. A good person.' Mack's face coloured. It was clear it had taken a lot for him to admit this.

'Thanks, Mack. You're all right yourself. I guess.' Her smile transformed into a laugh, and at that moment, Lindsay returned with her arms full of bedding.

'What's so funny? she said.

'I think your partner may have finally forgiven me, Lindsay.'

'Jesus, you two. Well, I'm glad you've both finally matured enough to get over yourselves. Now try to get some sleep. Tomorrow's going to be another mad day.' Lindsay pushed the bedding at Mack. 'What are you doing tomorrow, Connie?'

'Oh, I thought I'd do some of my own detective work.'

An expression of horror passed between Lindsay and Mack.

'I wouldn't go digging where you shouldn't—'

'Lindsay. Don't stress. I won't make a nuisance of myself. I only want to do a bit of research. I want to find *my* Alice. I have a feeling she is in need of serious help.'

CHAPTER FIFTY-FOUR

Connie

The house was quiet – the bedding neatly folded at one end of the sofa. They'd left without waking her. Part of her felt annoyed, but at least it meant they weren't going to talk her out of trying to find the fake Alice. Connie gathered the blankets and pillow and took the bundle upstairs, squashing it into the airing cupboard on the landing. The moment between her and Mack last night had been a relief. A clean slate, perhaps. Her and Gary's mistake now fully in the past.

The ten-minute walk to Coleton station was pleasant – the sun pierced the clouds giving a brightness and a more optimistic feeling to the day ahead. Two clients this morning, then a free afternoon. Hopefully Lindsay would update her later on about when they planned to visit HMP Baymead. Connie couldn't help but feel a bit apprehensive though, aware it was her initial leak about seeing Kyle's mum which had most likely triggered the attack on Alice Mann. Would Lindsay and Mack uncover another reason, so she might be let off the hook?

Connie was alert, her eyes scanning the platform, the café and the passing trains. She wasn't entirely sure what she was on the lookout for – a glimpse of the fake Alice? Or to spot someone watching her? Apart from Deborah Taylor, the only other potential lead Connie had as to where she might find fake Alice was the support group. If it was even real. She sighed loudly, the man standing near her shooting her a sideways glance. If fake Alice had lied about who she was, wasn't it also likely she'd lied about everything else?

Maybe it would be impossible to find her and Connie would never uncover the truth of who she really was, why she'd taken on another woman's identity.

The Plymouth train drew into the station and Connie was bustled towards the carriage door by a group of people with suitcases who had all moved close to her as the announcement had come across the tannoy. For a moment, anxiety consumed her – a sense of claustrophobia as strangers' bodies pressed against hers. She wanted to push them away from her, give herself air, her own space. The train would be stationary for about five minutes before it moved off – its ultimate destination, Penzance. Thankfully, the Totnes stop was the first, and only eleven minutes from Coleton. If the train was packed, at least it wouldn't be a long journey to suffer.

Connie headed in the other direction to the group of travellers, finding a seat in the relatively quiet D carriage. She sat by the window, staring out. A figure beside the steps to the bridge taking pedestrians across to the other side of the station drew her attention. A man in an overcoat, a scarf obscuring most of his face, seemed to be looking right at her. She sat upright, pressing her face against the cool glass to get a better view. The train jerked into movement, progressing the opposite way to the man. She'd been experiencing the feeling of being watched again for over a week. Maybe it was Luke keeping an eye out for her. Coming here would be a huge risk though, and she knew her father had put his foot down, categorically stating they couldn't have contact. Why would Luke chance it?

It could be because he knew she was in danger again. Goosebumps appeared on her arms at the thought of what she might have started. She couldn't blame her dad for anything this time. If she was in any kind of trouble, it was entirely her own making.

After her last client had gone, Connie's thoughts drifted. She had a nervous ball in her stomach; a growing anxiety she knew was related to Alice, to Kyle, to the other person who'd been involved with Sean Taylor's death. If he'd never been implicated, he'd been free all this time to create more damage. More victims. Had Alice Mann been his victim? She was in a bad way when she was found; Lindsay said it had looked like a frenzied attack. Someone who'd been angry. The writing on the wall, now confirmed as being a mix of Alice's own blood with an animal's, supported this. Whoever hurt Alice knew who she was. Connie hoped the poor woman would soon be well enough to be brought out of her induced coma, be able to tell the police who attacked her. Connie was worried Kyle knew the perpetrator – that it was the same person he'd been protecting. Even more worrying was the thought Alice might not be the only victim. Would there be more?

To get answers, Connie had to begin with Kyle Mann's case. Although she knew a lot from the psychology and prison records, she hadn't searched the internet. She could rectify that now. She went down to the kitchenette, grabbed her shop-bought sandwich from the fridge, made a coffee, and then settled herself in front of the computer. She typed 'Sean Taylor murder' into the search bar and watched in astonishment at the amount of hits Google returned. She rubbed her eyes with the heels of her palms. This was going to take some time. For now, she would concentrate on the court case; find any pictures she could. Maybe her Alice had been present during proceedings, might have been captured in a photo. She'd been so knowledgeable about the case, about Kyle and Alice Mann – she'd clearly studied it, and them. So, perhaps she'd been there, following the story.

Connie had to find her.

CHAPTER FIFTY-FIVE

Deborah

Now Alice is in hospital, I'm surprised to find I'm actually *missing* her visits – there's a gaping hole in my days. Twenty-four hours is a lot of time to fill, especially when only three or four of those are spent asleep. Work had been keeping me going – having a focus, the hours speeding past without thought, was important. I was needed. Being unwanted is not a good feeling. I'm not a mother, not a worker, and thanks to Nathan, I'm no longer a wife.

What am I?

Who am I?

I never envisaged it could be so easy to lose your identity. Although the 'what am I' is easier to answer. I am fifty-fifty: a half-sad, half-angry woman. The newspaper cuttings are strewn across the lounge floor. There's no likelihood of Nathan catching me with them now, so I don't need to hide my obsession. It's not only articles about my Sean that I cut out and keep; it's all the ones relating to a missing person, or attacks – the finding of dead bodies.

I pick up the one about a young woman who'd disappeared recently: Isabella Bond. I gaze at the pretty face which goes with the pretty name. Then there's the man found stabbed to death on the park bench in Torquay. Each person I read about leaves me wondering; each article I keep is because deep down I know what happened to Sean will happen again to someone else. It's only a matter of time before another bored gamer gets fed up with the fantasy of killing and wants to do it for real, or mixes the virtual world with reality. I'm compelled to keep check. I need to read about it when it happens. I don't even know why – what it is making me want to know about terrible things happening to others. I just know another family will be destroyed by one person's actions.

Or more than one. Something Alice said, moments before I lost my temper, comes back to me now. *You know it wasn't only my boy, don't you? Someone made him do it, Deborah. Someone manipulated him, I'm sure of it. And he has never been punished, just my poor Kyle.*

At the time, I flew into a rage, shouting and screaming at her: *Poor Kyle? POOR KYLE?* What about my son? He was left to die a slow, painful death all alone. Sod your poor fucking Kyle.

The look on Alice's face had told me all I needed to know about how mine looked.

She was afraid.

Of me.

I don't want to think about what happened after that. It's an unclear, mixed-up mess of images and sounds. A chill shakes my body. I don't want to remember.

Now, I look at the dozens and dozens of old and new cuttings and I wonder: was Alice right? Was there someone else – someone who helped kill my son?

I may have been blinded by her annoying perseverance to get me to like her. I discarded any possibility of it not being her fault. I was as bloody-minded as she was in my aim. I can see that now.

I straighten and catch my breath. What if Alice was being watched? She'd been outside my house, inside it – and I'd been to her house that day. I remember the figure by the bushes.

If someone *had* been watching, they could even know what I

did. They may have been watching me, too. Might be watching me now.

I leap up, the articles from my lap scattering across the floor, and run to the front door. I slide the bolt and then hook the chain across for good measure. I go to the back door and lock that, too.

I need to keep myself safe.

My own laughter startles me. How ironic. Less than twenty-four hours ago I was contemplating ending my life.

Now I'm in fear for it.

CHAPTER FIFTY-SIX

Tom

He watched her, silently, from the doorway. She was engrossed in the television; an episode of *The Chase*. She'd always had a thing for Bradley Walsh, and now, despite everything else going on in her life, she was giggling at Bradley's hysterics as a contestant gave a stupid answer. How did people watch this stuff, then have the nerve to slate those who played computer games?

She threw her head back, laughing. The sound was so rare, he couldn't even recall the last time he'd heard it. He did love her, in a roundabout way. At least, he *assumed* it was love. It was a fine line between love and hate, he'd heard. The line was as easily crossed one way as it was the other. He'd had moments in his past when he'd hated his father. Really loathed him. The way he made him feel so worthless, irrelevant. How he'd degraded him, embarrassed him in front of friends.

He'd *had* some friends, in the early days of secondary school – ones he wanted to hang with, invite to his house to play Xbox. Before his dad had started being a prick.

Tom had a flashback to being in his bedroom one day after school. He was shouting instructions to Chris Newman, who he'd allowed to play his *Call of Duty Black Ops* on Xbox because Chris wasn't allowed it at home. He'd thought Chris's parents were stupidly strict not letting him have 18-rated games. He'd felt sorry for him. Which was ironic, because later on, his own dad had dragged him by the hair from his bedroom for disturbing him, and it was Chris then who felt sorry for *him*. Things like that had been the reason why he'd stopped asking people round, why he spent more and more time in the privacy of his own room.

He'd come to guard his space. He valued it above everything else. At times, he'd even placed its importance over his mother. She didn't like that. But then, she should've done something before – to stop his father, prevent the beatings and humiliation – then he wouldn't have needed to hide himself away, barricading himself into the tiny room.

She'd had ample opportunity, and yet she'd done nothing. Instead, she'd waited until his dad had had enough, until *he* wanted to leave. The time after his departure was mixed with relief and hope, but also uncertainty. His mum had fallen apart. Tom had become all she had and she suffocated him.

He'd been back to not having his own space again.

That's when it started, really. When his moods changed, and his interests diversified.

Tom had also known of Kyle Mann from that time, although he'd been in a different tutor group at school and they'd never had any lessons together. Even though Tom had been a shy teenager, every time he'd seen Kyle in the school grounds at lunchtimes, he'd noted how Kyle appeared even more withdrawn than him – and weird, awkward. Tom never spoke to him, but he'd thought about Kyle – and years later, when he started online gaming, had looked him up. He'd observed him from afar, keeping a watchful eye on his online activities – the games he played, the people he interacted with. He'd unwittingly led Tom to Sean Taylor, someone Kyle clearly had issues with. The chatter between the both of them had gone far beyond playful banter – Sean had been verbally abusive to Kyle, slating his gaming ability at first, but then he got personal. It became apparent that Sean Taylor would make the perfect first victim. It hadn't taken an awful lot of time or skill to groom Kyle, convince him that this Sean needed taking down a peg or two. The rest was history.

Now though, despite having pushed his mother out, he didn't want her to come to harm. That wasn't part of his plan. He needed to stop her, silence her sometimes, but he'd only ever done it as a last resort. A quick slap – a back-hander was usually all it took. It had annoyed him big time when he realised she was seeing a psychologist, but when he'd followed her and found out she was trying to contact Kyle's mum, Alice – well that had been too much – a step too far. Alice would've put two and two together. She'd have found out.

She'd have uncovered the fact her son had been protecting the identity of the other killer.

And he couldn't have that. It was one thing Alice *suspecting* Kyle had been manipulated, but another to have the truth stare her in the face in the form of his mother. What had she thought she'd gain by meeting Alice? Was she *trying* to get him put in prison? No, he'd never be able to cope with prison. He'd been abused enough. If he got put away, his life would be over.

He'd learned to appreciate that at least his dad was honest, though. Yes, he'd lashed out, he'd been abusive – a right bastard a lot of the time. But what you saw was what you got, and Tom loved him for that. For his straightforwardness. He was uncomplicated. Unlike his mother. She pretended to love Tom, and then went around, sneakily, behind his back. She lied. Tom never really knew what was behind those eyes.

She was deceitful.

He shook his head as he stared at her. Still laughing like she didn't have a care in the world. She'd gone too far this time though, with her lies and tricks. He couldn't let anything get in the way of his game plan. Tom crept past the doorway and slipped out of the house.

185

CHAPTER FIFTY-SEVEN

Connie

Connie had set Friday aside to catch up with her admin, but as soon as she walked into her building, drenched from the sudden downpour, her mind was on one thing only, and it wasn't paperwork or filing. She chucked her umbrella in the kitchen sink, made a coffee then went up to her office. Once settled, her computer humming to life, she clicked on the images she'd saved to a file the previous day. She'd downloaded the most promising ones, and now, her face inches from the screen, she zoomed in on them. The photos had been mainly taken outside Exeter Crown Court during the trial, but Connie couldn't pick her Alice out of the crowds. She leant back in the chair, her hopes now diminishing.

She studied the photos of the real Alice, and immediately it struck her how much trouble the woman who'd been coming to see her had gone to in order to replicate her look. Her hair, her clothing, everything matched how the real Alice presented herself. Even if Connie had seen some photos beforehand, there was a strong likelihood she wouldn't have sussed out she wasn't Alice Mann at first. Why would you question someone who sought counselling because of a crime committed by their son? Connie had no reason to suspect she wasn't who she'd said she was. And even though Connie believed she was holding something back, at no point had it crossed her mind that *this* was what it was. What on earth was she gaining by pretending to be someone else?

Had Connie missed the telltale signs that she was outright lying? She wished she'd videoed her sessions now, so she could have looked back over them frame by frame to scrutinise her body signals, the way she spoke – the language she used, or didn't use, which may have given her away. The benefit of hindsight.

With the photos not bearing fruit, Connie went on to search Deborah Taylor. There were fewer hits, not so many online photographs. Strange how the murderer's mother seemed to have gained more press attention, more media curiosity, than the victim's mother. The pictures of Deborah were more guarded. In each one, she either had a protective arm around her, or her hand being held – always by her husband – named as Nathan Taylor, a local council planning officer. The articles were less sensationalised, more raw than those about Alice and Kyle Mann. The interest had been more for the perpetrator, his family. Not the victim. How did the Taylors' cope with that?

After hours of searching, Connie was no further forwards. She'd learned more about the crime from different perspectives than those she'd already known, and each victim – as inevitably in cases such as this there were numerous, not only the boy who died but his parents, family and friends – was ingrained in her mind. But she was no closer to finding fake Alice.

Would she still go to the support group, if it existed? Connie would work on the assumption that it did, as she had little else to go on. Even though Alice's identity had been compromised by the latest news – and she must know that – it might still be worth a shot. When were the meetings again? Connie lurched forwards, clicking on the therapy file for Alice. Scanning the notes, she found what she needed. The in-person meetings were held on the last Wednesday of the month, so Alice had said. Not long to wait. Although, first she needed to find out *where* they were held. It shouldn't be too difficult; there weren't that many places in Totnes suitable for such groups. She'd start putting out some feelers, but in the meantime, she should make a start with another option.

And her starting point would have to be Deborah. Connie would find her and ask her if she'd had contact with the woman posing as Alice. During her last session, Alice had stated it was her intention to visit Deborah – and for now, that was the only lead Connie had.

CHAPTER FIFTY-EIGHT

Angela

I watch as the rain drowns the back garden, huge rivulets of water tinged brown with mud run down the concrete path towards the back door. The weather forecast said it would only be a light shower this morning, so they got that wrong. I hope it stops soon, or it'll breach it, seep into the kitchen. I should put something in the way to block it. I would ask Tom, but I can't face him right now. I have so many questions I want to ask, but I'm afraid they'll all come spilling out at once and he'll become overwhelmed, angry. I have to go about things in a more subtle way, choose my time. Pick my battles. I've had lots of practice.

I tear my gaze away from the downpour, shut off my ears from the battering rain on the roof and against the windows, and take my seat at the table.

I suck in a huge lungful of air and open the laptop.

I'm going to brave the support group page.

My heart thuds. The sound of my breathing competes with the noise of the rain. The saliva I try to swallow forms a lump in my throat and threatens to choke me. Maybe it's what I deserve. To choke to death. Pay for my sins. Can I even turn to God now? Would He hear me, answer my prayers? 'It's better to beg forgiveness than ask permission,' I read once. Not in the Bible, but it still gives me strength.

The laptop has done its start-up routine and now my homepage glares at me. The icon for group support is in the correct position on the left-hand side. Now I'm diligently locking my laptop and have changed my password, Tom won't be able to access it so easily. I close my eyes after I click on the icon, but my mind has already begun to conjure the words I'm likely to see when I open them. *Lying bitch. Whore. Deceitful cow.* All terms David and Tom have called me before. But my group haven't, not my people. I couldn't bear the rejection from them.

I clench my hands into fists and allow my eyelids to open.

My hands loosen and my fingertips fly to the trackpad, and I furiously scroll down the message threads. I get to the end of the first page, then check the next. And the next. Then I go back to the beginning, calmer now, to start again – focussing on the topic of each message with more attention this time.

There's nothing.

Nothing about Alice Mann's attack. Nothing about me. No one hurling accusations or abuse, no angry tirades directed my way.

Why? Haven't they seen the news about Alice? No one is talking about it. Have I got away with it? For now at least? Maybe it is safe to continue being Alice – go to the next meeting even.

A relief, a happiness spreads through me.

'Love covers over all wrongs.' I smile as I cross my chest.

It's not over yet.

CHAPTER FIFTY-NINE

Connie

Connie replaced the receiver, and, tapping her pen against her mouth, considered her options. Having found out where Deborah Taylor worked, she'd rung the marketing company and asked to speak with her. They were less than helpful. It seemed Deborah was on leave. Judging from how the employee spoke, Connie gathered it was likely to be extended leave. Of course, they wouldn't give details out about her either, so Connie had no idea where she lived and didn't have a contact number. It was a frustrating early setback.

But a setback was all it was. *There's more than one way to skin a cat*, her mum would say. Outside of work, the employees of Complete Marketing might talk. There was always one loose-lipped idiot in every workplace – she knew that from experience. Connie would find them, see what information she could gain. In the meantime, it was possible she could get Lindsay to divulge some details – no doubt Deborah Taylor would be someone they were keen on talking to anyway, given the link between Alice Mann and her. She could even be a suspect, sad as that thought was.

Connie had been too busy contemplating how to find the fake Alice rather than thinking about who'd attacked the real one. Why would Deborah attack Alice though? Kyle had been imprisoned, justice had been done. Sean's murder was four years ago. So why now?

Connie's mobile vibrated, triggering it to creep across the desk. She picked it up, absently looking at the screen. Another message from Scott. Shit. She hadn't responded to any of them yet. He'd think her rude. Actually, if someone had failed to message her back after ten attempts, she'd have assumed they weren't interested and move on. But he was persistent. To the point of annoyance. Yes, he'd been a lovely guy, she'd enjoyed the company. The sex. But did she need a man in her life? She read his latest offering.

Hope you're OK? Worried I haven't heard from you. Thought you might want to hook up again. Xx

His messages were starting to become a bit needy; desperate even. But if she answered this one now, it would open the floodgates. If she ignored them, he'd soon get fed up and give up. This was the sort of mess she used to get in when one-night stands had been her thing. Having finally accepted that what had happened to her as a vulnerable teenager at that party was, in part, responsible for her poor coping mechanisms as an adult, she thought she'd moved on from that behaviour. The way of life that had become self-destructive. Did this prove otherwise?

She placed the phone back in her handbag, shutting it away from view. For the moment, ignoring the issue was all she could manage.

The security intercom gave a short, sharp buzz. Connie stretched across the desk and picked up the handset. She wasn't expecting a client.

'Yes, can I help?' she said.

'Just me. Are you free for a chat?'

Connie hesitated. Lindsay clearly wasn't with him – what did he want to chat about? Maybe Lindsay had sent him. 'I really need to upgrade my door entry system to include video, then I could screen my visitors before deciding whether to pick up.'

'That's a bit below the belt,' Mack's voice boomed. 'I was even going to offer to take you for coffee and a cake. But, if you're going to be like that . . .'

'Huh! Coffee and cake – has the police budget been given a sudden boost or something?'

'Well, I could do with a coffee that doesn't taste like shit.'

'Are you saying *mine* does?'

Connie heard a shuffling noise. 'No, obviously not yours. Christ's sake, Connie. Yes or no? I look a twat talking into this thing.'

She muffled a giggle with her hand. 'I'm not sure how to respond to that statement.' Connie imagined Mack hunched over the intercom, his mouth almost touching it so passers-by couldn't hear him speaking. 'Give me a minute, I'll be down.'

As she collected her things, a sense of nervousness crept over her flesh. Had Mack and Lindsay been to see Kyle? Was Mack here buttering her up with the offer of cake because something was up?

Mack was standing with his back to the door, his height practically blocking the daylight, as Connie flung it open. He spun around so quickly he almost lost his balance, his hand flying to his chest.

'Bloody hell.'

'Sorry,' Connie said, 'didn't mean to frighten you. I did say I was coming out.'

'Yeah – but so violently?' Mack said in a mock dramatic voice.

Connie laughed, the tension releasing itself.

'Glad to see the rain has stopped,' Connie said. She abandoned her umbrella inside the doorway.

'Yes, rain followed by sunshine. Good old Devon weather, eh? Can never prepare for it,' Mack said, shrugging. 'Where to for coffee, then?'

'Ann of Cleves? There, beyond the arch.' Connie pointed to the café a few buildings down from where they were. 'Look, you can see their amazing cakes in the window from here.'

'Good choice. It's almost like I'd scoped out the nearest place.' Mack put his hand on Connie's shoulder as they crossed the road. It felt strangely protective.

He had to duck to miss the low beams inside the café, and he looked awkward sitting at the round table, his legs packed in tightly beneath. She knew Lindsay often teased him about his height, but the jokes must have worn incredibly thin over the years. She refrained from commenting now. Instead, she jumped right in, asking him about Kyle, before he got a word in about the reason he'd asked her for a chat.

'Aha, what a coincidence,' Mack said, 'that's actually what I wanted to talk to you about.'

Connie's heart plummeted. 'Oh. I won't lie, that kinda makes me nervous.'

Her attention was taken by the waitress, asking them what they'd like.

Connie quickly glanced at the menu, although her focus was now gone. 'Er . . . I'll have lemon drizzle cake and a latte, please.'

The waitress scribbled in a pad, then took Mack's order. Connie stared at him while he spoke. His face had weathered over the past year: wrinkles gouged their lines from the corners of his eyes to the top of his cheeks. He'd grown more of a beard – no longer just stubble, it now had a thick coverage. Maybe to hide further lines, or a sagging jawline perhaps. It wasn't as grey as his hair, although it did age him. Connie liked it, though. It made him seem more friendly, approachable. Fatherly.

He turned back to Connie. She looked down at the table, feeling as though she'd been caught checking him out. Her face grew warm.

'Don't be nervous. I'm not going to ask you to do anything you probably hadn't already guessed at.' He raised his eyebrows as he leant in towards her. 'We didn't get a thing from Kyle – not a fucking word. Refused to even acknowledge our presence.'

Connie wiped her palms on her trouser legs. Yes, he was right, she had guessed.

'So?' she asked, even though the answer was obvious.

The waitress breezed up beside the table, politely interrupting the conversation, a plate in each hand. She placed the slab of lemon drizzle cake in front of Connie. Suddenly, it didn't seem so appealing.

Mack smiled at the waitress as she put his Bakewell tart down, and thanked her. He waited until she'd gone before delivering the line Connie had been dreading.

'We want you to go back in. See what you can get from Kyle Mann.'

CHAPTER SIXTY

Tom

He paced until it made him dizzy. The area was too small, what with the desk that ran the whole length of the room, his computer, three monitors, his gaming chair and his bed, all competing for space.

She'd had the nerve to confront him when he got home last night. She hadn't even backed down when he'd started shouting at her, screaming in her face. They'd been nose-to-nose and she'd stood her ground. He was losing his touch. Then she'd given him her 'soft voice' – the one she reserved for him when she was trying to talk him around. Or keep him calm. He had to admit, she was good at that. He'd always found his mother's voice soothing. Even during the dark days, the even darker nights when he'd wake in the throes of a night terror, petrified, and certain there were people in his room, people who wanted to hurt him.

When his mum had been there, stroking his hair, hushing him, telling him everything was okay, he'd believed her. A part of him wished she could do that now. Maybe her reassurances would make him believe it again. Although he had the feeling he'd gone too far for that now. He collapsed on his bed, staring at the computer screen. His server was open, his followers were playing the game without him. He wasn't in the mood, couldn't concentrate on online killing. He wouldn't for a while.

He had to come down from the high of last night's reality first. It hadn't happened as planned, but maybe that's why it'd been even more exhilarating than the first time.

CHAPTER SIXTY-ONE

Connie

Connie cut her cake into bite-sized pieces and slowly ate a couple of chunks. It was moist, a lovely zingy flavour, but it stuck in her throat; the thought of talking to Kyle again stealing her saliva. She took a gulp of her latte to wash it down.

'Why didn't Lindsay ask me? Why you?'

'I imagine it was due to the stress it might cause you, thinking about going back in. She said you were relieved when you'd finished the reports, didn't have to go there again. I guess she wasn't happy to ask this of you.' He shrugged, then took a bite from his tart, bits of pastry flaking off and dropping into his lap.

'But you are?' She narrowed her eyes at him. There she'd been, thinking they were getting on. Her optimism had been premature. This nicey-nicey 'take you for cake and coffee' routine was only to soften the blow.

'No, I'm not particularly. But even the prison psychologist said Kyle was only likely to talk to you. So . . .'

Mack drew back from the table and, reaching into his jacket, retrieved his ringing mobile. Connie watched as he nodded a few times, then shook his head. He gave a large sigh as he ended the call.

'I have to go. Are you up for helping us out, see what info you can get from Kyle?'

'Er ... actually ... I, er ...' Connie stammered, feeling flustered, as though she'd been ambushed. She wanted to say no outright – instead she settled for: 'Can I think about it?'

'Sure.' He rose from his chair and straightened himself, brushing crumbs from his suit trousers. 'But don't take too long.' He paused, looking intently at his phone, his forehead creased in a frown.

'What is it? Is everything all right?'

Mack walked to Connie's side, and bending right down, he whispered in her ear. 'A body has been found. I've got to go to the scene now. But I don't think we should delay speaking to Kyle Mann.'

Connie stared after Mack as he ducked down and out of the café door, watched as he strode past the window, back up the hill. Her hands shook. Lindsay and Mack had chastised her before, saying she kept getting herself involved in stuff she shouldn't be, and now they *wanted* her to. What if she said no, she wouldn't do it?

Mack had said they could only speak to Kyle informally. He wasn't a witness, and currently there was no evidence to suggest he'd done anything wrong. Unless they charged him with another offence, they couldn't have access to details of phone calls made via the prison phones. There was a PIN system – prisoners had a card with pre-arranged telephone numbers installed on it so the staff knew who they were calling. But it was well known that mobile phones were a real problem inside. They were often smuggled in – sometimes by staff members themselves. Even if the police had the information about who Kyle telephoned, Connie doubted he used the regular phone for anything but his family.

What kind of evidence would Connie help them get? She could make a recording of their session, but if Kyle was aware of it, he wouldn't cooperate, wouldn't speak at all. There was no way she could secretly record him, it would be unethical, not to mention inadmissible as evidence in court. So, wouldn't it all be her word against his anyway? Even if she got some information from him, how could the police use it? Unless they only wanted her to get names. If Kyle disclosed who might be involved, they could put surveillance on them. She didn't know for sure, but the way Mack had mentioned the discovery of a body made her think that this too was linked to Alice's attack.

Could Kyle's accomplice have already struck again?

CHAPTER SIXTY-TWO

Deborah

I'm still shaken from the call earlier. The police officer only asked a few questions, but it was unexpected. I didn't even consider they might contact me, which was naïve of me, given my link with Alice. I look over my shoulder every few steps, checking no one's following me. I'm probably overreacting, thinking someone would be bothered about me. But I can't shake the worrying thought that what happened in Alice's kitchen is going to trace back to me. I was careful, I thought, but it would only take one person to tell the police they'd seen me, heard me, and I'd be linked to her attack. Nathan was right. It's better to let things go, to move on and not let the past ruin the future. But when you believe there is no future, no real hope of experiencing a happy and fulfilling life, the past can be the only place to live.

I can't get over how Nathan has not only moved on from Sean, but from me, too. Does he see a better future for himself by letting what happened go? I should be glad for him, happy that he can forge a new life. Funny though, I'm not. Not glad, not happy.

Maybe I'm jealous.

But if I *could* let go, would I?

A car horn blares. I shake myself out of my thoughts; I'm in the middle of the road. I must've crossed without looking. I hold a hand up in apology and hear the driver's irritated voice calling me something unfathomable out of his window as he screeches off again. I need to be more alert to my surroundings. I parked in the car park on the outskirts of Coleton, thinking the walk into town would help blow away the cobwebs. I can't say it's worked. My head still feels woolly: abstract and random thoughts fight their way through strands of tangled yarn.

I need to talk to someone. Who, I don't know. I've alienated the friends I had. I hid myself away from the world after Sean's murder, refusing every offer of company and, eventually, they stopped asking if I was coming out. The only other friends I had were through Nathan. Colleagues of his from the council, wives of his golfing buddies. But I pushed them all away and threw myself into work instead. Now I don't have that, there's no one to turn to.

Christ. The realisation is like a smack in the face.

Alice Mann was the closest thing I had to a friend.

I stumble into someone who's stopped dead in front of me. I'm about to make a remark when I see she's not the only person who has come to a standstill. A group of people are congregating before the walkway running alongside the river. I back up slightly and make a move to go around them, but the road's blocked. A policeman stands in front of his car, which is parked horizontally across the pavement. There are murmurs from the gathering crowd, speculation as to what's happened. I am too short to see above the people, to see what they are looking at. All heads are turned one way.

I'm briefly intrigued – I try to squeeze through, go on tiptoes to see – but my interest is lost quickly. I retreat, turn away, and then cross the road. I'll catch the news later. A familiar structure looms ahead of me; I hadn't planned on coming here. My office. This was meant to be. I've found myself here for a reason. I check my watch. It's just after two-thirty. Marcie generally has a late lunch, leaving her desk around this time to go and get her favourite noodles from the kiosk in Market Walk. Maybe they've missed me at work, and she's regretting giving me an order to go on leave. If I play this right, I could get her to change her mind, tell her the time I've had off has been much-needed and therapeutic, but now I'm ready to come back to work full-time.

The thought bolsters my mood. I haven't spoken to Marcie since that day in Costa. If I can come across as bright, cheerful, and most importantly, 'together', she'll have to concede it's time for me to return. It could be the start of me pulling back from this dark cave I've entered.

I stand for what feels like an hour, but when I check my watch again, only a few minutes have passed. Marcie could be in a meeting, meaning I'm wasting my time hanging around here. My body tenses – there's movement; someone is coming out. I catch a glimpse of long, blonde curls moving through the glass doors. It's Marcie. She's added in more hair extensions. She's out of the building and I'm about to march up to her when I see she's not alone. Another woman exits the building after her and then catches her up. I hang back, ducking into a shop entrance to watch them. I don't recognise the woman Marcie's with as an employee. Unless she's my replacement. The bitch better not have replaced me. My chest hurts, the heart inside it feels as though it may burst. They disappear into Costa. Typical. Marcie obviously uses the place as a second office.

While I can't have a private chat with Marcie now, I can at least check out this other woman. I run my hands through my hair, neaten my clothes and cross the road. With my head held high, I walk into Costa.

CHAPTER SIXTY-THREE

Angela

My euphoria at having finally met Deborah – and in a totally unexpected and unplanned way in a coffee shop – is short-lived.

I think he's killed again.

I can't help but join the gawping crowd. Police tape stretches across the walkway, police vehicles block the road, and uniformed and non-uniformed services swarm the area. I can see part of what I assume to be a white tent jutting out from the dense bushes running alongside the river.

It's Isabella, I know it. A pain grips my heart, a moan escaping my open mouth. Bill. I silently pray to God I'm wrong. One, that it isn't her, and two, that it wasn't my son who took her life. Not again. It will be impossible to keep protecting him if he's responsible for this. They'll find him, take him away.

I can't bear to think about him in prison.

When I saw him in Coleton last month while I was waiting outside Alice's workplace to catch her and find out what she knew, I'd assumed he was following me, keeping an eye on what I was doing. My horror at possibly being caught with a member of my support group had overwhelmed me and I didn't consider he might have had other reasons for being in Coleton. Most of the time, Tom doesn't leave the house. He stays in the basement and I even forget he's there, living below me.

I hadn't noticed him coming and going from the house at all before last night, when I'd caught him sneaking back in. I'd thought that day in Coleton was a one-off. Thinking back now, he'd been angry with me afterwards. He'd raised his hand, smacked me across my cheek. I didn't question him about the reason for his outburst – he often loses his temper with me and I've been on the receiving end of one of his 'light slaps' on more than one occasion. I didn't think he'd seen me – I'd ducked behind Wendy – so didn't link the two events.

Has Tom been leaving the house regularly? I'm so stupid thinking he's safe inside his basement room. Happy to be left alone on his stupid computer.

It's my fault. Again.

I'm a bad mother.

I need to get home, *now*.

The journey's the longest I've ever experienced. My legs are barely able to hold my weight as I walk up the hill towards my house. I moved us here four years ago to escape the town where Tom's victim had lived. It's only eight miles away, I know, but I thought it would be enough. Give us both a fresh start. How foolish of me to think that was possible.

It takes a few attempts to get the key in to open the front door because my hands are trembling so much. It's quiet inside, as it always is. Either he's downstairs, or he's out. Why haven't I questioned this silence before? I told Connie I left him alone for an easy life, and that's the truth of the matter. I can't deal with any arguments, so I keep out of his way and pretend he's not here. How is that a good way to deal with him?

I've been wrong. All this time I've been focussing on trying to make things right, maybe even seeking forgiveness from those who've been affected by my lack of good parenting, when all along I should've been concentrating on Tom. On my relationship with my son. On making *him* right.

Seeing Deborah Taylor today has altered things. I saw her desperation for myself, witnessed her begging to get her job back. The pain in her eyes was as visible as it was the day Kyle Mann was sentenced to life in prison. I might've been a distance away then – high up in the gallery – but I could see enough to know she was in terrible pain. There'd been a sudden clarity in my thoughts when I saw her earlier, for the first time in four years: she is never going to forgive me. She will never give me the redemption I've been seeking all this time.

I've been so short-sighted. Connie was spot on with her assessment about not, under any circumstances, meeting with Deborah. How it wasn't a good idea for either person. I didn't get to speak to Alice in the end, so I don't have a clue what, if anything, she knows about the second person involved with Sean's murder – if she has any idea it was my Tom. Hopefully her silence is guaranteed – she's still in a coma and may remain that way. Even if she does have information which could damage Tom, and me, it will forever be locked in her sedated mind.

I walk with more purpose now, to the door leading down to the basement. It's locked of course, always is. I take a deep breath and hammer my fists against the wooden panels. I don't stop. My hands burn, but I keep going. I know it's pointless: he has sound-proofing on the walls and his headphones will be on. I don't even know if he's definitely down there. But I can't stop.

Hot tears and snot run into my mouth.

Years of guilt and anger continue to pelt the wooden door.

CHAPTER SIXTY-FOUR

Connie

The train ride from Totnes to Coleton passed in a blur. Connie
hesitated as she was about to pass the taxi rank. Her house was
close to the station, and usually it was a pleasant ten-minute stroll
home. The day's events weighed heavily in her mind though, and
some of that heaviness seemed to have seeped out into her body,
affecting her muscles and making them tired. *Sod it*. She headed
to the first taxi in the line and climbed in.

As she got out of the car and turned towards her path, she
stopped. A large bouquet of flowers obscured the top step.
She looked up and down the street but there was no one in
sight, and no delivery vans. Would they be for her or Lindsay?
Connie reached across them to unlock the door, then hauled
up the bouquet and took it through to the kitchen, placing it
on the worktop. Amber rubbed against her legs.

'Hello, baby.' She scooped her up and gave her a cuddle, nuzzl-
ing into her soft fur. With Amber tucked under one arm, Connie
checked the card attached to the bouquet. It was addressed to her.
'Well, we weren't expecting that, were we, Amber?'

Letting Amber down, she pulled the small white envelope from
the plastic cellophane. The flowers were beautiful, a mix of the
exotic and the traditional, the colours vibrant. They could only

be from one person. It was that knowledge which gave her pause. Not put off by her failure to respond to a single text, Scott had clearly moved it up a gear. It was a stunning bouquet – must've cost a pretty penny, as her mum would say. She opened the envelope. The card only had three words on it.

Thinking about you.

She turned it over. Blank. Did he *assume* she'd know they were from him? Fairly presumptuous – she could have many admirers, as far as he was concerned. She shook her head. Odd though, having clearly spent a lot of money, to not even write *love from Scott* on it. And thinking about her how? Still, it was a nice surprise to come home to flowers, so she shouldn't knock it.

Pulling at every cupboard door, Connie tried to find a suitable vessel in which to arrange the flowers. Settling on a huge metal jug, one she'd almost thrown out last month, she began the process of transferring the artistically arranged bouquet into it. She'd never been arty, and once she'd finished, they looked nothing like how they'd been presented. She wished she'd taken a photo of them to start with now. *No justice done here.*

Even more tired after her efforts, Connie made a hot chocolate and headed for the lounge to sit down. She was exhausted. The blinking red light of the answer machine caught her eye and she pressed the button to listen. The voice, barely audible, was her mum's. Why was she whispering? Connie stood closer, dipping her head towards the speaker.

'Hi, it's Mum. Everything okay, love? Not heard from you.' She sounded muffled, like she had something over her mouth. Or maybe she had it on speaker and was far away from the handset. 'Hope everything went well at the prison and you're back to your own consultancy, are you?' Her obligatory long pause ensued as she waited for an actual answer even though it was a machine she was talking to. 'Did you see the news? I do hope the body they found wasn't that poor girl, Isabella. Awful business. Anyway, give me a call, or pop around. I've made your favourite biscuits.'

Damn it. The news. How could she have forgotten? She switched on the TV, but she'd already missed it. Flowers had taken her mind off a body being found. What did that say about her? She found the next news programme on the menu and pressed the remind button. A report about the body was bound to be on later. Connie sat down and took a tentative sip of her drink. So, even her mum was concerned it was Isabella. It was the natural conclusion really: she'd been missing for weeks and most people realised it wasn't likely to be a good ending. She reached for her mobile: a Google search might give her enough to go on until the next news programme.

A dull thud came from the hallway. Connie reluctantly heaved herself up from the sofa. A parcel in brown paper lay on the doormat. She hadn't ordered anything, and it was late in the day to receive mail. It had no address, just *Connie* scrawled in black pen. She threw the front door open and stepped outside. No one was close by. She squinted. A figure was disappearing around the bend at the far left of the road. All Connie caught was a flash of blue jacket, hood up. She shivered and went back inside, closing and locking the door behind her.

There was something about seeing her name written in black ink that rattled her. Probably always would, given a murderer had inscribed it onto a dead man's hand last year. Her heart gave a nervous flutter. She had an uncomfortable feeling that whatever the brown paper concealed, it would be bad news for her. She'd had enough surprise presents for one day. She should wait until Lindsay came home, open it in front of her.

Placing the parcel on the coffee table, Connie sat back on the sofa. As she stared at it, she drummed her fingers on the sofa arm, going through the various possibilities of what it could be. She sat forwards and grabbed it, gently shaking it from side to side. There wasn't any movement. It wasn't heavy. She squashed the package between her fingers, it felt like bubble wrap beneath the paper.

It was no good. She had to open it.

Carefully unpicking the tape at one end, she slid out the contents. Then unravelled the bubble wrap.

A Nokia mobile phone fell into her lap.

CHAPTER SIXTY-FIVE

Tom

A distant, soft drumming noise infiltrated his ears. It wasn't anything in his room, or in his basement. He didn't usually hear the rain; his soundproofing insulated him from the world outside. He lay down his headphones, scooted his chair away from the desk and opened the door. The soft drumming changed to loud, urgent banging. What the fuck was going on?

He took the steps from the basement two at a time. Jesus, she was hammering at the door like a madwoman. That didn't bode well. He could hear sobs between the pounding.

She knew.

The news had got out. The body must've been found.

It was a good thing. He didn't want it hidden away for no one to ever find, or for dogs to eventually sniff it out weeks later. He didn't want to get caught, but at the same time, he didn't want what he'd done to be unknown. It was complicated; a fine line. There had to be a pay-off for his efforts, for his impeccable game play, one that gave him a sense of achievement and knowledge that he was good at something. Knowing people would be talking about this non-stop, that his actions would be discussed, analysed and reported for weeks to come gave him such a buzz.

Right now though, she threatened to dampen his mood. He

leant against the door, feeling the vibration from each thud course through his body. She'd have to tire soon. Then he'd open the door. She'd be easier to deal with if she'd expended all her energy. Although he'd guessed she would find out, and had considered how he'd handle it when the day came, the reality now gave him cause for concern. She was already displaying a reaction he hadn't anticipated. She hadn't been physically angry last time. This was new. Did it mean she wasn't going to protect him on this one? An uncomfortable sensation pulled at his gut. She'd failed him once, and promised never to let him down again. He'd believed that. Counted on it.

If she threatened to hand him over to the police now, how was he going to manage her?

The banging was slowing down, with more time between each fist hitting against the door.

Still he waited.

Waiting for her to completely calm down would give him time to think about what he was going to do with her.

CHAPTER SIXTY-SIX

Deborah

At least the woman wasn't my replacement. It's all the silver lining I can gain from the mistake I made today. The way she looked at me made my skin crawl. Her face was familiar, although I couldn't place her. She'd said she was a friend of Marcie's, but the look which passed between them when she introduced herself as such was enough to make me realise it was a lie. The woman – Angela, I think she said her name was – seemed a bit of a frump. A cardigan wearer. Not a professional-looking person, probably a home-maker. It was the only reason I decided she couldn't be about to take my job. I can usually read people quite well. Like I did with Alice. There were similarities between Angela and Alice, now I think of it, but Alice's face was more open. What you saw was what you got. I had the impression Angela was insincere, secretive. Not to be trusted. Why the hell *was* she with Marcie?

Oh well, it's not my concern. Now, back at home, sitting at the island in the kitchen reflecting on my coffee shop performance, I'm cursing myself for my lack of control. I thought I'd hold it together, show my strength. Instead, more emotion flooded out. Thankfully I didn't cry. But I did hear myself begging. Pleading Marcie to let me return to work, and all in front of that other woman. My cheeks heat up with shame.

I scratch at my arms, leaving harsh red lines. The stinging pain releases my frustration. I hate myself right now.

I hear the front door opening.

I'd locked myself in, hadn't I?

I spring from the bar stool, launching towards the knife block on the worktop. I slide the largest knife from its wooden slot, holding it up, ready to confront the intruder.

'Shitting hell, Deborah!'

Nathan backs away, one hand on his chest, the other outstretched, palm up in a defensive position. It hadn't crossed my mind that it could be him.

I let out a long breath, and lower the knife.

'Why didn't you call first?'

'Sorry, I didn't realise I needed permission to enter my own home.'

'Don't be stupid, Nathan. Of course you don't. But seeing as you haven't set foot in this house for over a week, some warning would've been appreciated. I thought I was being burgled.'

'Well, thankfully that isn't the case.' He moves towards me, slowly removing the knife from my hand and replacing it in the block. His skin is insipid; weary-looking. He doesn't look like he's slept.

'So, to what do I owe the pleasure?' Regardless of my desperation for Nathan to come home, I can't keep the bitterness from my voice.

He plonks himself down on the bar stool, slumping his upper body across the shiny black marble worktop covering the island, his head buried in his crossed arms.

Bloody hell, now what?

I hear words, but they are deadened by his jumper.

'I can't understand what you're saying,' I say, irritably.

He lifts his head and looks directly at me. 'I said, I miss you.'

My heart suddenly feels like it's tumbling. 'I miss you, too.' My voice crackles and breaks. Does this mean the other woman is no longer an option for him? Or is he having a minor wobble and will leave after he's unloaded his guilt?

'Do you? I mean actually miss me, or do you just miss the company? The knowledge that someone else is here.' His sad eyes focus intently on mine. I'm not sure I know the answer. My pause seems to have served as a reply, because he leaps up and begins to pace, his hands grabbing at his hair. This is so unlike him. Why has this started happening now?

'I . . . I miss you. I miss us . . .' I stammer. I want to say the right thing, but I don't know whether it's for his benefit, or mine.

'But you miss Sean more,' he says. His words aren't harsh – he's not accusing me, he's stating a fact. For the first time, I can see he's hurting too.

'Yes. I do, Nathan. Me and you aren't tied by blood. Me and Sean are. Were. I grew him *inside* of me.' I grasp hold of my stomach, remembering the feel of him, the lashing out of tiny limbs, the lurching sensations of his body flipping over in mine.

'And you think that means you miss him more than I do, that you loved him more?'

I shrug. It *is* what I believe.

Nathan walks towards me again, his hands outstretched. He takes hold of mine; they're warm, and my own feel cool enveloped in his. 'I'm not sure you can love me without him being here, can you? You saw me as the father of your child, and now that role's defunct. You can't – or don't want to – have me just as a husband.'

'That's not true.' I shake my head, not altogether sure I believe my own statement. 'But the fact I'm no longer a mother has changed me. You've changed too. It's like we have to adapt. To be something different. At the moment, I don't think either of us are making those changes. But it doesn't mean we won't ever be able to. It's going to take time.' I slip my hands out from his. 'Anyway, you're the one who left. You're the one who needs to decide whether you want this other woman in your life instead of me.'

'It's not as simple as that now.'

I shrug. 'No. It never is.'

CHAPTER SIXTY-SEVEN

Angela

I collapse on the floor, all my energy zapped. I've cried more tears than I think possible. My eyelids are heavy, so swollen they are almost closed. I have nothing left.

The lock rattles and the basement door edges open. Through the bleariness, I see my son. The murderer. My mouth is paralysed, no words can pass through my lips. He crouches down in front of me.

'I'm sorry, Ma,' he whispers. He looks like he did when he was little. Small. Scared. In need of my love and support.

I reach my arm out. He takes my hand, turning it over in his, studying the red skin. Then he sinks further down until he's on the floor beside me. He rests his head on my lap, his legs curled up like he's in the foetal position. Instinctively, I begin stroking his hair at the temple.

'I'm sorry too,' I manage to say. And I am. Sorry for a lot of things. Sitting here now with him, I'm reminded of how he'd been such a sweet, loving child. Always keen to help others, cheerful, energetic. He didn't have lots of friends, but those he did have, he seemed to go all out for. He was loyal. Then he became a teenager; the hormones kicked in. He and his father were continually at loggerheads. The arguments became heated. Then the beatings

217

followed. I didn't know how to handle it. So I shied away and let David manage things his way.

It was after David left that Tom came out of his shell more. With that came his confidence – but not in a positive way. I could see he was developing his father's abusive tendencies.

So, despite David finally being out of the picture, for us, Tom and me – for our relationship – it was too late. By the age of sixteen, he had realised I was weak. He took over where his father left off. Just as I'd told Connie.

See, I did tell some truths amongst the lies. I wasn't trying to bury all the real facts. Hide away from them, maybe; twist them to make them easier to bear, perhaps.

Rather than ignore Tom's behaviour in the hope it was a one-off, which clearly it's not, I'll have to help *change* him. It's obvious to me now. Although I can continue to seek some kind of redemption, Deborah isn't going to be the one to give it to me – it'll have to be through my group somehow. Maybe if I help Bill through his grief, that will be good enough – as close as I can get. I can no longer make things right with Deborah, but I can with the father of Tom's second victim. Because it is Isabella. I can feel it. And the way Tom is being now only confirms my fear.

Being Alice helped me. Gave me some redemption.

And this Wednesday I'm going to be Alice again.

218

CHAPTER SIXTY-EIGHT

Connie

Connie pushed her hand deep inside the envelope – there was no accompanying note. She stared at the pay-as-you-go mobile, half-expecting it to suddenly ring despite currently being switched off. She swallowed the lump in her throat and reached for it, gently handling it as if it might explode.

Someone had hand-delivered the package, meaning they knew where she lived. Could this be Scott's doing? He'd shown himself to be persistent, so it was a possibility this was an extension of the texts and flowers. Deep down she knew this wasn't the case. It felt different.

Connie checked the time. Ten-thirty. Surely Lindsay would be home soon. She would wait for her, get her to turn on the phone and find out what it was all about. Connie did not want to do it on her own. She pulled her legs up onto the sofa and lay her head on the arm. Surely it wouldn't be long to wait.

A crashing awoke her. Connie bolted upright, fear preventing her from moving off the sofa. She'd fallen asleep. She held her breath, straining to hear foreign noises. There was nothing. She felt disorientated, her head fuzzy with sleep.

Connie's muscles unclenched, her mind relaxed. It must've been a dream. Checking her phone for the time, she was shocked to see it was two-thirty in the morning. Why wasn't Lindsay home yet? She uncurled herself and stretched, her neck stiff from her position on the sofa. She couldn't believe she'd managed to sleep with all the worry swimming about in her head. She looked to the coffee table, to the mobile phone – its silence, its stillness somehow menacing. It was mocking her. With a sinking feeling, Connie reached forwards and picked it up.

She pressed the power button – her curiosity couldn't wait for Lindsay. She was obviously tied up with the body that'd been found; she might not even bother to come back now, choosing instead to stay on for the rest of the day. In the meantime, Connie had to find out why the mobile had been delivered to her.

The phone buzzed into life, the vibration sending shocks, like icy shards, across her skin.

When she'd been a teenager, her and her friend Tracey had watched the horror film *Carrie*. Connie recalled with absolute clarity the moment the scene came on the TV where a girl was standing at Carrie's grave. Connie had turned briefly to Tracey and said: 'I bet a hand comes out of the ground now.' And it did, as predicted. Connie had screamed, even though she'd been certain of what was going to happen. It was the same now: she knew that when the phone started up, a message would be on it. One that would cause as much fear as when Carrie's hand had burst from the ground. Only this time, there was no friend to join in with the screams; no friend to hold tight in horror. No one to comfort her.

One new message.

If she opened it here, now, she would be facing its content, and its repercussions, totally alone. She wasn't sure if it was courage or stupidity, but Connie allowed her fingers to open the message.

220

Do not go to the police. If you do, those you care for will come to harm. I need to talk to you. You have to come back. Make it happen. Delete this message after reading. K.

She breathed out a long, slow breath. It wasn't as bad as her imagination had conjured – although the 'those you love will come to harm' part kicked her heart rate up a few notches. In reality, however, it was only her mum she had to worry about – her dad was more than capable of looking out for himself. As for Luke, would anyone even be able to track him down? Connie rested back against the sofa. So, Kyle Mann wanted to talk to her, and had gone to a lot of trouble to deliver the message. He needn't have bothered. Didn't he realise she'd be dragged into this anyway? His refusal to speak with the police had pretty much guaranteed that.

The question, though, was *why*? It must be something he felt was urgent – he'd taken a huge risk sending a mobile phone to someone on the outside. Connie turned the phone over in her hand, half-expecting it to ring. Was this single message all there was, or did he intend to continue contacting her via it?

An uneasy sensation ran through her body. Someone else was involved. Kyle couldn't have delivered the package; he must've enlisted help.

And they knew where she lived.

CHAPTER SIXTY-NINE

Connie

Connie grabbed the Nokia from the coffee table and slipped it under the sofa cushion as the lounge door opened and an exhausted-looking Lindsay sloped in. It was just after 3 a.m.

'God, what a day!' She threw herself on the armchair, her head flopping against the chair back, and yawned widely.

Connie sat up, carefully positioning her legs to conceal the phone's hiding place. 'I wasn't sure you'd be home. I heard a body's been found . . .' Connie allowed the sentence to trail.

'It's the girl, Connie. Isabella Bond.' Lindsay's eyes were dull – through tiredness or the sad news, Connie wasn't sure. Probably a mix of both. Her usually shiny red hair was matt, unclean – held back from her face in a messy ponytail. When had she last washed it?

'Yeah,' Connie sighed, 'thought it would be. Even my mum left a message about it earlier.' Damn. She hadn't rung her back. She must remember to do it first thing in the morning. Well, when the sun was up – it was already morning. She rubbed her temples, the same time as Lindsay rubbed at her eyes.

'We're a right pair, aren't we?' Lindsay said.

'At least I've had *some* sleep. How are you still standing?'

'I'm not, I'm sitting.'

'You know what I mean.'

Lindsay smiled. 'I know you worry. About me, about everything. But I'll be fine. I have to keep going. We need to get to the root of this before someone else gets hurt.'

Connie's cheeks flushed – the mobile lying beneath her, tucked away, was making her feel guilty. Should she tell Lindsay now? But the warning words: *If you do, those you care for will come to harm,* flashed in her mind. Lindsay wanted her to go in and speak with Kyle anyway, there was no need to tell her about the mobile at this point. She'd see what he had to say first, find out what other reason he had for delivering the phone to her. If need be, she'd inform Lindsay afterwards. At least now her mind was made up: she *was* going to go back into the prison.

'Yes, of course I worry. I care about you. This job has drained you.' She wanted to add 'mentally and physically', but held back. Somehow this wasn't the right time for Connie to share her concerns about Lindsay's choice of career – point out how it could be damaging her. That was a conclusion Lindsay would need to come to herself – other people telling her would only make her defensive and push in the opposite direction. And maybe Connie wasn't the right person to talk to her about it anyway, given her own history.

'It's swings and roundabouts, Connie. After this case, it'll probably be boring again for ages. I'll catch up with sleep then.'

'Hah!' Connie shook her head. 'I don't know, Linds, I'm beginning to think we should both have a change of career. How do you fancy running a nice little tea shop by the seaside?'

Lindsay burst out laughing. 'Us two, in a tea shop? That's the best thing I've heard all day.' She wiped delirious tears from her eyes.

'Yeah, okay. Possibly a bit far-fetched. But still, I'm getting bloody fed up with criminals and hassle. A quiet life wouldn't be a bad idea.'

'I don't think I could leave all this, even if I wanted to. It has hold of me now. Anyway, I love it, mostly. It still feels great when bad people get what they deserve. I still get pleasure in knowing I've helped take another scumbag off the streets and made the place a little safer to live in. No other job could give me what this one does.'

Connie shrugged. 'Well, I don't think I'd miss it. Your job, or mine. When I'm more awake, I'm going to be seriously re-evaluating my career path.'

Lindsay stared at her for a while, saying nothing. Then she sat forwards. 'Mack spoke with you earlier?'

'Yep. Took me for coffee and cake. Your idea?'

'Good God, no. The old charmer.' Lindsay raised an eyebrow. 'And?'

'And obviously, yes. I'll speak to Kyle. No choice in the matter, really.'

'You've always got a choice, Connie. We all have choices.'

Yes, she was right. Everyone had a choice whether to say yes or no, whether to take one path or another. Whatever the factors involved, she did have the option to say no. Maybe a part of her didn't want to say no because she was too invested now. In too deep. She wanted answers. She could tell Lindsay about the phone. What could Kyle do from inside prison to harm those she loved? Even with outside contacts, the police would protect her and her family. She knew that. Was she taking the easy option by concealing the truth? Life would get very complicated if she confided in Lindsay right at this moment. Connie remembered something fake Alice had said during a session: *I went for the easy life, the easy option.*

Rather than having to face the upheaval that the truth would undoubtedly cause, and despite feeling ashamed about wimping out, the easy option was exactly what Connie was taking now.

CHAPTER SEVENTY

Tom

They'd talked for a long time. Surprisingly, Tom was able to regain some confidence – hope that his mum would carry on protecting him rather than give up on him, hand him over to the police. Her disappointment was evident, but he could get over that. Make her come around again.

She loved him. He was all she had.

He could use that.

She told him she'd stopped seeing the psychologist. Good news for him. The fewer people his mum came into contact with, the less likely his involvement with the murders would come out. Next, he had to cut her off from the stupid support group. The links there were the most dangerous. Apart from physically preventing her from leaving the house though, he was stumped at how he could achieve it. He'd hacked her laptop a number of times, gained a lot of information. It'd been a great source of help. But he didn't need help any longer. He had to sever his and his mother's ties with it.

His next mission was to eliminate the enemy. He'd have to think carefully how he could achieve it. It wasn't going to be easy, there were so many of them. Killing wasn't an option – far too risky. He'd have to use mental warfare, not physical. It was going to take superior skill. He remembered the time he'd followed his mum into Coleton. He'd seen her there with a fat woman, later finding out it was some loser called Wendy, who attended the group meet-up. Her messages on the online group page were laughable: *He's swearing at me all the time – what should I do? He's refusing to get help for his addiction – what can I do? He's threatening to punch me – what should I do?*

She was pathetic. Weak. It was obvious. She'd be easily manipulated.

Maybe he could start with her.

CHAPTER SEVENTY-ONE

Deborah

I've been married to Nathan for twenty-six years. You can't be with someone for that amount of time and not come to learn how they cope with challenging situations. The way Nathan acted yesterday, here in this kitchen, was out of character. This other woman had thrown him off keel. But how? What crap had she been feeding him? I can't grasp it, but something isn't right with this picture. He'd said it wasn't as simple as choosing between her and me. I should've made it simple for him. Told him to go to her.

I didn't though.

The kettle clicks off and I pour the boiling water into the teapot, remembering the times I did this for Alice. There's no one here to impress, but the tea always tastes better from my mother's bone china pot. I wish my mum was here with me, sitting at the island in the kitchen, wittering on about her latest ailment. Listening to her would take my mind off my current worries. She'd loved Sean so much, he could do no wrong in her eyes; she adored him, and he her. To the point I'd sometimes felt jealous. He often confided in her when he wouldn't in me. At the time, I felt hurt. The fact he didn't feel able to talk to me in the same way, that stung. Now they've both left me, I can see their relationship was how it should've been. I take some comfort in imagining them together now. Not enough to stop the pain entirely, only enough to soften the rough edges.

While I wait for the tea to brew, I take the latest newspaper and a pair of scissors. I carefully cut around the story about Isabella Bond, the young woman found dead in Coleton. I'd been there, at the scene on the walkway near the river, but other things on my mind had made me leave, and that's when I'd seen Marcie – and made a fool of myself for the second time. Looking at the dead girl's face now, I imagine what she must've gone through. The fear, the pain, the hideous realisation her life was about to finish. I hope she didn't suffer for long, like Sean did.

I don't know why I do this to myself. Is it to keep my own pain alive? To forget what Sean had gone through would be to forget the horror, to forget how someone, or some people, needed to be punished.

The article says the person who killed Isabella is still at large.

The bastard.

When they get him, they'd better not fill the pages of every newspaper with his image, his story. I don't want Isabella's family to have to go through what we did – seeing the face of your child's killer staring at you day in, day out. He doesn't deserve that attention, for people to read about the reasons he did it – feel any ounce of sympathy for how his depravity was the result of a broken family, poor upbringing and all the other bullshit the papers like to spout. That wouldn't be fair. Or right. But I don't hold enough hope that this murder, this killer, will be portrayed any differently from the ones that came before.

I take the cutting and place it with the others in the box. I pour my tea and think about the killer. Remember Alice's words about the one that got away. Coleton is a small town by most standards.

Could Isabella's murderer have been involved in Sean's death?

CHAPTER SEVENTY-TWO

Angela

I have both longed for and dreaded this Wednesday. The plastic chair slides from my hand, hitting the wooden floor with a crash. I wipe my palms on my skirt and pick it up. The trembling isn't only from the cold. What if it's a trap? The online group page had been going on as normal: people starting new threads, supporting each other, the same as ever. They had all said they were attending the meet-up today. If they knew about Alice Mann, they were keeping it to themselves. Waiting for the moment to confront me in person?

It's a chance I'm taking. I have to, so I can see Bill, offer him all the support I can give him. I swallow the rising bile. I couldn't eat this morning, butterflies playing havoc with my stomach; last night's vodka consumption probably didn't help either. I check the wall clock for the millionth time.

Ten minutes to wait.

Part of me feels exactly as I did when I stood here weeks ago, waiting, wondering, hoping. I felt an element of dread then, but nowhere near the same as now. I lean on the back of the chair, trying to take some slow, deep breaths. If worst comes to worst, I'll have to make a run for it. I almost laugh at the thought. Coward.

I imagine the chairs in the circle all filled with my group members, and I look out across their trusting faces and say:

'Hi. I'm Angela Killion, and I'm a liar and a coward.'

My voice is louder than I expect. I turn quickly to make sure I'm alone, What if Wendy had turned up early, like she's done on the other occasions? But the action of saying those words out loud has lifted a dark cloud. There is something to be said about the catharsis of honesty. Shame I was speaking to an empty room.

Protecting your children is the hardest job of all; everyone about to enter this church hall would agree. Protecting them *from* harm, protecting them when *they* harm – is equally challenging. Me, I'm attempting to do both.

I hear the creak of the external door and screw my eyes up. My breaths are shallow, the noise of the air expelling from my nose seems too loud.

Please, God, let today go well.

It's Wendy. Of course it is. She's always first to come in, last to leave. I'm reassured by the routine of this moment. I smile, and with my arms outstretched, move forwards to greet her. As I close in, I check for signs of mistrust; awkwardness. If she stiffens at my touch, if she pulls back from my friendly embrace, I'll know she knows. I am almost crushed by her arms. She pulls me in too tight and holds me there. I hear her tears.

'It's . . . so . . . awful,' she says between sobs, her words spoken into my neck. I can feel the wetness collect in my clavicle. I gently pull her arms from me. She's talking about Isabella, I realise. My relief is momentarily displayed as I find myself smiling. I amend my expression quickly, so concern is all I show.

'I know, I know.' I take Wendy's hand, patting it as I walk her to a seat. 'Terrible times are ahead for Bill, but he has us. We are his network of support and we'll help guide him through his grief.' I sound like a preacher, some do-gooder, and I think the words sound staged, insincere. But they're not, not really. I do want to help Bill. I have to.

'But what if he doesn't come today?' Wendy asks.

'He will. I'm sure of it.' Although I'm not, and I hadn't really thought about what I'd do if he didn't. The whole point of taking this risk, being here today, is for Bill. If he doesn't turn up, it'll have been for nothing.

It's time.

The chairs are all taken bar one. Bill isn't here yet.

I glance at the clock. It's bang on 3 p.m. When I look back to the circle, the faces are all on mine. Do any of them seem angry? Are any of them waiting to confront me? I daren't dwell on these thoughts right now – I need to get started.

'As you are all aware, this last week has brought dreadful, sad news,' my voice shakes, but the group will assume it's emotion. 'I'm sure we're all shocked at the death of Bill's daughter—'

'The MURDER!'

A heat flushes up my neck. I turn to the source of the shout. Bill is standing in the doorway, dishevelled, ashen. I jump up, moving towards him as quickly as I can without appearing to run.

'Bill, dear Bill. Come in,' I say quietly as I squeeze his arm. I want to embrace him, as Wendy had me minutes before, but refrain. It might be too much. We haven't become that close yet.

He holds his head in his hands, and he wobbles. I'm afraid he'll tumble to the ground, so I ask the group to help me take him to the empty chair in the circle.

One by one, my group members offer Bill their support. They share their shock and anger at what's happened, and he begins to make eye contact. He starts to open up about how he's feeling. I'm the only one who hasn't spoken – and now, as he looks to me, I freeze. The knowledge my son has caused this numbs me. How can I help him?

The group are doing a great job – I suddenly realise he doesn't need me. I can't offer anything more than these people. I'm nothing special. Now his life has been touched by a murderer, does he also look at me differently? I've gained the group's support, they all know my son is a killer – and although they think he's in prison,

231

paying for his crime, the fact remains Bill's perspective will have been changed. Others may follow. Even if they don't find out I've lied to them, they may well withdraw their support now this has happened. How much sympathy can a murderer's mother warrant?

The rest of the session passes in a blur. The voices surrounding me seem like they're a distance away, coming at me through a long, narrow tunnel. I try to focus on the good I've created. I started this group. Whether they change their opinion of me, given Bill's circumstances or not, they can't take away what I've already accomplished.

I watch the others as they talk, but it's like watching a TV programme. Then I sense the room has fallen silent. All eyes are on me.

I open my mouth, but no words come out. What did I miss?

'Alice?' Bill says. 'Are you feeling okay?'

Before I can stop them, tears are rolling down my face. Chair legs squeak on the floor and I feel half a dozen hands on my shoulders.

'I'm sorry,' I hear myself say. 'You all must hate me.' I drop my head, keeping my gaze on my lap, not able to look any of my group in the eye.

'We're here for you, Alice. We came together because we've all been affected by our children's behaviour in one way or another.' Bill's voice sounds thick with emotion. 'You've always been so brave in your honesty about what your son did. We aren't going to turn on you now.' This statement comes as a relief, but my guilt rages inside me like a hot rod being dragged through my intestines. Somehow having their support suddenly seems worse than having their disapproval.

Once everyone leaves, I stand in the silence and gather my thoughts. I must take the positives from today's meeting: no one has found out the truth, Bill has gained a wealth of support, and they still want me as their leader. The fact I am now left with a guilt almost as overwhelming as it was *before* I began trying to make things right in the first place is something I have to manage myself. How, I don't know.

My fingers fumble with the key for the internal door in the church hall, they clatter as they hit the ground. I stand back up after retrieving them, and I'm about to lock it when I'm aware of a presence behind me. A foreboding stops me from turning around.

'Hello, Alice.'

My pulse quickens. I know the voice.

I have no place to run. There's no option but to turn; confront whatever is about to happen.

I force my body to move – it shuffles around, slowly.

'Hello, Connie.'

CHAPTER SEVENTY-THREE

Tom

Not drawing attention to himself had proved more difficult than he'd expected. A young man in a hoody may not generally be an unusual sight, but hanging around in one spot attracted lots of stares from passers-by. The church was in Totnes's main street – why had his mother chosen somewhere so bloody obvious? He'd waited in the doorway of the shop opposite until he'd become too conspicuous. Once he witnessed what appeared to be the last group member entering the church hall, he'd wandered off, having almost two hours to kill before they all came out again. Before he could approach Wendy. It was during that time the idea came to him.

Now, sitting on a dirty old blanket he'd stolen from a bin at the back of the market, a plastic container in front of him, he was confident he'd be largely ignored. How many people stopped to look at a guy begging in the street? It was the perfect cover.

Head bowed so as not to make direct eye contact with anyone, Tom raised his eyes slightly. A woman who'd been walking down from the East Gate Arch stopped at the window of the shop opposite, where he'd started off a couple of hours ago. She didn't pay him any notice; her gaze was on the passageway leading to the hall door. He couldn't make out her details without it being obvious he was staring at her, but he could see she was biting her nails, and every now and then she turned to look at the window display. She was probably someone who wanted to join his mother's group but was too shy to go in.

Footsteps to his left alerted him to the end of the meeting. People were making their way down the path adjacent to the church and would be on the pavement in seconds. He had to time it carefully, make sure Wendy was alone when he spoke to her. He gathered his homeless kit together and stood. The woman who'd been waiting opposite now crossed the road and headed towards the hall. His attention left her once she'd passed him, not even giving him a fleeting glance, and settled upon the obese woman who now proceeded right, down the main street.

Tom followed, keeping a good distance behind her. It wasn't as if she was walking fast – she lumbered, her size restricting her speed – so she was easy to keep up with; easy to keep in his sights. An easy target. As long as she didn't get on a bus before he had a chance to speak to her, it would be fine.

Wendy was heading in the direction of the bakery at the bottom of town, near the waterside. Perfect. It was fairly quiet there – usually only good weather brought larger numbers of people that way. If he was lucky, she'd take a walk on the grassed area running alongside the river.

As Wendy left the bakery, a white paper bag clutched in her hand, Tom took a cut-through between the two shops to get to the rear of the buildings. He managed to position himself on the first bench just as she turned the corner and came into sight.

He waited for her to walk near him.

'Hey, love, do you have a light?' he said, leaning forwards on the bench towards her. She turned to face him. Her mouth opened, then closed again without words coming out. She continued onwards. Tom jumped up from the bench and sidestepped beside her as she walked. 'Sorry, didn't mean to alarm you.' He smiled, but Wendy wasn't playing as he'd hoped, and she carried on walking, ignoring him. That pissed him off, feelings of inadequacy flooding his body. It was like being back at school, kids all huddled in their groups at lunchtime, ignoring his attempts to insert himself into their conversations. Losers.

He'd have to go for the stronger approach.

'You go to the support group in the church, don't you?'

Wendy stopped. He'd got her interest.

Now all he had to do was get into her head.

CHAPTER SEVENTY-FOUR

Connie

The woman's shocked expression disappeared quickly, replaced with a smile and an attempt at appearing normal. But the colour had drained from her skin, leaving it waxy-looking, and her eyes gave her away. The fake Alice had been caught out – and she knew it.

Connie stood in silence for a few beats, allowing her surprise entrance to sink in before she spoke. She hadn't really planned what to say in this moment, she had half-expected the woman she knew as Alice wouldn't be at the meeting. Facing her now, Connie wasn't sure how to confront the situation: subtlety or bluntly. She didn't want to frighten her off – she might not get another chance to speak to her. Whatever her reasons for lying about who she was, it was obvious she needed help in one way or another. Connie hoped she could be the one to offer her support. Get to the root of her issues. At the same time, she wanted to find out if and how she was linked to the real Alice Mann.

'Sorry to drop in on you unannounced, but you stopped coming to sessions and I was concerned about you,' Connie said. She'd made the split-second decision to begin with the subtle approach; test the water.

'Oh, well . . . um . . . I'm locking up now, got to rush off . . . sorry.' Her movements were jerky, flustered – her eyes darting around. Connie sensed she was looking for a quick getaway and feared she would push past her, scurrying off before Connie could offer her help.

'Look, I'm not here to upset you, or cause you a problem.' Connie raised both arms, palms towards the woman, trying to appear unthreatening. 'I want to help.'

'I said before, Connie. You can't help me.'

'You came to me. You must've thought there was a possibility I could?'

'I've no idea what I was thinking, really,' she said, her shoulders dropping. 'I guess I thought you'd be helpful in other ways. I knew you couldn't do anything for me personally, but your knowledge would be useful.'

Connie frowned. What *was* she talking about?

She must've noticed Connie's confusion and, taking advantage of her change of focus – and before Connie could say or do anything to prevent it – pushed her hard against the wall before taking off.

Winded, Connie gasped for air and attempted to follow her outside. The pathway running alongside the church was long enough that by the time she reached the road in her winded state, fake Alice was out of sight.

Connie leant back against the rail near the church, breathing deeply. *Well, that didn't go as planned.* She scanned the shops opposite, then looked up and down the road. She couldn't have got far, but Connie had no idea where to start looking – there were numerous shops she could've ducked into, and at least two roads off the main road close by she might've taken.

The hope she'd find out why her client had lied suddenly faded. The group meeting had been her only chance – she'd been incredibly lucky to find out where Alice held the meet-ups. Had her luck run out?

She hoped not – she'd need it tomorrow morning.

She'd need all the luck possible for her interview with Kyle Mann.

CHAPTER SEVENTY-FIVE

Connie

The taxi dropped Connie at the prison gatehouse. She was earlier than she'd arranged with Jen – who had written the movement slip for Kyle's appointment at Connie's request, stating Thursday 9 a.m – so Connie sat on the wooden bench outside, a bench made by the prisoners in the wood shop. They made beach huts too in the summer. She stared out across the grassed area running in front of the gatehouse. When was she going to see the back of HMP Baymead for good?

For all her attempts to stay away, eradicate it from her mind, she kept getting dragged back. The place haunted her. Now, the thought of seeing Kyle caused her to shiver. On the one hand, she wanted to help Lindsay and Mack in the hope it would shed some light on what was going on -- who'd attacked Alice Mann, and maybe even who had murdered Isabella. She'd been given a few more details about it from Lindsay and there were similarities between the cases she was keen to discuss with Kyle. But, on the other hand, he'd gone to great lengths to get the mobile phone to Connie, and the reason for it worried her. It could be that he wanted to speak with her to help the case, or himself – but it could also be because he wanted to warn her off, threaten her in person to make sure she didn't give more information to the police.

His goal may still be to protect the other, as yet unknown, person. And if that was the case, her visit was going to be a waste of time, as well as dangerous.

Her eyes were drawn to a car driving down the long entrance. She followed its progression into the staff car park and watched as Verity climbed out and began slowly walking towards her. At least Connie wouldn't have to get the OSG to call the psychology department now to get someone to come and meet her.

'Morning, Verity.' Connie stood up as Verity approached.

'Were we expecting you?' she asked bluntly.

'Yes, I arranged it with Jen.' Connie's brow furrowed. She was surprised by this frosty reception. She hadn't been particularly chatty when Connie was there last, but this was different.

'Oh. Sorry, didn't get that memo.' Verity's mouth twisted into a half-smile.

'You okay?' Connie walked behind Verity as she entered the gatehouse and they both waited for the OSG to release the door to the glass pod.

'Tired. Been really busy here,' she said, without looking at Connie. 'And I guess I'll be your key person *again* today.'

Connie smiled, but Verity's attitude was making her uncomfortable and she had more important things on her mind than trying to butter her up. She was clearly fed up with having to hand-hold Connie, going onto the block and running around after her. She wanted to tell her she was as fed up about it as she was, but it probably wouldn't help the situation.

Verity retrieved her keys with her numbered tally and once the OSG had released the door, they walked outside into the sterile area. Connie puffed out the air she'd been holding. The feeling she had – the griping contraction of her stomach, her pulse racing scarily fast – was getting more intense with each visit. This had to be the last time walking through that door, she decided. Even though part of her desperately wanted to get answers, to figure this whole thing out and help in the process, she realised it wasn't worth this personal trauma. Whatever today brought – whether Kyle was willing to talk, give names, or not – she didn't want to do this again. Kyle Mann could threaten all he wanted. She'd dump the phone – or give it to Lindsay – and take her chances. She'd had enough.

'You got my message then,' Kyle said as soon as he was seated opposite her.

Connie had arranged to meet him in the portacabin used by the offending behaviour programmes team. She'd booked the smaller room; the Thinking Skills Programme was running in the larger one. Connie felt safe knowing others were within shouting distance, but it was private enough to be able to talk freely. She'd positioned two low-back comfy chairs opposite each other with a round table separating them, making sure she was nearest the door, and the alarm.

'I did get your message,' Connie said, her voice steady.

Kyle sat forwards, resting his forearms on his knees and clasping his hands together. 'Sorry for the delivery method, but I didn't know how else to get you to come back. Jen said you'd done your bit and had left, and I only wanted to speak to *you*, no one else.' His words were rushing out at great speed and Connie wasn't sure if he was agitated or excited – or high. He looked pale, strained. She almost said she'd only come in because the police had asked her to, but stopped herself. It would be better if he thought she was there because of his instructions – let him think he was in control.

'Okay,' Connie said, her hands raised to calm him. 'Well now you have me here, what is it you wanted to talk to me about?'

'Firstly, my mum. It's shit being in here, getting the odd piece of information about how she is but not being given the whole picture. Not being able to go to her, be by her side, is killing me.' Kyle's jaw muscles clenched, his knee bouncing anxiously as he stared at Connie. She was surprised to see the intensity of the worry etched on his face.

'I imagine it's stressful.' Connie allowed herself to relax a little. Talking about Alice was her aim too, so it was a great place to begin the discussion. If that's all he wanted, she'd had no cause to be worried about the reasoning behind him sending her the mobile. 'What leads you to believe you aren't being told the full picture?' she frowned.

'I had two coppers turn up here, wanting to get information. They'd got the prison chaplain to tell me about my mum first, so when they came, all they did was accuse me of knowing who'd been responsible for her attack. Straight in they were, going on about my "contacts" on the outside. I knew what they were getting at.'

'Which was?'

'You need to ask? Come on, Miss. You had the same idea, didn't you? That I wasn't alone when I killed that lad?'

Connie did a quick weighing up in her head – should she come clean, or play dumb? Which option was her best shot at getting him to tell the truth? She decided to take a slight detour – answer the question with a question.

'But what's that got to do with the attack on your mother?'

'Plenty.' Kyle slumped back in the chair and turned his head towards the window. The portacabin looked out across one of the newer living blocks, the greys of the building giving off a depressing air. Kyle still looked like a teenager, despite being twenty-two – his skin was soft and smooth. Connie didn't rush him, didn't prompt him to elaborate; she had enough time to take this slowly, the wing officer knew where he was and Connie had marked 'lunchtime' as her approximate return time on the psychology office's board. Kyle turned back and sighed before leaning forwards. 'You know when you don't know what to do for the best anymore? When what you thought was the better option turns out to be the shittest?'

'Yes, Kyle – I'm aware of that kind of situation,' Connie admitted.

'I did what I told him I'd do.'

Connie sat up straighter. 'Did what who told you to do?'

'Well, that's the big question everyone wants answered, isn't it?' Kyle leant back again, crossing his arms, but kept his eyes on Connie.

'And now you're ready to answer?'

'I'm not sure *ready* is the right way of putting it. I'm not prepared for the consequences. But now something's happened to my mum, and I'm guessing he's tidying up loose ends – trying to stop his name from ever being linked to Sean Taylor. And there are only a few people who know, or think they know, he was involved. Me – and I'm safely locked up, and he knows I've always kept quiet, until recently at least – and my mum, who always knew something wasn't right. Then I fucked up because of you.' He rocked gently in the chair. It was clear to Connie she was at fault, but Kyle didn't appear to be blaming her. It seemed he was more mad at himself for taking the bait – for breaking his self-imposed silence in the first place.

'Because I told you about Alice coming to see me . . .'

'Yep, precisely. I panicked. I told him. Said my mum was seeing a psychologist. Partly it was to protect him, but mostly it was for her sake. I only thought about the fact she needed to stop seeing you, to stop talking about the bloody murder and banging on about someone else being involved. I didn't think he'd hurt her.' His voice caught. 'The bastard almost killed her. She still might die, mightn't she?' His eyes became glossy with tears.

'Doctors induced the coma, Kyle, to prevent any more damage to her brain. Once they get the swelling under control, ensure there are no more bleeds, they'll slowly bring her out of it. No one is talking about her dying.' Connie tried to sound more positive than she felt. Kyle needed to hear there was a strong possibility of his mum recovering. 'Are you sure it was him that did that to your mum?'

'Oh, he probably didn't do it himself. Not his style – not often he gets *his* hands dirty.'

243

Connie took a minute to process this. So, it wasn't just one person – there were others, pawns in someone else's warped game. 'How many people do you think are involved?'

He shrugged. 'He likes to play games. I mean, like computer games, only in real life. He draws other people in, gets them on his site, talks to them for months, building up his profile.'

'His profile?'

'You know, like his online persona. It wasn't until I'd been in here a few years I realised what he'd done, how well he'd played me.' He shook his head, tutting. 'I was the perfect gamer, Miss. And if he found me, he'll have found others. New players to groom, manipulate.' His face contorted as he hissed that last word, cracking his knuckles as if to release long-held resentment.

'What on earth did he hold over you to enable him to silence you for four years?'

'Trust. Loyalty. Friendship. Fear. You name it. He's very clever. Very dangerous.' Kyle gave a snort. 'You wouldn't think it, would you? Being afraid of a nerdy gamer, huh! Pathetic.'

'It's not always the ones who *look* scary that we need to be scared of.'

'No,' he nodded vehemently, 'ain't that the truth.'

'Does he know you've been talking to me?'

'He knows you came to see me, yes. Obviously, I went off on one when you told me about my mum seeing you – her talking about me and stuff. I told him too much.' He lowered his head.

Connie wanted to ask outright the name of the unknown male accomplice but was compelled to come clean with what was on her mind first. She took a deep breath. She wasn't sure how Kyle would react to her disclosure but felt it safe to assume he wasn't going to be happy.

'Kyle. I have to tell you something, but I want you to know, I didn't lie to you.'

His face darkened. 'Go on.'

'When I told you your mum was seeing me, it's what I believed.'

He shifted forwards, his eyes wide. 'What are you saying?'

'I'm saying an Alice Mann was coming to me for counselling,' Connie started, but then hesitated, knowing there was no coming back if she carried on. She let her head loll back. She had to say it: 'But it was not your mum.'

'What the fuck . . .' Kyle's eyes widened, the whites of his eyes showing his shock. And probably, Connie realised, anger. She had to tread carefully.

'I didn't find out until your mum was attacked. When I saw her picture in the paper, that's when I realised. The woman coming to see me knew everything about Sean Taylor's murder, and talked about you being her son. She spoke of how she'd set up a support group for other parents, everything. I didn't have a single reason to question her identity.'

Kyle was frowning so hard that deep furrows appeared across his forehead and his eyes were lost beneath his brows. Connie held her breath, waiting for whatever outburst might come. She shifted her legs, turning her body slightly more towards the alarm.

Minutes seemed to go by, and still Kyle remained silent. Then he pushed himself from the low chair. Connie flinched, then stood herself, moving to the doorway, expecting him to bolt from the room. He didn't though. Instead, he walked to the window, standing with his back against it. She forced herself to relax, the increased distance between them now putting her at ease again – at least momentarily.

'Unbelievable,' he said, finally, shaking his head.

'I'm sorry, Kyle. It's my fault—'

'No. No, it's not your fault. It's mine.'

'I've no idea why someone would pretend to be your mum, I . . . I still don't know who she really is.' Connie couldn't find any other words to help the situation.

'Oh, I have a good idea who she is.'

Connie raised her eyebrows. His declaration was unexpected. 'Really? Who?'

'I think the woman you've been seeing may be *his* mum.'

Connie wasn't sure she was following Kyle's train of thought. 'Whose?'

Kyle slumped back in the chair, running his hands through his hair. 'Jesus. It makes sense now – why you thought you were seeing my mum. It was her. Had to be. What the hell is she playing at?' It was like Kyle had forgotten Connie was there, and was talking to himself, muttering under his breath.

'Kyle?' Connie took a step forwards, her eagerness for him to continue palpable.

'Tom's mum,' he said, his voice nothing more than a whisper. His gaze travelled to the door. Connie knew he was about to bolt.

'Tom who?' she asked.

Kyle was too quick – he jumped up and darted through the door. Connie didn't try to stop him.

She'd got a first name, and an acknowledgement someone else had been involved with Sean Taylor's murder – the person who was still free to kill again. And she knew she'd met his mother. No wonder she wasn't keen on talking to Connie any longer.

Now she could relay this new information to Lindsay and Mack and they could take over.

Her work here was done.

CHAPTER SEVENTY-SIX

Angela

Bill would've been an ideal dad for Tom. Tough, but caring; strong, yet capable of emotion. Nothing like David. Tom has ruined any attempt I could've made now. Tom has ruined a lot. But the fault is mine. Can I stop him from doing more harm? I have to try.

I carry the mug of tea down the steps to the basement. He's kept that door open for the last few days. Not his door though, that remains locked – but small steps. I give three sharp knocks and wait. I almost spill the tea as Tom flings the door open.

'Morning. Thought you'd like a cuppa,' I say, holding the mug up. I smile.

For a second, he stares, unblinking. 'Cheers.' He takes it and moves to close the door. I take a step forwards, putting one foot between the door and the frame.

'What do you want?' he says. He's irritated with me already. It doesn't seem to take much.

'We need to talk, Tom. About what happens next.'

His skin blanches. 'What do you mean, what happens next?' His hand falls from the door. I make the most of this opportunity and gently push my way into his room. It's the first time I've been in it for months. It's immaculate. Not like a teenager's room. But I guess he *isn't* a teenager anymore. I just feel like he is. Maybe I've treated him like one for far too long.

'I mean, where we go from here. You've done another bad thing, Tom. Unforgivable. You can't go unpunished – or at least, untreated.' I sit on the edge of his bed. He's still standing by the door, but has turned to face me.

'Unpunished? Untreated?' His face glows reds. 'What the fuck do you mean?'

'I protected you before, but you've let me down. I can't keep on doing this. You have to stop.' I hold back from sharing my sense of the net closing in around us since Connie confronted me yesterday. If Tom carries on hurting people, I, alone, won't be able to protect him.

'I will. I told you that!'

'It's not as simple as you *saying* you won't do it again. You said that the first time. You need help, Tom.'

I want to ask him what he did to Isabella – how he got to her, how he took her life. Fear of the answers stop me. Or maybe in my heart I believe that by not knowing the details, I can't be made to divulge them if the time comes. If police ever come knocking. The less I know, the better, in some ways.

'Enough now, Mum,' he says as he firmly pulls me towards the door, and I allow him to steer me out. I'll save my strength for another day.

Telling Tom he needed help was only the beginning. I know he needs it, and so do I. But how? And who is going to give it? To access mental health services would mean him having to talk about his past, talk about why he was seeking treatment. Everything would come out and I'd lose him. If I got rid of his computer, kept him in the house, that would temporarily stop him from getting to other people. As had been discussed at the group meet-ups though, when Bill was sharing how difficult it was keeping Isabella from going out, preventing them leaving the house is not easy, or even a viable option.

Unless . . .

Tom has his own bedroom door in the basement, and it's a heavy-duty one – not the usual hollow internal door in most houses. Then there's the door to the basement itself, in the hallway. If I get the keys to both of those, lock him in . . . the soundproofing would prevent anyone hearing him.

The idea swirls in my head. Longer term, it isn't a great plan. But while I wait for things to blow over and try to think of something better, it could work. If I could get the keys. If he doesn't have spares that I don't know about. Too many 'ifs'?

But it's something; a start.

The laptop lies open on the table. Taking my own cup of tea and a bowl of cereal, I sit and scroll through the group support page while I eat.

Something's up.

The last message on each separate thread are all the same. My heart leaps; my spoon drops with a clatter against the china bowl.

They are all from Wendy.

Don't talk on here, I'll private message you.

What's going on?

CHAPTER SEVENTY-SEVEN

Deborah

I wait by the door to the intensive care unit, my palms sweating. The last time I was at this hospital was when Sean was here. But he was in the morgue; dead on arrival, therefore no ICU, no attempt to save his life. It had been too late for that.

I hadn't expected a buzzer system – I thought I would be able to sneak in to see Alice without asking permission. I imagined it would only be family allowed to visit, so didn't bother phoning to ask if I could. I'm not family; I'm not even a friend.

I sit in one of the chairs outside the entrance and, taking my mobile out of my bag, I type 'Torbay Hospital ICU' into Google. Results only tell me about how the new state-of-the-art unit was opened in February last year and has fourteen beds.

What was I thinking, coming here? I'm not going to be able to see her – the place isn't big enough to go in unnoticed, and no doubt the nursing care is one-on-one with the nurse being with her practically all the time. My shoulders drop. I'm wasting my time. I don't even know why I want to see her. To check the damage for myself? To find out if enough pain has been inflicted on her? Will any of it make me feel better? I doubt it. Actually, I don't think either of those things are the real reason I'm here.

I lift my head as a figure slowly moves past me. An elderly man, stooped over, shuffles his way to the door – to the buzzer. Without much thought, I jump up and stand to the side of him.

'Good morning,' I say.

The man turns towards me. His eyes are sunken and his skin hangs loosely from his jawline. 'Morning.' His voice is a husky whisper, barely audible, and he points to his throat.

'Do you want me to buzz?' I ask as I lean across him.

He nods, then takes something from his pocket. The name Veronica Mills is written in block capitals on it. I smile and press the button. When it's answered, I state the name. The door clicks open and we walk into the ICU together. A nurse at the end of the short corridor nods her head towards the door. My heart drops. She knows I'm not really with this man and she's telling me to leave. She points to the door. It's useless, I'm going to have to go. But then I follow her gaze and spot the dispenser on the wall. Relieved, I place my hands underneath it and a squirt of gel lands in them. I smile at the nurse as I stand still, rubbing my hands together. Seemingly happy with that, she rushes off in the opposite direction. I wait for the man to dispense the gel himself and then walk with him as he heads to see Veronica. I've no idea which bed Alice is in, and in a moment this man is going to make it clear I'm not with him. I have to find her quickly. Eyes darting around, I try to take in the layout of the unit: how many nursing staff and doctors there are, and how many visitors.

A woman in scrubs walks towards us. The man I'm with turns to the left – he obviously knows where he's going. I hesitate. Should I follow him? I put an arm on the gentleman's elbow and lean in as if to speak to him. The woman smiles at me before disappearing behind some curtains. I hear my own breath rush out. 'I hope your visit goes well,' I say to the man, and I stand for a moment watching him hobble up to his wife's bedside.

The beds are widely spaced, probably because there are so many bleeping machines attached to the occupants that the large surrounding areas are a requirement. It doesn't make finding Alice any easier, though. Some beds have the curtains pulled around them, so I can't tell if one of those is her.

I feel a hand on my shoulder and jump.

'Sorry, are you all right? Who are you looking for?'

I immediately blurt, 'Alice Mann,' then regret it. I should've said I was looking for the toilet or something, bought myself some time.

'Bed four, over by the window,' the man who I assume to be a doctor says, pointing.

'Thank you,' I manage to say, my mouth as dry as sandpaper.

My heart races as I walk towards Alice, my leaden feet making the short journey difficult. Each step closer allows me to see more – the yellowing bruises, the tube protruding from her mouth. The damage is obvious; my guilt will be too. The nurse at the end of her bed turns his attention to me.

'Here you go.' He positions a chair as close to Alice's head as the machinery allows. 'I'm glad someone's able to visit today, Edward was concerned she'd be on her own. Did he ring you?'

'Er . . . yes. Yes,' I say, 'although I was planning on coming in today anyway.' I give a smile. I know it has come across as unsure, because that's exactly how I feel right now.

'I haven't seen you before,' the nurse says.

'No. I hadn't plucked up the courage until now.' That, at least, is the truth.

'It can be a shock, seeing a loved one in this condition. Don't feel bad about it, you're here now. I'm Graham, by the way – Alice's named nurse. I'm always about. I'll be popping over regularly to look after Alice's needs, but I'll give you some time now with her. The bell is there,' he points to the table beside the bed, 'but as you can see, we're all just a holler away if you're concerned, or need anything.'

Graham gives me a reassuring smile, replaces a clipboard on the unit at the end of Alice's bed, and leaves.

My muscles, tense from the anxiety of getting in here, now loosen. I've done it. I'm left alone with Alice. I don't know what to do. As usual, in situations where I feel awkward, I begin to talk. And before I'm really aware of it, I've told Alice everything.

CHAPTER SEVENTY-EIGHT

Connie

Finally, after what felt like months of eating alone, Lindsay was sitting opposite Connie at the dining table. As they tucked into a Chinese takeaway, Connie relayed her conversation with Kyle between mouthfuls.

'It's not much to go on, though. *Tom*.' Lindsay shrugged. 'But thank you. It's a start, and more than we were getting from him. Although now I think we have a way in – I'll get Mack to talk to him again officially, see if a threat of a longer sentence might make him drop his bizarre sense of loyalty to this low life.'

'Also, if fake Alice was telling the truth in her initial session with me about moving to Totnes, we know he lives locally. There's the footage from my security camera too – I'd forgotten about that.' Connie got up from the table and retrieved the SD memory card from the drawer of the coffee table. 'I was meant to watch it, see if it was possible to get a good still from it.'

'Good, yes. We'll take a look in a minute.' Lindsay popped the last of the chicken balls in her mouth.

'Do you think this Tom could be Isabella Bond's killer too?'

'There are similarities – the locality, age of victim, the use of a bladed weapon, together with what Kyle told you,' Lindsay said, shrugging. 'I'd say it was a strong possibility, wouldn't you?'

'Certainly seems to fit the profile – the links can't just be coincidental.'

'The links are good, but at this point only circumstantial,' Lindsay said. 'Solid evidence might be harder to come by.'

'Didn't the murder scene give you much?'

She shook her head. 'No murder weapon. There were a few fibres, but nothing identifiable at this point, the heavy rain showers the day she was found didn't help matters, and only the victim's blood was at the scene. It seems like a straightforward slit-of-the-throat-with-gloved-hands job. The blood spurt from the wound might've splashed him, but I suspect he burned his clothes after the attack.'

'So, he *could* get away with it? Again.' Connie slumped back down into her chair and pushed her rice around the plate.

'If we can link him to Isabella it would be a start.'

'Kyle said he met Tom through online gaming. Didn't you say there was something on Isabella's laptop, a gaming site she'd been on? Conversations outside of the game with someone called "The Boss"? Have your techies come up with any leads from that?'

'Not as yet. But if we get more info from Kyle, they might have a better idea where to look, what to concentrate on.'

'And if you can't get anything else from Kyle?'

'We have a place to focus on, and if we can find Alice . . . fake Alice . . . then that would be a bloody fantastic start. Fancy her going to see you, pretending she was Kyle's mother. I can't get over that.'

'I think she has many unresolved issues, not least a huge guilt complex.'

'So she bloody should, Connie! Jesus, if we're right about all this, her son has murdered two people, maybe more.' Lindsay's eyes widened.

'I know, but I suppose she was trying to . . .' Connie faltered. Trying to what? Cover up her son's crimes? Protect him from prison? 'Trying to be a good mother.'

'I think your thoughts on being a good mother and mine are vastly different.'

'Like I said – she came to me for help, and although she lied about who she was, I think the majority of *what* she told me was actually true. She's the mother of a murderer and she feels guilty about not realising sooner that his behaviour was becoming more deviant. I'm assuming the part she told me about her husband being abusive and then leaving is also true. That was *her* life. So, she's been dealing with a lot – with no outside help from social services – for some years. How else could she talk about what was happening to her without giving her son away? By setting up a self-help support group she was trying to redress the balance; make things right.'

'How can you possibly make murder right?'

'In her mind, she was undoing some of the wrong her son had done. Picking up the pieces of his mess. She didn't think she'd been a good mother; she allowed abuse to happen right under her nose, and she felt responsible for the way he turned out. Trust me, Lindsay, fake Alice is a psychologist's dream. There's so much going on in her head to untangle.'

Connie and Lindsay lapsed into silence, both lost in thought while they finished off the Chinese.

'Right,' Lindsay said as she pushed back from the table. 'Let's watch your CCTV footage, shall we?'

CHAPTER SEVENTY-NINE

Connie

Lindsay had invited her to the pub after she finished work, saying she was going to The White Hart with her colleagues for a swift one and that Connie was welcome to join them. As it might be the only time Connie would have a chance to catch up with Lindsay this weekend, she'd quickly agreed.

Nursing a half-pint, Connie's eyes searched the bar for a familiar face. No one from the station. Must be running late. *Nothing new there.* This wasn't one of the pubs on her list of regulars; Connie tended to head towards the town centre when she was out on her own. Lindsay often mentioned this pub though – it was close to the station, so convenient for the team.

Connie turned to the sound of the door opening. *Shit.* How could her luck be that bad? Scott immediately looked in her direction as he walked in with the group of men Connie had first seen him with at The Farmer. It was too late to pretend she hadn't seen him, too obvious to choose this moment to go to the bathroom. She'd have to face him. How embarrassing – she had completely ignored all his texts, and not even thanked him for the flowers. This was going to be awkward.

She smiled as he approached her.

'Well, you didn't strike me as the hard-to-get type?' His opening line was slurred. Drunk already? He pulled out a dark-wood Admiral chair and sat himself next to her.

Connie bristled. Yes, she should've answered his messages, even if only to tell him she didn't want to see him again, but the sarky 'hard-to-get-type' line was uncalled for. Any hope this guy might've had of pulling it back with her evaporated.

'And *you* didn't strike me as the stalker-type,' she said, her smile of greeting dying on her lips.

Scott's upper body straightened and jolted back, as if the force of her words had impacted him.

'Wow, Connie. Perhaps we should start this conversation over? Maybe we have our wires crossed.'

Connie pursed her lips, shaking her head gently from side to side. 'You know, I think not. Our lines seem pretty straight to me.'

He took a breath. 'Look, I'm sorry. I'm a little worse for wear, and me coming over to you like this and starting off on the wrong foot wasn't on. I guess I was a bit hurt – all my approaches being spurned and all that – I gave you my full arsenal of witty texts and romantic gestures, you know . . .'

Connie wasn't quite sure how to respond. If that was his best, there wasn't much to look forwards to. A shame, really – the sex had been great, and he was extremely good-looking. But sex and good looks did not make a relationship. There was only one option. Scott had to be marked up as just another one-night stand.

'I'm sorry too,' she said, smiling again now to soften her next words. 'But I'm afraid I'm not ready for a relationship.'

'Oh,' he said, his composure momentarily faltering before twisting his mouth into an unattractive smirk. 'Really? Not *ready*? Aren't you, like, forty?' His eyebrows met in the middle as he delivered what he must've thought was another witty line.

'No, actually. But age aside, I don't want to get into anything right now.'

'Right. I get it. I see now. You're a lezzi really, you and that copper you live with.'

'Just because I've turned you down, I must be a lesbian? Get over yourself, Scott.' Connie pushed her chair back and put both hands on the table to get up.

Scott pressed his hands down over hers, stopping her from leaving. 'Me get over *my*self? You think you're something special, don't you? Leading men on, then ignoring them. Make you feel good, does it, keeping guys hanging?' The pressure of his hands on hers was uncomfortable. She hadn't expected things to turn nasty. Clearly too much alcohol had a bad effect on this man. She hadn't been privy to that the other night. She was glad she hadn't taken the relationship further now.

'Get. Off. Me,' Connie said steadily. 'Unless you want me to make a scene.'

A memory flashed through her mind – hands on her, holding her down. Her body, weakened from too much alcohol, unable to fight against them. Her head fuzzy; a voice screaming: *Get off me.* Hers. The weight of one body, then another pressing down on hers. Connie blinked the images of that night away. The image of the hospital room, her mother holding her hand as Connie waited to be called in for the termination two months later, was harder to disregard.

'All right, mate. Come on, take your hands off her and walk away.'

Mack's voice brought her back to her current situation. He towered over Scott as he leant across and prised Scott's hand off Connie's. Scott looked as though he was about to argue, then thought better of it and did as he was told. He glared at Connie for a few seconds before turning and storming out of the pub.

'Why did you do that?' Connie snapped.

'Er . . . because the guy was hassling you. Or did I misinterpret his grip on your hand and the heated words as him being friendly?'

'I was handling it,' Connie said, rubbing the back of her right hand with her left. 'I'm not a teenager needing to be saved by her dad.' She moved to the bar and ordered another lager. Mack followed her.

'Pardon? Your *what*?'

'You were acting just like my dad would've, Mack – stepping in as if I wasn't capable of dealing with the situation myself.' Her feelings of being a helpless drunk teenager had rushed back. She *had* wanted someone – her dad – to save her back then. But no one had. Is that why she got herself into these situations? To prove she could save herself if needed? Or was she really after someone else to step in, to be her knight in shining armour? Being a psychologist enabled her to help others, analyse their behaviour, come up with theories as to how and why their lives were affected by their past. Why then was it so difficult to untangle the reasons for her own behaviour?

'I wasn't coming to save you, and I certainly don't see myself as your father figure, Connie.'

Connie's stomach dipped when she looked at Mack. His eyes were soft; his expression had taken on a hurt look. Even his height seemed diminished. She didn't know what to say. She walked back to the table and waited for Mack to sit next to her.

'Where's Lindsay?' She needed a change of subject.

'She had to take a call, told us to come on ahead. Just as well, isn't it? I mean, not that you needed any assistance, but . . .'

'Thank you, Mack. I'm sorry I was ungrateful, he rubbed me up the wrong way.'

'Clearly a dickhead.'

'Yup,' Connie gave him a wry smile, 'it seems he turned out that way.'

'Why are men these days such immature idiots? Going around picking women up in bars without knowing how to treat them . . .' Mack's neck flushed red. He took a sip from his pint and turned his attention to the rest of the team as they piled in.

'So I should go for more mature men?' Connie said. Even though she meant it in a jokey way, she too felt a flash of heat burning her cheeks.

Before Mack could answer, Lindsay walked in and headed straight for them.

'You'll never believe it,' Lindsay said in her harsh monotone. 'They've only gone and ghosted Kyle Mann.'

CHAPTER EIGHTY

Tom

He'd managed to get into Wendy's head all right. He'd calculated the common factor of the bunch of people who attended his mother's group was weakness. That's why their kids had become problematic – even criminal in some cases. It was the bloody parents. Their fault. If only they'd been stronger, not pathetically standing by and allowing things to happen. How were their children meant to grow up to be balanced and accepted in society when *they* were the ones with the most issues? Some people should never be allowed to reproduce.

We didn't stand a chance.

I *didn't stand a chance.*

Tom pushed back from his computer desk and unlocked his door. He needed to check on his mum, make sure she was complying. As he reached the top of the basement stairs he could hear the rhythmic bubbling of water bouncing on the inside of the kettle. Her back was to him as he walked silently into the kitchen.

She'd aged rapidly over the past few years. Her spine was showing signs of curvature; her shoulders constantly slumped. There was a frailty, despite her only being in her fifties. It made him sad, really. What kind of life had she had? He blamed her for a lot of what had happened, but then she'd been getting it from all angles. He couldn't help but wonder how things would've been different, had she sent his father packing as soon as the abuse began. He'd never know now, so there was no point in dwelling.

An anger bubbled away inside him, like the kettle – except his was always on the brink of boiling point. He had to control it. Sometimes he was more successful than others. Now, here in the kitchen, watching his mother make tea, he managed to flick the switch off. He must be careful not to upset her right now. He needed her on his side. It would take more this time; more effort from him to keep her happy. What could he do to seal the deal – to ensure she wouldn't go to the police, make sure she continued to protect him? He had to give her something so she believed she was doing the right thing not handing him in.

He'd tell her his plan to seek help. He knew she was concerned about him going to professionals, bearing in mind they'd need to know what exactly he'd done in order to treat him. But he could tell her he'd go online – anonymously – like she had done. That would be a start and would keep her sweet for a while. To make it really authentic, he could join a group for real – maybe to help with an addiction. He knew his gaming was addictive – he could pretend to get help for that part at least. He would tell her he wanted to change. If he cried, it would add in another layer. He'd make a big thing of it – remind her of the times his father had hurt him. That would have a big impact. He'd lay it on thick, talk about how his dad had made him who he was today. That would keep her feeling guilty enough not to let him down again.

He walked up to where she was standing, stopping inches away from her turned back. 'Morning, Ma,' he said.

She jumped, spinning around to face him, then made a sign of the cross on her chest. 'I didn't hear you,' she said, her voice breathless.

'Sorry. Look, I need to talk to you. I've been thinking . . .' He trailed off, and, taking her hands in his he began to speak the words he'd formed ready in his mind.

As planned, tears swelled as he delivered his speech.

CHAPTER EIGHTY-ONE

Angela

I'm not sure whether to believe him. Trusting him feels like something I *should* do, but it's not as if he's given me good reason to in the past. He put up a convincing argument, said the right things, seemed genuinely willing to change this time. His dad does have a lot to answer for. So do I. Did I think this last time? I can't even remember. Is he playing me for a fool?

For Tom's sake, I hope he's telling the truth.

I'm still going to plan the lock-in, though. As a backup. Because if the time comes, I have to be ready.

And there's something else on my mind too. Wendy's messages on the group support page on Thursday have been niggling at me; the anxious feelings intensifying ever since. I was awake for ages last night, sweat laying its wet film over my skin as I wrestled with the bed sheets hour after hour. Going behind my back – how dare she? She'd seemed so sweet, harmless. Now though, she's up to something. Perhaps she's trying to overthrow me.

She can't be group leader. It's not her group! If she ruins this for me, I'm left with nothing. And no way of making things right.

I won't let her take this away from me.

CHAPTER EIGHTY-TWO

Deborah

Visiting Alice has become easier since my first time on Thursday; I'm more confident, so look like I belong here. No one's questioned me the last three days – in fact, the staff greeted me with a bright 'hello' today.

I brush Alice's soft, ash-blonde hair; it seems longer than before. Fascinating how the processes of the human body continue – her hair and nails growing – despite her coma. Apparently they continue to grow even after death. I wonder how long Sean's hair is. Before he died he'd had it cut – a grade two all over – he'd had the pleasure of telling me when I'd gasped at the shock of seeing his almost-bald head.

'It'll grow back, Mum,' he'd said, giving me a hug. 'Don't you think it makes me look tougher?' He'd laughed. So had I. But I hadn't liked him with it so short. I preferred the boyish good looks his shoulder-length hair gave him. I wipe away my tears.

Maybe I'll paint Alice's nails tomorrow.

Her bruises are lightening, revealing her porcelain skin tone beneath.

'It's lovely you're spending so much time with Alice,' Graham says. I start at the sound of his voice – I'd forgotten he was there. He's standing quietly at the foot of the bed, writing his observations of Alice in her notes. He peers at me in between strokes of his pen.

Something is bothering him.

'Well, I enjoy being here, actually,' I falter, feeling my words catch in my throat. I cough. 'I like chatting to her, hoping she can hear me . . .' I suddenly feel self-conscious and lower my head.

'Edward only just left before you arrived. Did you see him?'

'Erm . . . no. I must've been in the lift or something.' I keep my eyes averted from Graham's. I can't very well tell him how I watch and wait, like an animal hunting its prey, for Edward to leave before I enter the ICU each day.

'He was thrilled when I told him you've been reading to Alice, that you've spent a few hours here for the last few days.'

I look up briefly and smile, unsure of what to say. Scared of what is coming. I turn my attention back to gently pulling the paddle brush through Alice's hair. He might go off, do something else. He doesn't. I can see him out the corner of my eye, watching me.

'Although,' Graham says, standing with the file of notes against his chest, a perplexed expression on his face, 'he said he doesn't know anyone called Diane, and, as far as he's aware, neither does Alice.'

My heartbeat gallops. Of course he doesn't know a Diane. I'd been afraid of giving my real name when Graham had asked, as I imagined it would get back to Alice's husband. And it was better for him to not know a Diane than it was for him to recall Alice mentioning a Deborah. She might've told her husband that she'd been visiting *the dead boy's mother* for tea and forgiveness for all I know. But now, on the verge of being found out, I feel a panic rising. How can I get out of this?

'Oh, that's strange,' I manage to say, 'but then, I haven't met Edward in person, only heard about him through Alice. She often spoke about him when she came over to my house for tea and a chat.' I might have overdone it with the 'often'. I smile again and place Alice's hairbrush with her other belongings.

Please go away now.

If they begin to question me, start digging and find out who I am, they'll also query why I'm here, visiting. Then they'll ensure the police look more closely into my movements on the day of Alice's attack – I'll be asked for my alibi. When the police phoned before, they'd been quite vague, only asked a few general questions. I could tell they didn't suspect me of anything, or they would've got me into the station, wouldn't they? Asked me to make a full statement or something.

I shouldn't chance being here, at the hospital. But I can't tear myself away now. It's become part of my day – part of my healing. It helps sweep away some of the guilt. I want to make the most of it, because it can't last for much longer. Graham says the doctors are planning to bring her off the ventilator soon, monitor how it affects her vital signs. If good, then they will keep her off longer. Permanently, with any luck. Then my visiting days will be over; I'll be back to my own company. My own demons. It's been therapeutic spending time with Alice, my one-way conversations have made me come to different conclusions – enabled me to see things more objectively. Something I never thought would happen.

In fact, I think I've come to forgive her. Everything I've done has worked, somehow.

But, will *she* ever forgive *me*?

CHAPTER EIGHTY-THREE

Connie

The timing of Kyle Mann's ghosting from HMP Baymead was odd to say the least. He'd been there almost two years, and had two years at the Young Offenders Institute prior. During that time he hadn't caused any problems whatsoever – no involvement in security issues, drugs, anything. Why now? Had something happened to force the governor to get rid of him to another prison quickly, without warning? All they'd told Lindsay was that, for security reasons, he'd had to be moved. Connie had a nasty suspicion security reasons meant a threat – Kyle's life in danger from another prisoner, or prisoners.

Could Tom somehow have managed to get to him through someone else on the inside? She flipped the small mobile phone over in her hand, again and again. She could try texting him, although the likelihood of him still being in possession of his mobile after being ghosted was slim. It would probably be in someone else's hands by now. Connie sat forwards. Someone who might know more about what went on and why? Well, it was worth a go. She had nothing to lose. The worst that could happen was that whoever had the mobile now didn't know anything, but threatened to use Connie instead, for their own purposes. All she had to do in that case was to destroy the phone. They wouldn't know who she was, unless Kyle had told them. And Connie doubted that.

With one ear listening out for Lindsay's footsteps, she hammered out a message. She'd keep it simple, in case Kyle wasn't the one reading it.

What happened? Has he got to you?

Connie placed the mobile back under the cushion and settled back on the sofa. Not that she'd be able to relax now – she'd have to constantly check if she'd received a message back. She'd put the phone on silent to prevent Lindsay finding out about it, although maybe now was a good time to mention its existence. Now Lindsay had finished work perhaps she'd be more relaxed and so Connie's confession wouldn't create as big a shitstorm. She'd been in the bath for the last half-hour, attempting to soak away her stressful week. Connie could tell the cases were getting to her – it was unusual to have two big ongoing cases linked in the way these were. And the fact they also connected to an older, and presumably 'solved' case, was even more unsettling.

They'd managed to get a half-decent image of fake Alice from the CCTV footage. Lindsay had taken the memory card into work, saying her techies would be able to tidy it up and enhance it. Connie's determination to find her was intensifying. She'd been annoyed at herself for letting fake Alice get away from her last Wednesday, and now she didn't have a clue where to look for her. Even if she did return to the group meeting, it wouldn't be until the last Wednesday of *next* month now. Too long. What else might lead her to the woman? She'd be keeping a low profile now, no doubt. She must realise the net was closing in, her lies had been found out. She'd be panicking that her son could be revealed as the Coleton murderer. Double murderer even. What on earth would make her believe she could keep this from getting out? That she could possibly continue to protect her son?

'That feels better,' Lindsay said. She walked in, a towelling robe wrapped around her, and sat on the sofa beside Connie.

'Good, you deserved some relaxation time.'

'What are we watching?' Lindsay looked to the television. 'Looks depressing.'

'Something about losing loved ones to cancer, but I'm not really watching it.' Connie had been too busy concentrating on the mobile and thinking about fake Alice to focus on the TV.

'Fancy a film then? I could do with something uplifting . . .' Lindsay was already flicking through the movie channels before Connie even replied. 'So you gave that bloke the brush-off?' Lindsay kept her attention on the menu on-screen.

'Scott? Yep. Kind of got forced into the situation. I wasn't expecting to bump into him when I was waiting for you lot to turn up at the pub. I should've done it sooner.'

'How come? He seemed all right when I met him on the way out of the house . . .'

'Yes, well – he came across a bit needy in the end. Wouldn't stop texting, wouldn't get the message that perhaps I wasn't wanting to take our one night any further.'

'And Mack came to your rescue—'

'He did *not* come to my rescue. I didn't need him butting in, I was dealing with it fine.'

'Ooh, okay, sorry.'

'Why does everyone think I need saving?' Connie got up. 'I'm making a drink; do you want one?'

'Hot choc, please. And don't get annoyed. You know it's only because you have people who care about you, Connie.'

'I know, and I appreciate that.' Connie smiled, trying to lighten the atmosphere as she headed for the kitchen. 'But give me some credit – I can look after myself. After all, I'm an adult . . .' She was overreacting. Lindsay and Mack had every reason to want to protect her.

They'd be even more protective if they knew she was in possession of a mobile phone sent to her by a murderer.

Lindsay fell asleep before the film ended. Connie watched her: her head was lolled back, her mouth drooping open, her steady breaths audible above the TV.

Connie swept her hand beneath the sofa cushion.

The Nokia's display read: **1 new message**

Connie swallowed hard. Glancing up to make sure Lindsay was still asleep, she tapped the button to open the text.

Nothing happened. I lied. It was only me, no one else involved. Sorry.

Connie's brow creased; she shook her head. No. Either Kyle had written this under duress, or it wasn't him at all. A shiver ran over her skin. Could it be from Tom? But how would he have ended up with Kyle's phone? Although she *had* been given this mobile, delivered to her by God knows who. The same person might well have smuggled Kyle's phone outside the prison too and got it in Tom's hands. But for that, they would've had to have been in the know – and ghosting meant that Kyle would've been transferred without warning, no time to arrange a phone delivery. Unless he had insider knowledge – or help from a member of staff.

Connie switched the phone off without responding and pushed it back under the cushion. It was no longer safe to text him – if it ever had been in the first place.

'Hey, sleepyhead,' Connie said, gently rocking Lindsay's arm. Lindsay jolted awake, sitting upright almost headbutting Connie.

'God, sorry. Some company I am.'

'I was going to say the same.' Connie laughed. 'But I'll forgive you. You'd best get yourself up to bed.'

271

'Yeah, I should get a few hours in before it all kicks off again tomorrow,' Lindsay said, rubbing her eyes.

'Do you think there's a decent chance you'll be able to find fake Alice soon, now you have a photo?'

'It's not exactly a wide search area, but when someone doesn't want to be found, it can make our job tricky.' Lindsay headed out of the lounge.

'Yes.' Connie's throat tightened, the thought of Luke being one such person flying through her mind without conscious effort. 'That's true. Night, Linds.'

Connie couldn't even think about sleep now – her mind was alert with questions and theories.

CHAPTER EIGHTY-FOUR

Angela

I'm braving going out today. I must go shopping; the cupboards are seriously depleted. I didn't know whether to stick to the smaller Totnes shops – the ones closer to the house, where my presence might be more noticeable – or be one of an anonymous crowd of people shopping in Morrison's. Either option makes my stomach twist with nerves. There's no reason why random people should notice me, or know who I am. But the paranoia is setting in. I'm sure people are looking at me as I walk down the road, like they know my secret. Do I want to risk being spotted in a supermarket? What if one of my support group sees me? I hope that's unlikely because most live outside the area, or at least they wouldn't regularly come to Totnes unless it was for our meetings.

The group are never far from my mind. None of them have spoken to me online – it appears they're giving me a wide berth. What could Wendy have possibly said to them? I feel isolated. This is the first time since I started trying to put everything right that I've felt so negative. It had all been going in the right direction. Tom's actions have jeopardised everything. I know things are sent to try us, test our faith and ability to overcome obstacles – to be worthy. But I've had my fair share now. Why am I continually being tested? When will it be over?

Am I damned to spend my life, such that it is, in a state of guilt? Hiding away from the world in my house with only my son?

I haven't dared venture into Coleton since Isabella. I don't even know how Alice Mann is doing, whether she's recovering from her attack or not – it's all gone quiet. Even Isabella's murder has lost its prominence in the news, other things now taking its place. But I wonder about Alice, whether she's still in a coma. Maybe it's better for her to be in a state of nothingness, her mind free from guilt and worry. She'll be better off if she never regains consciousness.

I decide on Morrison's. I want to be anonymous right now. Thankfully I don't need to go past Connie Summers' building to get there; I can bypass the main Totnes road, although it does mean a longer overall trip. I'll have to get a taxi home with my shopping bags. My funds are almost as depleted as my food cupboards. I'll have to be careful what I buy. Tom hasn't given me any money for a few weeks now. I'm assuming he's not collecting job seekers allowance anymore – but although I'm not seeing a benefit from it, I think he has other means of making money. It won't be by legal means either.

I've turned a blind eye.

The story of my life.

CHAPTER EIGHTY-FIVE

Connie

Connie stared into every shopfront as she walked up the hill. She was hoping for a small miracle, but even if she spotted fake Alice, she wasn't sure how best to approach her. If she should approach her at all. Her instinct was to talk to her rather than phone the police, but would that be the right thing to do? If she frightened her off, lost her again like last time, an opportunity would be wasted.

She should leave it all to Lindsay and her team. They were on the right track – one which was hopefully going to lead them to a murderer. So why was Connie feeling so conflicted? The woman had come to her, lied, and broken the law by harbouring a criminal – but she was a mother; she was protecting her young. That was her job, her role in life. How did Connie know she wouldn't be doing the same if she were in Alice's shoes? If she'd had the opportunity.

Whoever 'Alice' was, whatever she did – or didn't do – she deserved help. And for a reason Connie couldn't quite figure out, she felt she should be the one to help her. Maybe it was her link with Kyle and the first murder, or because she had some empathy – Connie was concealing enough lies herself, after all. Some things were not simply black and white. There was an awful lot of grey in this case.

Stopping at the foot of her consultancy steps, Connie turned and gazed up and down the road. Cars drove past her within inches. The road was narrow, the traffic one-way going up the hill at this point. Connie tutted. She hadn't even thought that the fake Alice could be in a car. She hadn't been looking at drivers – only pedestrians. Totnes might only be a small town, but it was still like looking for a needle in a haystack. It was even possible the woman had got spooked and left altogether. She could be anywhere by now.

As Connie settled in her office, she thought about ways of tracking her Alice down. She'd not got far with finding Deborah Taylor – her boss had been reluctant to give any personal information when she'd spoken to her, which was fair enough. She hadn't asked Lindsay if *they'd* spoken to her. Surely, as the mother of the victim of the first murder, she'd be high on their list to contact. How stupid for her not to have discussed this with Lindsay. But then she wasn't meant to be part of this investigation, even though she'd been in the loop when Lindsay and Mack had spoken about the case at her house and they'd asked her to speak with Kyle. They'd had their reasons for those times; she doubted they'd do that again. As Lindsay had said to Connie's mum, she didn't tell her *everything*. After her morning clients, she'd ring Lindsay, disclose fake Alice's urge to contact Deborah Taylor.

If she was lucky, Lindsay might even reveal something about the case's progress.

CHAPTER EIGHTY-SIX

Deborah

I have a story prepared if Graham or one of the ICU team ask me who I am, why I'm here. But no one has enquired so far today. A new high-dependent patient has moved into the bed beside Alice overnight and there's been a lot of attention on her. Although Graham is here again, still looking after Alice, he doesn't appear in the mood for idle chit-chat, getting on with his work without saying more than a few words to me. I sit by Alice's left side and eat the packet sandwiches I bought at the hospital shop.

Edward appeared pale, tired, when he left just before lunchtime. Instead of immediately entering the ICU as soon as I knew it was clear, like I usually do, I followed him. I don't know why – it wasn't as if I planned to stop him and talk to him. When he walked out of the main hospital entrance, he took his mobile phone from the inside of his jacket pocket and made a call. I walked a little further on from him and hesitated – I made a big deal of searching through my handbag, as if looking for something, so that I could stand and listen to his conversation.

As I sit here now, watching the mechanical rise and fall of Alice's chest, I wonder where Edward is. Did he go to see the person he was speaking with? Probably another woman. Has he given up on Alice? Or had he already, even before her attack? The percentage of couples who survive trauma: death of a child – or in their case, the incarceration of theirs for murder – is low. It's no wonder relationships crumble under the pressure; the guilt. Me and Nathan, Alice and Edward. Are we all now destined to become statistics? The thought makes me sad. But, I tell myself, it doesn't have to end sadly – there are still things within my control. When Alice wakes up, it would be great if her husband was here, wanting to spend the rest of their days together. If I can find forgiveness, it may have a positive impact on others. Maybe we can all come out of this better people, with a brighter future.

'We're going to have to ask you to leave, Diane.'

Graham's tone sends a chill through my bones. Have I been caught out?

I bundle my things together, hands shaking. 'Oh, okay. Is everything all right?' My voice displays a tremor.

'Yes, but Alice's consultant and team are on their way. Today's the day,' Graham declares with a broad smile.

Oh, shit. They're going to take her off the ventilator.

Today might be the day Alice Mann talks. What will she remember?

CHAPTER EIGHTY-SEVEN

Tom

His mum had been acting strange. More so than usual. The only reason he hadn't been concerned was because she hadn't ventured outside the house – she'd been holed up inside for days watching daytime TV and pottering about, cleaning things that didn't need cleaning. He hadn't even noticed her on the laptop; he assumed it was due to his warning to that Wendy woman. So, while she was in the house, separated from any other people, she couldn't be doing any harm. Talking to people who she shouldn't be.

Tom left his room and ascended the basement stairs, the creaking sounded loud in the relative silence of the house. Too silent. He quickly checked the rooms.

She'd gone out.

It unnerved him. Like a foreboding, it made his heart race as he imagined what might happen to him if he was left totally alone. Like when he was growing up. The skin on the back of his legs prickled, his nerve endings jumping with the memory of the leather belt. When his mother left was when that bastard would come for him.

Danger always came when she wasn't with him.

For him back then, but for others now.

He should try to take his mind off his mother's absence for

now. His growling stomach acted as a diversion. He was hungry, so he headed back to the kitchen. When had he last eaten something other than a Pot Noodle or crisps? Flinging open cupboards and the fridge and freezer, Tom rummaged through the sparse contents. Nothing to even make a sandwich from.

A relief washed over him. That was it, she'd only gone shopping. She hadn't gone to tell someone; she wasn't handing him over to the police. She was getting food. He hoped she'd be quick. One, because he needed to stop the hunger pains, and two, because being outside too long could be a problem. God knows what damage she'd already done going to that psychologist, talking to those pathetic group members. The thought of her being in contact with Isabella's dad was something he'd been trying to put to the back of his mind. Hopefully he'd limited any fallout from that now.

At the time, his mum's links with 'the damaged' was useful – he'd been handed Isabella on a plate. But once Isabella had told him she'd completed the first job she'd been tasked with, Tom quickly realised she wasn't as good at real-life gaming as she was online. She hadn't been aware that he knew she'd taken the easy way out. Smearing some blood on the wall was a nice touch, but nothing passed Tom by, and he was angry that she hadn't made the cut. Angry that he'd been wrong about the fact he thought she *could* have made the cut. His ultimate goal, his end game, had been to make a kill *with* Isabella. But she had evidently been unable to make an actual kill.

Isabella had served a purpose at least. And killing her on his own had been a bigger thrill than he could've ever imagined. He'd taken more of a backseat in Sean's killing, once he'd set things in motion – his kick coming instead from the power he'd had over Kyle, how he'd forced him to do most of the lead-up work. Tom had still had the pleasure of plunging the knife in, though – delivering the wound that would prove fatal. He couldn't compare it to Isabella's murder, though. He knew now that there was even more thrill to the kill if he put all the work in himself – it was more deeply satisfying to know he was the only one to have snuffed out her life. Still, it was a shame it had to be her as she'd been better than Kyle in some ways. Certainly more intelligent. Just not as trustworthy. Although even Kyle was now breaking. For four years he'd kept his silence, protected Tom. And he would again. But in a blip, which had created a huge issue, Kyle had opened his mouth.

Now the job had been done, and Isabella had been disposed of, his mother's link to that group was risky.

Kyle and the psychologist were now his biggest problems. And they needed sorting. Fast.

CHAPTER EIGHTY-EIGHT

Deborah

Since being asked to leave the hospital I've been wandering aimlessly around town – it's better than going home to an empty house, even if it does mean I keep thinking about work, or rather *not* working. I've already passed my building several times and had to consciously force myself not to go in. Now I tread the pavements, head bowed. How did it get to this? I hadn't thought my life could get any worse.

I knock into the woman, hard; my mind too preoccupied to notice her ahead of me. Had I seen her in time I would've crossed the road to avoid her because now it looks suspiciously like I've been stalking her.

'Umph,' we both say at once.

'Sorry, I was in another world.' Marcie holds up her mobile as way of explanation. 'Oh, Deborah, hi!'

'Hi, Marcie. Me too,' I say. I go to move around her, carry on walking, but her hand's firmly on mine. In this moment of awkwardness, I decide I should make the most of the accidental meeting. 'You well?'

'A bit fraught, if I'm honest – the office is madness at the moment, we're trying to land a big new commercial deal.'

'Oh?' I burn with curiosity, but refrain from asking who or

what. 'A bit short on the ground, are you?' The words are out of my mouth before I realise they could sound sarcastic.

'Yes, actually. Look, Deborah, do you fancy coming up now? We could have a chat, work out some kind of back-to-work plan.'

'Really?' Damn. I sound too grateful; desperate. 'I'm not sure,' I add quickly. I check my watch. 'I haven't got the time right now, could we do it tomorrow?' Yes, that was better. Coming across as busy is a good idea, more 'together'.

Marcie looks surprised. 'Er, yes, that should be fine. Around lunchtime?'

'That works for me, yes,' I say. And then I ask the question that's has been bugging me for a while. 'That woman, the one you were with in Costa last time I saw you, were you lining her up for my job?'

'God, no!'

'Oh. She was just a friend then? Sorry, I thought . . .'

'No, not a friend either. Weirdly, she was asking about you. You were popular that week,' Marcie brushed her long blonde hair from her face, 'a few people were asking after you.'

Marcie must've seen me frown, because she adds, 'I was really pleased about the other woman asking after you, the psychologist. It's great you've finally decided to seek some support – therapy – for your loss. It shows you're serious about getting better and back to work.'

'What psychologist?' I push aside Marcie's other condescending comment, for now.

'Um . . . what was her name again? Can't remember. Something about the seasons, ah yes – Summer, or Summers. I hope I haven't spoken out of turn, Deborah. I'm honestly very pleased you've taken positive action.'

'Yes, yes. It was about time.' I smile, then leave quickly before my confusion registers with Marcie.

Why was a psychologist asking about me? I've never even approached one for sessions, despite my doctor's recommendation

283

for bereavement counselling after Sean's murder. And why would they go digging around and asking about me at my place of work, anyway?

As soon as I'm out of Marcie's sight, I sit on one of the metal benches running through the centre of the pedestrianised walkway in Coleton's main shopping street. I rummage in my bag to get my mobile, and click on the Google icon. I type *Summer, Psychologist* in the search bar. The results show various counselling websites. I click on the one saying *counselling directory.* I scroll through the list of psychologists in the area.

There. This must be her.

Connie Summers, Totnes.

Whatever the reason this psychologist was nosing around, I'm going to find out.

I don't have anything else to do now I've been banned from Alice's side. I head back to the car park. This afternoon I will visit Totnes.

CHAPTER EIGHTY-NINE

Connie

'Yes, we have already spoken with Mrs Taylor,' Mack said.

Connie put him on speaker and began pacing the room.

'Oh, okay. I assumed you might have. Just thought I'd best mention what my Alice had said about attempting to see Deborah. Could be relevant.'

'Yes, definitely. Thanks, Connie.'

Mack sounded as though he wanted to end the call, was about to say bye, and hang up. But Connie wanted more.

'Did you get any good information, any leads from her?'

She heard a hiss of air; a sigh, she guessed. 'No, not really,' he said.

He clearly wasn't keen on giving her anything else.

'What about the link with her and Kyle now he's given a name and practically confirmed someone else was involved in Sean Taylor's murder? Does Deborah know this?'

'Look, try to calm down. Lindsay has spoken with her about it. Suffice to say, she was upset by the implication, at least at first, but then she seemed to accept that there'd been more to her son's murder – even back then there'd been questions, I suppose. Certainly, from what she said, she'd had the feeling that it wasn't just Kyle Mann who was responsible.'

'Right. Yes, all the stuff I read online, and the prison notes, all pointed to there being more than one person. No evidence though, and obviously Kyle took the fall. Is Deborah a suspect for Alice Mann's attack?'

Mack gave a nervous cough. 'Er . . . Connie, I can't—'

'Sorry. No, of course.' Connie sat back down and put the phone to her ear. She hadn't spoken to Mack since he 'saved' her, albeit unnecessarily, from Scott in the pub on Saturday and had made a weird comment. One Connie hadn't known how to react to. At least this call had broken the awkwardness. She hadn't expected to speak to Mack, she'd asked for Lindsay.

'Anyway, with luck, we might hear it from Alice Mann herself soon.'

'Oh? Is she out of the coma?'

'Her consultant informed us that the plan was to begin the process of bringing her out of it slowly today, run the necessary tests to see if her vitals remain stable, check how she copes. Fingers crossed, eh?'

'Brilliant. I know it's likely to take some time before she can tell you anything – and it depends on whether she's suffering from memory loss; post-traumatic amnesia can be common after a head injury. But yes, fingers crossed.'

The buzzing of the intercom brought a halt to the conversation.

'Sorry, Mack, got to go. Speak soon.'

Connie pressed the button. 'Hello, can I help?' She wasn't expecting a client for another hour.

'I hope so, yes. Are you Connie Summers?'

'Yes.'

'Good. Right, I'd like to know why you were asking questions about me?' The female voice was hard; accusatory. Connie's heart dipped, her mind scrambling for a memory.

'Who is this?' she asked.

'Deborah Taylor. My boss informed me you'd told her you were my psychologist.'

The penny dropped. Connie hadn't specifically told the woman she was Deborah's psychologist, but when she'd assumed that, Connie hadn't put her straight.

'That's not strictly true.' Connie spoke the words as quietly as she could, given she knew the conversation might be heard by passers-by on the street.

'Maybe you could let me in and we could argue the point face-to-face?'

Connie wrestled with the part of her brain screaming at her to not let this woman in, just in case the encounter became confrontational. But right now, Connie didn't see that she had much choice. She *had* wanted to meet Deborah, so this was as good an opportunity as was likely to befall her.

She pressed the door release button and waited.

CHAPTER NINETY

Angela

Luckily I hadn't got anything frozen from Morrison's – my impulsive detour making the return journey longer than expected. Now, as I stagger inside the house with my bags, throwing them onto the floor just inside the door, I pause to catch my breath. The taxi driver had been helpful in deviating from the route when I asked, but less so when it came to assisting me with my shopping.

I sneak the hardware store bag away from the others and hook it on the coat stand underneath my long raincoat. I'll retrieve it when I know the coast's clear and then conceal it in my room somewhere until I need its contents.

The shopping trip was uneventful – no tricky meetings with people I knew, no stares from strangers. Maybe this will all blow over, like last time. We could be all right. I note the disarray of the kitchen as I place the bags on the worktop, but no sign of Tom. I begin putting away what I've bought; I'm on automatic pilot, not really thinking as I place the tins in the cupboard. I have this weird empty feeling: a hollowness in my stomach, a void where my heart should be. I'm so very tired. My arms ache with the repetition of reaching into the cupboards and suddenly my entire body feels heavy. I'll finish this later. I need to sit.

My laptop beckons as I seat myself at the table. Half fearful, half curious, I fire it up. I have numerous notification emails, all from the support group, stating that I've been tagged in topics or threads. I also have private messages waiting to be read. A shudder rocks my body. It has been so quiet since Wendy's private messages to all the members. No one's spoken to me. Why are there so many messages now? My curiosity wanes. I don't think I want to know. The fear of what they might say is overwhelming.

I can't catch my breath. A pain grips my chest.

I can't deal with this now.

My legs shake as I walk towards the basement door. Tom's left it unlocked again. I open it, then stand and listen for a while. It really is quiet with the soundproofing he's got, although it's not like he's making much noise. I descend the steps cautiously, then knock at his bedroom door. This door has never been left unlocked. Tom swings it open.

'Have you only just got back? Where the hell have you been? Why were you gone for so long?' His eyes are wide, his pupils dilated like a cat about to pounce.

'Calm down, Tom,' I say, wearily. 'I was shopping.' Before he can question me further, I add: 'You must be so hungry. What would you like me to cook you?'

He visibly relaxes. Maybe he'd got himself worked up about where I was, who I was speaking to. Hopefully he'll be satisfied now – happy I wasn't up to anything to put him, his freedom, at risk. His reaction to my absence makes me realise it's not going to be easy. Imprisoning him in this room will take more than restraints. He's too strong for me. I'll have to use something to drug him. I have unused packets of sedatives, although they are probably out of date by now. Or, maybe if I knocked him out, I'd have enough time to tie him up. If I do it so he has just enough length of chain to get from his bed to computer, that should be fine. Although on second thoughts, I'm sure he could still inflict damage via the internet, so maybe not too long a chain. Then I'll attach the locks and bolts to the *outside* of his door.

I will keep my son safe.

I will ensure no others come to harm.

'Hatred stirs up conflict, but love covers over all wrongs,' I mutter to myself as I close the basement door, shutting my son away again.

CHAPTER NINETY-ONE

Deborah

My heart clatters against my ribs as I take each step up the stairs. The woman who must be Connie Summers is standing at the top, waiting for me. I've no idea what this is all about, why she was talking to Marcie, why she implied I was her client. But a deep, aching knot inside me tells me it's something to do with Alice Mann. I don't know how I know this, but the way everything has played out – the things that have happened – have all been because of her, or her son, so surely this must be too.

I had no time to check my hair, my face, before entering – and now seeing her towering above me at the top of the stairs, there's no opportunity to quickly titivate. I can imagine that Connie Summers has already made an assessment of me based on what she's found out from my boss though, so my appearance is unlikely to change it.

Anyway, what you see isn't always what you get. Her presumptions will be wrong, I can bet on that.

'Come on in,' she says as I get to the top and she stands aside, her left arm outstretched indicating an open door.

The room isn't big, but it's light and airy and smells of jasmine – sweet and aromatic. Connie takes a seat behind a melamine desk and leans her elbows on it, steepling her fingers. Interesting.

She seems more nervous than me. What is going on here? I take the comfy chair opposite her and settle as best I can before getting straight to the point.

'Why did you tell my boss I was your client?'

Connie Summers purses her lips and takes a long breath in through her nose; I watch as her chest rises, then slowly falls again. I maintain eye contact with her while I wait for her response. For a moment, I wonder if what she's going to say will be a lie. But then I see it in her eyes. Whatever she's about to say is the truth – she's merely weighing it up in her mind first, thinking about her choice of words rather than spewing out the first thing that comes to her. She is measured. Intelligent. I wait patiently.

'I'm sorry I gave that impression to your boss. It wasn't entirely my intention. However, I *was* trying to get information about you. I wanted to find you, to talk something over. Something important.'

She pauses now, and I'm not sure I want her to continue. I feel a surge of panic. Was Alice seeing Connie? Had she told her about coming to chat with me? Maybe Connie saw me that day, outside Alice's house. I take a deep breath myself now. I must stay calm, not jump to conclusions. I swallow and then readjust myself in the chair before speaking.

'What exactly is so important?' I hear the hint of arrogance in my voice. I'm trying to sound hoity and I don't really know why. My defence mechanism kicking in?

'Do you know Alice Mann?'

Shit. So this *is* about her. I was right.

I frown, make as though I'm thinking about it. Who am I kidding?

'Yes.' A sigh involuntarily leaves my mouth. 'I do. Why?'

'She was the reason I was trying to find you. I wanted to . . .' Connie looks away, her gaze appears to be on the window, to the world outside, then she lurches forwards slamming her elbows back on the desk. 'I don't know. I shouldn't have done it, I'm sorry.'

Her initial controlled demeanour slips away. Now she rubs her face and gives me a defeated smile.

'I have no idea what's going on right now,' I say. 'I think you need to start at the beginning, Miss Summers.'

CHAPTER NINETY-TWO

Tom

She'd cooked him a decent meal; they were even sitting together and eating at the table in the lounge. That was the first time in about ten years. The TV was on quietly in the background creating a comforting atmosphere. Normal. Almost. Tom devoured the chicken pie, his stomach gurgling with the pleasure of proper food, not just crisps and snacks. He could feel her eyes on him while he ate. She only picked at her food.

'Not enjoying it?' he said.

His mother smiled. 'It's fine, but I'm not very hungry. It's good to see you wolfing yours down though.'

'It's lovely,' he said, his mouth full.

Tom knew she was itching to have a deep, meaningful mother–son conversation – it was why she'd cooked him his favourite meal. Why else were they sitting together at the table, pretending to be just like any other family? He'd allow it, once he'd cleared his plate.

He sat back, rubbing his stomach. 'That's better. Thanks, Mum.' He really wanted to go back to his room now, back to his gaming. His mind was alert, so he should make use of it. But instead he waited. She seemed calm, which bothered him a bit. Like she knew something he didn't. Was that a smug look on her face? What did she have to be smug about? He knew how to wipe that look off. He leant forwards, locking his gaze on hers.

'Why didn't you stop him?' he said. He noted his mother taking a deep breath, and then she averted her eyes. She wasn't going to get off that easily – she was the one who wanted a deep and meaningful. 'Were you afraid he'd hurt you, too?'

Finally, she settled her eyes back on him. 'I was frightened of him, yes. But him hurting me wasn't what prevented me from stepping in. It was fear he'd take it out on you even more. Harsher punishments, longer ones. If I kept out of it, the beatings weren't as violent; his anger was intense but quickly blew over. The few times when I'd shouted, physically pulled him from you, his rage doubled and it made the whole situation worse. For you. By not getting in the way, I thought I was protecting you from something even worse.'

'Protecting me?' His nostrils flared as he breathed in sharply. 'Protecting me would've been you taking me away from him, being just the two of us.'

'Yes, I see that now,' she said, her voice quiet but steady. 'I did what I thought was right at the time. I know I made so many excuses for why I stayed, why I put up with him.'

'You should've been braver.'

'I'm not sure it was anything to do with bravery, or lack of it, Tom. I've spent many years believing I was weak, that I allowed things to happen to me – to you. And maybe it is weakness, I don't know. All I know is that I let you down back then. I won't again. I'm not going to be weak now. I'm not going to let bad things happen anymore.'

Tom wasn't sure if he should feel comforted by these words, or afraid of their intensity. If he wanted her to protect him, keep his secrets, then her being braver and stronger was key. Yet that same strength might well be a problem. It could mean he'd lose his control over her.

Tom excused himself from the table and hurried down the

basement steps into the security of his room. Locking himself in, he went straight on his computer. But instead of logging onto his gaming site, he opened the search engine. Once he'd found a suitable company that did same-day deliveries, he clicked on their homepage placing an order using one of his alternative accounts.

Now, more than ever, he had to ensure there were no other loose ends.

CHAPTER NINETY-THREE

Connie

The fact that Deborah Taylor had found her, rather than Connie being the one to seek *her* out, had thrown her at first. Watching as the well-dressed woman ascended the stairs, Connie had felt a twinge of nerves. She'd have to explain why she'd allowed the woman's boss to believe she was Deborah's psychologist, why she was asking questions about her. Basically, why she was sticking her nose into Deborah's business.

Her being here saved time, though. Connie had assumed she wouldn't be able to find Deborah on her own – and, as it now appeared Lindsay and Mack were shutting her out of the investigation because they'd got enough information from her and no longer *needed* her, she'd have been unlikely to get Deborah's address from them.

Having Deborah turn up in her office was a positive, Connie decided, and it meant she *might* be a step closer to finding Alice. Now, after Deborah's opening question, Connie began from the beginning.

'The woman I believed to be Alice Mann came to see me for the first time back in February. She wanted counselling regarding her son's conviction for . . .' Connie hesitated for a second. 'For murder. She had, *has*, huge guilt issues.'

'Sorry, who you *believed* to be Alice?'

'Yes. Turns out she wasn't who she said she was. I found out when the real Alice was attacked.'

'Why would someone purport to be another person?' Her eyes narrowed.

'My question exactly. During one of our sessions, she talked about you.' Connie noted Deborah flinch slightly but carried on. 'She told me she was planning to go and visit you, have tea.'

'She did. Have tea with me, I mean,' Deborah said.

'Really? You had tea with fake Alice Mann?'

'Sorry, I mean the real one, not the one you're talking about. She kept hanging around; I'd catch a glimpse of her outside my house every now and then. One day she rang the doorbell, practically invited herself in. I was too stunned at the time to even stop her. It was weird. It angered me, really. A bit.' She shrugged.

'What a coincidence that the real Alice was clearly doing the same, or similar, to what the fake Alice wanted to do. Tea at yours could've got very complicated.' Connie smiled awkwardly. Joking wasn't perhaps the best thing to do under the circumstances, but this new information stunned her.

Connie relaxed back in the chair. How would that have played out – if both the mothers of the killers turned up at Deborah's house at the same time? The anger would've been immense, surely.

'Exactly how angry were you, Deborah?'

'My anger subsided. Once I realised it had taken a lot of bravery for her to approach me, I calmed down.' Something in Deborah's tone was at odds with her words. Connie didn't think she *had* calmed down. In fact, she had the distinct feeling the opposite was more likely to be true.

'I'm sure it must've taken some courage, to face you knowing her son had destroyed your son's life. *Your* life.'

Deborah stared defiantly into Connie's eyes, as if she knew where Connie was going with this conversation.

'You didn't tell me why you were snooping around asking my

boss questions,' Deborah said, her chin tilted up – the change of topic intended to direct attention away from herself.

'Like I said, the Alice who came to see me talked about meeting you, she said she wanted you to know she was suffering too, that she could understand your loss, because she too had lost her son, albeit in a different way. I told her it was a bad idea. After my Alice didn't show up for her appointment, and I heard about the vicious attack on Alice Mann, I obviously assumed they were one and the same person. Then when it became clear I was wrong, I wanted to find Alice's imposter – because I really feel she needs help, and fast. The only thing I had to go on was the link with you. So I tried to find you. I got hold of your work, but they said you were on leave. My only other option was going to your office and finding someone there who'd tell me where you lived.'

'Marcie didn't tell you, though.'

'No. But in chatting with her I accidentally gave her the impression I was your psychologist. I'm sorry about that. I only wanted to know where I could find Alice. I thought you were my best shot.'

'And now you realise I'm not?' Deborah uncrossed then recrossed her legs.

'Oh, I still think you are, Deborah. I think you've more to tell, and together we can figure out who this Alice really is – and what, or who, she's hiding.'

CHAPTER NINETY-FOUR

Connie

Connie's pulse had raced for a good hour after Deborah had left – after telling her some of what she knew, or what she believed to be true: that fake Alice was protecting her own son. Having been taken in by the lies of the woman pretending to be Alice though, Connie was overanalysing now. She half-believed the things Deborah had told her, but not enough to dispel her suspicions entirely. She, too, was clearly holding onto things – guilt, half-truths and secrets. She was guarded and, Connie sensed, afraid. Her boss had hinted at there being ongoing issues with Deborah, saying she was still grieving for her son. But would that grief have found an outlet?

Mack had told her they'd spoken to Deborah – in fact, that day. Was Deborah riled by that conversation? Is that why she'd chosen to seek out Connie now?

As usual, there were more questions than answers. The biggest questions remained.

Who was fake Alice?

And where was she?

Connie's walk home from Coleton train station was impeded by the weather. A sheet of rain, blowing horizontally by gusts of wind, had met her as she stepped off the train. Now, literally two minutes after beginning the ten-minute walk, Connie was soaked. She pulled her hood up and held onto it to stop the wind blowing it back down, her hand going numb with the cold. Damn the British weather.

Her mood did not improve as she finally reached her house and lifted her head.

'Oh, for God's sake!' Connie stopped at the foot of the steps. Obscuring the bottom half of the door, again, sat a huge bouquet of flowers. Why would he do this after the pub scene? It could be an apology, she guessed. But still – he should let it go. Couldn't he take the hint?

Connie leant over to unlock the door, then bent to retrieve the dripping flowers. With a sigh, she plonked them on the kitchen worktop, droplets of water flying upwards, then scattering all over the place. She tutted. What a complete loser. Yanking the soggy card from the cellophane, she roughly opened it.

Stop looking. Check your phone.

Connie flipped the card over. Nothing else was on the reverse. She read the words aloud, frowning. Had Scott sent more texts? She peeled off her coat, leaving it hanging over the top of the door, and grabbing a towel, dried her face and hands. Then she rummaged in her bag for her phone and scrolled through her messages. A missed call from her mum. Jesus, she'd not responded to her poor mother for ages – she must call her in a minute before she forgot again. There were no new messages from Scott though. What did he mean then? He was so infuriating. She stabbed out a text, short and to the point:

Why the hell are you sending me more flowers?

Connie slung the phone on the side and filled the kettle. A large cup of coffee was required. It hadn't even boiled before a ping sounded.

That was quick. Connie snatched the phone up and opened the message:

Wasn't me. You must have another admirer ;) Scott xx

Really? The reply puzzled her – she could tell he was still keen from the almost immediate response, but she believed he hadn't sent them. So, if he hadn't sent this latest bouquet, then who had? And what did the message on the card mean?

Her heart gave a sudden jolt.

Running to the lounge, Connie swept her hand beneath the sofa cushion.

With shaking fingers, she jabbed at the power button. It seemed to take forever to vibrate into life. Her breathing shallowed. *One new message.*

Stop looking. People will get hurt if you don't stop. Do you want more blood on your hands?

Connie paced the room, the phone gripped in her hand. The tone of the message didn't sound like Kyle's. She'd worried the phone had fallen into another's hands – she'd even considered the possibility of Tom having it. Whether it was Tom or Kyle though, the fact was, those flowers were not from Scott.

Tom or Kyle knew her home address.

The memory of being held captive, beaten here in her house the year before, flooded her mind. Once again, she felt unsafe within her own property; her *home*. Her sanctuary. Anger fizzed through her veins.

She'd waited too long to tell her, but now Connie rushed back to the kitchen and grabbed her mobile. She had to speak to Lindsay.

CHAPTER NINETY-FIVE

Deborah

'It's definite, Nathan. There were two of them.'

I've had several glasses of wine, and I think I might be slurring my words slightly. The conversation with Connie Summers has played over in my head since I left her office. I had to call Nathan. I needed to talk this over with him. I know it's not like I hadn't thought there was another killer, and the police had informed me when they rang again of their suspicion that the latest murder of that girl, Isabella Bond, is linked to Sean's – but now the reality's hit me. A murderer is free – has not been punished. He can, and probably will, strike again. Alice – the one who had been seeing Connie – is hiding him. Protecting him. That's what Connie implied, anyway.

We have to find her; find *him*. He has to pay.

'How do you know?' Nathan's voice is strained.

'The police told me, for one. Although it's a psychologist who filled me in.'

'I don't understand. You're going to have to explain properly, Deborah. Are you drunk?'

He's caught on, heard the drawl of my words. I can't be bothered to lie.

'I've had a few. It's been a stressful day.'

303

'My God, it's only six o'clock! I'm coming over. I'll be there in fifteen minutes.'

He cuts me off.

I wander into the kitchen and put the kettle on. I'll make some tea, try to appear more stable for when he gets here. I don't want him judging me. How much shall I tell him? Should I admit to what I've done? He'd understand, wouldn't he? I was angry. I didn't mean to do what I did.

I'm more alert by the time I hear the key in the lock.

'Are you okay?' he asks as soon as he sees me, concern fixed on his face. I must look awful.

'I'm struggling with it all, Nathan. I thought I was coping. I'm not, though, am I?'

It isn't a question that requires answering.

'Tell me what's going on. What's happened?' He leans against the kitchen worktop, crossing his arms, and stares at me. I can't read his expression; he has an odd look on his face. His manner seems off.

'What's wrong with you?' I ask.

'I want to know what's caused this,' he throws a hand up, directed to me. 'What you've been told.'

'But you seem odd.' I can't let it go. There's something he's not telling me.

'Deborah, for fuck's sake! Tell me what you know.' His anger surprises me.

'I told you – there's another person responsible for Sean's murder.'

'Yes, I know that, but what about this psychologist? What's she got to do with it?'

'She had been seeing a woman, someone called Alice—'

'Alice Mann?' Nathan's skin pales.

'That's what she said.' I realise I'm not explaining myself well at all. I'm about to tell Nathan about fake Alice, but he disappears from the kitchen. 'Are you leaving? Where are you going?' I follow him, but he doesn't head for the front door – he walks into the lounge and sits heavily in the armchair. This is a lot for him to take in, and me blurting it all out in a rush won't help. I need to slow down. 'Sorry, I'm not making sense, I know that,' I say apologetically.

'It's my fault,' he says quietly. Then he buries his face in his hands.

'What is?'

'I wonder how much Alice told the psychologist. Did she tell you?'

I'm losing the thread of the conversation now. He's speaking like he knows who Alice is, but she only came to the house when I was here on my own. Nathan never met her.

'I'm sorry, Deborah, really I am. I should never have followed you. You were acting so weirdly, secretively. I had to know what you were doing, why you weren't going to work.'

Oh my God – he's known the whole time.

'You followed me? Where?' I sit, before my weak legs give out.

'I already knew about her coming here.' He's wringing his hands together, avoiding eye contact. What the hell is happening?

'Right,' I say, shaking my head, confusion and worry fighting for attention. 'Go on.'

'I'd been seeing her too.'

Finally he looks at me, his eyes filled with tears.

'Seeing Alice?' A hot ball burns my stomach, my heart bangs fast and I hear it in my ears. I want to scream. A darkness clouds my eyes. 'You mean *she* was the other woman?'

I hear words, muffled, far away – Nathan's face swims in front of mine.

I close my eyes and put my hands over my ears.

I don't want to hear any more.

CHAPTER NINETY-SIX

Angela

What they're saying isn't even true.

My fear of them finding out I'm not really Alice is quickly supplanted. That isn't what they're saying. They know I can still access the online group support page – they haven't struck me from the group, or blocked me – so they must want me to read this. After all the secret messages Wendy sent each member in private DMs, now it seems there's one everyone can see. My eyes skim furiously over the words.

> She pretends to care about us all, but she doesn't: she's an evil, selfish woman. Her son isn't even in prison, much less a murderer. She's got a mental disorder – she's a pathological liar who's been manipulating us, telling us she's this brave victim of her son's crime – all for the attention. Alice is not to be trusted.

It's hugely exaggerated. She's taking pleasure in spreading vicious lies about me and everyone's jumping in, adding their ridiculous assumptions to the thread.

I have to keep moving, my muscles are jumping with annoyance;

anger. I pace the room as far as the kitchen door and back. Where has this come from?

Of course. There's only one person who could've told Wendy this pack of lies.

My son.

Why is he doing this to me? I get he's got unresolved issues about how I didn't protect him from his father, but to go to these lengths – and all these years later – after everything I've done for him, is cruel. Evil. He saw me that day in Coleton with Wendy. How long had he planned all this? My stomach rolls, a sickly sensation spreading upwards.

I'm going to vomit.

I'm not going to confront him, there's little point. Nothing will be gained. My group won't believe me even if I try to repair the damage Tom's done. I knew time was running out, and it's even more apparent now. It's real.

I don't think I can keep this up.

I know I've lied to myself for a long time; I'm not even sure what the truth *is* anymore. It's never been to purposely deceive anyone, apart from myself, perhaps. Self-preservation. Seeing Connie had begun to make a difference; I'd delved inside myself, questioned my decisions, my reactions to events – to things I thought were beyond my control.

They weren't. I know that now. Maybe Tom is right. I deserve to be punished for not protecting him. Everything that happened, that's happening now, is because of me. Why have I kidded myself into thinking I could put it right? Maybe I really am as deluded as the support group messages are saying.

And I *did* pretend to be someone else. All this time I've thought it was Tom who needed help – but maybe it's me.

It's quiet in the basement as I pass by the door. I can sneak out without him knowing. He's got food down there so he won't emerge for a while. I'll have enough time to finish getting what I need; I hadn't wanted to draw attention to myself when I was in the hardware store yesterday by buying everything in one go.

Only a few more items and I'll be ready.

CHAPTER NINETY-SEVEN

Connie

Neither Lindsay nor Mack were at the station when she'd called yesterday evening. Connie hadn't wanted to talk about the phone message with anyone else, so she'd hung up. This morning, having realised Lindsay had pulled an all-nighter – her bed unslept in – Connie decided not to bother calling the station, instead taking a different path. She dialled HMP Baymead.

'I need to speak with you, Jen. Are you free after work?'

Connie heard Jen umming – she sounded flustered, distracted. She'd obviously not caught her at a good time. Eventually, she said, 'I think it should be fine. Can you meet me in Coleton at four-thirty?'

'Great, thank you – in the Country Table café?'

'Yep.' And she hung up.

Connie held the phone away from her ear, staring at it as if it held something more. The dead tone was proof there was nothing further. Jen was obviously busy, but it didn't excuse her brusqueness. It wasn't like her. Had Connie done something wrong? She'd refused to go into the prison again following the last meeting with Kyle, but she'd completed her report satisfactorily. Maybe it was something to do with him being ghosted. The timing had been coincidental to say the least. Hopefully, come this afternoon, she'd have some answers.

While she was in the mindset to make calls, Connie dialled her mum. The ringing carried on for ages. She mustn't be home. Either that or she was in a mood with Connie for not contacting her for so long, and was ignoring it. Just as Connie was about to cut the call, she heard the receiver being picked up. She'd have to pile on the pleasantries, apologise quickly for her lack of communication, for being a rubbish daughter – get in first before her mother could chastise her and make her feel worse than she already did.

'Mum? I'm so sorry for being useless and not calling. How are you?'

The silence stretched. Connie's heart thrummed.

'Mum, are you there?'

Stop looking. People will get hurt if you don't stop. Do you want more blood on your hands?

The words echoed in her head. *Shit.*

'Hello? Mum?' Connie's words wobbled.

'Connie?' Her mum's voice was strained.

Was someone with her? Was someone going to hurt her? Tears burned Connie's eyes.

'Mum!' she shouted.

'Sorry, love. Was trying to get my cake out of the oven, thought I'd hit the speaker button . . .'

'For fuck's sake,' Connie said breathily.

'Connie! No need for language like that.'

'Sorry, you scared me. I thought there was something . . . something wrong.'

'Well, you've not bothered to call for so long, anything could've been wrong and you wouldn't have known, would you? Could be stone-cold dead in bed, the neighbour's cats all taking chunks from me . . .'

'Oh, Mum, that's disgusting.'

'I read about that very thing happening, you know. In Hampshire last year.'

Connie butted in before the conversation deteriorated any further. Her heart rate had settled now she knew her mum was safe. It was silly her thinking that Tom could've got to her. The mobile message, the flowers – they were scare tactics, that was all. He wouldn't risk further exposure, surely? The police were after him for suspected murder; he'd be stupid if he wasn't keeping his head down, maintaining a low profile right now.

After a fifteen-minute conversation, mostly about Isabella Bond and Connie's job, the call ended. It was a relief to know her mum was safe, although hearing the pain in her voice when she spoke about Isabella was almost unbearable. Some wounds never mended – particularly deep ones that were never allowed to heal before the scab was picked at again. Her mother's lost son was one such wound. Knowing she had information that could repair it, leaving only a scar from the past hurt, was something Connie was struggling to live with. Each time she spoke with or saw her mum, the need to tell her grew ever stronger.

CHAPTER NINETY-EIGHT

Connie

Connie chose a table at the rear of the café, the low one with the small leather sofas either side. It was cordoned off at the back because it was near to closing time, but the owner, who Connie knew well, said she and her friend could sit there and be undisturbed for an hour or so.

Jen breezed in through the door spot on four-thirty. She gave Connie a kiss on each cheek before sitting down. Her usual calm persona had slipped, her face appearing hard, weary. Connie got the impression all was not well at HMP Baymead.

'Thanks for coming,' Connie said.

'Sorry for my abruptness on the phone. It's all a bit cloak-and-daggers at the moment.' Jen was sitting stiffly on the edge of the sofa, her gaze not settling on Connie.

'What's going on? Is it to do with Kyle being ghosted?' It was best to get straight to the point, and she knew Jen would be the same if the roles were reversed.

'Well, you know my old saying, "What's the worst that can happen?" – it appears that the worst might be me getting the sack.'

'No way, really? What the hell . . .' Connie's mouth dried. The moment she'd gone back into Baymead, seen Kyle Mann, she'd opened a can of worms – and now she was afraid what Jen was about to tell her was somehow due to her.

Jen rubbed her hands over her face, making a low groaning noise. 'I didn't see it, not until it was too late.'

'See what?'

'What he was doing. How could I have missed it, Con? I'm a trained psychologist, and the signs were all there. It was obvious: the manipulating tactics, the conditioning . . .'

Connie put her hand to her mouth. Jen couldn't be talking about herself, surely? She shook her head.

'I don't understand, Jen. What has happened?'

Jen leant forwards conspiratorially, talking in a hushed whisper. 'Kyle was ghosted for security reasons. He'd been beaten in the showers, and the same men grassed him up as having drugs and several mobile phones.'

Heat rushed to Connie's face. Mobile phones. *Shit.*

Jen finally made eye contact. 'When the officers sprung his cell though, they only found one mobile. But it's not that uncommon really, is it? And usually it's an adjudication and time added to their sentence. I didn't think it was such a big deal; didn't contemplate getting involved past the usual risk factor assessment and writing it in a report.'

'I'm taking it that somehow you *are* involved though?'

Jen didn't answer her question. 'I'd been so busy. You know how stressful that place can get. I haven't slept properly, and the workload is ridiculous for our small team. When it happened, I'd been spending more hours there than at home. It's not as if we get paid any extra, is it, Con?' Jen stooped to pick up her drink, then carried on. 'It's when mistakes happen, when we're tired, not really concentrating – that's when we might not realise prisoners are manipulating us.'

Connie didn't like the direction the conversation was heading. She was afraid Jen already knew about Connie being given the mobile.

She was even more afraid it was Jen who'd delivered it to Connie's house.

CHAPTER NINETY-NINE

Tom

Now the excitement of the past two months had slowed right down, Tom's mood crashed. As far as he could tell he'd covered all bases, but his mind wouldn't let him rest – it kept swilling names around his brain, morning and night. He couldn't escape them. Sean, Kyle, Isabella, Connie . . . Sean, Kyle, Isabella, Connie . . . then, every so often, *Mum*. At least two of the names were permanently taken care of now, only their ghosts could plague him. But Kyle, Connie and his mum – they were very much alive and, despite the measures he'd taken, there were no guarantees they'd keep their mouths shut. He wasn't even sure how much the psychologist knew; how much his mum had told her. Maybe nothing of importance – in fact, his mind kept reminding him that he'd probably drawn attention to himself, made things worse by intervening.

You're an idiot, Tom. Why are you so fucking dumb? His father's nasty, needling voice wormed its way into his head at every given opportunity.

Ultimately, it was Kyle's fault. If he'd stayed quiet, as agreed, none of this would be an issue now. He never imagined it would be Kyle who let him down, although if he was honest, he could understand it to a point. Fucking psychologists, getting in your head, messing with your mind. She'd broken him by using a dirty, underhand tactic. Dragging his mother into it was low. Tom felt bad for what happened to his mum. The mother–son bond was a complicated one. Kyle's mum wasn't bad – she'd looked after him, kept him safe. Kyle had had huge problems with his old man too, but *his* mum had ensured he'd never got physical with Kyle. She'd *protected* him.

It was a shame Alice had to come to harm.

But Tom's need for another adrenaline rush, to kill again, had been too risky; his belief that he was invincible was faltering. He had to make a new plan to figure out how he was going to get away with what he'd done. There was no scapegoat for Isabella's death like there'd been with Sean.

Tom's chest tightened. For the first time, he realised that no plan, however clever, would ensure he got away with it. There were too many uncertainties, variables he couldn't control; he'd involved too many people. In trying to cover up what he'd done, stop others talking, all he'd accomplished was to lengthen the list of people who could bring his world crashing down.

He banged his fist against his temple again and again until it was numb.

The answer to his problem screamed inside his skull. He may not have any other alternative.

It was time to do a runner.

Connie

Connie took a few sips of her latte, giving herself a bit of time to compose herself before speaking to Jen again; she didn't want to give too much away by rushing in with questions that made it obvious she was in possession of a mobile sent by Kyle. She had to think carefully. Realistically, if Jen had agreed to take the phone out of the prison for Kyle and deliver it to Connie, then she'd have been sacked already, surely? Unless they didn't know. Jen had said Kyle had been accused of having several phones, but only one had been found. Maybe there hadn't *been* another one. Could Kyle have manipulated Jen into supplying the mobile to give to Connie, then told Tom the number so he could also contact her directly? As much as Connie didn't want to know, she felt she had to. If she played it carefully, even if she'd got it wrong and her mobile delivery had nothing to do with Jen, she shouldn't implicate herself.

'I'm scared to ask really, Jen. But how exactly are you involved in this?'

Jen looked over her shoulder, her gaze flitting around the café. 'I'm not sure I should say, Con. I've said too much as it is and I'm in enough shit.'

'No one can hear us. It's not as if I'm going to sell the story to the papers, you *know* that!' Connie was on edge, impatient to know – her anxiety levels increasing by the minute.

Jen smiled. 'Don't even joke.' She tucked her hair behind her ears. 'It's been such a horrible few days. I'm a rubbish manager.'

'No, Jen, you're not. You're under pressure, that's all. Mistakes happen when there aren't enough staff and resources. Some prisoners are quick to spot weaknesses and take advantage. If you've done something wrong . . .' Connie couldn't finish the sentence. If Jen had done something wrong, she'd be hung out to dry. Like Connie had been. She had no words of encouragement. Not ones she believed in anyway.

'Do you still have Kyle's mother as a client?'

'No,' Connie said. Jen was changing the subject and Connie wanted to get it back on track. If she expanded, telling Jen that all along it had been someone else, not Kyle's mum, she'd get embroiled in a different conversation; get further away from the topic of the mobile phone. 'Was Kyle using the mobile to contact his mum, do you think?'

'Oh, I don't know. I'm not sure they could tell – phone numbers were saved to SIM, and they didn't recover that.'

'So,' Connie said, squinting, 'I still don't get what this has to do with you?'

Jen gave a long, drawn sigh. 'Like I said, I didn't realise, didn't *see* it. Right under my nose, and I failed to notice.'

'What? Notice what?' Connie was beginning to lose patience.

'Okay, look. I'll tell you in a roundabout way and you can make the obvious link. *Someone* was caught taking in contraband for prisoners.' Jen flung herself back against the sofa.

Connie pursed her lips tightly. The obvious link would be Jen herself, given all she'd said so far. Connie blew out air.

'Wow, Jen. This is big.'

'Yes. And I feel responsible. Well, because I'm the manager, I *am* responsible. That's why I think they'll sack me.'

The relief oozed from Connie. Jen *wasn't* talking about herself.

Good job she hadn't jumped right in with her accusation. She felt terrible even considering Jen would do something like that.

But if it wasn't Jen, then who had it been?

'It'll be a capability hearing first. You know how much they love those.' Connie shivered at the thought. 'I'm sorry all this has happened. I'm sure you did your best under the circumstances. You can't keep an eye on your staff all the time, not when they're all over the prison delivering one-to-ones and sessions. It's impossible when the prison is so low on the ground, staffing-wise.'

'Yes, that would be true. *If* it was a member of staff whose role involved prisoner contact . . .'

'Oh, shit.' Wherever this was going, it wasn't good.

'Yup, it wasn't even someone who was meant to be dealing with inmates.'

Connie's mouth gaped. The penny dropped.

It was Verity.

'I can't believe it, how—'

'Don't say her name!' Jen widened her eyes at Connie.

'No, I won't. She lives near you, doesn't she?' Connie whispered.

'A few doors up, in the new block of flats. It's a bit awkward to say the least. We've been told we can't have anything to do with her – I've had to unfriend her on Facebook and everything. I feel so guilty, Con. When I should've been managing her, I was too busy using her to run errands.'

Heat flamed at Connie's cheeks. Verity had been escorting *her* around the prison, she'd been in close contact with Kyle on each of those occasions, and Connie couldn't swear to it that they hadn't spoken. At some point, he'd obviously seen a way in, or out in this case, and he'd picked someone who wasn't used to dealing with prisoners. Someone more naïve than most. It was *her* fault. If Connie hadn't pushed Kyle into talking – by revealing information about her client she should never had revealed – he'd have had no need to draft in outside help. The way Verity had gone from bright, bubbly and chatty to moody and quiet made more sense now. *That* was the reason Verity had acted oddly the last time she'd seen her – she'd just delivered the mobile to Connie's house. The poor girl had probably been petrified of being caught out.

Connie would have to go to Torquay and see Verity, not only to apologise for exposing her to Kyle, but to find out who else she'd been pressured into delivering mobile phones to.

CHAPTER ONE HUNDRED AND ONE

Deborah

We'd talked through the night and for most of today. The pot of tea I'd made to see us through sits unfinished in the centre of the coffee table; the bone china cups contain undrunk tea, a film of milk clinging to their sides. The words we spoke were too important to interrupt with sips of warm liquid. I slump against Nathan on the sofa, silence now falling around us. The revelations have simultaneously lifted us, and weighed us down. Why did we wait so long for this honesty? Why did it take something so bad to happen again before we realised?

I'm glad this has all come out now. I think it's right we both know the full story. We owe it to each other – to Sean. I stare at his photo, his face young and bright; full of wonder. I sense Nathan doing the same.

I don't know where to go from here.

My eyelids are heavy from lack of sleep and swollen from crying. I allow the warmth from Nathan's body to comfort me.

Before decisions are made, before mine and Nathan's lives are changed even more – and irreversibly – I think I'll go and see Connie Summers again.

Tomorrow.

For now, I'm going to close my eyes. Lie here with Nathan.

For one last time.

CHAPTER ONE HUNDRED AND TWO

Connie

The pendulous black clouds crowded in, forcing out the light, making the early evening sky look as if it was night already. Connie told herself it was the weather making the block of flats look so ominous. The reason for her visit didn't help.

Jen hadn't given any specifics about which flat was Verity's, and she hadn't dared ask. It couldn't be that difficult to find her though, as, usually, the outer door had a list of occupants alongside a door buzzer. Worst case scenario, Connie would have to ring thirty-odd buzzers before she got the right one. Standing at the entrance, trying to decipher the names, Connie realised she should've called Lindsay first. Or Mack. But she was here now, and there was little point in wasting any more time.

The name **V. Payne** was halfway down the list. The surname immediately stood out; she remembered seeing it alongside the list of names on the whiteboard inside the psychology portacabin at Baymead. Connie pressed the button and waited, shifting her weight from one leg to the other. Verity probably wouldn't let her in. She'd realise Connie had found out, so why would she knowingly unlock her door to her?

A click sounded. Connie pushed the door.

She frowned. Verity had let her in without even asking who it was. Connie looked above the entrance before walking in. There must be a camera, and Verity had seen her. But she couldn't spot one, which gave her cause for concern. Why would she let someone in before checking their identity? Connie hoped it *was* Verity who had operated the door's release. This thought gave her pause and she hesitated, holding the door for a moment, considering her options. Why *wouldn't* it be Verity? Connie let the door slide from her grip, hearing the clunk of it locking behind her. She was being overdramatic, she needed to get a grip of herself. She mustered her confidence as she continued inside.

As much as she hated lifts, the stairs felt like one hassle too much, so she took it. It looked clean, decent. As she stepped out on the eighth floor, she was greeted by a blur of movement, a pull on her arm and the sensation of being dragged backwards.

'You weren't followed?' a nervous voice in her ear asked.

Connie yanked herself away and stood facing Verity. 'No, I wasn't.' She straightened her jacket.

'Good. Hurry up.' Verity disappeared around the end of the corridor. Connie followed.

The flat was fairly open-plan with a small kitchen off the square lounge area. Verity closed the door as Connie walked through, locking it and sliding a chain across. Her behaviour jangled Connie's nerves. Verity moved further inside and began rearranging the sparse furniture. Sitting on a leather cube, she looked tiny. Vulnerable. She indicated for Connie to sit on what appeared to be a single chair-bed. She waited for Verity to compose herself, watching as she took a few slow, deep breaths. Finally, Verity's posture relaxed, her face losing the tension visible moments before. Connie gave her what she hoped was a reassuring smile, then began asking questions.

From what Verity said, she didn't openly blame Connie. She said she'd been stupid to even speak with Kyle, let alone run an errand for him, however innocent it'd seemed. After a few minutes of talking, Connie found out it had all started when Verity had accepted a letter from Kyle. A simple enough request: *Can you post this out for me, Miss?* He'd cornered her while Connie was with another prisoner. When no one else was watching. Verity had been shocked he'd spoken to her, thinking he would only ever speak with Connie. She'd said that in a way she was flattered; the fact she'd gained his trust made her feel important, her role more significant than usual. Of course, Kyle knew full well it was against the rules. The post was given to the wing officer and sent out at specific times. If a prisoner missed the post, it waited until the next lot went.

'I didn't *think*!' Verity said. 'He seemed so genuine. I was so worried the card wouldn't get to the hospital in time – he was scared she'd die before he got to say he loved her. So, I felt sorry for him, took it, said I'd post it for him – I couldn't see the harm.'

This one simple act of kindness was all it took. Once she'd done one thing, he had her. The next thing he asked her to do was bring him in cigarettes.

'When I said I couldn't do it, that's when he got funny. Said I'd already done something illegal for him . . .' Verity shook her head. 'When he explained what I'd done with the letter was wrong, how I would get the sack if he told the other staff, I realised I'd made a huge mistake. And, of course, I then brought in contraband for him because I was scared of what he'd do if I didn't. When he asked for the next thing, I knew I was in the shit, that there was no turning back. A mobile phone. He even offered me money.' She gave a dry laugh. 'By that time, he said that if I didn't agree, he'd inform my manager. No skin off his nose, he said. It would be an adjudication for him, a few days added to his sentence. Didn't matter, he wasn't ever getting out anyway.' Tears dripped off Verity's chin, she swiped at them with her hand. 'What a mess.'

Verity had brought in two mobile phones for Kyle as instructed. A prison sentence for her if she was caught. She knew she was in too deep then, and didn't know what to do, who to turn to. She said she was going to go off sick, but the fear of what Kyle would say while she wasn't there kept her going to work.

'He said taking the mobile to your house was the last thing he'd ask of me.'

'But it wasn't?'

'I went to my friend in security, wanted to tell him, indirectly, that I'd got involved in something bad. But he ended up mentioning that Kyle was going to be ghosted. I was walking back to the psychology office when Kyle approached me again. God, I dreaded walking the grounds on my own. Anyway, he was bruised, said he'd taken a beating and thought something was going down. Oh, God, Connie! I told him. Said he was about to be ghosted. He gave me another mobile – I assume it was the one he was contacting you on – he told me to get it out of the prison and await instructions.

'And what were the instructions?'

'To wrap it in a bin liner, take it to a specified area, and leave it. He said someone was going to pick it up. Said that was it, all I had to do, and it would be over.' She took a deep breath. 'I was so relieved to know he'd be leaving, and believed it really was over, Connie.'

'Where did you have to leave it?'

'The text I got first said Baker's Park, in Coleton. But I got a second, about twenty minutes later with a change of plan. I had to go to Totnes, leave it in a bin near the top end of town.'

Connie's pulse tapped hard against her wrist. 'Where, *exactly*?'

'Castle Street, near Totnes Castle. Why?'

Connie didn't think it was a coincidence it was a Totnes drop; pinpointing a specific location might get her a step closer to finding fake Alice and her son. 'Did you see anyone when you dropped it?'

'I didn't hang around, really. I did see someone – nothing more than a figure walking up the hill from the opposite direction I was going in.'

Connie took her mobile phone from her pocket and clicked on

Google Maps, then thrust it in front of Verity. 'Show me where he was.'

Her gut feeling was that it must've been Tom. It all fit. So, he did have the phone, and it was him who'd been sending the messages. The threat. The flowers. There were more questions Connie had to ask Verity – she had the feeling leaving the mobile hadn't been the end of her involvement.

As soon as this visit was over, whatever she found out, Connie would *have* to call Lindsay.

Connie was cold, her fingers and toes numb. It had taken longer than she'd hoped to get a train back to Coleton from Torquay; several had been cancelled and she'd had to wait on the platform for an hour for one that would be stopping at her station. She kicked her shoes off as soon as she walked into her hallway and padded into the lounge, her freezing feet sinking into the soft carpet pile. The house was quiet. Disappointment flooded her. No Lindsay.

She'd left Verity on the phone speaking to the police. Her heart ached for the poor woman – it was a terrible situation to be in. But by the time she'd finished going over all the options with her, Verity had concluded herself the only thing she could do was inform the police. Connie had agreed it was the safest option – if she didn't, she'd always be targeted, open to being blackmailed. Connie had agreed to give a statement at a later date.

With the TV on mute and finally feeling some warmth curled up with Amber on the sofa, Connie closed her eyes. As she drifted, she thought she heard the buzz of a mobile. Whether it was hers or the hidden one, she couldn't tell. She was too exhausted to look.

Connie

Lindsay's bed had not been slept in for the second night in a row.

Connie closed the door on the empty room and went back downstairs. She'd awoken a couple of times in the night, the unfamiliar shadows created by the lounge furniture disorientating her. She'd thought about going up to bed but had obviously fallen asleep again each time. The stiffness in her joints and muscles proved she'd at least managed a few hours.

She'd really wanted to talk over the evening's developments with Lindsay. At least the police had been contacted though, so she'd done her bit. Almost.

Guilt twisted her gut. She'd encouraged Verity to go to the police with what she'd done, but asked her to leave out the part about taking a mobile phone to Connie's house. It wasn't that she wanted to withhold information – she knew she had to tell them – but she'd rather talk to Lindsay or Mack, explain it to people who knew her. Would understand.

After picking at her breakfast, Connie showered and dressed. She had two clients booked in for the day; unfortunately, they were spread out. She'd try to change one, bring their appointment forwards so she had the afternoon free.

Approaching her counselling office, Connie spotted someone hovering outside.

Deborah.

Connie didn't really need the distraction, but if she was here again so soon, something must be on her mind. Maybe she'd found out who and where the imposter Alice was. She quickened her pace, rushing across the road in between the slow-moving cars.

'Hello,' Connie said. 'Wasn't expecting to see you.' She walked up the steps, putting her key in the front door.

'Before you go in,' Deborah said, tugging on Connie's arm, 'can we take a little stroll?'

A little stroll. Connie hesitated, then pulled the key from the lock again, resigned to the fact her morning wasn't going to go as she'd planned.

'Where was Alice, the fake one, holding those support meetings you told me about? Can you show me?'

'Well, yes, I guess. It's not far from here.'

Connie turned to her left and began walking back down the street. Deborah kept up beside her. Neither of them spoke until Connie stopped outside the church.

'The hall, up the alleyway,' Connie said, pointing to the narrow walkway that ran alongside the church itself.

'Why?' Deborah stood stock-still, her voice a whisper.

Connie didn't answer, assuming it was rhetorical.

'Why did she lie about being Kyle's mother? I don't get it.' Deborah turned now and faced Connie. 'After four years of keeping her son's crime to herself, she chances him being found out by pretending to be someone she's not. Why would she do that? What was the point?'

'I think the support group was her way of making amends. Or something along those lines.' Connie tried to explain how Alice's guilt, her misplaced sense of making things right, had compelled her to take actions most people wouldn't even consider.

'As I told you on Monday afternoon at my office, she thought she had a connection to you because you'd both lost your sons.'

'That's exactly what the *real* Alice Mann said.'

'I imagine they're going through the same patterns – trying to forgive themselves via the real victim of the event. You.'

'But, according to what you said before, you believe that fake Alice hasn't lost her son at all. She's hiding him.'

'I think she must have thought she knew him, who he was. Had brought him up, believed him to be a certain type of person, then he turned out to be something quite different. In a sense, she *did* lose her son.'

'How fucked up the three of us are,' Deborah said, staring off into the space behind Connie. Connie turned, almost expecting to see someone directly behind her, then realised Deborah's eyes had glazed over. What was behind those eyes?

Secrets. Lies. The truth.

'When did you last see Alice Mann – how long before her attack?' Connie put her face in front of Deborah's to regain her attention.

'What?' Deborah blinked repeatedly, then focussed on her. 'Um . . . I can't really remember.'

'I'm trying to put some pieces together that don't quite fit yet—' The ringing of her mobile interrupted her. At first she was annoyed at the bad timing, but then she saw it was Lindsay calling. 'Sorry, Deborah, two secs.' Connie pressed Accept, and angled her body slightly away from Deborah's. 'Good, I've been trying to get hold of you. Why haven't you been home the past two nights?'

'Sorry, Connie, no time to explain now. Alice Mann has fully regained consciousness and we've been with her, waiting for her to talk. What she remembers about her attack is *very* interesting.'

CHAPTER ONE HUNDRED AND FOUR

Deborah

Hearing just one side of the conversation makes me nervous. Connie has turned away from me, but I catch snippets of her dialogue:

What does she remember?

Is her memory to be trusted?

There are some gaps, I assume?

Connie shifts further away from me, and I lose her words. She's now at least five paces ahead. Then she stops, turns, and I catch something. I'm frozen to the spot.

I had a feeling there was more to it. What do you want me to do?

Alice *has* remembered. She's told them.

I have to leave now.

While Connie continues to talk on the phone to decide what she's to do with me, I make a break for it, sneak away with a family group heading up towards the centre of town. I keep in step with them.

What precisely has Alice revealed?

I might not have long. I must call Nathan, warn him of what's to come. I stop walking with the family, and turn to check if Connie is in sight. Good, she's not. I continue to the top end of

Totnes, creating as much distance between us as possible – it's the furthest point from the car park where I've left the car, though. I only put enough money in the machine for an hour, so I'm bound to get a ticket. I'll worry about that later – it's the least of my problems right now. I duck into a narrow side road, Castle Street, I note from the sign, and dial Nathan.

'Nathan, it's me.' I hear his breathing, can almost feel his chest rising and falling. I'm glad we spent last night together. At least we had that before the truth came out.

'What's the matter? You sound out of breath.'

'I'm sorry, Nathan. I think it's time.' I screw up my eyes, but it doesn't prevent the tears from escaping. 'Alice Mann is out of the coma. And I think she's told them about the attack.'

'Oh.' He sounds defeated. 'Are you sure?' his voice monotone.

'I was with Connie Summers when she took a call from the police. I heard her. It's over, isn't it? Can we run from this, do you think?'

'No. No, love, we can't. We discussed this yesterday – the probability of it happening. I'll wait here for you to come home. We'll face this together.'

My arm goes limp, the reality of the situation numbing my muscles, and the hand holding the mobile bangs against the wall, sending my phone flying across the road. I lurch forwards to get it, almost knocking into a woman walking along the pavement opposite. We make the briefest of eye contact, but in that moment, I recognise her. I've seen her somewhere before.

It takes me a minute or so to remember, but then I'm sure. It's the woman from the café – the one who was with Marcie. The one who's been asking questions about me.

'Hey!' I'm yelling. Yelling and walking quickly after the woman. Some other people are staring at me, looking to see who I'm shouting at, who I'm following. I don't care. This woman, whoever she is, needs to answer my questions.

Angela

She's not going to give up easily. I hear her shouts following close behind me as I attempt to scuttle away. I knew I shouldn't have chanced making another run to the hardware store. I had a weird feeling it was a mistake. I thought it'd be safer if I got one more lock. For peace of mind. Tom's restraints hadn't lasted once he came around. I'm worried his repeated banging, and throwing himself – and furniture – at the door, will weaken it and he'll escape. Lord knows what he'll do if he gets out before he's calmed down. I hadn't intended to do it, but the opportunity arose, so I had to take it. If I hadn't, he'd have left; run away. A few weeks will give him the chance to consider what he's done. Time to reflect. Keep him away from temptation. It'll give me time to figure out what our future holds.

My heart pumps so hard it feels as though it'll burst from my chest. Deborah's footsteps get closer. She's got almost ten years on me; she's fitter. She's going to catch up with me unless I can lose her. It's my own fault. After Alice's attack, I'd had to carry on my plan without involving her – if I hadn't been so intent on meeting Deborah, and been seen speaking to her boss, she'd have been none the wiser. She would've walked on by now, instead of chasing me down. I wonder what she knows? Does she have any idea who I really am?

Part of me is intrigued. After all, I'd wanted the chance to talk to her for so long. My whole plan of approaching Alice first, facing Deborah together, somehow trying to make right what Tom had done, had been all-consuming. All I thought about. Now I have the opportunity, and what am I doing? Running away.

Running away. Ignoring the issue. I'm weak. I need to be stronger. Face up to the reality.

I stand still, breathing heavily, heart still banging noisily in my ears.

What can she do to me? We're in a public place. Perhaps I'll ask her to go for coffee, talk things over just like I'd planned before things turned sour. I could get my chance at redemption after all.

Deborah

It's her. It's got to be – she looks remarkably similar to Alice Mann, like she's imitated her. Her hairstyle and colour is almost identical. For a moment I'm stunned into inaction, then a surge of adrenaline pushes me forwards once more. She's stopped running from me now. I stand opposite her, staring. Wondering.

'You're her, aren't you?'

She looks quizzically at me, but it's brief. The pretence falls from her expression.

'Shall we get a coffee?' she asks.

The moment couldn't be any more surreal. This is fake Alice. *This* is the mother of Sean's other killer. The one that got away.

'What's your real name?'

'It's Angela. Angela Killion.' She utters the name like it's alien to her tongue; the first time she's spoken it. Perhaps it is, for a while at least.

'Okay then, Angela. Well, you know who I am, and I know you've been wanting to talk to me. So, let's do this.' I walk purposefully towards the main shopping street, to the closest café. Angela follows.

*   *   *

The similarities between Alice Mann and Angela Killion end at the colour and style of their hair and clothes, and the fact both their sons are responsible for Sean's murder. There's something dark about Angela – an unnerving quality about her. It puts me on edge; chills the blood in my veins. Alice Mann's motives for meeting me were clear, obvious, and although she wasn't exactly straight with me on our initial meeting about who she was, or later when she failed to mention she'd been seeing Nathan, she exuded a genuineness. Something I'm not sensing now from Angela.

Angela has a different agenda.

'This isn't how I saw things working out,' she says.

I bite the inside of my cheek while I try to form a reasoned response in my head. I clench and unclench my fists underneath the table.

'Oh. In what way?' It's not exactly how I envisaged my life going either. But I don't think she's talking about the bigger picture.

'I'd wanted to talk to you for the longest time, had planned it all out, knew just what to say. Of course, the whole plan went awry when someone attacked Alice. I thought if we came to you together, you'd see we were all the same.' Angela's eyes are so wide that she seems almost manic. I'm glad we're in a public place. I think she's unpredictable. I also think she's unwell, even more troubled than I'd imagined – and that's the only reason my anger, my hatred for this woman, has dampened now I'm sitting with her. I wish Connie was here. But if I hadn't run off from her, I'd never have met Angela. Fate has done this.

'If you'd come to me together, I'd have turned you both away,' I say with a tight smile.

'Oh, but I wasn't going to say who I was, not to begin with. I was going to be there as support for Alice.'

I can't help but frown. I've no idea what was, *is*, going on in Angela's mind. She's not making sense.

'To be honest, Angela, I'm not sure I understand – or that I want to understand.'

334

'It's because I *couldn't* be honest, you know? Not while I was protecting my son.'

'So, what was your point then? The reason you went all around the houses to try to meet me?'

Angela wriggles in her chair and leans her upper body across the table, closer to me. I instinctively inch away from her.

'Okay, well, I couldn't come and see you on my own, could I?' She lowers her face slightly, and I see her take a deep breath. I feel she's about to say something I'm not going to like. I keep my eyes steady on hers as she speaks again. 'How would I be able to talk about what happened to your son, what my son did? I needed a way in.'

I hear my own sharp intake of breath. Does this woman have any idea of how the words she is uttering will affect me? Isn't she afraid of what I might do? As it is, I can't *do* anything – it's as though my body has frozen. I have little choice but to allow her to carry on.

'Alice Mann is in the same position as me,' Angela continues, now in full flow, 'although Kyle is in prison, obviously, and I wanted to convince her we were in the same boat by telling her my son was also in prison for murder. If I could get her to trust me, open up to me about her guilt and talk about the fact we are *all* experiencing loss, then I could talk her into meeting you to help her with her guilt issues. Maybe even get your forgiveness. And by proxy, *I'd* be getting your forgiveness too.' Angela sits back, her speech delivered. She's smiling, as though she's proud of herself, of her plan.

I've been sitting, listening, mouth gaping with increasing disbelief. And now, seeing the smile still playing on her lips, my initial shock subsides. I finally recognise the hot, crushing pain in my chest – the one I experience when I'm looking at my newspaper cuttings – as my rising anger.

This woman is deluded. More to the point, she is selfish and evil. She wants *me* to forgive her and her son to make *her* feel

335

better – so she can redeem herself. And she was all up for manipulating me and Alice by lying to us to get what she wanted. To protect her murdering bastard of a son.

I have to let some of this out. 'Angela, that is the most ridiculous thing I've heard. You need help.' I have to get away from this woman, and quickly, before I do something else I regret. I get up to leave, but she snatches my wrist and pulls me back.

'Please. I'm sorry my son did what he did. He's not a bad person—'

I yank my hand from hers and lower my face so it's directly in front of hers. 'Don't. Touch. Me.' Spit lands on her cheek. 'Your son is a murderer and hasn't even been punished. He is every bit a bad person. As are you. Neither of you have my forgiveness.' My heart is drumming so hard I feel faint, but I manage to turn and walk out of the café with my head held high.

I escape a parking ticket despite being over my time. A tiny bit of good fortune in an otherwise bad day. I replay the bizarre chat with Angela Killion over in my head as I drive out of Totnes. She's obviously protecting her son, and I get that – to a degree. But it should be out of her hands now. He has to face justice. I had waited, hidden inside a shop, for Angela to exit the café, then I'd called the police anonymously from a payphone after watching her disappear down Castle Street, the road I'd first seen her on an hour prior.

I couldn't hang around to see how it played out. I have my own troubles to face.

On the radio, 'Ironic' by Alanis Morrissette plays, and I laugh. I drive the rest of the journey home to Coleton in a cloudy haze. Flat. Emotionless.

When I see Nathan, it's like a dam bursting and spewing its contents in one huge torrent – years' worth of emotion let loose. Sobs erupt from me uncontrollably, like violent hiccups. His arms fold around me. His grip is tight, reassuring. I feel the weight of his head as he rests it on mine. It takes a few minutes for me to recover; Nathan waits patiently until I quieten.

'You've been a long time, I thought you were coming straight home after you called me.' His lips brush against my hair as he speaks, sending little electrical sparks shooting across my skin.

'I ran into the mother of Sean's *other* murderer,' I say, my voice thick with the remnants of mucous and tears.

He pulls back from me, his eyes wide. 'What?'

'I know. It's been a hell of a day.' I rip off a sheet of kitchen roll to wipe my nose.

'What did you do? Did you call the police?'

I give him a sympathetic smile. 'I did, but anonymously. I could only give them a rough idea of the direction she was headed, I didn't want to waste time following her. I needed some time with you before the police come here. They're probably on their way now. I half-expected squad cars to be lining the pavement when I drove up.'

'I'm so sorry, Deborah. For everything.' He runs a finger across my cheek.

'I know. I'm sorry for jumping to conclusions. But you never put me right when I accused you of having an affair . . .'

'I know. I said I *could* have, if I'd wanted to. And like I told you yesterday, the temptation was there. I came so close. But ultimately, I couldn't do it. You're all I want. But I want all of you. Not merely the shell, the pretty exterior.'

'And just as we've finally been honest with each other, it's going to be torn away from us. I'd been so afraid of Alice waking up, telling the police what I'd done. I'd no idea you were terrified of the same thing.'

'I really didn't mean to hurt her,' Nathan says. He looks away from me briefly. I know it's because he's ashamed.

'I know, I know.' My tears begin again – I am surprised I have any left. His admission late on Monday night came as a massive shock. All the time I'd been blaming myself for Alice's condition, it had been due to Nathan. If I hadn't heard it from him, there'd be no way on this earth I'd ever have believed it.

'The strength came from deep within me. It came with the anger – a rage I didn't even know I was feeling. You know I've never hurt a woman before.' Nathan's eyes are pleading, and tears prick at my eyes as I give the briefest of nods in acknowledgement.

'I'm so scared, Nathan.'

'Me not coming forwards isn't going to help my case either, is it? God, if only I'd walked away when you did. Followed you home, confronted you, rather than gone into Alice's house.'

'Our lives have been filled with *if only* and *what if* ever since the day those bastards took our boy. We're not to blame, *they* are.' I walk to the window, convinced I hear sirens. 'What are we going to tell the police?' I ask.

'The truth. Alice wasn't badly injured when you left her, Deborah. She was just in shock from you lashing out at her, so there's no need for you to feel afraid. I'll tell them what happened, that I was attempting to get her away from me, but she kept coming at me, wanting me to hold her, comfort *her*. Like she was the one hurting. God, Deborah. Something inside me snapped. I grabbed her, shook her. One second I was shouting at her and the next, she was falling away from me. It was like time suspended for a few seconds as she hung, helplessly in the air, her arms flailing trying to grip mine to stop herself from falling backwards. I didn't help. It was me who caused her head injury. You and I know all too well what it's like to have been affected by others' hideous actions. I have to take responsibility for mine now.'

Isn't it ironic, plays inside my head.

338

CHAPTER ONE HUNDRED AND SEVEN

Angela

There isn't much time.

All the rushing I've done today has made me dizzy, sick; and I'm so very tired. I bend over the kitchen sink retching, but nothing comes up.

Things are falling around me. Caving in on me and Tom.

Tom.

I make a sign of the cross. Dear God, if ever I needed guidance, it's now.

When *they* come, which they will now Deborah knows who I am, they will find him locked in his basement room. He'll look awful. He's bound to have bruises, and it'll look like I've beaten him, somehow taken him prisoner. Although that part is quite true. It was *for* him, for his own good. For the safety of others.

They'll understand that, won't they?

They won't understand Tom, though. Why he did what he did. That it's not really his fault. My stomach gurgles with worry. This isn't how I wanted it to end.

I push back from the sink and drag an almost-empty bottle of vodka from the back of the cupboard and take a swig. The liquid is welcome, the burn as it goes down feels good. It's not going to help my dizziness, but right now I need courage.

There's no noise coming from the basement as I press one ear against the door in the hallway. Of course, there wouldn't be. The soundproofing does its job well. I unlock the wooden door, tentatively stepping down into the basement, then creep across to Tom's bedroom door. No banging, no throwing of furniture. He's worn himself out. Either that, or he's succumbed to thirst and finally drank the water I left for him – the crushed sedative pills dissolved in the bottle should be enough to ensure he won't have much awareness of what I'm doing.

What *am* I doing?

Why did it have to come to this?

I step away from his door. Maybe there's another way.

I walk back up to the lounge and pick up the phone.

Connie

Connie had cut Lindsay's call short when she realised she'd lost sight of Deborah, saying she'd call back shortly. She'd scoured the streets for a while but had to get back to the office for her next client. She couldn't believe Deborah ran off like that while her attention was taken talking to Lindsay. She was the one who'd sought Connie out after all, so why suddenly disappear without warning? Maybe Deborah had caught wind of the discussion – Connie couldn't remember what she'd said, whether she mentioned Alice's name during the call. Had Deborah been spooked by the fact Alice had regained consciousness?

She had a while to wait for her final client, so she took the opportunity to ring Lindsay. She answered on the first ring.

'Oh, wow, you must've been sat on the phone. Right, sorry to have ended the call so abruptly earlier—'

'Don't worry, but speak quickly, Connie – things are moving rapidly here.'

'Oh, okay,' Connie said, flustered by Lindsay's statement. 'I wanted to say something about Verity Payne, the woman who took in contraband for Kyle Mann.'

'Yes, we've taken her statement. She's going to be charged, Connie.'

'Will it be taken into account she was conditioned? That she shouldn't have been in contact with prisoners?'

'She's got a solicitor. She'll be well briefed, I'm sure.'

'Right, well I'm not sure if she said, I'm guessing not, but I was the one she gave a mobile phone to, so that Kyle could message me. I think Tom now has Kyle's mobile – he contacted me through it the other day.' Connie sucked in a lungful of air, waiting for the reprimand.

'Jesus Christ, Connie. Really? Well, that's fan-bloody-tastic, isn't it? Why didn't you tell me? Withholding information—'

'I didn't know it was in Tom's hands.'

'But you knew Kyle was breaking the law having a mobile phone in prison, Connie. Shit, I haven't got time for this now.'

'I'll give a statement,' Connie said. 'Don't get angry.'

'I'm not angry. Well yes, actually, I am.' There was a pause – Connie could hear Lindsay take a deep breath. 'Hopefully there's no harm done,' she resumed, her voice calmer. 'We had a breakthrough with the gaming community: someone came forwards to say they'd been targeted – groomed, pretty much. And they gave details, which, together with Verity's evidence and an anonymous call giving a rough location as to the suspect's possible whereabouts, means we've got a solid lead.'

'You know where Tom lives?'

'We've narrowed the area significantly – surveillance teams are there now along with Mack. I don't think it'll be long before we pinpoint his precise location.'

'So, you know who the fake Alice is as well then?'

'Look, I'll fill you in once it's all over, okay? All you need to do is stay well away from everyone involved, Connie. Can you manage that?'

'Well, yes. I don't know where she is, do I? Therefore, I can't get involved.'

'No, I guess not. Anyway, have to go, our team's getting ready to move. See you tonight.'

The words *See you tonight* echoed in Connie's ear. Lindsay sounded confident she really would be home. That this case, and its linked one, would be tied up. Connie had her fingers crossed that Lindsay's optimism wasn't misplaced.

The caller ID on Connie's mobile was withheld. That wasn't unusual – it was the case with many prospective clients. But when Connie answered and heard the voice on the other end of the line, she took a sharp intake of breath.

'Help me, Connie.'

The words sent a shockwave through her.

'Hello? Alice?'

'It's Angela.'

'Angela,' Connie repeated – saying her name to imprint it in her mind. Finally, she had the real identity of fake Alice. 'How are you?'

'Been better,' she said. Her voice sounded echoey. 'I'm a bit lost, Connie, you know?'

The sadness in Angela's words tugged at Connie's heart. Yes, she could imagine she did feel lost, afraid of what her future held – of what Tom's did.

'Where are you now, Angela?' Clearly, Lindsay and her team hadn't got there yet.

'At home. Sitting outside Tom's room.'

Connie realised this was the first time her client had been completely honest with her, not obscuring her own or her son's identity. What she was telling her now was the truth. Was it because she knew it was over, because she felt defeated? Connie tried to remember things Angela had told her over the sessions. She quickly accessed the notes she'd made in 'Alice's' client file on the computer, her shoulder cradling the phone against her ear.

'What's Tom doing?' Connie asked as she scanned the file.

'He's sleeping.'

'Are you sure, Angela? It might be that he's out, and that's why it's quiet?'

'No, no. He's definitely in there. I made sure of that. Didn't want him to harm anyone else. Didn't want harm coming to him.'

That sounded ominous, but Connie pressed on. She didn't want her to put the phone down.

'Okay, well, it's good that he's safe. Are *you* safe, Angela?'

'Yes, I'm fine. I wanted to know if you could help us? Keep Tom from going to prison?'

'I can help in a way.' Connie needed to be careful what she said, she didn't want to give false hope, promise something she couldn't deliver. 'I can talk to the police and tell them about your reasons for not coming forwards. I can also write a statement about how you felt you were let down, how when you tried to get help with Tom you were turned away. But other than that, I'm afraid I can't stop the police from taking Tom into custody, Angela. He'll be assessed there though, he'll get the support he—'

'But they'll take him from here, from me, won't they?' Connie heard the desperation in her voice as it cracked. She must feel as though her control was slipping away.

There was no point Connie lying. 'For the moment, yes.'

'I've let him down, then.'

'You haven't let him down. He is an adult, he's made his own decisions, acted of his own accordance – you didn't make him do the things he's done.'

'But we both know I didn't stop him either, and even when I knew he'd done wrong, I didn't do anything about it. There were no consequences to his actions. Not until now, anyway.' The power came back to her voice as she said this, and Connie sensed the shift in her state of mind. Without seeing her, she couldn't be sure, but it seemed to Connie that there was every possibility Angela may act rashly. Could she talk her through this episode – at least keep her on the phone until Lindsay's team arrived there?

'And the consequences now are?' Connie had to keep her talking.

'I've drugged him. Tied him up, locked him in his room. And today I met Deborah, and she knows who I am. She's bound to have called the police. They're going to be coming now. Those are *his* consequences, but what are mine?'

'I really don't know, Angela.' Connie's mind scrambled for the right thing to say. It sounded as though Angela had come to a critical point; the fact she'd drugged and bound her son showed an escalation in her thinking – panic. In that frame of mind, she could be dangerous. Connie wanted to blurt out questions: what had she done to Tom, where was he, what had she given him, when? But in order to help him, Connie had to play it safe – and talking about Deborah would buy some time, perhaps keep her calm. After all, it sounded like she'd finally achieved her goal after months of trying. 'You say you met Deborah? How did that go?'

'Not as I wanted. You were right. I knew you were, but when the opportunity was right there, I had to take it. I had to try. I knew she might not forgive me, but I thought she'd at least understand where I was coming from. I thought she'd accept we are alike, that we've both lost our sons, you know?'

There was a gap – a silence followed by a bang – then Angela's voice came back louder and more urgent.

'She didn't, though. Maybe one day she will. After.'

'After what?'

There was no response from Angela, but Connie could hear movement, shuffling. A key in a lock?

'Angela, what are you doing?' she shouted.

'He's coming round, Connie. I have a chance to save my son. I have to take it.'

'Angela, don't do anything hasty, I can get you help, I can. But Tom can't be trusted to stop killing. Don't let him go, let the police take him. Please, Angela. He needs professional assessments. Let me get that for him, for you. Where are you? I'll come to you right now.'

Angela's voice, slow and steady, calm, stated her address, then added, 'You'll be wasting your time, though. Tom will be long gone.'

The phone went dead.

Connie

Connie didn't waste time putting her coat on or phoning Lindsay; she'd told Connie her and the team were about to make a move, so she wouldn't pick up the call anyway. Running up through the town centre, pushing past people, dodging cars as she crossed the roads, Connie's mind worked quickly. She had to try to assess the situation as soon as she reached Angela's house. She had to ensure she wasn't putting herself or Angela – or the police's investigation – in jeopardy. As loud as Lindsay's voice was in her head – the one screaming 'leave well alone, do *not* get involved' – Connie's instinct remained stronger. With luck, the police were already there preventing Angela from helping Tom escape. But she had to make sure.

If she could get there quickly, then she might be able to give her professional judgement – at least see that Angela was handled correctly before they took her away, too. Having Connie there as support, a familiar face, might go some way to easing the situation.

As Connie approached Castle Street, she could see police vehicles at the end of the road, their lights flashing, casting blue shadows on the walls of the surrounding houses. She ran, and as she reached Angela's house, caught sight of Mack.

'Mack!' she shouted, her breathing shallow from the running. 'What's happening? Where is Angela?'

'What are you doing here?' Mack's voice was harsh.

'Angela called me, about ten minutes ago. She needs help, Mack. I think you should let me go in first.'

'No way, Connie. That's out of the question. We don't know what we're dealing with yet and Lindsay would rip my nuts off if I let you in. Tom Killion could be armed, so you're not going in there, putting yourself and the team at risk.' He grabbed Connie's arm, pulling her clear of the doorway.

'She said she'd drugged him,' she panted. 'She locked him in the basement. But she said he's regaining consciousness. I think she's going to help him escape.'

Connie watched helplessly as a team of armed officers prepared to enter the property. Mack moved away from her, informing the team of this new information. Connie followed him.

'Let me in after them, Mack, please. I can be of assistance here.'

'With respect, Connie, you're more likely to get hurt, and I'm not having that on my conscience. Sorry. Lindsay told me to secure the house with my team. I'm not having you make me look a twat just in time for her to see when she reaches the scene in a minute. Now, move.' This time, he grabbed both of her upper arms and shifted her away from the cordon.

348

CHAPTER ONE HUNDRED AND TEN

Angela

I knew Connie would be helpful. It's such a shame I didn't start seeing her earlier, before things got out of hand with Tom. It's too late for her input now, she won't get here in time. Anyway, as much as she believes she can help, she can't – speaking to her confirmed that.

There are no noises coming from inside his room now. I think something must've just fallen; it wasn't Tom coming around at all. I need to go in and check him, though.

I fetch the keys to all three external locks – the basement light catches them as I turn them over in my hand; they are shiny-new, a bright silver. The locks are tight.

As I finally unlock and unhook the last padlock, I hesitate.

What if Tom's behind the door with a heavy object, waiting to pounce and attack me? I quickly pop the padlock back, click it in place. I'll get a knife, just in case.

As I return from the kitchen with the large carving knife, I see blue lights glowing through the glass of the front door. Am I too late?

Adrenaline shoots through me and I run down the basement steps with a new purpose. Armed and prepared, I unhook the lock once more and, my breath held, gingerly open the door. He's on his side on the bed, eyes closed. I continue to stare from the doorway, listening for rhythmic breaths which might indicate he's asleep, not merely pretending. The water bottle lies empty on the ground beside his bed.

He must've drunk it. I wonder how long ago; how long I have until he wakes.

Whether I'm waiting for him to wake, or for the police to burst through the doors, it's painfully obvious I haven't got long with him. I perch on the edge of the mattress, looking down at his face. He's perfect: his skin soft and blemish-free, his hair thick. His long eyelashes rest on the tops of his full cheeks. He is my baby. My flesh and blood.

I brought him into this world on Wednesday 16th November 1994. He'll be twenty-four next birthday.

As I stroke his face with the backs of my fingers, he stirs and mumbles. I grip the knife more tightly.

'Please. Let me out,' his voice slurs.

He has no energy. His limbs move slightly, but they seem loose and useless. I think I gave him too much sedative. I let the knife drop to the floor. I'm not going to be needing it – I'd only brought it in to shock him anyway, and maybe gain some time. He's not going to hurt me.

'Darling, I can't. You know that.' I bend my head to kiss his cheek. 'I have to protect you, like you want – you said it's what you wanted, didn't you?'

'But . . . not—'

He loses his words. Instead he moves his eyes to look at me. I see the pain, the pleading within them. I can't bear it.

A noise from upstairs.

A banging.

They're coming.

I get up, shut Tom's door and lock it from the inside.

They'll take him, imprison him for the rest of his life. He stares at me, and an understanding passes between us.

'Mum . . .' He's attempting to lift his head, trying to get up. 'Let . . . me . . . go.'

There's only one way I can do that.

Hatred stirs up conflict, but love covers over all wrongs.

'I brought you in to this world, Tom.' A pressure consumes my chest. I reach across him and pull the pillow from under him. 'I'm the reason you're in this situation . . . It's up to me to get you out of it.' I grip the corners of the pillow, my knuckles as white as snow-capped mountains. 'This is for the best. I love you, Tom,' I whisper into his ear, before placing the pillow over his face.

He struggles beneath me, but I'm stronger than him this time. Maybe he doesn't have enough fight in him. This is what he wants – he too must know it's the right thing.

I feel his muscles slacken.

I hold his body next to mine as the life slowly leaves him.

Forgive me God, for I have sinned.

Connie

The firmness of Mack's words, and his grip on her, convinced Connie to back off.

'Okay, okay, Mack. You can let me go now.' She rubbed at her arms.

'Make sure she stays there, will you?' Mack instructed a uniformed police officer. Then he followed the team in.

Connie moved her weight from one foot to the other, her heart still racing. She checked her watch, straining to hear what was going on. Minutes later she saw members of the team rush out.

Had they been too late? Had Angela and Tom escaped?

'What is it, Mack?'

Mack's expression was neutral, but his features seemed to have lost shape, his jawline slack. Connie could hear a mixture of sounds and voices, police radios, and now, creeping closer, ambulance sirens. She watched as paramedics were ushered inside the house, itching to get inside too, to see Angela. Was she hurt? Or had she done something reckless, like attempted to take her own life?

'Let me go in, Mack.'

'No, Connie. It's a crime scene.'

'Did he escape? She let him bloody go, didn't she? I tried to get here quickly to stop her—'

'Connie.' Mack's hands grasped her shoulders firmly and he lowered his face to hers. 'He didn't escape. Not in the way you mean anyway.'

Connie frowned. 'What do you mean?' But the question hung unanswered in the space between them as her attention shifted to Lindsay and DC Clarke getting out of their car. Connie took a deep breath awaiting a reprimand as they rushed over to her and Mack.

'What are you doing here?' Lindsay's eyes narrowed at Connie, before shooting a contemptuous glance in Mack's direction. But she didn't give her time for a response. 'Stay out here, Connie. You're not here in an official capacity.' Lindsay turned her back and prepared to enter the house with Mack and Clarke.

Connie's mind raced. What on earth had happened in there? People were going in, but no one was coming out; there seemed to be little urgency. More people in white paper suits littered the small lawn, some taking photos, some preparing to go inside the house.

Connie waited. She should probably go home, watch the unfolding events on the news, but she couldn't. Not now; she was committed. She had to know. The time passed slowly, with Connie walking back and forth along the narrow road, not daring to venture far from the scene in case she missed something vital. Finally, there was movement – figures were exiting the door with a gurney between them. But it wasn't the paramedics. She followed the progression of the zipped body bag as it was carried then placed just inside the plain black transit van. Connie burst forwards, running towards it.

'Who is that? Is it Angela? Tell me!'

'I'm sorry,' the older of the two men said. Connie presumed he was the police's designated undertaker. 'Who are you?' He spoke softly, probably aware of the fact she may be a family member or friend.

'I'm Connie Summers, Angela's psychologist.'

'You'll have to speak with the SIO, sorry.' And the undertaker turned away from her as he slid the body fully into the back of the vehicle. Connie continued to watch in shocked silence as a police car escorted the van, and the body, away from the scene.

What the hell had gone on inside that basement?

'Connie!' Lindsay's voice cut through the crowd.

Connie pushed through to get to the front garden, the policeman giving her a warning look not to come too near the scene.

'What's going on, Lindsay?'

Lindsay stayed on her side of the police crime-scene tape. 'Angela Killion is fine. The paramedics are still tending to her here, and then she'll be taken to the hospital as a precaution.'

That came as more of a relief than Connie had imagined. Losing another client would've been too much to contemplate.

'How did Tom . . .' Connie began, but Lindsay's hand, held palm up in front of her, made her stop.

'We'll discuss this back at the station. I'm going to get Clarke to take you now, wait for me there.'

This time Connie didn't argue.

'Mack's rounding everyone up,' Lindsay said as she handed Connie a coffee from the police station vending machine.

'What do you mean, everyone?'

'Loose ends, Connie. We have a few people to talk to yet, and there are still some suspects in connection with Alice Mann's attack.'

'Oh, yes. Our conversation earlier seems so long ago now, I'd almost forgotten what you said about Alice's memory of her attacker.'

'I thought we'd head to the hospital now, actually. I know it's late, and it's been one hell of a day, but Alice is keen to talk to us. Are you up for it? It might be good for you to see the real Alice Mann.'

Connie was surprised Lindsay was involving her. 'I thought you'd want me as far away from the case as possible?'

'Well, in this instance, I think it would be useful to gain your professional opinion.'

'Sure, but aren't you busy with Angela Killion?'

'We will be, but not yet. We can't see her at the moment. She's being checked out by a doctor, then undergoing a psychiatric assessment.'

'I'm glad of that, she's clearly a very troubled woman.' Connie swallowed the last of the coffee, the bitter taste making her screw up her eyes. 'I really wish I could've helped her, seen her sooner – or even realised what was going on. I find it so hard to believe this all ended with her taking her son's life like that. It all seems so tragic.'

'I don't think you can take any blame – no one would've figured out her lies. If it wasn't for the real Alice being attacked, it's likely she'd still be getting away with pretending to be someone she wasn't. Makes me shudder, Connie, thinking about how she was protecting Tom, knowing what he'd done. If she'd informed police, done the right thing, poor Isabella Bond would still be alive and so would Tom, then justice could've been served properly. Somehow, this all feels like an easy get-out.'

'Not for Angela Killion,' Connie said with a sigh.

Connie and Lindsay headed for the police-station door just as Mack was reaching there from the opposite end of the building.

'I'm going to the Taylors',' Mack said to Lindsay. 'I'll meet you at the hospital.' He held the glass door open for Lindsay, and Connie followed, ducking underneath Mack's arm. Lindsay was already at the Volvo before Connie stepped outside. 'Hang on a sec.' Mack placed a hand on Connie's shoulder.

'Everything okay?' she asked.

'I wondered, if you were up for it, whether later on you'd like to—' He shook his head, sighing. 'No. Of course not. Stupid question, sorry.' He turned his reddened face away.

'What exactly are you asking, Mack?'

'I thought, given the way I ruined your possible future relationship with that idiot in the pub by jumping in where I clearly wasn't wanted, whether I could make it up to you by taking you for a drink? It would be nice to unwind a bit after all this . . .' His words left his mouth in such a rush that Connie almost laughed, assuming he was joking. The coy look on his face informed her he wasn't.

Mack and her having a drink. Socially. Alone. Without Lindsay.

Why would he even *want* to have a drink with her?

'Um . . . it's been a really long day . . .'

'Another time perhaps.' He turned away and strode towards a police car where DC Clarke was waiting for him, his smirk obvious even from where Connie was standing. She went to walk away, then hesitated. If she'd learned anything from the last few weeks, it was that she was still holding onto too much of her past. She'd accepted that what happened to her at that party when she was a teenager was a huge factor affecting her adult life: her actions, thoughts and beliefs – but she hadn't *dealt* with it, or done anything concrete to overcome the problems. It was this holding her back, preventing her from forming a steady, serious relationship. Not that Mack was suggesting anything other than a friendly drink, of course – after all, she'd had a fling with his son. But, having seen, through Angela, how badly things could go when you didn't effectively deal with the past, maybe now was as good a time as any to begin to rectify it.

'Mack!' She shouted after him. 'You going to bother waiting for me to finish my sentence?'

'What?' He turned so suddenly his legs twisted and Connie thought he was going to fall over himself.

'I was going to say, it's been a long day, so yes – a drink would be perfect.'

His face creased with a surprising grin. 'Excellent.'

Connie smiled. The first move made. She climbed into the passenger seat next to Lindsay.

'You can take that smug look off your face, Wade. It's a drink, that's all.'

'Absolutely. Wasn't going to say a word.' And she switched on the engine and they drove out of the station car park.

Alice

My hospital room is filled with people. I was moved to a private room once ICU staff were happy with my progress. I'm still in pain, but the morphine pump helps a little. The police have brought a psychologist with them. And Deborah Taylor. At first I was confused, but the nurses said it was her name I spoke the second I was brought out of my coma. They must've presumed there was a reason I mentioned her name.

Now they hand me some photos – a few different ones depicting what seems to be the same person but taken at varying angles. My head throbs, and my vision hasn't returned to what it was prior to my injury. But I recognise the face they're showing me.

'This is the face I remember hovering above mine. A wide smile as she took my head and smashed it down onto the floor.' My mouth dries so quickly that I have to pause to take another sip of water. My eyes flick from the photograph to Deborah, and back again. 'There was a split second of searing pain, then nothing.'

'You are certain this is the person who attacked you?' DI Wade asks me.

'Yes, that's the woman who attacked me.' I say with almost 100 per cent certainty.

Almost.

I smile across at Deborah. She's endured more pain and sorrow than anyone should have to bear. She's suffered enough.

My ICU nurse, Graham, told me she visited me regularly; practically every day.

Tears sting my eyes and hurt my skin as they travel down my bruised face.

Deborah puts her hand on mine. I reach up and pull her into a hug.

She forgives me.

I feel forgiveness releasing us both.

Connie

'These look fantastic, Bev.' Lindsay took a chocolate muffin from the plate being offered.

'I hadn't seen you or Connie for so long, I thought I'd better treat you. You might visit me more often then.'

'Oh, Mum. You don't have to bribe us with baked goods!'

'I don't know, the offer of food's the only thing that appears to have worked so far.' Despite her mum's jokey tone, Connie squirmed a little. She had felt guilty enough about her lack of communication and visits to her mum, without her openly chastising her.

'Must be a huge relief to have got this case over, Lindsay?' her mum continued.

'Yes, it's been a very emotional case all round. So many lives affected. I'm pleased with the eventual outcome, although it's a shame we didn't wrap it up sooner, before more people were harmed.'

'It's the *what ifs*, isn't it?' Her mum looked thoughtful. 'You can't go through your job, life even, thinking in that way. Believe me, Lindsay, it can drive you insane.'

Connie looked away. How long could she avoid her mother's eyes and dodge the elephant in the room – the one her mum didn't even know existed?

Her mum jumped up. 'I forgot the tea. Sorry, will go and make a pot now. You two talk amongst yourselves.'

'It's easier said than done, not thinking about the what ifs though, isn't it?' Connie said, her fingers pulling the ruffled paper cake case away from the muffin.

'I know you're going to tear the whole thing apart, analyse it, and worry about what you could've done, what you should've done – and probably what you *shouldn't*, but at least the truth has finally surfaced.'

'Well, there's still the outstanding matter of me withholding information,' Connie said.

'You've put forwards a convincing case – firstly relating to client confidentiality, then your fear of possible repercussions if you spoke out about the mobile phone. Those factors will be considered. The worst is over. Maybe everyone can move on now.'

Connie sighed. 'I imagine some of those involved have been able to find closure, one way or another.' She took a bite of the muffin.

'Speaking of being able to move on,' Lindsay said, her voice low. 'What about . . . you know . . . do you think it's time?' Lindsay gave an awkward nod.

'I'm not sure,' Connie said with a mouthful. 'You know, I've been having this sensation of being watched again?'

'God, Connie, no. You didn't mention it.'

'To be fair, we've been a bit preoccupied with other things . . .' Connie raised her eyebrows then continued. 'At first it frightened me, because of last year, obviously, but also because of everything that happened with Kyle and Tom. Then the fear went, and I began to wonder if it might be Luke.'

'You really think he's back here, despite what your dad said?'

'I don't know, really. But it's weird – I feel calm. Protected. Like Luke's keeping me safe from harm.' Connie noticed Lindsay suddenly sit bolt upright. Her mum walked back in with a tray in her hands.

361

'You're talking about Luke,' she said. It wasn't a question. 'I'm not deaf as well as daft, you know. If Luke's name is mentioned, I hear it above the sound of any whispered conversation.' She placed the tray on the table, then slumped down on the sofa, her eyes not focusing on Connie's but instead gazing into the distance. 'Loss affects people in many different ways,' she said after a moment. 'I'm still coming to terms with it after all these years. I can even understand Angela's actions in a sense. Protecting your children is so natural, it's all I'd wanted to do. What I wish I'd accomplished. I mean, I know she took her job of protecting her son to the extreme, but I don't suppose her intentions were all bad.' A sad smile flitted across her face.

'I agree, partly,' Connie said, shooting Lindsay a wide-eyed glance. 'Angela needs help – her reasons for doing what she did were skewed, not a normal reaction to events. I hope she's fully assessed while in custody, and can access the services she requires.'

'She'll be lucky.' Her mum reached forwards and began pouring the tea into the mugs. 'Very difficult to escape the past. It's always affected me. However hard I've tried over the years, the pain has never gone. I'd do anything to turn back the clock, make different decisions.'

A horrible sensation, empty yet painful, made Connie grasp her stomach. She had to be brave and tell her mum everything. The fallout from the decision she and her dad had made not to tell her had haunted Connie for the past year. Her concerns had been for her mum first and foremost, for herself, maybe even her dad – for the far-reaching consequences of telling the truth after all these years. Connie's biggest fear – the one her dad held over her – was what the shock of finding out might do to her mum.

But it wasn't her secret to keep, and it should never have been up to her, or her dad. Her poor mum shouldn't have been put through years of grief, believing her son had been killed when really he'd been hidden away, taken, and given a new identity by her own husband, for his own selfish reasons.

She had to think of her mum, and of Luke. She could regret this, but now, sitting with her mum, it felt right.

'Mum,' Connie said, looking directly into her mother's eyes. 'There's something really important I need to tell you. Something I should've told you last year, and I'm so sorry I didn't. Please believe I held off telling you for what I thought were the right reasons. What was best for you.'

Connie wrung her hands, grasped then unclasped them, wiping the sheen of sweat into her trousers. Lindsay placed a hand over hers, squeezing it, then got up and left Connie and her mum alone in the lounge.

Connie expelled a lungful of air.

'It's about Luke.'

CHAPTER ONE HUNDRED AND FOURTEEN

Deborah

'It's over, Nathan.'

As I walk through the door and sling my handbag on the kitchen worktop, he looks up. His eyes are dark, swollen. He shakes his head, eyes narrowing – the confusion evident on his pale face.

'Are you alone? Where are the police?'

I smile and take his face in both my hands. 'Alice Mann has made a positive identity. Isabella Bond – the missing girl who was later found dead. *She* was the one who attacked her.'

'I . . . I don't understand.'

'Alice said she remembers Isabella coming in, standing over her and smashing her head onto the floor. She must've been waiting for you to leave before going in. Apparently she was linked with Tom Killion, the other boy involved in Sean's murder alongside Alice's son. He was using this Isabella to help him eliminate the people who might've been able to expose him, but once she'd done what he wanted, he killed her. The policewoman, DI Wade, said it fits with the evidence they already had. It's over. We're going to be okay.' And for the first time in a long while, I truly believe this.

I lower my face, gently kissing his forehead.

Two weeks later

I've dressed in my favourite plum dress with its matching bolero jacket clipping me in at the waist, creating the perfect silhouette. I feel positive as I walk into the foyer with my head held high – and as I catch my reflection in the glass, I see my new cropped hairstyle and a surge of extra confidence races around my body. I've got this.

'Morning,' I trill as I sweep past my colleagues already at their desks. I'm late. That was intended – I wanted to make an entrance, show them I'm back.

And I *am* back.

I'm not the same person. I know I never will be. But that's all right. After long discussions and heart-to-hearts with Nathan, we've realised we can still function. I can't pretend I'm not still reeling from his confession about spending time with Alice. My stomach contracts painfully when I think about him telling me he'd been attracted to her at their first meeting at the tax office, where she worked part-time. From his account, it'd been a purely coincidental meeting – he'd been there to evaluate the new extension plans, and got chatting to her on reception. Coleton is a small town. Too small, it seems. Nathan reassured me the relationship never went further than meeting after work at his council office and having long chats. She made him laugh. Although he admitted to me he was tempted to begin a physical relationship with her, he'd been unable to go that far. He said guilt, his marriage vows, prevented the ultimate betrayal. He'd no idea who she really was until he followed me to her house and confronted her. His anger at finding out she was the mother of the boy who'd taken his son away had been too much to bear.

Knowing those who took our son's life have paid, one way or another, has given us some closure. I, for one, no longer feel the intense hatred I once did – the events of the last few weeks have somehow extinguished the flames that burned inside of me. That's a good thing – I can now give that space to healing.

Nathan and I will remain a couple and we'll make every effort to mould ourselves into different roles. We were parents, and no one can take that fact away from us. We had a son, and Sean will always be a part of our lives. Now though, he's firmly in our past. We can't take him with us into our future, not in the way I'd been trying.

Today is the first day of my *new* future.

Monday 6th August 2018

'It took approximately three minutes for Tom Killion to die.'

That sentence, stated in court last month, plays over in my head on a loop. A few minutes, though. Not hours. A much better ending than Sean Taylor had. I've killed two birds with one stone, really. I protected my son *and* I ensured justice for Deborah's son; for Bill's daughter.

I am finally redeemed.

The cell isn't bad. I have a bed, a table, a toilet.

Most of all, I have peace.

I'm sitting at the table now, writing a letter. It's an important one.

I'm writing to Deborah.

We share a loss, you see. The death of a son.

I feel sure we can help each other through.

Author's Note

This novel is a work of fiction – however, there are some real locations mentioned. For example, I talk about the wonderful historic town of Totnes in Devon – a place I know well. While real, I've used it in a purely fictitious manner, and to this end, have slightly altered some of the geography to fit my story.

Acknowledgements

Huge thanks to my agent, Anne – your encouragement and support is first-class. My editor, Katie – your enthusiasm, keen eye, wonderful ideas and support kept me on track and prevented me tearing ALL of my hair out, so Thank You! *One Little Lie* is a novel I'm now extremely proud of. Thanks also to Kate from Kate Hordern Literary Agency and Rosie and Jessica Buckman for your hard work – I feel blessed to be with an agency that gives such fantastic personal attention! A big thank you to Rachel, Sabah, Elke and the rest of the brilliant team that make up Avon, HarperCollins – you are a fabulous bunch and I'm grateful for all your efforts. You are all professional, super enthusiastic and work tirelessly to get the novels into the hands of as many readers as possible.

As ever, I couldn't do this without my trusty writing companions and good friends Lydia and Libby. Also, the two C's – Carolyn and Caroline – I've had a great time getting to know you both over the past year and know we have made a lifelong friendship. The four of you make writing a less solitary job!

I'm very lucky to have great family and friends who continue to encourage and support my writing journey. Far too many to list, but a special shout-out to Celia, Pete, Stacey and Charlotte;

Tracey and my god-daughter, Katie; J, San and Jess; Jo and Keeley; Nicci and James: Aldyth, Jen and David. The greatest support obviously comes from my little family, so the biggest thanks to: Doug – for your attempts to sort out my own space for me to write and for your words of encouragement. Danika – you're always so proud of me, it makes my heart swell. I miss you, you've left me here with all these boys! But thank you, Josh, for making her happy. Louis – I'm so very proud of your achievements this past year, and thank you for still talking through plot issues with me. Nathaniel – this is going to be your year! Thanks for your gaming expertise (any mistakes in this novel are mine) and for trying to ensure I'm left in peace to write. Oh, and just to make it clear, this novel is in no way based on you or Louis . . . Thank you all for believing in me and encouraging me every day.

Many thanks to my book club girls: Charlotte, Izzy, Tara, Luisa and Laura, for allowing me to stay in the club despite not always reading the chosen book, and for being interested in, buying and recommending my novels! Your support means a lot to me. And my thanks to Lauraine (you are missed at book club!) and Russ, for answering questions about removing bodies from a crime scene and the like!

Bloggers play a huge role in spreading the word about novels and I've been very fortunate to have gained support from many established and professional bloggers. They are worth their weight in gold – thank you all. Special mention to Kaisha (The Writing Garnet), Anne (Random Things Through My Letterbox), Katherine (BibliomaniacUK), Jen (Jen Med's Book Reviews), Vicki (Off-The-Shelf Books) and Jacob (Hooked From Page One) – but many more supported the blog tour for *Bad Sister* and were kind enough to review or offer a guest author spot on their blogs, so a massive thank you.

My thanks to Angela Killion, whose fantastic winning bid in a charity auction organised by Tracy Fenton (THE Book Club), meant she got to name a character in this book. Thank you for allowing me to use yours!

Getting messages from readers who have loved my books is one of the best things about being a writer. Thank you to everyone who has bought my previous books, read them and reviewed them. I read all the reviews I get and am very grateful for people taking the time to let me know their thoughts.

Thank you to my readers – from ones who've read my previous books to those who have picked this one up as their first. I hope you enjoy *One Little Lie* as much as I enjoyed writing it.

I never feel confident that I've thanked enough people – there will be some individuals I haven't mentioned that I should have! Don't worry – I'm sure I'll remember by the time I come to write book four's acknowledgements . . .

That, of course, might be a lie.

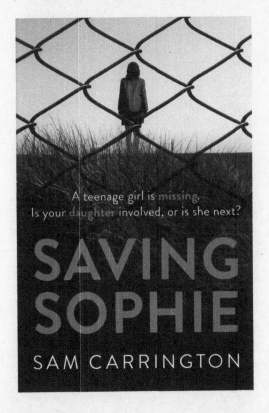

If you play with fire . . .

. . . You're going to get burned.

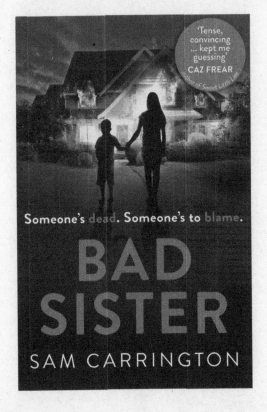

Someone's dead. Someone's to blame.

BAD SISTER

SAM CARRINGTON

Available now in ebook and paperback.